CALL of the PENGUINS

'Sparkles with wit,
courage and kindness.'
CELIA ANDERSON

'A wonderful story, full of twists
and turns. Outstanding.'
SAMANTHA TONGE

'Just what the doctor ordered . . .
Funny, wise, touching. I loved it.'
TRACY REES

'So many readers are set to fall in love
with this charming story.'
PRIMA

'The perfect fireside read. Hazel Prior's
novels always make me smile.'
TRISHA ASHLEY

'Beautifully written
by a born storyteller.'
LORRAINE KELLY

Praise for

AWAY with the PENGUINS

'This year's *Eleanor Oliphant* . . . Funny,
bittersweet and wholly original.'
DAILY EXPRESS

'A glorious, life-affirming story. I read it in a day.'
CLARE MACKINTOSH

'This adorable tale will put a smile on your face.'
GOOD HOUSEKEEPING

'A warm-hearted and life-affirming tale about
ageing, human kindness, old-fashioned values
and protecting our planet.'
CULTUREFLY

'A touching, uplifting tale.'
JO WHILEY, RADIO 2 BOOK CLUB

'Veronica McCreedy will
capture your heart.'
TRISHA ASHLEY

LIFE and OTTER MIRACLES

Hazel Prior

PENGUIN BOOKS

TRANSWORLD PUBLISHERS
Penguin Random House, One Embassy Gardens,
8 Viaduct Gardens, London SW11 7BW
www.penguin.co.uk

Transworld is part of the Penguin Random House group of companies
whose addresses can be found at global.penguinrandomhouse.com

Penguin
Random House
UK

First published in Great Britain in 2023 by Penguin Books
an imprint of Transworld Publishers

A CIP catalogue record for this book
is available from the British Library.

ISBN 9781529177039

Typeset in 11/14.5pt Sabon LT Pro by Jouve (UK), Milton Keynes.
Printed and bound in Great Britain by Clays Ltd, Elcograf S.p.A.

The authorized representative in the EEA is Penguin Random House Ireland,
Morrison Chambers, 32 Nassau Street, Dublin D02 YH68.

Penguin Random House is committed to a sustainable
future for our business, our readers and our planet. This book
is made from Forest Stewardship Council® certified paper.

LIFE and OTTER MIRACLES

1

Narnia

PHOEBE LISTENED. IT wasn't so much a song as a collection of voices weaving around each other. They chortled, they gabbled and they whispered. She glanced up at the sky and then down at the ripples. The Darle wasn't like the green, sluggish rivers she used to know. It ran swift and clear. The current, split by rocks, was alive with white sprigs and swirls and skittering bubbles. It was the river that had enticed them here in the first place. It fascinated her: the shining beauty of it, the way it managed to be both playful and deep.

Next to her, Al lifted his wrist and took a peep at his watch. He breathed a sigh of relief. It was only his third day in the new job, and he must be neither too early nor too late. Timing was everything, he'd told her. That and being polite. He would, she knew, do better on the politeness than the timings.

'Still early,' he said.

It was rare for Phoebe to be awake at this hour, let alone active. Whoever suggested that moving to the country was a good idea? Birmingham traffic had never disturbed her slumbers, but Devon cows? To indulge in a noisy bout of mooing before six in the morning . . . They were plain rude.

Fresh coffee smells had then unfairly seduced her down to the kitchen. Al, already up, dressed and zealous, had slapped breakfast in front of her: too much toast and not enough coffee, but she could hardly complain. Not only was breakfast accomplished in record time, he had somehow persuaded her into the garden as well, albeit with her pyjamas still on underneath her jacket and tracksuit bottoms. Her father firmly believed in the power of fresh air.

She had pretended more enthusiasm than she felt. Phoebe Featherstone had spent most of May pretending. She had pretended so hard that she felt weak from the effort. Smiling, laughing, producing jokes; it should be easy. But she wasn't a natural pretender and, in spite of all the practice, she still found it a strain. She wasn't sure whether Al was taken in or not. She put on a reasonable act, but he'd known her for a long time. Nineteen years, in fact, ever since she'd come into existence. He had seen all the changes.

Phoebe huddled into her jacket. She gazed at the rushing water and flinched at the thought that it could be a metaphor for her own life slipping by.

'What are you thinking?' Al asked, as he often did.

'Just listening to the river,' she said. 'Can you hear voices in it?'

'Sort of. Can't tell for the life of me what they're saying, though.'

'*I* can.'

'What, then?'

'They're passing on gossip to their fellow water molecules downstream. They're talking about us.'

'Nice things, I hope.'

'Shhh . . . I'll tell you . . .' She angled one ear riverwards and translated for him in a low, fast chatter. '*Psst. Did you know those are the two newcomers? The Featherstones. Townies, I'll bet. That skinny one's the daughter.*' What could she say about herself? '*Bad haircut, stares into space a lot. Still living at home. You'd have thought she'd have launched herself out into the world by now, got herself a job or be studying, at least. She looks as if she doesn't know what's hit her.*'

That was quite enough about her, Phoebe decided. She swallowed and moved on.

'*The other's her father, Al Featherstone. A real oddball.*' She darted him a sly glance. '*When he's not busy on his rounds of Darleycombe and the surrounding villages, he's often digging in the garden or wandering down here by the bank. Awful dress sense, he's got,*' she added, flicking her eyes towards her father's baggy jeans and jumper with holes in the elbows.

Al tutted. 'Cheeky little molecules!'

Soon, unlike her, he'd be meeting actual people, whizzing along the country roads, leaving a trail of satisfied

3

customers in his wake. No doubt he'd simultaneously be carving out a social life for himself. Not that she was jealous. In her opinion, socializing – like Sudoku, Christmas and olive oil – was vastly overrated.

It had taken Al under a week to find work here. He was hopeless at blowing his own trumpet, but what he lacked in boastfulness he made up for in immediate likability. That didn't stop her worrying about him, though.

He looked longingly towards the low mossy gate at the edge of the garden. He'd been miles beyond already, of course. He consulted his watch again. 'Another hour before I have to go and collect today's packages. Shall we go a bit further? That path goes through to a sort of glade. I think you'd love it, Phoebes. It's really picturesque, like a little Narnian enclave.'

It was too tempting. Phoebe (who had spent much of her childhood checking out the backs of wardrobes) still fostered faint hopes that Exmoor would turn out to be a grown-up version of Narnia.

Al pushed open the gate and they wandered along the bank, into a spinney of hazels, alders and young birch trees. Ferns curled at Phoebe's feet and sticky strands of goosegrass clung to her trousers. Her father ploughed ahead through the web of light and shade, beating back the undergrowth. He bounced a little as he walked. She lagged behind him on the path.

'It's not far at all,' he assured her, looking back, all encouragement.

'You've already said that twice.'

It was further than she had anticipated, though. A ploy?

'Here we are,' he said at last, leading her out into the open.

The glade wasn't as idyllic as she'd been led to expect. The sun wasn't yet high enough to cast golden dapples and show off the place at its best. The canopy hung low and dense, like lumpy knitting. Patches of mud showed through the scraps of vegetation and there were far too many nettles.

As it happened, none of this mattered at all. Because what they found there was almost as good as Narnia.

2

A Delivery from the Darle

'WHAT DO WE do?' said Phoebe.

'We can't just leave it. It's all alone. And it's a baby.'

'Do you think it's safe to pick it up?'

'Oh . . . I don't know . . . It might bite.'

'Perhaps if I used my jacket?'

'You'll freeze. You're only wearing your jimjams and trackie bottoms underneath.'

'Well, give me your jumper, then.'

He yanked it off and passed it to her. She'd already slipped the jacket off her shoulders, and now she pulled his jumper over her head. It hung loosely around her, but it was deliciously warm and gave off a faint whiff of earth and bonfires. She crept forward, one step in front of the other, as slowly and quietly as she could, never taking her eyes off the tiny creature. It rose to its feet, wobbled, squeaked, then looked up at her, big brown eyes gazing out of a fuzzy, round face; quite fearless.

Her heart gave a squeeze. She crouched in the grass, flung the jacket around the cub, scooped it up and cradled it in her arms. It seemed to trust her and nestled into her chest.

In this moment, Phoebe felt it for the first time: a curious concentration of joy that had nothing to do with her own state, that was activated by focusing wholly on the baby otter. It was like an inner sun blasting through clouds. It was a new and glorious phenomenon. It should have a name. Perhaps she would call it 'the Otter Effect'. Like the Butterfly Effect, only much, much better.

Phoebe whispered to her father, 'Have you ever seen anything so impossibly adorable?'

'Nope.' He leaned forward and stroked the soft fur of its chin. It nuzzled his hand. It was less than a foot long from the tip of its broad, pinkish nose to the end of its long tail. 'I hope it's okay,' he said. 'I guess we need to take it back home, and then . . . Well, we know a place that can help. We'll have to be quick, though. The parcels won't wait.'

Phoebe was reluctant to relinquish her charge but knew they could get on faster if she let Al carry it. He accepted the otter tenderly and rolled it up a little more securely in the jacket.

They scrambled back as fast as they could through the bobbing fronds and over the twisted tree roots, accompanied by the river's gurgles of excitement.

Phoebe was gasping for breath by the time they reached

the garden of Higher Mead Cottage. Al handed the bundle over to her again as he unlocked the back door.

'I'll ring the sanctuary,' he said. 'Maybe you should give the little fella some water or something?'

She followed him into the kitchen and ran some cold water into a bowl, cuddling the young otter under her other arm. She held it so that its muzzle was just touching the edge of the water. It twitched its nose but didn't drink. She noticed it had a little smudge of white fur just above its mouth.

'Damn,' said Al, throwing down the phone. 'No answer. Look, Phoebe. It's getting late. I have to go and pick up those parcels, but I'll be back in half an hour. Do you think you could keep ringing this number, and look after the cub in the meantime?'

'Of course I can.'

No sooner had she said the words than he had dashed out of the house again. She heard the car door slam and the motor start up.

'Well, it's just you and me, now, little Floof,' she crooned to the cub. 'I'm going to take care of you. Don't you worry about a thing.'

The cub scrabbled gently at her hand with its paws. She carried it around the house with her, stroking it while she looked for somewhere safe to put it. The empty, oblong log basket in the sitting room might do. She placed her new furry friend inside it and put down the water bowl too, encouraging it to drink. It shrank into the corner, curling its long tail around its body. It started chewing and nibbling at its fur.

'Are you hungry?' she asked.

Her phone was on the windowsill. She grabbed it and quickly searched *What do otters eat?*

Google informed her there were thirteen species of otter, and she concluded this must be a Eurasian one, or (she made a mental note) '*Lutra lutra*'. *British river otters eat trout, carp, eels, frogs, crustaceans and molluscs such as snails and slugs. Occasionally, they will prey on moorhens, rodents and rabbits.*

'I don't think we have any of those things in the fridge, my friend.' She went to check. 'Yesterday's chicken curry? Black olive tapenade? Baked beans? Cheesecake? Probably not your thing. Sorry, baby. Not a frog or moorhen in sight. But you're very young. Do you fancy some milk, maybe?'

Google was less helpful on that front. She poured a trickle from the milk carton into a dish, then thought she'd try the otter sanctuary again first, using the landline. The sanctuary was the single tourist attraction in the area. She and Al had seen signposts to it and had planned to take a look sometime, when they were more settled in.

They had been living at Higher Mead Cottage for over a month, but most of their possessions were still in boxes. They'd agreed that the pace of life ought to be slower now, and nobody had visited yet, so where was the hurry? Anyway, time seemed to work differently in Darleycombe, like a stolid tortoise after Birmingham's frantically zigzagging hare.

Al had done nearly all the house-hunting, zipping down to Devon on Saturdays and returning completely exhausted. When he came back with an *I think I've found the one* smile, Phoebe had agreed to accompany him for the second viewing.

The old couple who had owned Higher Mead Cottage had shown them around with chatty enthusiasm. The wonky chimney had been that way for decades, they said, so Al and Phoebe need not worry. The rooms were low-ceilinged, unassuming and cosy. Several had tiny fireplaces fitted with wood-burners. On the minus side, the window frames struggled to keep out the draughts and there wasn't even a hint of a mobile signal. There was broadband, though, as the former owners had pointed out with pride. Apparently, their children had made them have it installed, although neither of them had ever used it.

They were charming. So was the house. Although a lot messier now. Al couldn't claim to be the tidiest of people, and neither could Phoebe. 'But what does it matter, really, in the great scheme of things?' Al had said.

Her eyes on the otter, Phoebe let the phone ring for a while, but there was still no answer.

When Al returned, Phoebe was kneeling over the log basket. Her posture reminded him of paintings of the adoration of the Magi.

'Dad, that was quick.'

'Yes, wasn't it?' he said, his voice self-congratulatory but edged with worry. 'Just made it in time. Everything was already offloaded from the lorry and I transferred it across in the car park.'

His daughter had finally got herself dressed and was layered in sweatshirts, which helped bulk out her tiny frame. She had also lined the basket with newspaper and added a few sprigs of bracken to make the otter cub feel more at home. It was now curled up, fast asleep.

'Great job,' he said. 'Any luck with the sanctuary?'

Phoebe shook her head.

'Well, I have to get my load delivered asap. I'll deliver the otter while I'm at it, on the way out. We'd better put him or her into a shoebox once I'm ready. This is going to make me even later, though.' He cracked his knuckles. A knot of stress was forming in his stomach. 'Now for the tricky bit.'

He tried to look nonchalant, but she knew he was hinting.

'Like some help?' she asked.

'Well, if you're offering . . .'

For the job, Al had been told to download an app, and he'd been swearing at his phone ever since. Phoebe was a lot better at computer stuff than he was. It had taken her all of three minutes to grasp how it worked. He had managed sorting the deliveries for the first two days, but now that there was the pressure of time he could really do with her help.

Al unloaded the parcels from the car, armful by armful, and placed them in a semicircle on the sitting-room carpet. They varied from huge reinforced boxes to Jiffy bags, cardboard book envelopes and the classic 'brown paper packages tied up with strings'.

Al warbled a couple of lines from *The Sound of Music*. His Julie Andrews impression was rather good, he thought. However, Phoebe put her finger against her lips and said he would wake up the otter cub if he didn't cut it out.

She swiftly read out the postcodes in a low voice, supervised as he shuffled the deliveries into a sensible order, and calculated his route for him. Some of the parcels had the shop's name printed on the packaging and she muttered her guesses about what was inside. Multivitamins in bulk, chocolates, cosmetics, wellies, stationery . . . Other boxes were more mysterious.

'Mr Crocker, Mr Dobson, Ms Penrose, Reverend Daws. I wonder what they've all ordered?' she mused. 'I bet you could work out masses about our neighbours from what's inside these packages.'

'Yup. I bet *you* could,' Al said, emphasizing the 'you'. 'I'm in too much of a flurry to even think about it, so I'm going to mind my own beeswax.'

As Phoebe transferred the otter cub to a shoebox, he hastily stacked the parcels into the car in reverse order of delivery. He came back in once more to fetch the box.

Phoebe followed him out.

'Are you coming too?' He was surprised she wasn't back in bed by now.

'Dad, no way am I *not* coming.'

She scrambled into the passenger seat and he handed her the precious package. She cradled it with devotion as he started up the engine and eased out into the lane.

'Drive carefully, won't you?'

He cast her a sideways glance and grinned.

A scuffling sounded inside the box and a shiny nose peeped out from under the lid. Phoebe held the box with both hands, careful to keep it steady as Al drove over a hump in the road. The nose twitched then disappeared again.

Darleycombe spread out on both sides of the river and stretched halfway up the hill. Its buildings were a mix of crooked, thatched idyllic, blockish eyesores from the seventies and flimsy modern structures that were classed as affordable housing (were any houses actually affordable these days?). A cluster of houses perched high up, proudly above the rest, looking over the view. On a clear day like today the purple tints of heather-covered moorland were visible in the distance.

They passed through the pretty part of the village, over the bridge, beyond the council houses and out the other side. The river meandered off into a stretch of woodland then returned to run alongside the road.

Phoebe huddled over the shoebox and opened it a chink again, unable to resist another look inside. The round, whiskery face peeped out, and a tiny paw crept over the edge. She pushed it back just in time.

'Best not do that too much,' Al warned. 'If it escapes and leaps down my neck, I might just drive into a hedge.'

They were nearly there. They turned right, following the sign, and drew into a car park. Phoebe let Al carry the box to the gate but walked closely beside him.

The place was not open yet, but when he pressed the bell a woman came out almost immediately. She stood with her body barring the entrance. She was in her early sixties, short and compact, with thick grey hair gathered in two bunches that rested on her shoulders. Her wellies, jeans and jumper had a lived-in look, but she wore them stiffly, as if they were a uniform.

Al did the introductions.

'Pleased to meet you,' she replied, although she didn't look it. 'I'm Carol Blake. I run the otter sanctuary.'

She eyed the box with suspicion.

13

Al held it awkwardly, tapping the lid with one finger. 'We found this down by the river.' He allowed her a quick peek inside. 'We were out walking early this morning and saw it toddling about in the grass. We thought at first it was maybe a stoat or a weasel, but then . . .'

'Once we got a proper look, we knew straight away it was an otter,' Phoebe put in. 'Stoats and weasels aren't as chubby-faced or cute as this.'

'We watched for a while,' Al continued, 'and it gave a whistle, almost like a bird, as if it was calling, but there was no answer. It was nosing about, and seemed to be looking for its parents. There weren't any others around at all, though, and it looked so young and helpless. We picked it up really easily and took it back home. We brought it here because we . . . Well, it seemed like a good idea.'

Carol's mouth was a flat line. He would have thought they'd done exactly the right thing and she should be pleased. Apparently not. He'd also been hoping Phoebe would get an invitation to see the other otters, which she could enjoy while he whipped around the countryside delivering parcels. Instead, Carol said, 'You didn't give it any milk, did you?'

'No, we brought it straight here.'

'Well, that's something. Otters are lactose intolerant, so if you had, you'd have made it very ill.'

A small, almost imperceptible squeak sounded in Phoebe's throat.

'Wait here,' said Carol, and disappeared back inside. Al muttered something about 'cold fish' under his breath. He tried not to think about the clock ticking.

Carol was back a moment later, wearing thick leather

gloves and carrying a cat basket and a map of the local area. She indicated that they were to open the shoebox. They had scarcely blinked before she had grabbed the otter cub by the scruff of its neck and transferred it across to the cat basket.

She surveyed them severely. 'You assumed that, because you didn't see an adult, this little one is an orphan. That's probably not the case. The most likely thing is that its mother was around, hiding in the undergrowth and just waiting for you to go away.'

'Oh,' said Phoebe, crestfallen. 'We've messed up everything, then.'

'Well, we shall see,' Carol answered. 'Otter fathers are terrible and leave the females to do all the work, but the mothers are very caring and attentive. I've asked Rupert to babysit the sanctuary.' Al assumed Rupert must be her husband. 'I'll take this young one back to the exact spot where you found her,' Carol continued, 'if you could show me where it is. I'll put her back there in a temporary pen, and I'll keep watch. If the mother comes back, I can release her straight away, and she'll be fine. If, over the next twenty-four hours, there's no sign of a mother, I'll bring her back here to the sanctuary.'

'You said "she". Is it a female, then?' Phoebe asked.

Carol shrugged her shoulders. 'Hard to say, and I'm not going to examine her now. It's just that I often get a sense about these things.' She unfolded the map. 'Show me the place.'

Phoebe stabbed the map with her finger, immediately able to locate Higher Mead Cottage, that stretch of the river and the glade itself.

'I'll drive there now. It's not far from the top road.'

Al dug his hands into his pockets. 'Since you're going that way, I don't suppose you could give Phoebe a lift back home, could you? I've got a ton of parcels to deliver and I'm running unbelievably late.'

'All right,' said Carol in a monotone.

'Am I allowed to come back to the glade and watch for the mother otter with you?' Phoebe asked.

Carol shook her head. 'No, I'm afraid not. The fewer humans around, the better.'

There was clearly no point in arguing.

3

Haste, Not Speed

AL FELT BAD leaving his daughter in the company of the less than friendly Carol Blake. Still, if Carol ran an otter sanctuary, she had to be a decent type of person, didn't she?

He gave them both a wave as he backed the car and zoomed away from the premises. Soon he was on his official route again. He whistled as he drove, glad that Phoebe had taken such an interest in the otter, hoping that, wherever it ended up, it would survive. And that Carol would keep them posted.

He put his foot on the accelerator. The road flickered with filigree patterns of grey and gold as he sped through a tunnel of beech trees. He came out into the open again and sunshine burst through the windscreen. On either side, the verges were a tangle of buttercups, cow parsley and feather-headed grasses. Birds perched and chatted together on the few telegraph wires; were they swallows or swifts? He kept forgetting the difference. He would ask Phoebe later. She'd know.

Al's round (more of a squiggle, really) covered a few outlying farms and several villages. In his experience, roads tended to get shorter the more you drove along them, but the Devon lanes were still long. And twisty. And very, very narrow. In the first week here he'd involuntarily breathed in, and even now he felt the hedges might tickle him as he passed.

He dropped off a supply of horse equipment at a smallholding and several smaller packages across three hamlets, darting out of the car to leave the goods and hurrying away again before anyone could engage him in conversation, desperate to make up for lost time. He had to reverse several times to let cars or tractors pass. The satnav had a wicked sense of humour and everything was taking far longer than the blasted app said it should. Luckily, people had been forgiving so far. On the whole, they seemed pleased to see him. He came bearing gifts, after all.

It was hard to believe he was actually being paid for this. It was a lot less per hour than the job he'd given up, but the joy of maths teaching had ebbed away over the last few years.

Al Featherstone considered himself young, although others might not. He had a boyish manner and a good, thick crop of hair that was only sparingly peppered with grey. It was just the stresses of the classroom that had worn him down. On top of that, he had been given heaps of admin, and if there was one thing that drove Al to despair, it was admin. Nobody had blinked when, at fifty-three, he'd suggested an early retirement. Semi-retirement, anyway. The decision was first prompted by a flyer through the door that read, 'Choose the funeral you want from just £15.97 per month.' It had been like a slap in the face. Although he managed to bumble along and was, on the whole, a man of cheerful habits, Al's heart had been crushed long ago and what remained of it beat to the rhythm of his three children. For their sakes, he had no intention of playing the starring role in a funeral any time soon, bargain or no. He might be an empty shell, but he hoped that at least he was a useful one.

Essentially a shy person, Al had no idea how popular he'd been as a teacher. Many of his pupils were sorry to see him leave and sorry they hadn't been nicer to him, a realization that came too late. At school he'd been called Mr Featherstone to his face but was always known affectionately (he hoped) as Big Al behind his back. The 'Big Al' worked in much the same way as 'Little John' in the Robin Hood stories and was the wittiest name the students had managed to come up with. It could have been so much worse, but it had riled him a little. Not that he was touchy about his height. He wasn't noticeably small, merely below average for a man. But the 'big' somehow made it more of an issue.

When he had suggested the move, Phoebe had given a little crow of excitement, which was enough to stir him to action. Their Birmingham life had felt congested. He'd been craving green fields and fresh air, and surely countryside would be good for her, too? Properties on Exmoor were relatively cheap, and it wasn't far away from his other daughter, Jules, who was studying in Plymouth. His son, Jack, currently in York, had nearly finished at university and might be settling anywhere else soon . . . Or, more likely, not settling at all.

Since their arrival, Al had committed himself to the dual pleasures of scruffiness and vegetable gardening. He quite liked his new, unironed look. He'd got into the habit of being smart in the early days of his marriage; Ruth had appreciated such things and it was necessary for his job anyway. Yet now he'd relaxed into a less spick-and-span edition of himself, and he had to admit he felt more comfortable being just a little bit crumpled.

At last, he was returning to Darleycombe, the village he could now call home. He followed the twists and turns of the valley, drove up a steep incline, then pulled up in a driveway. The house had a large square front and heavily curtained windows. A Vauxhall was parked outside the lean-to garage. As he strode to the front door, Al startled a posse of plump, red-brown chickens. Their heads bobbed up to view him momentarily before they resumed their pecking and scrabbling.

He had to knock twice. The door opened a chink and he caught sight of a pair of bulbous eyes and two or three strands of hair scraped sideways over a bald head.

'Just a delivery!' Al called cheerfully.

The door opened a little wider. Al observed that the man, a Mr Crocker, according to his parcel, wasn't wearing any shoes, just a pair of thick, green socks. He took the package in a swift, greedy movement.

'Sorry, I have to take a photo of it,' said Al, fishing out his phone. 'Not of you, just it,' he assured the man, who had shrunk back into the hallway. He focused the lens downward on the parcel and clicked.

'So you'll be the people who've moved into Higher Mead Cottage?' Mr Crocker pronounced the words meditatively, as if he was working them out as he went along. Al guessed he had gleaned the information from the village shop, where he'd already introduced himself. He smiled at the way Mr Crocker said 'people', since there was clearly only one of him standing here on the doorstep.

'Yes, just me and my daughter, Phoebe.'

Mr Crocker shook his head. 'Not much happening here for a young person.'

'She won't mind.' Al pictured Phoebe with her hair mussed up and her down-at-heel slippers. 'We both like the quiet.'

'Plenty of that going on,' the man said with a wry grin. He extended a surprisingly smooth hand, which Al shook. 'Anyway, I'm Jeremy Crocker. Retired policeman,' he seemed to think it necessary to explain.

'Al Featherstone,' said Al.

'I wish you both all the best in your new home.'

'Thank you so much.'

Al was just turning to go away again when Mr Crocker held up a hand to stop him. 'Wait here.'

He disappeared. Al hoped he wouldn't be too long. Although there were only a few more deliveries to go, he was disastrously behind schedule now. Mr Crocker re-appeared carrying an eggbox.

'Take these, won't you? From my girls.'

'Your girls?'

'Yes. They're free-range, you know.'

Ah. The chickens. Al had recently stocked up with eggs but thought it prudent to accept anyway. 'That's generous of you. Thank you.'

'Right you are. If there's anything else you ever need, please don't hesitate to contact me.'

The door was closed firmly with no more chitchat, to Al's relief. He had the impression of kindness, though, and made a mental note to factor in an extra five minutes for Mr Crocker in the future.

As he took off again, he thought about Mr Crocker's comment that there wasn't much going on here for a young person. Had Al done the right thing by Phoebe?

Higher Mead Cottage was already throwing so many challenges at him. The window frames were rotting away and the beams were riddled with woodworm (it had apparently been treated, but Al wasn't convinced. There was some suspicious-looking powdery stuff under the one in the bathroom just this morning, he'd noticed). The hot-water system regularly erupted into wild clanking noises and the only way to make it stop was to turn the heating on and off again several times. The electrics were dodgy, too. He kept promising Phoebe he would fix the flickering light in the hall, but he hadn't got round to it yet. Then there was the garden, which was far more time-consuming than he'd bargained for. There was a real art to staying on top of things, he reflected. It was something he'd never quite mastered. It would all be so much easier if Ruth was still alive.

What would Ruth have made of all this? Jules and Jack were doing their own thing now and didn't mind much what he did, but Phoebe was still so dependent on him. At least she was fond of her new bedroom.

Phoebe had been in favour of the move, yet now she seemed to have sunk into a kind of torpor. Despite his cajoling, she'd hardly left the house at all. Since their arrival he'd coaxed her out on a single short expedition, to a National Trust property. The formal garden, a chequered pattern of box hedges and borders, was encircled by woodland in which the ceiling was an emerald canopy and the floor a glory of rippling bluebells, yet Phoebe had scarcely registered any of it. To his dismay, she had even said she'd sit in the car while he looked around, a suggestion he wouldn't accept since the trip had been for her benefit in the first place. Her lack of interest had shocked him. It had both sapped away his own appreciation of the place and accentuated his inner sadness. She used to like history and antiques, but when they traipsed round the manor house the only enthusiasm she had shown was for one of the ornate four-poster beds. 'I wouldn't mind sleeping in that,' she'd said.

It was hard to gauge how Phoebe really felt. He supposed he was lucky he wasn't living with a *moaner*, but an occasional little moan for purposes of clarification would actually be welcome. His other daughter, Jules, never had an issue with such things. Phoebe wasn't a great one for sharing, though.

He had made her promise to try to get out and meet people here. At the village shop he'd seen a notice about a local yoga class and had suggested she might go. With a shrug and a slight grimace, she had agreed.

The baby otter, though, had lit her up like a sparkler. It

23

was ages since anything had enthralled her like that. He only hoped they hadn't seen the last of it.

He was jolted out of his reverie as a car careered round the bend ahead. Al punched his foot down on the brake. Something screeched. His body slammed back against the seat. As he was flung forwards again, images of his children hurtled through his head. Jack and Jules would manage, but . . .

I can't die. I mustn't. If I die, who will be there for Phoebe?

When his breath returned, his thoughts whisked by in rapid succession: *I'm not dead. Neither is the other driver. Thank God! No blood shed, no bones broken. Both cars are damaged, though. Damn. At least it's not a company vehicle . . . but I'm going to be ridiculously late for the last few deliveries now. I may get sacked, and in my first week, too. I've really let Phoebe down. At least she still has a father. My head hurts like hell. This woman looks furious.*

From the way she'd sprung out of her own car, the other driver couldn't be hurt, but she was clearly agitated. She was striding towards him in long leather boots. Her orange pashmina and her handsome swathes of dark hair blew in the breeze. Her eyes flashed with anger. He could see her mouth shaping swear words as he struggled to undo his seatbelt and get out.

The stunned sensation in his neck was probably mild whiplash. He gingerly walked round to survey the dent in his car. The other car, a purple Peugeot, had a sister dent.

'Didn't you see me?' the woman demanded.

It was a stupid question.

24

'No. Didn't you see me?' he returned. Then he added, 'Are you okay?' because she really might not be.

Wrinkles kept appearing and disappearing on her brow. She clenched her teeth and looked away.

'Yes, I'm fine . . . That is . . .' She glanced back at him and glowered. 'Just don't!'

'I only asked if you were okay. Are you?' It was hard to know what to make of her.

She turned away again. 'No, not really. No, dammit, not at all. I could have done without this.' She waved a hand at the two cars straddling the road at a skewed angle, bumpers kissing.

'I'm sorry. I don't actually think it was my fault,' he added, hoping the insurance companies would agree, 'but I'm sorry anyway.'

'Sorry doesn't really help, does it?'

Now she seemed close to tears. He fumbled in his pocket for a handkerchief, found one, but decided against giving it to her. He'd blown his nose on it earlier and it wasn't looking its best.

'This can easily be fixed,' he said, attempting a tone of reassurance. 'We just need to get the cars out of the road for now because they're causing a blockage. I think they're both still driveable. Did you need to be anywhere? I could give you a lift, if you want, if you're too shaken. Do you know if there's a mobile signal here?' His voice was running on and on, inane words, but it would be a chance for her to gather herself.

'Rrrrra,' she said, which didn't answer any of the questions but clearly helped her vent her frustration. 'Ignore me! Just having a moment. It's not you. It's not even this.'

She indicated the cars. 'It's everything.' Her words spurted out. Her cheeks were flushed.

It might be time to introduce himself. He stuck out a hand, determined to be pleasant.

'Anyway, it's nice to meet you. I'm Al Featherstone,' he said.

The woman frowned at his hand and didn't take it.

4

Sherlock

WAS IT POSSIBLE to care too much? If it was, her father was surely guilty. He had cared about every single boy and girl in that Birmingham school, including the mean ones. He'd tried so hard to teach them maths, even though they weren't in the least bit interested. And he cared about Phoebe way more than she cared about herself.

Take her bedroom, for example. It had previously been a blank, square space, but now it resembled a colourful and chaotic palace. Al had even rigged her up a four-poster bed. That is to say, he'd managed to screw four posts around her bed and draped them with a thick, shiny fabric in turquoise, her favourite colour, adding gold tie-backs with tassels. He had invested in a heap of new and beautifully mashable pillows. And he'd bought a rubber stamp of an elephant, so one day soon after the move they had spent the morning stamping mini golden elephants over the headboard.

All this because she'd made a passing remark about a four-poster bed when they visited a National Trust property, and he had remembered it. She loved to draw the curtains around her, cocooning herself in with her thoughts. Al had put down turquoise fluffy rugs to match, strung fairy lights around the bookcase and hung up the treasured ukulele she never played. Her computer was connected to a screen positioned at the end of the bed, with the handset on her bedside table so she could binge-watch *Strictly*, *Bake Off* and detective dramas on playback whenever she liked.

Al had overspent on both money and energy. The rest of the house was having to wait.

This afternoon he had got in even later than expected, only to tell Phoebe that he had to go out again. Due to a prang with some rude woman driving a Peugeot, he needed to get the car fixed.

Phoebe sighed. She'd have to get used to being on her own again. Unfortunately, since Carol Blake had taken the cub, the Otter Effect seemed to have faded. Now she just felt a dull, sinking sensation in the pit of her stomach. She lay in bed staring into space for a while. At least when you were alone you didn't need to pretend *at all*. You could be as miserable as you liked.

The move had seemed such a romantic idea, and she had assumed that everything was going to be (even if not a hundred per cent Narnian) significantly better in Devon.

Yet now they were here she couldn't shake off the feeling that she had just been buried for ever.

She kicked her shoes off, climbed on to the bed and picked up her phone. Ignoring the warning voice of her own common sense, she made herself do an online happiness survey. Her score came out as three out of ten. The questions had been stupid, though. How often do you go outside? (Seldom.) How often do you socialize? (Hardly ever.) How much time do you spend on your hobbies? (Hardly any.) Do you have something to look forward to? (No.)

Cataloguing her woes was fatal. Phoebe knew that. It would take her on a downward spiral leading to a deep morass of self-pity. She must try harder to be happy here. She owed her father that much.

At last she heard the front door opening, followed by Al's whistling as he moved about the kitchen. A few moments later his footsteps sounded on the stairs. By the time he poked his head around the door her smile was back in place. He had two mugs of coffee with him, which went some way towards lifting her spirits. Life was so much better when you were wholly and deeply caffeinated.

Phoebe accepted one of the mugs, wrapped her hands around it and waited for the usual question.

'So how are you?' asked Al.

'Completely galluptious, thank you,' she answered without hesitation. 'And you?'

'Oh, very mixolydian indeed,' he replied.

It was great that he was prepared to misuse vocabulary

with her on a daily basis. Doubtless people living closely together always developed their own quirky ways of communication.

'Can they fix the car?' she asked.

'Yes, but not immediately. I've got a hire car for now. Any news about the otter?'

'Still nothing,' she said.

They both looked pointedly at her phone, but it refused to ring.

'Ah, well. Maybe a bit of *Sherlock*, to take our minds off it?'

'Good plan.'

She pulled herself a little higher on the pillows and switched on the TV using the handset. Al settled in the chair to watch with her.

A distraction was definitely needed and, if anyone could do it, Sherlock Holmes could. Phoebe liked Professor T., Endeavour, Poirot and Hetty Wainthropp, but nobody – *nobody* – would ever come close to Sherlock Holmes. She had watched every incarnation of him from Basil Rathbone to Benedict Cumberbatch. She possessed all the stories on audiobook, too.

As they watched, Al punctuated the mystery with comments such as 'Oh, it's a spooky one, isn't it? I seem to remember that character. Can't for the life of me remember who did it, though.'

Phoebe would have appreciated her father's comments more if they had been timed better. Too often he shared his opinion just at a crucial point in the drama.

'Did you get that one?' he asked when the programme finished.

'Yup.'

'Smarty-pants. I was miles off,' Al admitted.

Phoebe had watched so many episodes she knew most of the plots inside out. Even if she forgot, she had trained her brain to tick alongside Sherlock's and so could fathom out the mystery without too much effort. Only occasionally did she fail to work it out, when the red herrings were extra clever or her head had fogged up. It was frustrating when that happened. Her brother and sister used to call her the brainbox of the family. It was ironic that they were the ones now studying at university.

She picked up Al's phone, which was lying on the bed, and listlessly flicked through his photos. Most of them were images of parcels being delivered.

'If I was Sherlock, I could deduce so much from these.'

'Like what?' he asked.

'Like . . . well, this one, for example.' She held up the photo he'd taken at Mr Crocker's house. It didn't show much apart from the parcel itself, held in Mr Crocker's hands. In the background below was a corner of Mr Crocker's left foot, with dark-green socks and no shoes on, and a small area of his porch with the edge of some wellington boots visible.

'I can tell you that this man has chickens.'

Al gaped at her. 'What? How the devil did you know that?' He was sure he hadn't mentioned it in conversation.

'You really don't notice anything, do you, Dad?'

He rubbed a hand over his brow. 'No, I've never been observant. I don't know where you get it from, Phoebe.'

His shoulders bowed. A moment of silence passed

between them. They both knew she had inherited it from her mother.

'It's all about context. See here?' Phoebe said, pointing to the photo. 'There's a tiny feather stuck to the toe of that wellington boot. It's a reddish-brown colour. Chicken-coloured.'

'So it is. You're quite right. Mr Crocker is the proud owner of several chickens. He calls them his girls.'

'Sweet. Also, I believe Mr Crocker has a problem with his foot. Probably an ingrowing toenail.'

'What makes you say that?'

'The fact he isn't wearing shoes. And I can see a slight bulge under his sock in the area of his big toe, which looks as if there's a plaster there.'

'I don't know whether to be proud or horrified at your powers of perception,' said Al.

'Proud, Dad. Proud.'

Al stretched his knuckles, and they clicked loudly. It was a sound that might grate with some people, but Phoebe associated it with being loved and comfortable.

The rowan tree outside waved its fleecy blossoms as if trying to brush the windowpane. Al stretched and went to open the window, determined that Phoebe should get another dose of Devon air. She drew the duvet around her ears as a fresh breeze penetrated the warm fug of the bedroom. Al stood, silhouetted, admiring the view. The strip of land that was their back garden, flanked by his new vegetable plot, dipped down to the riverbank. Hills rose beyond a line of woodland in dozens of different shades of green. The sky spread above it all, a smooth sheet overlaid with a thin layer of cotton-white clouds.

'Ruth would have loved all this,' he muttered, so softly Phoebe wasn't even sure he had spoken.

She closed her eyes.

When she opened them again he was still standing there. Was it her imagination or did he flick a tear from his cheek?

'Are you okay, Dad?'

'Yes, yes, of course.' He gave himself a little shake. 'Oops! I've just remembered the washing's still on the line. It's been there three days.'

She had known this. She hadn't reminded him because she'd wanted him to remember on his own.

'Silly old me,' he said with an eye-roll. 'Well, I'll get it in later. It's Featherstone time now.' He crossed the room to switch on the computer.

Every week, they met with Jules and Jack via Zoom. Jules was studying hospitality, tourism and events management in Plymouth while Jack was in his final year of environmental science at York University.

'Can we not mention the otter yet?' Phoebe suggested. 'Until we know what's happening?'

'If that's what you want,' Al replied with an air of disappointment.

'It's just that Jules will . . . you know . . . make a big drama of it. Tell the world. Demand photos. Post it on Twitter and TikTok and Instagram. And I sort of want to keep it between us at the moment. I just want to own it for a bit longer, if that makes sense?'

'It does. I won't tell, I promise.'

In fact, Jules and Jack, both more talkative than Al and Phoebe, packed the half-hour with their news. Jack raved

33

about his new romance, a 'seriously hot' sociology student he'd met at a sailing club. Jules described an incident during a university ball when a friend's boyfriend had thrown a shoe from a fourth-floor window and it had bounced off the bonnet of a car passing below. Jack laughed along to the story, inserting comments and comparisons. Al beamed on.

Phoebe hoicked up the corners of her mouth and tried not to come across as sullen. So they were having a wonderful time. Great. Pleased as she was for them, the brightness of their lives cast hers into deeper shadow. Friendships (and boyfriendships) were a distant memory for her, and Jules and Jack had no idea how much they were rubbing it in.

'And what's going on with you two in Darleycombe?' Jack asked.

'Not a lot,' said Phoebe.

'How's the job, Dad?'

'Great,' Al said. 'Great, except that my satnav is evil and I keep getting lost. And today I got delayed and was late for everything and a cross woman in a Peugeot banged into me.'

'Oh, Dad!' they chorused.

As soon as the call was over, the phone rang, as if it had been waiting politely for them to finish.

Al and Phoebe looked at each other.

'That'll be Carol.'

Phoebe put a foot out of her bed, but Al was faster. She hadn't wanted a house phone upstairs because it might disturb important things like sleep, but now she was beginning to regret her decision. She pulled the duvet

34

back around herself and listened impatiently. She could hear her father's side of the conversation from upstairs but couldn't quite make out the words. The call went on and on. If she didn't find out about the otter soon, she would burst.

Finally, she heard Al's footsteps on the stairs. His face appeared at the bedroom door. His expression gave nothing away.

'Well?' she demanded.

'Well what?' he asked with a nonchalant air.

'You know perfectly well what.'

He could be the most annoying person in the world when he put his mind to it. He stuck his hands in his pockets. 'I take it you'd like to know about our furry friend?'

'C'mon, Dad! Tell me before I thump you!'

He took a step back, a smile playing on his lips. 'Carol says the little one is doing fine. She was observing it all day in the glade. It played and snuffled around, but there was no sign of any other otters at all.'

Phoebe sank back on her pillows. 'So it will stay in the sanctuary now?'

Al nodded. 'Yes. For whatever reason, it seems to be motherless.'

That last word hung between them, exuding sadness. Al pulled his head back as if trying to distance himself from it.

Phoebe cleared her throat. 'Poor little otter.'

'Carol said thank you to us both. She sounded a bit grudging, but she assured me she would make a temporary home for the cub at the sanctuary. It's only about eight or nine weeks old and is a female, apparently. She's already called in the vet to give it the once-over, and it seems okay, just a little dehydrated. She has managed to get it eating and drinking with the help of a baby's bottle. She wants to keep it well away from the public eye, though. She hopes to be able to release it again once it's older. In the meantime, it'll be fed and cared for and learn how to fish and fend for itself.'

'Can we see it again?' Phoebe asked quickly.

'That's exactly what I asked. I had to wheedle, but yes: Carol has agreed that we can go and visit later in the week. She went on and on about not getting too attached, though. The idea behind the sanctuary is to release otters back into the wild, but some become too used to human company and then it's no longer possible.'

Phoebe wished they hadn't been quite so hasty in taking the cub to the sanctuary. Yes, Carol was the expert. All the same, she felt that she, Phoebe Featherstone, would make an excellent substitute otter mother.

5

Aardvark, Cat, Leech and Otter

Phoebe couldn't believe she'd agreed to this. She was dreading it.

It wasn't that she disliked people. There were some that she liked very much indeed, and she found all of them quite fascinating. It was just that they were such *hard work*. They required focus, they required energy, and she felt obliged to behave a certain way whenever they were around.

She'd only turned up because Al had made her promise. So here she was, clinging to the radiator in the village hall. The room was tediously beige and full of hard surfaces that amplified any sound and seemed to accentuate the chilly edge in the air. She shivered. Life had been a lot warmer in the days when she'd had all those layers of fat, even if they hadn't done much for her image.

With her best toothpaste-advertisement smile, she ran her eyes around the room to examine the other participants. Just like her father's deliveries, you could guess a lot about a person from the packaging. Whether it was lumpy, smooth, heavy or bright. Whether it rattled or smelled funny.

There were only four in the yoga class, and the others were much older than Phoebe. The teacher was in her early forties, and, after a quick appraisal, Phoebe decided she was the most interesting person present. Her dark hair was in a high ponytail fastened by what looked like a fat purple caterpillar. She was wearing a tie-dyed T-shirt over her leggings and her fingernails were painted jade green. She was the type of person, Phoebe thought, who was a vegetarian borderline vegan, believed in the power of crystals and dabbled in pottery.

Chatting with the alternative yoga teacher was Darley-combe's vicar, Reverend Daws, who everyone seemed to call Rev Lucy. She was in a pale-pink tracksuit, which, coupled with her sweet smile and frizzy blonde hair, gave an impression of innocence and niceness. Phoebe put her down as the type of person who changed her sheets every Saturday, knew how to make a quiche Lorraine and had a window box of geraniums that she never forgot to water. She'd have a quiet husband who stayed firmly out of church affairs and two children who were polite but slightly spoilt. Her sermons would be brief and apologetic.

The other two participants were grey-haired ladies in Lycra, who Phoebe mentally dubbed 'Serene' and 'Melancholy'. Melancholy's facial expression suggested she had quite honestly given up on most things in life but was doing this class to please someone else (presumably, Serene. They seemed to be friends). The two of them had looked at Phoebe curiously when she came in. They were probably thinking, *How nice to have someone young in the class.*

'Hi, I'm Christina,' said the probably vegetarian yoga teacher, pouncing on Phoebe, who caught a slight whiff of aromatherapy oil when she approached.

'I'm Phoebe.'

'Great to have someone new here. Brave of you. Hope you enjoy it.'

'I'm sure I will,' Phoebe answered, not sure at all.

'Got any medical conditions, Phoebe?'

'No,' Phoebe answered swiftly. 'Have you?'

Christina looked amused, as if this was an unsuitable question for her, the teacher. It ought to go without saying that she was super-fit.

Serene and Melancholy were at the front, so Phoebe took her place at the back behind Melancholy and next to Rev Lucy. She was relieved that she didn't have to tie herself in knots, and much of the session was taken up in merely lifting the arms in slow motion and breathing. She guessed Christina was longing to do more but felt limited due to the age and relative stiffness of Serene and Melancholy. Melancholy had unnaturally loud breathing, as if she was following a technique she had learned in a former lesson which she was keen to show off.

Christina had removed her shoes and did the exercises in bare feet. Her sinuous body flexed and twisted. Her students followed with clunkier movements. When they were asked to stand on one leg, Phoebe wobbled violently.

Fretting that she would topple over and draw attention to herself, she willed her left foot to grow roots into the floor and keep her upright. The room was beginning to go blurry.

'Now we're going to do the Cat,' said Christina.

'Are you all right?' asked Rev Lucy.

Phoebe thought she was addressing her, but then realized she was looking at Christina, whose face had suddenly creased up.

'Never mind me,' Christina answered huffily. 'Let's just get on.'

They were taken through the next series of movements. Along with the others, Phoebe crouched with her back arched: easy. She bent her head upwards: not so easy. Summoning extra willpower, she levered her muscles into the required positions. Thank goodness everything was in slow motion.

'How did you manage, Phoebe?' asked Christina when they had finished.

'Good, thank you.'

'Do you feel energized now?'

Hardly. She could have collapsed on her mat right there and fallen asleep if it hadn't been so cold. Luckily, Christina didn't seem to need an answer. She was now bustling about, chatting to the others.

'Is there any news of Miaow?' the vicar asked her.

'No, nothing at all.' At once Christina took on a look so tragic it out-melancholied Melancholy. She noticed Phoebe listening.

'Miaow is the name of my cat,' she explained. 'I called her that because I thought it was only right that she should be able to say her own name. She's been missing for three whole days now. I'm desperately worried about her.'

Phoebe couldn't help smiling at the name, although she sympathized. 'Oh, I'm so sorry. What does Miaow look like? I'll keep an eye out for her.'

'She's a tortoiseshell. Sweet, but bossy with it. She firmly believes she rules the universe. She has a toffee-coloured smudge on her nose and a streak of white between her eyes. But you'll know her if you see her, anyway. She's the only cat in the village. There must be about ten thousand dogs in Darleycombe, but she's the only cat.'

Christina was evidently fond of exaggeration. She sighed. 'She's never disappeared for this long before. I've put up notices and sent it out on the village email. I've even offered a reward, but no luck so far. I live alone, so I'm missing her a lot.' She swallowed hard. 'Anyway,' she said, rallying, 'I don't want to burden you with my problems. Tell us all about you, Phoebe.'

Phoebe suspected that Miaow led a far more interesting life than she did.

'Dad and I moved to Darleycombe last month. He thought I should try something new, so here I am. This yoga session has been an experiment, really.'

'Well, it's lovely that you came. There isn't much else on around here, I'm afraid. What other things are you interested in doing?'

'Oh, not a lot,' Phoebe assured her. 'I'm trying out an art class on Zoom, but I'm terrible at it. Otherwise, I'm happy with just reading and telly.'

'I love art too!' Christina exclaimed, delighted that

they'd found something else in common. 'I've done hundreds of art classes over the years. And I make jewellery. I made these, in fact.' She pulled at her earrings, which were made up of green and silver beads. 'I have a little shop in Porlock and, at the moment, I'm making pieces for the otter sanctuary to sell, too. You know about them, of course? I've started experimenting with silver otter earrings and I've already done some pendants and bracelets.'

'I've been to the sanctuary,' Phoebe said. 'I haven't looked round, though. Dad and I were dropping off a baby otter.'

'Really?' Christina's eyes blazed with interest.

'We found an abandoned cub down by the riverbank and took it in.'

'Wow! How marvellous! I wonder if the otter is your spirit animal.'

'Oh no, I doubt it.'

'Aha! You already know what your spirit animal is, then? Do tell.'

There was something childlike and endearing about Christina. Phoebe sifted through various creatures in her head and tried to think which one might be representative of herself.

'A leech,' she answered at last.

Christina burst out laughing. 'That's far from flattering. No, I'm sure you're wrong. It might be an otter, you know. Otters are symbolic of all sorts of things. When I started on the otter jewellery, I looked them up online, and I'm quite the expert now. It's highly significant when an otter appears in your life. It indicates you've been overthinking things and you need to rediscover your inner child.'

'Ha ha,' Phoebe said nervously.

'Otters herald a time of exploring feminine mysteries. And medicine,' Christina asserted.

'Medicine?' Phoebe echoed faintly.

'Yes, medicine. And healing and mysticism. Both the Indigenous Americans and the Celts saw magic in the otter, along with a good dollop of humour. Otters are so playful, you see. In Ireland, the otter is sacred to Manannán mac Lir, a sea god, and in Wales, to Ceridwen, the great Mother Goddess.'

'Okay.' Phoebe was sagging now. The grey-haired ladies were long gone and the vicar had packed up her bag and was on the point of leaving. She waved on her way out.

Christina was unstoppable. 'In Celtic tradition, the nicknames for the otter mean Brown Dog and Water Dog, implying loyalty and unyielding love.'

'It was my father who spotted the otter first,' Phoebe pointed out. Loyalty and unyielding love were Al's traits rather than hers.

Christina waved away her comment. 'Phoebe, it's time to assess whether something in life is pulling you down to the point of drowning. Your otter is a sign that you shouldn't take things so seriously. This is a time for personal liberation and renewed joy.' She laughed again, noting Phoebe's cynicism. 'Forgive me for nattering on. I got a bit carried away there. It happens sometimes.'

Phoebe liked people who could laugh at themselves. 'What's *your* spirit animal?' she asked, curious.

'Oh, mine's an aardvark.'

Phoebe didn't know much about aardvarks. Weren't they piggy things that stuck their snouts into the earth and ate termites?

Christina didn't stop to explain. 'Tell me more about your rescued otter.'

'It's a female and an orphan, and that's all we know. But Dad and I will be going to see it again on Saturday.'

'How wonderful! I often go there to sketch. I can meet you, if you like, and you can show me your baby otter and I can introduce you to the other otters. And the people, Carol and Rupert.'

'Oh, I don't know,' Phoebe stammered. This was all moving a bit fast for her. 'We've already met Carol, and I'm not sure if she'll be okay with it.'

'Don't worry yourself about Carol. She's a teddy bear in disguise, and Rupert is great, too. A real old-fashioned gentleman. Do come!'

She made it impossible to say no.

Al was waiting for Phoebe in the car park when she came out.

'How was it?'

'Good.'

'You took your time. I was wondering if I should come in and rescue you.'

'No. I was just chatting. I met a rather lovely person.'

'Who was that, then?'

'Christina, the yoga teacher. She says the otter is my spirit animal.'

'Nice.'

Phoebe reflected on what else she'd said about otters. The words 'loyalty and unyielding love' kept repeating themselves in her mind. She swivelled in the front seat and looked across at her father as she did up her seatbelt.

'Dad, did you remember to bring the washing in?'

He slapped his brow. 'Oh no! It's still out there. It's been on the line nearly a week now. Ah well, at least it's been thoroughly rinsed and aired.'

'I'll give you a hand with it when we get back in.'

'No, no. Don't even think about it. I'll do it. Just don't let me forget again.'

She felt a surge of affection towards him, for all his foibles, for everything he did for her. It was high time she did something for him.

Al was single. At one stage, Phoebe had speculated about him and the French teacher at the school where he had taught. If anything *had* been going on, it was short-lived and unacknowledged. That had been years ago. Otherwise, he'd formed no romantic relationships at all since her mother's death. He had devoted himself solely to his children. Now that Jules and Jack had left home, he poured his energies into looking after Phoebe. And, year by year, he seemed to shrink a little more. It wasn't right. It wasn't fair.

Al had started mumbling about the voracious community of Darleycombe slugs that had invaded the vegetable garden and selfishly consumed several of his beloved courgette plants. It was just as well there were some seeds left in the packet. He would plant them in the hope they wouldn't meet a similar fate. Fingers crossed they would catch up with the others. What a shame Higher Mead didn't have a greenhouse.

Only half listening to him, Phoebe pondered on Christina again and the fact that she lived alone with just her cat for company – and, at the moment, without even her cat.

6

Coco

AL WAS PLEASED on two counts. First, that Phoebe seemed to have found a friend at yoga, and second that she was raring to visit the otter sanctuary. He couldn't remember when she'd last been so enthusiastic about anything, especially anything that involved going out.

They were to meet Christina in the car park. This Christina had arranged for them to look around early, before the place was officially open. She made jewellery, some of which was sold in the gift shop, and she knew Carol Blake quite well. Phoebe had gone on and on to him about the lovely Christina. She was 'one of the most interesting people I've ever met', 'incredibly sparky', 'with a great sense of humour', 'closer to your age than mine, but really young at heart' and 'super-fit'. Since these were words chosen by his daughter, he understood that 'super-fit' referred to sportiness rather than sexiness. In spite of this, his imagination had naughtily added long legs, ripe lips and excessive curves to Christina's other qualities. He drove to the sanctuary in a state of pleasant anticipation.

When they drew up in the car park, Phoebe pointed out of the window.

'There she is. That's her.'

The person waiting was nothing like the adorable character he'd imagined. Standing by the entrance, wrapped in a cape thing that looked like a pair of curtains, was the rude, forthright woman who had careered into his car last week. He wilted. It wasn't that she was unattractive – she had her own quirky, zingy brand of beauty. But her presence felt like a test that he knew he'd fail.

'Oh, it's you!' she said when Phoebe introduced them.

'Yes, it's me,' he replied, without warmth. 'How's your car?'

'Fixed, thankfully. Yours?'

'Ditto.'

She was at least making a gesture towards politeness, but her face implied that the incident was his fault, which it definitely wasn't. Still, she had been kind to Phoebe.

His daughter was standing back, surveying them both. 'So Christina was the person you pranged on your rounds. How funny!'

Al replied defensively: 'Excuse me, but I don't think I was the main pranger here.'

Christina opened her mouth as if to argue, then shut it again.

'Anyway, here we all are,' said Phoebe, speaking fast. 'Shall we go in?'

*

48

Crestfallen that her father had pulled the shutters down on his usual charm, Phoebe asked Christina if there was any news of Miaow. There wasn't.

'There's nothing worse than not knowing whether she's alive or dead. I can't even give her a decent burial,' she moaned. 'I'm glad we're here, though. The otters will take my mind off it.'

At the entrance of the building, they were greeted by Carol Blake. She seemed less dour than she had been before, perhaps due to the presence of Christina. She even managed a tight smile.

Phoebe asked if they could see the rescued baby otter before they did anything else.

Carol nodded. 'Just briefly, mind, and you must be quiet. Not you,' she added to Christina, whose face fell.

'Oh, can't I just—'

'Too many of us,' Carol said firmly. 'I'll let you see the cub next time, Christina. Go and talk to Rupert. He's in the office.'

She led Al and Phoebe out of the back door of the building, across a yard and down a short track flanked by holly hedges. At the end was a small run containing a wooden hutch. Carol held a finger to her lips as they peeped over the barrier. The cub was just outside the hutch on a patch of grass, with a ragged teddy bear. ('Charity shop,' muttered Carol, by way of explanation.) She had one paw resting on the teddy's stomach but was sitting in a curved position, nose to tail, busily grooming her own fur. She was even tinier than Phoebe remembered.

And there it was again, the Otter Effect, like bright bolts of sunshine streaming into her heart.

'You can name her, if you like,' Carol conceded, addressing them both in a whisper.

Al, whose grumpy expression had been ousted by sheer delight, looked at Phoebe, delegating the job to her. 'Any ideas?'

She gazed at the cub, deep in thought. 'There's something very determined about her. She seems quite an individual, quite a character. She's grooming herself so thoroughly, and what a beautiful, perfect coat she has! So I think I'm going to call her Coco, after Coco Chanel. Or as in the drink, cocoa, because her fur is almost that colour.'

Carol nodded. 'Well then, Coco it is. And it's time to feed her. It's important to handle her as little as possible, but at this stage it's inevitable. She can't feed herself yet and she'll be missing her mother a lot.'

She shooed Coco into the hutch and lowered the door, then opened the roof and gently picked her up. To Phoebe's amazement, she found herself being handed the cub.

'Just this once,' said Carol.

Phoebe cuddled Coco, and the sunlight inside blazed stronger. What was it that triggered such a strong reaction? Was it some kind of misplaced motherly instinct? Was it the knowledge that she had saved Coco's life? Or had she simply been overcome by this stratospheric level of cuteness? She didn't know. She gazed down at Coco's features: the soft, chocolate-coloured fur on her head, the cream-coloured velvet under her chin. The white marking on her upper lip that looked like a milk moustache; the molten brown eyes, wide nose and minute, perfectly rounded ears; the bristly whiskers that stuck out from rows of tiny holes and looked like freckles; the webbed paws that clutched at her sleeve like delicate miniature hands. Coco had put immediate, total trust in her. To be appreciated by a baby otter was an incredible compliment, far better than the compliments of human beings, who were probably less perceptive and definitely less honest.

'Here, give her a few squirts of this,' Carol said, now producing a baby's bottle from her pocket. 'It's warm puppy milk.'

Phoebe did as she was told. Coco seemed to know what to expect and opened her mouth, the inside of which was very pink. She sucked and gulped down the milk, her eyes closed in bliss. Her tail wagged, dog-like, from side to side. Then she looked up at Phoebe and gave a series of happy little squeaks. Phoebe would have liked to squeak back at her but didn't feel she could in Carol's presence.

'Okay, that's enough,' Carol said. 'Put her in the run now, if you would.'

Back on the ground, Coco pottered round to the other side of the hutch, chirruping softly to herself. Her gait was slightly wobbly and her head swayed from side to side as if she was looking for something. Spotting the teddy, she pounced on it. She dragged it by the back leg to the entrance of the hutch, then lay down, resting her nose on the tatty seam of its stomach.

'She looks a bit lonely,' said Al. 'Can't you put her in with the other otters?'

'Not a good idea,' Carol answered, her voice still hushed. 'Those pens are too close to the public. But you're

51

right. Otters are sociable animals, and normally there will be two or three cubs in a litter, so she could do with some company. I've contacted the nationwide otter community and there's another orphaned cub of a similar age in a wildlife park in South Wales. A member of staff will be transporting that cub here to join us soon. It's a male and it's called Paddy.'

'Doesn't sound very Welsh,' Al commented. 'Perhaps he has some Irish ancestry?'

Phoebe conveyed to him with her eyeballs that he was not to indulge in any of his *Father Ted* impressions, least of all the Mrs Doyle one. She laughed hard at his manic Mrs Doyle in private, but Carol would doubtless not be amused.

Carol had ignored his comment anyway. 'Coco and Paddy will grow up here together until it's time for their release.'

'And when will that be?' asked Phoebe.

'Not for another ten months or so. We'll see how they get on, but the idea is to let them out on to the banks of the Darle as soon as they can fend for themselves.'

'Can I help look after them?'

Out of the corner of her eye, she registered her father's gesture of surprise.

Carol's frown intensified and filled her whole face. She ushered Al and Phoebe away from the enclosure and back down the path so that they could talk at a normal volume. When they had reached the yard, she halted, turned around and started listing all the reasons why Phoebe couldn't and shouldn't get involved.

Many of the otters here were used to people, liked

interacting with people and felt safe when surrounded by people. Those otters, content in captivity, would never survive in the wild. Otters due for release were a completely different matter. They would be monitored by means of a video camera and had to be left to their own devices as much as possible. They must not, once past a certain stage, be handled, spoken to or played with. Phoebe was welcome to see the domesticated otters whenever she liked but should stay away from Coco.

Phoebe, in a hot rush of determination, argued back. It was not fair that they, who had rescued Coco, should be deprived of her company. She and Coco had formed a bond and she knew the otter trusted her. She was willing to learn and super-keen to help.

She heard the insistence in her own voice, felt the beat of her indignant heart, knew somewhere deep inside that this would be important.

'They need to be fed, don't they?' she protested. 'I can at least pop in to feed the two of them every so often, can't I?'

Carol sniffed. 'Coco and Paddy will need to have their food left downwind, so that they're not aware of a human presence.'

'Not a problem,' said Phoebe bluntly.

'Once they're weaned, their food will be made up of raw fish – smelly and disgusting,' Carol pointed out.

'Again, not a problem.'

'You will become fond of her. It will be very hard then for you when she is released into the wild.'

'I know. I want to do it anyway.'

Phoebe crossed her arms, aware of Al waiting,

watching, knowing his daughter wouldn't budge. He had always admired her tenacity.

She planted herself squarely facing Carol. She did not let herself blink. Nor was she going to be the one who looked away first.

'Oh, all right,' Carol said wearily. 'Once in a while I'll let you do the feeding. It might be a good thing in some ways. At least it will be a change of human, so they're less likely to become dependent on me.'

Phoebe resisted the urge to punch the air. 'Great,' she said. 'Sorted.'

Christina was in the office, drinking tea and deep in conversation with a long, beaming man.

'This is Rupert,' she said. 'Rupert Venn.' He jumped up and shook their hands.

Al had only known him a matter of seconds – too short a time for any real judgement – but he immediately liked him a little less than when he'd been seated, due to his extreme height. It was never pleasant to be looked down upon by your fellow men.

Rupert, too young to be Carol's husband, must be a member of staff. His pale-blue eyes looked out of a very clean-shaven face. His hair, fading at the temples, was smartly trimmed around his small ears. Christina had clearly been telling him all about Al and Phoebe.

'I'm fairly new to the village myself,' Rupert told them. His voice was cultured and creamy smooth. 'I used to do purely office work, but life here is much more interesting. Not that I have much to do with the actual otter care – I leave that to Carol. But I help with the accounts and in the shop, and I do odd jobs, like pulling up nettles and repairing the fences.'

Al noticed the prominent Adam's apple that kept moving up and down his long neck whenever he spoke.

Christina busied herself making more tea. She was full of questions about the otter cub and delighted to learn that Coco was soon to have company.

'Coco and Paddy will make a great team, I know it already,' she cried. She turned to Carol, thrusting a mug into her hand. 'Hey, Carol, how about telling your guests how you set up the sanctuary?'

Carol hugged the mug close to her chest and spoke rapidly. It had all started six years ago when she discovered an injured otter on the road. She hadn't known what to do with it, but she came from a farming background, so knew about animals generally. She had brought it home, consulted with the local vet and somehow managed to nurse it back to life. A friend had helped and they had learned a lot in the process. News of their success had spread around Darleycombe and the area. Then suddenly people had started bringing them injured and orphaned otters.

'But last year my friend unexpectedly met her true love. Late in life, you might think, seeing as she was in her sixties, like me. Anyway, off she went to live with him in Scotland, leaving me to look after the otters. Fourteen of them. There's an otter community across the country, you see, and I have ended up with some non-native otters too, that were passed to me from other wildlife parks. They attract tourists and keep the money coming in. It was a lot to manage on my own, and I didn't cope very well. You wouldn't believe how complex otters can be – well, not otters themselves, they're not complex – but running a business is quite a minefield. And as for the public . . .' She grimaced. She evidently preferred otters to people. 'Luckily for me, Rupert arrived here six months ago, and now he helps with the business side of things.'

Rupert coughed modestly.

'Always pleased to help you, Carol, and we all love otters, don't we?' he added to the assembled company.

'We had a few disasters last month, and I don't know what I would have done without you,' Carol said, unexpectedly showing a hint of vulnerability.

'What disasters?' Phoebe asked.

'A young boy poked his finger through the caging and got bitten by one of the otters. The child was okay, but it was a bloody affair, awful for everyone. Soon after, we had health-and-safety inspectors coming round, and they happened to visit just when the warning signs were down, being cleaned. So the sanctuary got a big black mark. I did explain, but it looked as if I was making excuses. Such bad luck.' Carol swirled her tea and took another gulp. 'Then we had a break-in at the sanctuary – £200 cash, stolen from the till.'

'It was very shocking, because all the money goes to looking after the otters,' Rupert put in. 'Unbelievable that anyone would do such a thing. We discussed getting CCTV in for the entrance and gift shop after that but, sadly, we just can't afford it.'

Al wondered if this was a hint. Were they hoping for a donation? An image of the unpaid bills he'd left on the windowsill at home rippled uncomfortably through his head. He laid down his mug and cleared his throat. It must be time for them to look at the other otters. Rupert seemed to read his mind.

'Shall I do the honours, Carol?' he asked.

'Yes, yes. Do, Rupert. Christina, you've been here enough times, you can help.' She disappeared through a side door without saying goodbye. Al had the impression she was relieved to escape their company.

Rupert, however, was keen to show them around. The whole area backed on to the river, which was just visible behind the barriers. Every available wall space was covered in signs with information and warning notices: *Otters bite. Please do not try to touch or feed them. Parents, you are responsible for your children*.

The enclosures were surrounded by caged fences. On the human side, a circuit of wooden walkways led them across small bridges, viewing platforms and ramps for wheelchair access. On the otter side were playgrounds made up of branches, rocky ramparts, tunnels and old tyres. Every enclosure had a pond or a tub of water and some had a little waterfall. Otters gambolled through the grass and dandelions. They rolled and wriggled on their backs. They slid into their pools and coursed through the water. Silver V-shapes trailed in their wakes.

Phoebe and Al looked on, enraptured.

'That's Rowan,' Rupert told them as a lithe brown otter popped his head out of a tunnel then dashed up to perch on a rock. 'He's a Eurasian otter, found locally.'

Rowan had leaped off the rock again and was now lolloping along the edge of the pond. He was joined by a second otter, and they chased each other around for a couple of circuits before sliding into the pond.

'That one who's just joined him is Quercus,' Rupert said. 'Carol went through a phase of naming them after trees, and Quercus is the Latin name for oak.'

Phoebe nodded wisely and Al could see she had known this already.

Quercus pelted along, just as fast as his companion but in a more lopsided fashion.

'Does he always run like that?' asked Al.

'Yes. It's an old injury, but it doesn't bother him at all,' said Rupert.

They moved on to a lower walkway where the otters could be watched behind glass as they swam in huge tanks. Two otters were engaged in watersports, twisting and spiralling through the bottle-green water. Their names were apparently Twiggy and Willow. They were sisters, Rupert said. They had been offered mates several times but were completely uninterested in boy otters.

Further on, Holly and Hawthorn (a couple of North American river otters) were playing in and out of a branch that lay on the ground.

Al was glad to see how energized his daughter seemed to be by the whole experience. Christina kept pointing things out to her, fizzing with excitement, even though she'd apparently been here dozens of times before.

Rupert was very informative. He told them how everything was kept as close to the otters' natural environment as possible. The water came straight from the River Darle. No detergents were used when cleaning, just the natural water.

They were introduced to a gang of small, ginger-coloured otters in another pen, who were swarming around in circles. These, Rupert told them, were a family of short-clawed Asian otters. They were non-native and were here mainly for the tourists.

An otter broke off from the group, snatched a pebble, tossed it into the air and nimbly caught it again.

'Look, he's juggling!' cried Al.

The otter seemed to be putting on a show specially for his viewers.

'They have a good sense of humour,' said Christina. 'They love to make us laugh and entertain themselves at the same time.'

Rupert resumed his spiel. 'There's a pulley system for opening the otter doors and shutting off different areas. Not like some wildlife parks, where they have automated systems operated by push buttons. We're not a big, sophisticated set-up.'

He gave Phoebe a wink that Al knew she would find patronizing but would forgive anyway because it was kindly meant.

Al was now beginning to suffer from information over-load. They had been there less than an hour, but he noticed that Phoebe had fallen silent. He looked at his watch as if they had another appointment and suggested that it was time they left.

Christina turned to Phoebe as they headed for the exit. 'Why don't we meet up when you next come in to see Coco? Then you can join me sketching the otters? You said you liked drawing, and it would be so much fun if we could do it together!'

Al was clearly not included in this little scheme, a fact that he didn't mind at all.

Phoebe studied her feet. 'Oh, thank you . . . But I really don't think that's for me.'

Christina surveyed Phoebe curiously but didn't pursue it.

7

Unreasonably Lovable

IT WAS COCO this, Coco that, and Coco everything else in the Featherstone household. Al had never seen his daughter so obsessed. Coco was so much adored and discussed between the two of them that she even cropped up in conversations where no otter should naturally belong. When Phoebe looked at herself in the mirror, she exclaimed, 'Messy hair. Too messy. I need to take a leaf out of Coco's book.' When Al said he'd switch on the hot water for a bath, Phoebe told him Coco hadn't learned how to swim yet – rather a *non sequitur*, although he could see a vague connection. When they watched an episode of *Sherlock Holmes*, Phoebe commented that Coco's philosophy on life was much better than Sherlock's. (Did an otter even *have* a philosophy on life? Al asked himself.) And when Al apologized that he still hadn't sorted the dodgy light fitting in the hall, Phoebe said it didn't matter since Coco lit up their lives anyway.

Phoebe had already been back to the sanctuary for a lesson from Carol on otter care. Al had loitered while his daughter warmed some milk, fed Coco, bathed her and dried her in a towel. Since Coco was still small and needy, one otter cuddle had been permitted while Phoebe was bottle-feeding. Al was also allowed a quick turn, which touched his heart far more than he let on. How could he help it? Coco was so excessively, unreasonably lovable. Despite her fur and long, tapering tail, he was reminded of holding each of his own babies in his arms soon after they'd been born. It was strong, this instinct to care for whatever was sweet and vulnerable. He caught Carol looking down on Coco, noticed her eyes had widened and her whole face looked softer. He suspected that, under her unsmiling exterior, Carol might also possess a gooey inside.

She had stressed again the importance of balance. There must be just enough interaction so Coco would be stimulated and not feel lonely . . . but not enough to make her dependent. When the second cub, Paddy, arrived there must be no more cuddles. Phoebe didn't seem to mind this. She had made it her mission to make Coco self-sufficient so she would thrive in the wild when the time came. Much like good parenting, Al thought.

'As the cubs grow, we'll gradually give them more solids,' Carol explained. 'Their adult diet will be a variety of fish, including roach, trout, eels and a special mix of fresh minced beef and biscuit meal. They'll get dead day-old chicks, too. It's a useful source of roughage.'

Al had flinched at this. Phoebe hadn't.

At this stage, however, Coco needed milk every three hours, day and night. Al had the impression that Carol would rather have got on with the job herself without Phoebe's intervention.

'How often do you want to come?' she asked.

Phoebe couldn't drive, so she would need his cooperation. She hesitated, weighing things up.

He scratched his chin. 'I'm afraid I won't have the time to drop you off here every day, but we could arrange for you to visit and feed Coco on alternate days?' he suggested.

'Thanks, Dad, that would be great.' She turned to Carol. 'Would that be okay? Maybe I could come in the evenings when it's quiet, sometime after the sanctuary closes to the public.'

Carol didn't answer. She heaved a huge Tupperware tub out of the fridge and upturned it on to an equally huge chopping board. A mass of grey fish slithered out. Some were already dismembered; others were whole. She handed Phoebe a knife. It was evidently a test to determine whether she had the stomach for this sort of job. Al was proud to see his daughter's firm resolve as she set about slitting the fish open and chopping them up. He saw her grit her teeth, saw her eyes watering, and so did Carol, although it wasn't for the reasons she assumed. The knife banged down again and again. Al wanted to intervene, to step in and say he'd do it himself, but he knew Phoebe would never forgive him. She forged on, exposing slimy pink innards, severing grisly fish heads. The smell turned his stomach and made him retch.

Carol continued talking as Phoebe sliced. 'Soon after I started out, I discovered the fish farm eight miles down the river. I approached them to ask if they were willing to contribute anything, but I didn't have any luck there. Fish farms don't warm to otters much, which is understandable, seeing as otters deplete the river's fish supplies. More recently, Rupert has been down there in person several times to try and reason with them, without success. But we're lucky. The chippy in Porlock is extremely generous and regularly supplies us with fish heads, tails and anything else they don't need. That's free food for the otters and a free ticket here for the chippy staff.'

She glanced down at Phoebe's handiwork. 'Well, your fish-chopping skills are pretty good – almost as good as Rupert's and mine. We'll be seeing you the day after tomorrow, then.'

At last Phoebe was applying herself to something. She'd been down for a long time, and it was wonderful to see the old spark blazing again. Al felt lighter and brighter himself because of it. Phoebe's appetite for life was flooding back before his eyes. She had a name for it: the Otter Effect. Otters really should be prescribed on the National Health Service, he reflected.

Phoebe had also been quite preoccupied at home. She seemed to be spending hours in bed poring over Google Maps of the village. Al had no idea what she was up to. Every day that he brought home packages to be sorted, she examined them carefully.

It was extraordinary, the amount of stuff humans liked to amass. Some of the packages contained necessities:

tools, food, clothing. Many had contents that, in themselves unnecessary, were seen as life's essentials thanks to the advertising industry; items such as beauty products, iPhone accessories and goods made irresistible by the addition of a designer label. They existed to promote self-esteem, the esteem of others, a point made, a position in society underlined. Others were pure indulgence: luxury bath salts, chocolate truffles, pretty knick-knacks. Then there were those items that seemed to exist almost on another plane, such as books, films, art and music . . . The things that made people feel and imagine, that helped them escape from the petty round of trivial existence and transcend to a different level.

Nature, he reflected, was far more minimalist in its wants and needs. Otters were blissfully unbothered about anti-wrinkle cream or bestselling novels or topiary shears.

Sometimes Phoebe asked if she could check out the photos of the parcels being delivered. Bewildered, Al let her inspect them. After all, he hadn't signed any contract to say he mustn't.

She kept asking all sorts of questions about the neighbourhood. Who had a car? Who went out a lot? What sort of gardens did people have, and were there many trees around? Outhouses?

To please Phoebe and to be able to report back, he had begun to observe all sorts of little details that he never would have noticed before.

Now, for example, as he pulled into a driveway, he registered the peeling white paint on the gates. They must be permanently propped open, since the hinges had rusted into their sockets. The sign that read *Vicarage* was relatively new, though. As he marched up the drive with his two parcels, he noted the crunch of gravel underfoot. The garden was shaded with laurels, he would inform Phoebe later, and the back wall loomed over a small, sagging trampoline. He looked up at the ivy-coated Victorian building. It had generous proportions, suitable for tea parties, he imagined. Reverend Lucy Daws, who Phoebe had apparently met at yoga, lived here with her husband, children and dog. It was always Rev Lucy herself who opened the door, accompanied by a sweet black Labrador. He hadn't seen the children, although he sometimes heard them playing upstairs. The husband seemed reluctant to show his face in public. ('I can understand that,' Phoebe had said.)

'One for you and one for Mr Daws,' Al informed Rev Lucy at the door.

She was too young and too female to be a vicar, he couldn't help thinking. Her fluffy blonde hair was scraped back, held off her forehead with two plastic clips. Her complexion was blotchy, but her features were fine and delicate. Her very blue eyes suggested sensitivity. She was wearing her dog collar with a dark, plain dress. She immediately switched on a smile and asked after Phoebe.

'She's doing all right, thank you,' he replied. (When he'd asked Phoebe how she was this morning, she'd said, 'Mellifluous, thank you. And you, Dad?' To which he'd replied, 'Quite antediluvian, thank you.' But he wasn't going to try to explain this to Rev Lucy.)

Al stooped to stroke the Labrador, who nuzzled his hand with a wet nose, gazing up at him. Was it his imagination, or did the dog look rather sad?

Rev Lucy took both the parcels and submitted to them being photographed as they were passed over.

'Oh, this will be the book I ordered, *God and Coping with Disaster*. I'm always on the hunt for wisdom I can regurgitate for my parishioners.'

He liked her honesty.

She placed the other parcel on the hall table. 'I have no idea what this is.'

The package for her husband had issued from a company called Smelders. ('They manufacture hoop earrings and thick, rope-like necklaces,' Phoebe had informed Al. 'Very bling.') He hoped the Smelders box contained a nice present for Rev Lucy. She didn't come across as a bling type, but maybe that was just a vicarly front. Maybe she and her husband had romantic evenings in which she unleashed herself from that uncomfortable-looking dog collar, let loose the enthusiasm of her hair and festooned herself in glittery stuff. He hoped so.

'Anyway, I'd best be off,' he said. 'Loads to deliver this morning.'

His next address was right in the centre of the village, only five minutes away. He had to brake for a troop of mallard ducks as they crossed the road and waddled towards the village green before plopping into the pond one by one.

The package for Mr S. Dobson was hard and heavy. A DIY manual, Phoebe had reckoned. Mr Dobson's house was one of three that all looked pretty similar and were of indeterminate age. They stood neatly lined up, their bland, pebble-dashed faces fronting the Darle. He knocked several times on Mr Dobson's door. There was no answer, just an eruption of barking from within the house. He would have to leave the parcel somewhere. He was searching for a suitable place when he spotted a figure pruning an unruly sprig from the ruler-straight hedge of the neighbouring garden.

Thanks to a delivery last week he knew the man was called Mr G. Bovis.

'Morning!' he cried. 'Sorry to trouble you, but would you mind taking this for Mr Dobson?'

G. Bovis, a portly man with a florid face, looked sour.

'Just leave it there. He'll find it all right.'

'Right you are.'

Al propped the parcel against the front door, took the compulsory photograph, and retreated as another explosion of barking sounded from inside.

'Blasted dog, never shuts up,' grumbled Mr Bovis.

'Nice hydrangeas,' Al commented, appreciating them over the hedge.

Mr Bovis brightened. 'Thank you. They are, aren't they? My pride and joy! That and the fishpond.' He waved his secateurs in the direction of a large, ornate pond with lilies, guarded by a stone heron. Beside it stood a pristine, octagonal summerhouse.

'Partial to a bit of gardening myself,' Al said. 'But mainly vegetables. Proud of my beans.'

Mr Bovis's lawn was a manicured expanse of parallel mown lines in a strikingly artificial shade of green. It was a very different style of gardening to his own. Still, it was nice to find something in common with his new acquaintance.

Today's rounds were nearly finished. Just one more house to go.

He stopped beside a property on low ground which, like his own, backed on to the river, although on the other side. The tiny cottage resembled a child's drawing, with steep gables, square windows and front door boldly painted in cobalt blue. A young apple tree stood in the garden. Windchimes hung from its branches, twisting and tinkling in the breeze.

He knocked on the door.

Christina looked as surprised to see him as he was to see her. He'd checked the name on the package, of course, but it had not occurred to him that Ms C. Penrose could be her.

Her hair was wet and smelled lemony. She had a towel around her shoulders and she was draped in a buttercup-yellow sarong that almost reached the floor.

Thrown by her dampness and her sudden proximity, he stammered: 'Oh, hello. Hello there, Christina. Just dropping off a parcel.'

'Ah,' she said, eyeing the package dolefully. 'My cat-food order. Thanks. Not that I need it now.'

'Do you want to send it back?' he asked. It was part of his remit to return parcels as well as delivering them.

She hesitated. 'Listen, Al, I've just washed my hair and it'll go epically wild unless I smother it with gunk and get a hairdryer to it straight away. But please do come in for a moment.'

'Well, I . . .'

He could escape now by saying he needed to get on with his work, but in fact this was the last delivery today. And, peculiar as she was, something about Christina piqued his curiosity. As he wobbled between his wish to stay and his wish to rush off, she flapped him inside.

'We need a cuppa. I do, anyway, and you look like you do. I'll put the kettle on, but you'll have to do the rest.'

Although the outside of the house was plain, the inside was a different matter. He glanced into the living room and saw that she had covered virtually every surface with an exotic throw. Needle-felted hangings filled the walls, in among what he assumed must be her own drawings. Some were lifelike sketches of wild animals while others were blobby and abstract.

Christina ushered him into the kitchen and whisked around, pointing at cupboards. 'Teabags. Mugs. Tin containing home-made apricot and almond slices. Help yourself. I'll be back in a mo.'

After a hasty exit, she poked her head back in and pointed at the fridge. 'Milk. It's probably out of date so consume at your own risk. None for me, thank you.'

Al noticed a cat basket on the floor. It was lined with a rug covered in white, black and ginger hairs. A couple of clean cat bowls sat beside it.

He made the tea and settled down at the kitchen table. The tablecloth was tie-dyed and the curtains resembled Indian saris. The mugs, hand-painted with swirls, flowers and butterflies, were from a local pottery. Christina evidently loved her artisan stuff. She was refreshing, he decided; wacky and just a little bit scary.

The milk did turn out to be out of date and his mug of tea was swimming with little white flecks. Luckily, it tasted normal. The apricot and almond slice was delicious in a gritty, low-fat, low-sugar sort of way. As Al ate, he looked out of the window at the back lawn, a couple of woven willow structures and a rustic-looking seat beside the Darle. He could hear the stirrings of the river from here.

His eyes kept flicking back to a framed picture that stood on the windowsill. A smiling young family: man, woman and baby. The man had Christina's dark hair and sweeping eyebrows. Her brother?

By the time the distant moan of the hairdryer had finished he was on his last mouthful.

'Meh,' Christina said, reappearing. 'Sorry to keep you waiting. My hair was putting up a real battle.'

He wondered if he should say how nice it looked – which it did – dark and abundant and super-glossy – but decided against it. He didn't want to sound like a creep.

'So there's no news?' he asked politely, indicating the empty basket and cat dishes.

'No, nothing. Poor Miaow! I couldn't bear to hoover the sofa this morning because tufts of her hair were on it and . . . I don't think I'll ever see her again.' Christina's voice snagged and her face underwent a range of different contortions. 'Don't you dare say she's only a cat!'

'I wouldn't dream of saying any such thing,' Al protested.

'Oh. Sorry. I didn't mean to be rude. It's just that a lot of people don't understand.'

She seemed deflated now and sank into a chair. He was amazed at the way she flicked from one mood to another.

Al remembered her distraught face when he'd bumped into her car and realized she had been desperately trying not to cry. Her anger had been a cover-up for grief. It might be wise to change the subject.

'It's all very arty here,' he said.

'I'd rather be arty than artificial.' She had taken it as a criticism, which wasn't how he'd intended it. He pushed her tea towards her and tried again, pointing at the photo. 'I've been admiring that. Are they your family?'

'Yup, my son, Alex, with his wife and my grandson.'

Al hid his surprise behind a cough.

'They live in Switzerland, so I don't see much of them.' She took several gulps of tea and cast her eyes down.

Al wondered about the history, but didn't feel he should ask.

'You'll be wondering what happened to my ex,' Christina said.

Al's throat made another small noise that could have been a yes or a no.

She put her mug down again. 'Life didn't pan out the way I expected. When I was very young and stupid, I fell madly in love with the boy who played Macduff in the school play. Macduff said he loved me back but, unfortunately, he lost interest when I fell pregnant. I did my best to bring up Alex on my own. I did actually marry – twice – after that, in my twenties, but I somehow got it all wrong again. And again. You're talking to a double divorcee here,' she added with a mirthless laugh.

It was hard to believe.

'You're married, I presume?' she asked.

'Was. She died.' Al felt the sharp sting that happened whenever he thought about Ruth. His body curled in protectively around his heart.

'Oh. I'm so sorry.'

It was what everyone said. What else could they say?

Christina looked into his eyes searchingly. He had a

sense that she was treading gently around his sorrow, viewing it from different angles, careful to give it respect but seeking ways to soften it.

'It was a long time ago,' he said, to make her feel better about it. She shouldn't be wasting any worry on him.

He remembered all the cards of condolence that had poured in: cards from the hospital where Ruth worked, from Al's school, and from all the friends who came round for dinner. The cards were well meaning, but he had hidden them away because he thought they'd be a continual reminder to the children. The friends and senders of sympathy had long since moved on with their own lives. But the shock of Ruth's death had left him confused and raw. Even now, eight years later, he still felt confused and raw.

'What was she like? Your wife?'

People didn't normally ask. He appreciated the fact that Christina had risked it. But how to sum up a whole life in just a few words?

'Ruth was . . . She was a mediocre ukulele player. She worked in a hospital. She was a loving mother. She went to evening classes in tap dancing and she knew the names of butterflies. Blue really suited her. She was good with people, and she wrote to-do lists and she kept a pot of pencils that were always sharpened. She smoothed out everyone's problems. She made great apple chutney. She liked netball and swimming and Waldorf salad and chess. She was . . . just lovely.'

Christina nodded, her eyes glistening.

Al's throat constricted. He needed to change the subject again.

'Thank you for meeting us at the otter sanctuary the other day,' he said. 'Phoebe really enjoyed it.'

Christina pulled subconsciously at her earlobe.

'Bah, it's nothing.'

'It's not nothing. She loved it, and it meant a lot to her that you were there too.'

'I do wish I could persuade her to come and draw the otters with me. I enjoy her company, and I think she'd have fun, too.'

Al pushed the crumbs around his plate. He didn't want Christina to think of Phoebe as a nonentity. He wanted her to know that his daughter would grasp life with both hands, given half the chance.

Christina examined him with new interest. 'Al Featherstone, you are looking shifty.'

Al twisted and untwisted his fingers, trying to decide whether he should say something or not.

She detected his doubt straight away, along with his need for lightness. Her face broke into a smile. 'What's up? I insist on knowing. Tell me now what it is or I will' – she looked around for inspiration – 'hit you over the head with my frying pan. And believe me, it is not your lightweight Teflon rubbish. It is solid cast iron and it will hurt.'

He lifted his hands in surrender.

If she was to be a genuine friend to his daughter, Christina would have to understand what was really going on.

'Is there something I should know about Phoebe?' she asked.

Al met her gaze. 'Yes. There is.'

8

How Are You?

'Morning, phoebes, how are you?'

'Very molecular, thank you. And you?'

'Nicely gladiatorial, thank you.' They'd got into the habit of throwing out random adjectives in response to that unavoidable *how-are-you* question. Phoebe had initiated it because to say 'Fine, thanks' all the time was an outright lie, but to say 'Barely functioning' seemed churlish. She'd begged Al simply not to ask, but he couldn't help himself and had been feeling bad about it. So now this slightly bizarre exchange had become the way every morning began. Any adjective apart from 'fine' and 'well' would do, so long as it had no relevance to the current situation. The more obscure the word, the better.

Now he had matched his gladiatorial to her crepuscular, they could get down to the serious business of breakfast, which they normally had together in her bedroom. Al laid down the breakfast tray and nudged a plate of toast towards her. Before anything else, though, she glugged down half a mug of coffee, because nothing would be possible without it. She stretched.

She was still glowing from the visits to the sanctuary and her new responsibility of looking after Coco. She had fallen in love with all the otters, in fact: the charming family of short-clawed Asian otters; cheeky Rowan; Quercus with his slight limp and lopsided walk; the devoted sisters, Twiggy and Willow; the ageing but lively North American couple, Hawthorn and Holly.

Otters, she decided, operated on their own, possibly superior, level. As well as being beautiful and magical, they threw themselves at life with such attitude. They were all about *fun*, a concept she had pretty much forgotten.

Wouldn't it be amazing if the otter really was her spirit animal?

It might have been, once. Was it possible for your spirit animal to degrade into something else, if life inflicted limitations on you?

'Dad, tell me honestly,' she said, rinsing down her first mouthful of toast with another gulp of coffee. 'Am I more like an otter or a leech?'

Al guffawed and leaped in to reassure her. 'Not a leech. Far from it, Phoebe. If those are the two options, you're definitely an otter. I'd go as far as to say you're very otter-ish indeed.'

It was said with conviction but, as her father, he was obliged to try to boost her confidence whenever possible.

'Swift, fluid and joyous? Yup, that's me,' she answered, unable to resist the sarcasm.

How hard it was to avoid the self-pity that was forever lurking at the edges of her subconscious. She steered the conversation in another direction.

'Well, if I'm like an otter, I need "stimulation" and "enrichment" and all those other things that Carol says the otters require for their wellbeing. So you can be my eyes and ears, Dad. You get about everywhere in that vehicle of yours. So tell me more about Darleycombe, the people and the parcels you deliver.'

Her interest sprang not from any need to interact but from an intense natural curiosity. If there was one thing Phoebe craved it was knowledge, and no knowledge was more fascinating than other people's business. People were a challenge and a conundrum. She wanted to know about their values and priorities, the choices they made, the way their minds operated. Phoebe wasn't ashamed of her insatiable curiosity. In fact it was the thing she liked most about herself. (What she hated most about herself was her conflicted resentment toward her sister. But she needn't think about that now.)

She listened to her father's informative ramblings about Rev Lucy, Mr Dobson and Mr Bovis, taking in every detail.

She now had her own list of local acquaintances, which comprised the women from yoga, Carol and Rupert.

'Nobody you've met is anywhere near your age, though,' Al said, rubbing his hand over his brow. 'You should be spending your time clubbing and flirting, like your sister.'

Phoebe pulled a face. Clubbing wasn't her thing. And for the foreseeable future, there would be no flirting. Romantic relationships were not a viable option for her.

For her father, on the other hand . . .

At the otter sanctuary, he'd wandered around with that faraway look she'd been seeing on his face more and more. He was such a dreamer. She wondered if her plan to get him together with Christina could possibly work. So far, they didn't seem to have progressed much beyond their initial animosity due to the car incident. She decided to have a gentle pry and throw in some compliment about Christina if she could.

'What do you think of Carol?' she asked, as a starter.

'She seems down to earth and friendlier than I thought at first. I'd say she was completely herself and comfortable with it.'

Phoebe nodded. 'And Rupert?'

'He's very *tall*,' Al answered. Phoebe could detect a slight . . . what was it? Not jealousy or resentment, but a sort of grim acceptance.

She offered up her own opinion of Rupert.

'He is posh but nice.'

Al took another slice of toast. 'You're right there. Posh but nice. Absolutely the way to describe him.'

'And Christina?' she hazarded.

He shrugged. 'Well, she likes *you*,' he said. Which was annoyingly non-committal. 'I hope you don't mind, Phoebes,' he added with a shamefaced look, 'she invited me in when I called at hers with a delivery, and we got talking and I told her about . . . you know.'

'Dad, that's not fair!'

'I know, I know,' he said, hanging his head. 'I shouldn't have done such a thing without consulting you. I don't know how she managed to drag it out of me. She must be a witch or something.'

'No, she's just a very kind person, and I expect she realized something was wrong.'

Al nodded in a resigned fashion.

'Did you know she's a grandmother?' he asked.

Phoebe didn't.

'Makes me feel quite young,' he said.

'Not as young as Christina, though,' she reminded him. 'Or do you think being a granny automatically ages her?'

'In some ways, yes. More life experience. She's had two husbands, too, I gather.'

'Really?'

'Really.'

This gave Phoebe pause for thought. Maybe Christina wasn't very good at relationships. Maybe she was a poor judge of men? No, she refused to believe it. Everyone made mistakes, and Christina had proved she was a person who was prepared to take risks and go for it. Exactly the sort of person Al needed. Anyway, she'd have yardsticks now. Her history would have taught her about the potential pitfalls in a marriage, armed her with wisdom and shown her (if only by comparing and contrasting) what a good man was made of. Al was therefore bound to score much higher in the potential husband stakes than anyone else.

It was possible, of course, that Christina didn't want anyone else, but Phoebe didn't think it likely. There had been a real air of loneliness about her when she had talked about missing Miaow.

Cross as Phoebe was that Al had given her away, she wasn't as cross as she wanted to be. Christina had invited him in, which was promising. And he'd felt able to confide in her, which was pretty amazing.

Phoebe let on to very few people that she had been in chronic pain for the past three years. They didn't need to know how arduous even the simplest activity had become for her. What did it signify to them that bending to open a drawer sent torturous jolts down her spine? That writing down a single sentence was a major ordeal? That chopping a fish wrung tears from her eyes and made her gasp in agony?

Everyone suffered from pain at times, but for most people it was fleeting – a matter of minutes or hours. When it went on month after month and year after year, it changed you.

There were no bleeding gashes to see, no black bruises or swellings. The pain was invisible, but that didn't make it any less powerful. It changed in character and intensity, but it never left her alone. It was a drilling pain, a hammering pain. It kicked and bit and punched. It gnawed and eroded like a slow acid drip. It stabbed and prickled and clawed. It crushed her and left her utterly drained, often unable to operate on any level at all.

Her neck suffered most, closely followed by her head, although at times the pain invaded her whole body. Things that should be relaxing had now become frustrations instead. This morning, for example, the idea of a hot bath had been utterly delicious. How she'd longed to soak her groaning muscles under the kind softness of warm water. She had held an inner debate, weighing up the pros and cons (as she often did), and had decided in the end (as she often did) that it would be impossible without bending her neck one way or another . . . and that would hurt far too much. Putting her whole head under water was an option, but that would make her hair wet, so then there'd be the torture of drying it afterwards. (Going to the hairdresser's was a nightmare; they never understood the pain they were inflicting, which was why she hadn't been for so long. Desperate to keep her hair short, she frequently hacked at it herself.) So she had taken a shower instead, and spent ages trying to angle the hot water on to the sore patch between her shoulder blades. The wet dribble that wormed from the shower head was woefully unenthusiastic. Al still hadn't got round to doing anything about the awful plumbing.

Phoebe had sought medical advice again and again. Doctors had repeatedly produced platitudes and suggested paracetamol. Some had also referred her to physiotherapy, which had made no difference whatsoever. None of them had been able to give her a diagnosis. She had even begun to doubt herself at times, and glumly googled psychosomatic ailments. She was pretty sure she wasn't making it up, though. It was too real, too utterly, horribly life-sapping.

She had tried countless private treatments: chiropractors, osteopathy, cranial osteopathy, deep-tissue massage, then a few more alternative ones like the Alexander technique, the Bowen technique and emotional freedom techniques. She had risked acupuncture too and had gained nothing apart from a glimpse into the problematic lifestyle of a porcupine. Somebody had then recommended a sound-healing session, and she'd willingly attended. It had involved lying on the floor in a large, echoey room while a woman played gongs – a surreal experience that seemed to have little scientific backing, but anything was worth trying once. She had even gone to a therapy session where a bearded and sandalled guy had tipped salt over her and then played bongo drums while she sat cross-legged on the floor, as instructed. These things might be effective for some people, but none of them had worked for Phoebe. All they had done was to dig deep holes in her father's bank account.

No day could be borne without painkillers. They didn't kill the pain, but they dulled it, and she was grateful. Yet often the fibres of her body ached and burned so fiercely that she was useless for anything. All she could do was to shut herself in her bedroom and wait until she could face the world again.

Whenever Phoebe was asked about university or jobs, she changed the subject. Every dream and vision of the future had been packed away, the lid shut tight.

Most people, of course, had a good supply of sympathy. Nobody had endless quantities of the stuff; sooner or later, everyone ran out of it. It was as if you were only allowed to be ill a certain amount. After that, you crossed a barrier and they ceased to be interested. They decided you must be putting it on or exaggerating. You'd become a bore. It was time you pulled your socks up and got on with life.

It didn't work that way, though. You were stuck with it. You had no choice. No amount of sock-pulling would make the pain go away. It didn't care that it had become tedious. It just carried on and on and on . . .

Phoebe had her coping mechanisms well in place. Pretending to be fine had become a lifestyle. She worked particularly hard on smiling. Nobody seemed to suspect so long as she smiled a lot. If she blitzed her system with painkillers and saw people only for a very short time, they didn't notice anything was wrong at all. This meant that, even if she couldn't escape from the pain, at least she didn't have to talk about it. She didn't have to see that look of scepticism on their faces when she couldn't name her condition.

She also kept it to herself out of sheer stubbornness. Pain dominated her life quite enough as it was. It was doing its very best to *define* her, and she was determined not to let it. The last thing she wanted was for people to think of her as 'poor, ill Phoebe'. If she could drum up enough cheer and conversation to give an impression of normality the few times she met people, then the illness hadn't a hundred per cent won.

It was impossible, of course, to fool her own family, who saw her often. They all had some awareness that she was suffering, which was all the more reason to try to be bubbly in their presence. She effervesced whenever she could, as much as she could. Her brother and sister probably thought that much of her inactivity was due to laziness. Al, who was inevitably closer, had a truer picture. Even with him, she pretended hard and smiled hard. She knew that her hurt only resulted in his upset.

Now it had become necessary to apportion out small morsels of energy to Coco and the people at the sanctuary. That was pretty much all that was available. And that could only be achieved by pushing herself to her limits.

Much of the time, Phoebe was capable of thinking only one thought: *Ouch!* However, there was a lovely little slot each day when the pain ebbed enough for her to engage her brain the way she used to. She decided to put that time to good use.

'Are you all right to receive a visitor? It's Christina. I can get rid of her if you like?' Al offered.

Phoebe pulled herself a little further up on her pillows and put her book on the bedside table. 'No, it's okay. She can come on up.'

Her room was a tip and she was in her unicorn pyjamas, but she had a feeling Christina wouldn't mind. She heard Al retreat again, voices, a light step on the stairs, and then Christina entered her inner sanctum. She looked as if she was bursting to share some news. It didn't stop her from staring at the scene.

'Wow, that is one cool bed!' she announced.

'Glad you like it. Dad made it.' Al-appreciation emanated from her and spread throughout the room. Hopefully, Christina was absorbing some of it as she stood there.

'Phoebe, I'm not going to stay long, but I've got a present for you. You won't like it at all.'

Not sure how to take this, Phoebe produced her best *Mona Lisa* smile.

'Close your eyes.'

Phoebe closed them. She listened to Christina's footsteps going out of the room and coming in again, along with wild giggling and something that creaked slightly.

'Okay, open them now.'

Christina was wielding an enormous gift-wrapped object. Phoebe knew immediately what it must be by the shape. She tore off the sparkly paper, miming more enthusiasm than she felt. An artist's easel.

'It's amazing. Thank you so, so much!'

'I knew you'd hate it,' Christina said cheerfully. 'But you have no excuse now, do you? When you come to the sanctuary to see Coco, you can do some otter sketching with me. And do come into the countryside and draw some scenery, too. Whatever you like. I'll be totally offended if you don't use it,' she added.

Al must have told Christina how painful it was for her to look down while writing or drawing. Christina had given it some thought and come up with this as a solution. It would still be difficult to hold a pencil and draw, but the easel would certainly help.

'It's so generous of you,' Phoebe said, meaning it. She sneaked a peek at her father, who was loitering in the background, hoping he'd registered Christina's kindness.

'Don't worry,' Christina said. 'I didn't fork out for a new one. I'm not made of money. Car-boot sale.'

Phoebe had no intention of going out into the countryside to draw scenery. Drawing otters might be marginally more tempting, since she'd be at the sanctuary anyway. She considered. With sufficient painkillers in her system, she might be able to draw a passable bowl of fruit . . . but apples and pears didn't dash about everywhere. They stayed nicely put. She was sure otters wouldn't be quite so obliging.

Christina was waiting for her answer, all brightness and anticipation, her attention pinpointed on Phoebe. Her enthusiasm was focused in completely the wrong direction. It was Al who she was supposed to be interested in. Still, it would be rude to say no.

9

Barking

June sunlight beamed down on the top of Al's head. The grass, newly mown, sent a green perfume up into the warm air, mingling with the scent of roses and honey-suckle. A mixed ensemble of birds chirruped in the treetops. Al gazed around at the mosaic of colour that was his garden and let himself be enveloped by summer.

Phoebe stood beside him. She was in a thick jumper, despite the mild weather. He had managed to coax her outside for a picnic, although she would venture no further than the garden.

The back lawn was their chosen spot, since it was more private, but he'd insisted she came to look at the front first. It was crammed with flowers: a blousy pink rose bush, lilacs, hollyhocks and coiling periwinkle. Foxgloves had self-seeded everywhere and the breeze gently swung their purple bell spires to and fro. Weeds proliferated too.

Dry grasses, groundsel, boisterous dandelions and clouds of forget-me-nots erupted through the gaps in the crazy paving. It was shambolic. *Nicely* shambolic, though, Al thought.

Phoebe's mind must have been elsewhere because, having dutifully admired the flowers, she started questioning him about his deliveries. Al groaned inwardly. Once his morning's route had been run, his mind was reluctant to dwell on anything work related, but she was very persistent. Did any of today's parcels look interesting, she wanted to know?

He scratched his head. 'Interesting? How do you mean, interesting?'

'You know. Unusual. Telling. As though they might contain anything out of the ordinary.'

To him, the issue was not the contents of the parcels but their quantity, bulk and weight. Phoebe's mind worked on a different plane. He'd often thought that. He pondered. Al was not naturally given to gossip but was happy to stoop that low if it engaged Phoebe's interest. He lived for her sparks of enthusiasm.

'Well, it looks as if Mr Crocker has been ordering romantic gifts for a lady friend.'

'Mr Crocker?' she said, her eyebrows shooting up in surprise. 'The ancient, goggle-eyed, balding ex-copper guy with the chickens?'

'Yes, him.' Her dismissive tone peeved him. 'Phoebe, it's possible for even an ancient, goggle-eyed, balding ex-copper with chickens to be deeply passionate. Just because someone has a hard, wrinkled, old shell doesn't mean he can't have a tender heart that longs for love.'

He laughed abruptly, conscious that he might have overemphasized his point.

Phoebe fixed her father with a penetrating gaze. After a pause that went on a little too long, she asked him how he knew that Mr Crocker had a lady friend.

Al chose his words with care. 'Well, I can't be a hundred per cent sure, but he ordered a small box that had "Vivienne Westwood" printed on the packaging and, as far as I know, Vivienne Westwood doesn't produce chickenfeed.'

Another moment of silence passed between them.

'Ah well, let's have this picnic, then, if we're going to,' said Phoebe.

He fetched the rug and sandwiches and they made their way to the back garden together.

Al had begun to revolutionize the small plot, which the former owners of the cottage had left to its own devices. The part nearest the house was now an embryo vegetable garden: three raised beds with potatoes, courgettes and runner beans. He'd made the decision to go organic and had vowed not to use slug pellets. It made plenty of extra work. Every night he did a 'slug run', a tour of the garden with a torch on a quest for the pestilent critters. When he found them, he flicked them into a plant pot with a stick. He then carried them down to the riverbank, where they were emptied out, surprised but unscathed. He did wonder, though, if they were equipped with their own inner satnavs and promptly made their way back again, laughing at him with silent, slimy sniggers. The courgette leaves looked as if somebody had been at them with a hole-puncher.

Al often had the feeling he was sliding backwards in life. The list of things he wanted to achieve was getting longer, not shorter. What with the extra time involved in the slug run and his new job and all the cooking and cleaning and ferrying Phoebe to and from the otter sanctuary, he still hadn't found time to mend the hall light. Or sort out the plumbing. Not to mention unpacking most of their possessions. Ah well, those things could wait. It was important to enjoy nature's gifts, or what was the point in anything?

'Phorrr. It's smelly here,' Phoebe said, breaking his reverie.

'Don't be rude about my lovely compost heap,' he retorted. 'All that dead, rotting stuff is turning into rich food to nourish new life. It's an alchemy. A paradox. It's a kind of resurrection. In fact, I would say compost is nothing short of a miracle.'

'It's not a good accompaniment to peanut-butter sandwiches, though.'

She was right. They wandered further down the lawn towards the fresher air and the riverbank. Phoebe lowered herself on to a scarred tree stump, which was level enough to make a semi-comfortable seat. Al spread out the rug and settled on it. The river was twinkling, leaves were rustling in the breeze, and there were crisps and sandwiches to be consumed. Life could be a lot worse.

Then Phoebe started asking him about dogs.

Who had dogs in the village? What sort of dogs did they have? Did they have a *Beware the Dog* notice but no actual dog?

These were easy to answer. Al knew the dogs better

than their owners, in fact. While most were friendly, just a few had big teeth and a bloodthirsty aura, and with his type of work it was wise to be cautious.

There was the vicarage black Labrador, a gentle giant who licked his hands whenever Al passed over a package. There was Seth Hardwick's Alsatian, who always jumped up at him. There was Spike Dobson's snappy, yappy Jack Russell terrier. Then there were (he counted on his fingers) two spaniels, three sheepdogs, a bulldog (probably French), a couple of whippets and a Labradoodle, not to mention several breeds he couldn't identify.

Which dogs barked a lot, Phoebe wanted to know. He informed her that by far the barkiest dog was Spike Dobson's Jack Russell (much to the disgust of his neighbour, G. Bovis). Judging by her face, Phoebe was making careful mental notes about all of this. At the same time, she nibbled at a sandwich, treating it with great respect. Al had already wolfed his down. He never treated sandwiches with respect, despite the great affection he felt towards them.

He assumed the questions were over, but once she'd finished her mouthful Phoebe started afresh, on a theme of cars. Who in Darleycombe owned a car? Who went out a lot? Who had a garage?

'Phoebe, what's with the inquisition? Why all these weird questions?'

She took a long, slow swig of water before answering. 'I'm doing some detective work *à la* Sherlock. I'm trying to find Christina's cat, Miaow.'

'Aha. Why didn't you say so before? Now I see where you're coming from.'

His daughter seemed very keen to help this new friend. An image of Christina imprinted itself on to his brain, her hair dripping, her buttercup-yellow sarong clinging to her curves. Everything about the woman was vivid and emphatic, as if she was unwilling to be forgotten. But there was a certain vulnerability there which he found touching. Like him, she had been bruised by life, she was acquainted with loss, but she forged on anyway.

He looked out over the river. It was all green swirls and stippled brushwork and sunlit dazzle. Pale prongs of sunshine penetrated the depths. Furry, green waterweed swayed in the current.

'Listen, the river's speaking again,' Phoebe said.

She had always been fanciful, but he understood what she meant. In among the plops and splashes, a deep bass murmur combined with higher-toned voices in a torrent of conversation.

'What do you think they're saying this time?' he asked.

'Oh, I can hear them quite distinctly. They are saying, *Thank you, dear Featherstones, for looking after my water baby, Coco. Please return her to us as soon as she's ready.*'

Al shook his head. 'I don't hear them saying that at all.'

'What are they saying, then?'

'They're saying, *Mr Featherstone is looking very hungry. His daughter really ought to pass him another sandwich.*'

She took the hint and passed the plate over with a chuckle. It was her sandwich really, but she wasn't going to eat it and he hated waste. He wished she'd eat more. She had become so pitifully thin.

He posted four crisps between the slices of bread and cheese and polished the sandwich off.

A shaft of light slanted through the trees and shimmied on the water. The surface was teeming with silvery crinkles, passing in and out of each other in constant movement. A dipper bobbed rhythmically on a rock, its white chest swollen. They were rare, people told him, but here he saw them nearly every day.

'Coffee?' he asked.

'Good plan. Caffeine will focus our minds.'

She was evidently still thinking about finding Miaow. She seemed to be expecting him to be her accomplice: Watson to her Holmes, Hastings to her Poirot, Lewis to her Morse.

He helped her up, gathered the rug and picnic remains and accompanied her back to the cottage. While he filled the kettle, she took a jotter pad from the kitchen drawer. It had been an hour since her last painkillers, optimum thinking time for Phoebe, and she was taking advantage of the fact.

'I've compiled a list of possibilities. Shall I read them out?'

'Do,' he answered, tickled.

Phoebe cleared her throat. 'Title: *Where is Miaow?* Possible answers: *1. Stolen. 2. Dead. 3. Hiding. 4. Stuck.* Now for the analysis. *Stolen.* Highly unlikely. Miaow is not an exotic pedigree. She's a common moggy, valuable to Christina, of course, but nobody else.'

'Sounds logical to me,' said Al.

'*2. Dead. Subsection (a) Killed by a dog, or possibly a fox, or (b) Run over by a car.*'

Al winced. He passed plenty of roadkill on his travels and dreaded running some poor creature down.

'Both unlikely,' said Phoebe, 'since no one has found a body. Other causes of death: *(c) River.* I don't think so. She's lived near the river for years and never had a problem with it. Then we have *(d) Underlying health issue* – heart, kidneys, cancer, a stroke? She might have just crept away somewhere to die. Animals do that, I believe. And there are plenty of woods around.'

'In that case, we don't have much hope of finding her.'

'True. But she was healthy, according to Christina, and had been recently checked by Mr Pickles the vet, so death by these causes is improbable. Next, we come to scenario number 3. *Hiding.* Why would Miaow do such a thing? Christina feeds and loves her, and the love is, by the sounds of things, returned.'

'Oh, yes, I should say so,' said Al, recalling Christina's intense emotion when she talked about her cat. She was undoubtedly a very passionate person.

'Finally, number 4.,' said Phoebe. '*Stuck.* Up a tree? On a roof? Trapped in somebody's garage? I've come to the conclusion that 4. is by far the most likely. I'm going to work on this premise.'

Al placed a mug of coffee in front of her. 'Full marks for effort,' he said, trying hard to think of the cat rather than Christina.

Phoebe took a sip and continued, consulting her notes.

'Cats are very territorial. But also very curious. According to Google, the average cat roaming distance is between forty and two hundred metres. Bearing in mind that Miaow is the only cat in the village, I'm assuming her territory will be nearer two hundred metres.'

She unfolded a large sheet of paper that was tucked

into the notebook and spread it across the kitchen table. It was the printout of a local map.

Al marvelled at Phoebe's powers of analysis. She had always scored highly at school, and her teachers had praised her 'vivid imagination and unusually sharp mind'. She also had a sort of sixth sense about people, which her sister called 'spooky'. This, combined with a dogged determination to find the solution to any given problem, meant that Phoebe might achieve much in life . . . if only she was well. He was keen to help her. It would be neighbourly to try to help Christina, too.

Phoebe followed a pathway across the map with her finger.

'I don't think a cat would go anywhere near a house with a dog, certainly not a dog that barks a lot or a large, ferocious dog. That rules quite a few of them out,' she reasoned.

'Indeed it does.'

'And Miaow's not going to have crossed the river, is she? The nearest bridge is right opposite Spike Dobson's barky dog. So she must have stayed on this side of the Darle. She will either have headed towards the village green . . . or along the backs of the houses, passing through the gardens or the strip of woodland here. Do you want to know where I think she's ended up?'

'Tell me,' said Al.

10

Miaowing

PHOEBE WANTED TO come with him but had crashed again. He could see from her face that she was besieged by pain, so he told her to lie down. He could do everything she asked, no problem. He would report back to her, down to the last detail.

'Thanks, Dad,' she said, her voice scarcely more than a whimper. 'I need to save myself for feeding Coco later.'

She crawled back to the four-poster bed and pulled the curtains around her.

He knew it had been a hard decision. Although Phoebe had now subscribed to the feel-the-pain-and-do-it-any-way school of thought, in her life, something always had to be sacrificed for something else because there simply wasn't enough energy to go round. It wasn't fair. As he got into the car, a ball of rage flamed in his stomach. The steering wheel felt hot. He turned on the fan.

It hurt him to see his child in pain – he still thought of her as a child. She had become a ghost of her real self. In the past, she'd been a rounder, rosier person who sizzled with wit and fun; so much so that he'd felt dull in comparison. She had inherited it from her mother, of course. Ruth had been brisk and kind and clever and up for anything. Phoebe had been very like her, but with her own special add-ons.

With a pang, Al remembered Phoebe as a toddler. The way her sentences rose in pitch at the end as if they were questions. The way she always repeated new words to herself, trying to remember them. The way she gave names to everything – her two shoes (Belinda and Bethan), her hairbrush (Aslan); even the tap (Tina Turner). When she was sad, she'd puff out her cheeks as if holding the misery balled up in her mouth. When she was happy, she hopped up and down from one leg to the other.

It had been Phoebe who had held the family together after Ruth's death, even though she was only eleven at the time. She had taken on to her small shoulders the weighty responsibility of cheering them all up. She had been the pushy one then, ensuring they still made trips out together to cafés, museums and the cinema. They had all sought comfort in different things: Jack in dating girls, Jules in social media, clothes and make-up, Phoebe in food. Al himself had craved the countryside.

Phoebe had done everything she could to ease their sorrow. She had accompanied Al on long treks across the fields. Cried with him. Put her chubby arms around him. She had been funny and charming with Jack's shy girlfriends when he brought them home. She had patiently weathered Jules's teenage tantrums and told her how beautiful she looked in the new clothes and make-up. She had shown an exceptional capacity for sympathy and helped herself to another Jaffa Cake.

Phoebe had dealt with the grief better than everyone . . . at least, until a certain point a few years later, when she seemed to suffer a delayed reaction. She had suddenly become very quiet. She was not wanting to go to school (which she'd loved before), and she changed the subject when he asked about her day. That must have been the point when her illness began to take hold.

Sometimes when he was out on his rounds, Al shouted and swore. He had finally adjusted to the loss of Ruth, but to see his beloved daughter like this was hard to bear. She was still just nineteen and she was living like an old woman. She wasn't bitter – perhaps she was too tired to be bitter – but *he* was. All he wanted really was for her to be well again. He'd give anything for that.

If only he could do more. He wished he could share even this short drive with her, these views. Outside the car window, meadows rolled by, quilted with yellow and green. Hawthorns clustered in ragged glory, their blossoms drifting like snow. Wild roses and bramble flowers entwined the hedgerows. The river gleamed like molten silver.

Mind you, Phoebe recently seemed to have lost her appreciation of nature's beauty. It was as if even admiring things used up too much energy. Her focus seemed to be forever pulled back inwards.

He drove up the hill, turned into the driveway and narrowly avoided treading on a chicken as he got out. He rapped on the front door. Mr Crocker opened it speedily this time.

'Ah, Al Featherstone! Another delivery?' His face was alight with anticipation.

'No, I'm sorry, it's not that, Mr Crocker.'

'Jeremy, please!'

'It's not a delivery, Jeremy. There's a missing cat in the neighbourhood and I'm just asking . . . people' – he didn't want Mr Crocker to feel he'd been singled out – 'if they wouldn't mind checking their outhouses and garages . . .'

He glanced down and noticed Mr Crocker had pink socks on today, although mostly concealed within thick hiking boots.

'Ah, right you are. Just a minute.'

He disappeared back into the house then returned with some keys. Al followed him into the driveway, noticing he walked with a slight limp.

'Sorry to be slow. Toenail problems,' explained Mr Crocker. Phoebe had been spot on about that one.

He slid open the up-and-over door of the garage. His black Vauxhall was inside, and there wasn't much else to see. A few stacked boxes, a rake propped against the wall, a rusting toolbox on the floor and an old chest freezer.

They took a look inside the boxes but there was no sign of Miaow.

'Otherwise, there's only the henhouse.'

Phoebe had said specifically to check the henhouse.

'Quick look, just to be sure?' Al said, keeping his voice light.

Mr Crocker frowned, but as an ex-policeman he clearly believed in thoroughness. He led Al across the rough, grassy area. Several chickens eyed them before resuming their jerky-headed pecking.

The henhouse was a low wooden shed with a slanted roof and a smaller lidded section for the nesting boxes. Mr Crocker swelled with pride. 'It's got five roosting perches, a galvanized removable tray for easy cleaning and secure sliding latches. Only the best for my girls! I shut them in every night to keep them safe from foxes. They stay out during the day and wander at will.'

He opened the door, and the two men peered in. The interior was dark and Al could just make out corners and edges. A thick, strong smell of straw tickled his nostrils.

'Miaow?' he called gently, not expecting any answer.

But there *was* an answer: a very quiet, cautious 'mew' from one of the high perches.

'Good God!' exclaimed Mr Crocker.

Al could hardly believe it either. He held out his hand. 'Come here, Miaow!'

There was a soft thud of four paws landing on the floor, and a moment later he caught a glimpse of two green eyes. A furry face pressed against his hand. He pulled her out into the daylight. Her fur was rumpled and her eyes looked wide with alarm. He held her close and stroked under her chin. Relaxing into the caress, she stretched out her neck for more.

Mr Crocker gaped at her. 'Well, I'll be blowed. I haven't looked in here for a while, only in the egg department. I've been cleaning it out by means of the sliding tray, and I just popped more straw in via the roof. She could have escaped when I let the girls out every morning, but thinking about it, she was probably too scared. I normally give them porridge scrapings at seven thirty and bang a spoon on the pan and shout *Kakakaka* so they know to come out and get them.'

'*Kakakaka?*' Al wondered a little at his choice of word, but he supposed it must work for the chickens.

'Yes. Then I close the door behind them. The clatter and *Kakakaka* must've been a bit much for this little cat.'

'I should think it scared the living daylights out of her. No wonder she stayed put.'

Mr Crocker scratched his chin. 'I did think the girls were acting a bit oddly when I shut them in at night. Amazing, really, that I've not lost any of them.'

Al nodded. 'Well, if you don't mind my saying, they're big girls and Miaow isn't exactly huge. She must be pretty hungry by now. It's been six days. Still, maybe she found a mouse or two in there.'

'Quite likely.'

Al smiled and cracked the knuckles of one hand, which made Miaow jump and put her ears back. 'Christina will be over the moon to get her back. I'd better take you straight home, hadn't I?' he added to Miaow.

'Was she pleased?' asked Phoebe. She was sitting up in bed now, looking considerably better, even a little smug.

'She was over the moon,' replied Al. 'Delirious. I don't think I've ever seen anyone so happy. She flung her arms around me and Miaow together, so we could hardly breathe. Then she took Miaow and cuddled her for ages. There were tears of joy. In fact, Miaow nearly drowned. That is one very tolerant cat.'

Al had been touched by Christina's gratitude. He'd kept telling her that the reunion wasn't due to him, it was all due to Phoebe. After Christina's rapturous embrace, Miaow had guzzled down a whole packet of Whiskas. Al had then related how amazed Jeremy Crocker had been that his chickens had all been untouched. 'I wondered if Miaow might be vegetarian, like you?' he'd asked.

Christina had laughed. 'Nice idea, but unfortunately cats can't live off a fully vegetarian diet. Still, she's mainly pescatarian. I like to think I'm a good influence on her.'

Her joy was contagious. He was still basking in it.

'And did she invite you in?' Phoebe asked.

'Miaow didn't,' said Al, pretending to misunderstand.

'But Christina did?' Phoebe glanced at the clock. 'You didn't stay for long, though,' she said in a tone of slight accusation.

'No. I wanted to get back to make sure you were okay.'

'You should have stayed and celebrated with her.'

It was hard to win, Al thought. He had assumed that Christina would want to spend a bit of quality time alone with Miaow, but maybe he was wrong?

Was it possible she'd wanted him to stay longer?

Phoebe was much better at reading people than he was. Ah well. He'd done his best. And no doubt he'd be seeing Christina again soon at the otter sanctuary.

11
Trouble

THEIR SHADOWS STRETCHED behind them as they walked up the path. A hush had fallen over the sanctuary. The last tourist had left. Phoebe could almost sense the enjoyment of today's visitors still hovering in the air. She felt honoured to be here at this hour. Pleased, too, that everything seemed to be going according to plan.

When Al had dropped her off, he and Christina had exchanged numerous smiles (smiles ranging from sheepish to cynical to outright flirtatious). They had launched into cat talk and otter talk and small talk, and her father had only spoiled it slightly by cracking his knuckles during a gap in the conversation. She must have a word with him about that. He'd needed to get back to water the garden and cook dinner, so Christina had offered to take Phoebe home once they'd had enough of drawing otters.

Her father had now left, and Christina was enthusing.

'It's wonderful, Phoebe! This morning I woke up with my dearest, fluffy love-bundle snuggled up against me. Life is PURRY again!'

'How nice.'

'Do you know, I used to suffer from terrible depression, and I chain-smoked before I discovered yoga and mindfulness. When Miaow was missing, I could feel the darkness closing in on me again. I actually bought a packet of cigarettes. I hadn't got round to smoking them, but I would've lapsed very soon. I can't tell you how grateful I am to you and Al.'

'Especially Al.'

Christina didn't seem to notice this last comment. She was in full flow. 'I'm relieved beyond words. Giddy with elation. I want to dance and sing. A party is in order, at the very least.'

You could never underestimate the joy of a middle-aged woman reunited with her long-lost cat.

'What do you say, Phoebe? Shall we celebrate with veggie sausages and home-made relish?'

'If that's what you'd like to do, yes. Great idea.'

'A barbecue it is, then! Expect your invite very soon.'

Phoebe manifested enthusiasm as best she could by means of a quiet 'Yay!' The celebration sounded as if it might expand into something bustling with people, noise and expectation. But if she admitted to Al that she was too ill to go, he wouldn't go either, and that would be an opportunity missed.

In the building, Carol was busy locking doors, while Rupert counted out the day's takings. Phoebe and Christina headed straight to the video screen to check out

Coco. The cub was nestled in a bed of straw, sleeping curled up, not unlike a tiny cat. Her flanks moved gently up and down as she breathed. She rolled over and stretched out her back legs.

'I'll give her a feed if it's okay,' Phoebe said to Carol.

Carol nodded. 'And could you please feed the other otters while you're at it. You know where everything is.'

Carol evidently thought her passion for otter care would diminish in proportion to her exposure to dead fish. Phoebe knew it wouldn't. She wasn't squeamish at all. Chopping anything, though, was physically hard. Still, she was keen to prove herself to Carol, so she swallowed another painkiller when nobody was looking and fetched the raw fish from the fridge. She pulled on the plastic gloves, braced herself and laid into them with the knife, ignoring the barbs of pain that dug into her shoulders.

'God, that's repulsive! How can you bear it?' Christina asked, pulling a face as Phoebe threw sludgy pink innards into a bucket.

Phoebe forced a laugh. 'You feed Miaow, don't you?'

'Yes, but Miaow's food comes in neat, hermetically sealed pouches and it's disguised as miscellaneous splodge, so I needn't think of it as a creature at all. Those fishy bits are truly yuck.' She stepped backwards. 'Come and find me when you're done. I'll be setting up the easels.'

Coco woke at once when she heard Phoebe's approach. She lifted her head with a little squeak of excitement, aware that warm milk was coming. Phoebe lifted her gently and presented the bottle. She clasped her longer than she should, knowing that once Paddy arrived, human contact would be limited much more.

Hey, Coco. I seem to be getting myself a social life. And it's all because of you, I'm beginning to get a social life. How do you feel about that, then?'

Coco waggled her tail and continued to suckle at the bottle.

'Proud, are you?' Phoebe wasn't sure how she felt about it herself. It might be worthwhile, though, in the long run. 'Looks like I'm going to have to go to Christina's barbecue. Let's hope she doesn't invite too many people. And let's hope she keeps on being grateful to Dad.'

Coco looked up at her wisely, shifting the teat of the bottle to one side of her mouth and gulping the milk down.

'Tell me, Coco, when Christina drops me off, do you think she might stay for dinner? That would be great, wouldn't it? And I could feel ill and need to go to bed and leave them together. Ah no, hell, that's not going to work. Christina doesn't eat meat, and Dad mentioned beef stroganoff. Unfortunate. Oh, well, she might stay for a drink, if we're lucky.'

She set Coco down again and watched her scampering in search of the teddy bear. Heart aglow, she walked back to the sanctuary building to collect the bucket of fish.

In the gift shop she almost collided with a man who was carrying a large cardboard box. They both sprang back, apologized and coyly manoeuvred around each other. The man placed the box on the floor, an inch away from the wall and exactly parallel to it. As he straightened again, she was struck by his appearance. He had dark eyes fringed with thick lashes, coal-black hair and beautifully chiselled features. His expression was distracted, as if he had forgotten to turn something off at home. He was oldish – a similar age to Christina – but that didn't stop him from classifying as one of the most handsome men Phoebe had ever seen. Which made her even less inclined to engage in conversation.

'I'm just dropping off twenty-four oak leaves,' the man said, with an air of apology.

'Oh. Um. Right.' Then, as his words sank in, curiosity got the better of her. 'Why?'

'They are £11.99 each. Twenty per cent, which we round up, so it equals £2.40 per leaf for the otters and Carol. Eighty per cent, again, rounded to £9.59, for Ellie and me.'

It dawned on Phoebe what he meant. She had already admired the carved wooden leaves that were on sale in the shop. 'Is it you that makes them?' she asked him.

'It is.'

'They're fabulous,' she gushed, warming to him. 'Unique. I just love them.'

He ran a hand over his brow. He seemed anxious that she should understand something. 'I don't normally make oak leaves. That is the job of oak trees. But I made one once for Ellie for Christmas, and Christina saw it and said to Ellie, "Wouldn't it be great if there were some on sale here?", and Ellie reckoned that I should give it a go, so I did and it was, and here they are.'

Befuddled by the long sentence, Phoebe posted a bright Hollywood smile on her face and wondered what to say next.

'I know Christina,' she declared after a small pause.

He surveyed her with unblinking eyes. Another pause.

'Do you know Ellie?' he asked, suddenly very eager.

She shook her head.

'That is a shame,' he said. Once again getting in each other's way a little, they both headed out towards the public otter pens, Phoebe with the bucket of fish. She threw bits of fish over the fencing towards Quercus and Rowan, who galloped towards her. They pounced on the food and started chomping. Rowan sat on his haunches, holding a piece of fish between his front paws as he feasted. The wood-carving man lingered and gazed at the otter's face with intense concentration.

'Everything all right?' Phoebe asked.

'I'm just counting his whiskers,' he replied. 'It's hard to do because he doesn't keep his head still. Also because some of the whiskers are very much shorter than others. If I count only the long whiskers, I believe there are twenty-three on each side, making a sum total of forty-six. Including all the shorter ones, it must be closer to seventy.'

Phoebe was surprised. 'That many?'

'Yes. A good quantity, isn't it?'

She had to agree.

'Ah well, now that's done, I'd better be getting home,' he said, and in the same instant disappeared by way of the back door.

Phoebe discovered Christina with the two easels and chairs positioned by the enclosure of short-clawed Asian otters.

'I met the man who makes the wooden leaves,' she said.

'Ah, the gorgeous Dan Hollis,' Christina replied. 'Tall, dark, handsome. And different. And uncommonly lovely.'

Was there an attachment here? Phoebe thought it best if she came straight out with a question. 'Are you interested in him?'

'Not in that way, no. He's taken – by my oldest and dearest friend, too.'

'Would that by any chance be Ellie?'

'Ellie,' she confirmed. 'And anyway, he's not my type.'

'Who *is* your type?' Phoebe asked swiftly.

'Cads and tyrants, mostly. I have a terrible habit of falling for men who are oozing valour and heroism on the outside but turn out to be stinking wormwood on the inside.'

That did not sound like her father, Phoebe feared.

'To be honest, though, Phoebe, I think my man-eating days are done. I'm a mum and a grandmother, which is rather a lot of baggage, you know.'

Al had plenty of baggage too, though. Phoebe realized with a jolt that she herself qualified as part of that baggage.

Christina frowned and bit into the end of her pencil. 'I hardly ever see my baggage, though. My son and his Swiss wife and my gorgeous grandson live abroad. So it's just as well Miaow is back.'

She gave herself a little shake and pointed to the otters. 'There's lots of these Asian ones, so I thought we might have more chance of capturing them than the others.'

She threw down the pencil, picked up another from the array and started to draw; strong, sweeping lines across the page.

Phoebe finished her rounds of the otter pens, flinging fish to the joyous residents and wondering if this was the kind of satisfaction Al felt when he delivered his parcels. She returned the bucket to the building, informed Carol that the otters were fed and peeled off her gloves. Exhausted, she returned and settled in the chair beside Christina. She adjusted the paper on the easel.

Her friend's artwork was impressive. Christina had captured the animals' movement absolutely within the first few strokes.

'How did you do that?'

'Practice, like everything else in life,' she answered. 'Don't be scared of going wrong. Don't be self-critical. Just watch the otters and *feel* it.'

Phoebe watched. There were seven otters in this family. They poured out from the mouth of a tunnel and spread out, loping around in the grass. They ran round in a figure of eight. They clustered together and romped to the far end of the enclosure then hurtled back again. They weaved in and out of the welly tree. Play was clearly their first priority in life.

'Makes your heart soar just watching them, doesn't it?' said Christina.

'Yes. I call it the Otter Effect,' said Phoebe.

Her pencil hovered, not quite daring to touch the page. She longed to capture an otter in motion, but they were so fast it seemed impossible.

Christina glanced over and gave a faint, knowing smile at Phoebe's lack of progress.

'Don't try and get a whole otter this time,' she suggested. 'Start small. See that one, there? Just get your pencil to trace the curve of his back. The way the line bends down a little with his neck and then sweeps up to an almost hump shape then along a gradual gradient down to the tip of his tail. You need to relax and go with the flow. Fast and fun. Like the otters themselves.'

Phoebe set to work, sitting bolt upright. It really helped having the easel. She would never have managed all the neck-bending without it.

Soon Christina had amassed a selection of accurate, quick-fire sketches and one particularly striking otter looking out from the page, eyes inquisitive, a sheen caught on its tousled fur.

All Phoebe had was a series of random lines. She surveyed her drawings with disgust.

'Lovely work, ladies!'

Phoebe jumped. It was Rupert, looking over their shoulders at the easels. She covered up her drawings with both hands, ashamed. He transferred his attention to Christina's pictures.

'Well, those are amazing, I must say. Such sensitivity! Quite beautiful.'

'Why, thank you, Rupert,' she simpered.

'And how are you getting on with young Coco?' he asked Phoebe, crooking his back so as to be more on a level with her.

'Pretty well, thanks.'

'She's a dear little thing, isn't she?'

'Mmm.'

'Too bad Carol's so strict about not being able to hold her much.'

'Yes, she's very hard-hearted,' Christina complained.

'She hardly lets *me* see Coco at all. And she made Phoebe chop up a ton of revolting fish.'

Rupert looked impressed. 'You're a good sport, Phoebe. And it's great to have you around. Thank you so much.' He loitered some more, then said, 'Well, I just popped out to say toodle-pip.'

Christina giggled. 'Oh, toodle-pip, then, Rupert.'

He was good-natured but rather annoying. 'Why can't he just say "goodbye", like a normal person?' muttered Phoebe after he'd gone.

'Oh normal-schmormal,' Christina said, keen to assert her allegiance to anything that wasn't. 'I thought his toodle-pipping was quite funny.' She twisted her hair into a loose bun at the back of her head and skilfully prodded a pencil in to fasten it. 'Let's move on to Rowan and Quercus,' she suggested.

They set up again a few yards further on.

Phoebe scarcely looked at the lines she was making. Nearly all her attention was taken by the otters. When Quercus passed close to Phoebe, he stopped and gazed straight into her eyes with such intelligence that she really felt *seen*; more seen than she ever did when a human looked at her (which wasn't saying much).

Quercus yawned.

Christina had resumed sketching, absorbed in her creativity. Phoebe still feared her own marks on the paper looked like the drawings of a five-year-old.

She was surprised when she glanced at her watch and discovered that an hour had passed. Considering she'd been sitting in the same position for most of that time, the pain was negligible. Her spirits were unusually light, too.

It was nearly time to pack up. She fished out her rubber and started rubbing out most of what she had drawn.

All at once she was aware of a large, dark shape moving rapidly to her left. Before she had time to register what it was, it crashed into her easel, knocking it to the ground, then hurled itself over the wall and into the otter pen.

A voice called: 'Oh shit!'

There was a single, excited, high-pitched bark. The otters scattered.

In front of Phoebe was a blur of scampering paws and flailing tails. With horror, she registered that a dog, a monster of an Alsatian, was chasing Rowan around the enclosure. She heard a shriek from Christina on her left, and then they were both shouting madly. So was a lean young man in khaki who had appeared beside them. He started clambering over the barrier.

Rowan darted towards the hutch and managed to whisk away from the dog's reach, but it then turned its attention to Quercus. Hackles raised, Quercus faced his foe for a split second before turning to flee for his life. The dog charged after him, tongue lolling, saliva streaming.

'No!' Phoebe screeched. 'Oh my God, no!'

The young man had one leg over the wall. He was calling the dog and brandishing a leash, but, in his panic, seemed to be getting tangled up in it. It had somehow looped around his foot. 'Boz!' he yelled as he scrambled and struggled. 'Boz! Come here now!'

The dog ignored him. Its jaws were snapping within an inch of Quercus's tail. Phoebe's heart clattered in her chest. The rest of her was frozen in shock.

Footsteps sounded behind her.

Carol. She was in her wellies and her hands and arms were protected by thick leather gauntlets.

'Stop!' she bellowed, pulling the man back. Within seconds she had catapulted over the wall and into the middle of the fray. She hurled herself right into the path of the dog, managed to catch its collar and yanked it back. The three watchers fell silent, stunned by her force and composure.

She dragged the dog to the gate, unlocked it and came through.

'Take him, Seth,' she said to the man in a voice like thunder. His face had turned a deep shade of beetroot. He muttered an apology, untangled himself and clicked the leash on to his dog. He patted it on the head.

'Good boy,' he mumbled, presenting it with a doggy treat from his pocket.

'Good boy!' cried Christina, incredulous. 'Hardly!'

'Just go,' Carol said to Seth. Not raising his eyes to meet theirs, he obliged at once, the dog now trotting obediently after him, looking rather pleased with itself.

Carol fetched the bucket and started throwing fish at the otters to distract them from their recent trauma. Rowan and Quercus cowered in their hutch, but it wasn't long until the prospect of food coaxed them outside again.

Now, as if it had been saving itself up, an avalanche of pain rolled through Phoebe. She gave an involuntary groan.

Christina, who was gathering up the easels, dropped them again and threw an arm around her. 'I think we need some tea. Okay if I get some, Carol?'

'Of course. Rowan and Quercus are all right now. I'll come in too.'

They headed for the back room. Phoebe's stomach churned. As she sank into a chair, further bolts of pain shuddered up her spinal cord.

'Somebody left the back gate open,' Carol growled as she brought through a tray. She looked accusingly at Phoebe. Phoebe knew she'd closed the back gate after visiting Coco, but she felt too ill to defend herself.

Carol plonked down the tray. 'I can't believe this has happened again,' she said.

'Again?' Phoebe asked faintly, accepting her mug with shaking fingers.

'Never mind that now,' said Christina. 'Drink your tea and take a moment to relax, then I'll get you home.'

Christina had read her well. She couldn't cope with any more today.

When they stopped off at Higher Mead Cottage, Christina didn't stay, saying she had to get back for Miaow. Phoebe was met by a strobe effect in the hall. It made her feel worse than ever.

'Sorry,' said Al. 'I was determined to fix that light once I'd done the watering and dinner, but I've spent the last hour looking for the blasted screwdriver.' He looked at her, scrunching up his eyes. 'Hey, are you okay?'

Words eluded her for a moment, then one limped into her head. 'Subterranean,' she muttered. 'You?'

'I'm extraterrestrial, thank you,' he answered, pleased with today's choice of vocabulary. Then, registering her misery, he enfolded her in a warm hug.

Her need for sleep was extreme and desperate. She was

too tired to eat her stroganoff or even to tell him what had happened. She took two painkillers and went straight to bed, even though it was only seven o'clock.

She failed to sleep, though, her head pounding, her brain turning over and over what had happened.

12

Wonder and Beauty

AL HAD ACCEPTED a dozen free-range eggs from Mr Crocker. At the same time, he had been persuaded to go to a bell-ringing session. He hadn't quite liked to say no to the retired policeman. Bell-ringing seemed an activity that Jeremy Crocker took very seriously, for his eyes grew more bulbous than ever and his hands mimed rope-pulling whenever he talked about it. There were five bells in Darleycombe church and recently only four bell-ringers had been available, he'd explained gravely. Al Feather-stone had replied that he'd done a little bell-ringing many years ago. Having mentioned this, there was no escape.

Now he stood in the cold belly of the church tower, try-ing to keep control of rope number four. The other ringers were, by now, quite familiar to him. It occurred to him that their ringing style reflected their personalities. It was the lady vicar, Rev Lucy, who led with the lightest bell, the treble. She took her responsibility with an earnest expression, frequently checking her fellow ringers were all right and compromising on her own rhythm whenever it was required to meet their needs. Mr S. Dobson (whose first name, Al had discovered, was Spike) followed her on rope two. He was a man with a flattish nose, long waves of hair and a ginger-grey beard that was shaped like a shovel. If he hadn't been wearing a tracksuit, he would look very like a Viking. He frowned as he rang and yanked at his rope, as if he and it had longstanding issues with each other. Posh-but-nice Rupert Venn, who he knew from the otter sanctuary, was on rope three. He rang with ease, almost flippancy, and seemed to view the whole proceeding as jolly good fun.

Al was concentrating hard on following these three with an even pace on rope four. He did not feel as in control of it as he would like to be. Jeremy Crocker had claimed his position on the heavy tenor bell behind him. He maintained a steady tolling at the end of each round, but his goggly eyes held a transcendent expression, as if the sound lifted him away to a more magical place. Perhaps he was thinking about his chickens.

Al was managing pretty well when the bells were merely chiming in a downward order. He struggled more when the group embarked on something called plain hunting, which involved constantly changing the sequence. It appealed to his mathematical brain, but it was hard to speed the bell up and slow it down at the correct rate. It annoyed him when he couldn't keep the rhythm exact.

He was tired and relieved when the session was over.

'Time for a tipple,' said Rupert. 'It's a tradition for us to visit the pub after the practice, Al. Will you join us?'

'Gladly.'

Although it was summer, the bell tower was impervious to any warmth and Al welcomed the prospect of a swift pint in the Quarrymans Arms.

He dropped behind the others on the way out. Rupert was always affable, but Al didn't particularly like standing next to him. He wondered, not for the first time, what it was like to have such a good view of the top of everyone's head.

Rev Lucy was locking up with a giant bunch of keys, and Al found himself chatting with her.

'Don't feel you have to come to church just because you're part of the bell-ringing team,' she told him. 'Nobody else does, apart from me. And I sort of have to, don't I?'

Al chuckled. He wasn't religiously inclined. Still, he might give church a go one day, just to give her some support. She looked as if she could do with it.

'We're so pleased to have you, and a complete contingent of bell-ringers again,' she said as she closed the church door behind them and locked it with a metallic clunk. 'George Bovis used to be part of the team here, but he left six months ago and we've only been ringing the four bells ever since.'

'Why did he leave the team?' he asked. Mr G. Bovis was still very much a presence in the village. Al had spotted his portly figure mowing his lawn early that morning when he was on his way to pick up the parcels. As he gave him a wave through the car window, he'd been disappointed to note that the hydrangeas had finished flowering.

'Oh, you know, local politics,' Rev Lucy answered in a hushed voice, aware of the others within earshot.

'Ah,' Al answered, imbuing as much wisdom as he could into a single syllable, although he had no idea what she was talking about.

They trundled to the pub, which was a few yards down the hill, conveniently close to the church. As they went in, Al tried not to look at the two dead pheasants that were hanging up on a hook by the door. Otherwise, he liked the Quarrymans Arms. It was homely and traditional, with real ales, beamed ceilings and a fire that was permanently lit. He bought the first round, three pints of beer, a white wine for Rupert and a lager and lime for Rev Lucy.

'You're a decent guy,' bellowed Mr Crocker. 'Remember, if this village ever gives you any problems, just give me a call. I still have contacts in the police force, you know.'

Al would always think of him as Mr Crocker but managed to say: 'Thank you. Thank you. Appreciate that, Jeremy.'

'Jeremy keeps an eye on us all, so you'd better be on your best behaviour,' Rupert chortled.

'Oh, I'm pretty law-abiding and virtuous most of the time,' said Al.

'But you have to say that in this company, don't you?' Rupert indicated the retired policeman with one hand and the vicar with the other.

Al turned to Spike Dobson, who had been silently downing his pint. Al had made a few deliveries to his house but hadn't had many conversations with him, mainly due to being drowned out by the Jack Russell's barking. Now he asked after the dog, and was told, somewhat defensively, that it did get walked twice a day, come rain or shine.

Al congratulated him on his commitment.

'Is that an otter pendant you're wearing, Rev Lucy?' Rupert asked, noticing a glimmer of metal against her dark clothing.

She put a nervous hand up to her neck and fiddled with the chain. 'Oh yes, it's one that Christina Penrose made. I don't have pierced ears, and I wanted to buy something to support her – and the otters, of course.' She gripped the mini otter so tightly it would have been suffocated if it had been a real one.

'The thing with Peter didn't put you off otters, then?' Rupert asked.

'Peter was a very silly boy,' she said.

'Who's Peter, and what thing?' Al asked.

'Peter is my eight-year-old,' said Rev Lucy. 'There was an incident at the sanctuary, a while back now. He poked his finger through the caging and lost the tip of it.'

'Oh, Carol said something about that,' Al recalled. 'But I didn't know it was your son. Sounds nasty.'

'Yes. Peter was learning piano, too, and had to stop. Not easy with one finger shorter than the others. It was dreadful for him. He learned an important lesson, though. My daughter is better behaved, but it's so hard to keep an eye on them both at the same time. That's why we're grateful to have Kandisha now, who steps in to babysit on a regular basis.'

Al made a mental note that Rev Lucy had a babysitter

called Kandisha. Phoebe would want to know. He must also warn her to watch her fingers when feeding Coco.

Rupert gazed at the tiny silver otter. 'Christina is a very talented lady,' he said. 'And her contributions to the sanctuary shop are quite splendid.'

Al remembered the box of Smelders jewellery he had delivered to Rev Lucy's husband. Christina's handiwork was altogether a different style. Rev Lucy was a bit of an enigma.

They started to discuss otters generally. Rupert told them that, in Britain, they had nearly died out altogether because of otter hunting.

'It was an incredibly cruel sport. They used to chase an otter until it was exhausted, spear it and then fling it to the hounds. Otter hunting was finally banned in the seventies, and now the otter population is on the rise again,' he said. 'Which is great for everyone. Except, of course, for the fish farms.'

'Or anyone who happens to have a fishpond,' added Spike.

'Or maybe Seth Hardwick?' Al suggested. 'I gather there was an incident with his dog.'

Rev Lucy nodded. 'I heard about that too. Poor lad. Thank goodness the dog was okay. He dotes on that dog, just as he doted on the spaniel he had before. He was broken-hearted when it died. His parents had just split up too, I remember. His father lives in Brazil now with his new wife, but he still owns the house by the sanctuary. He lets Seth live there at a peppercorn rent.'

'What does Seth do?' asked Al.

'Some sort of clerical work, I believe. You'll see him

out and about on his motorbike or walking the dog. I honestly don't know what else he gets up to.'

Rupert was not ready to relinquish his pet subject quite yet. 'Did you know, otters can be found on every continent except Antarctica? In the Amazon, you get giant river otters. They're massive. Not like the cute, fluffy little chaps we have at the sanctuary. They're two metres long and have been known to hunt and kill alligators.'

Rev Lucy shuddered. She was doubtless very glad that the otter who had bitten her son's finger was just a small British one.

'There's been a kerfuffle.'

Phoebe pricked up her ears. 'What kind of kerfuffle?'

'A complaint about one of my deliveries.'

'A timing thing?'

'Why must you assume it's a timing thing?'

'Why do you think?'

'All right, point made. But, actually, it's not.'

Al sifted through the photos of packages on his phone, muttering to himself. 'Luckily, there's proof that I didn't do anything wrong. *Voilà*,' he declared. 'I left George Bovis's package on the garden table in his summerhouse, exactly as he requested.'

He remembered the package had been heavy and bulky. The picture showed it with the inside of the octagonal cedar summerhouse in the background. 'Here's the evidence, which I will send to the powers on high. They tell me Mr Bovis complained that it was left by the front gate! And then some dog had the bad manners to lift its leg against it . . .'

Phoebe was still tending to flinch whenever anyone mentioned the word 'dog'.

'I wonder if the culprit was the barky Jack Russell belonging to the Viking in the tracksuit, your bell-ringing chum. They're neighbours, aren't they?'

'Spike Dobson? Yes, I wouldn't be surprised. He apparently takes the dog out every day, come rain or shine.'

He had bumped into Spike in the village shop that afternoon, the Jack Russell accompanying him, as if to prove the point. Spike had apologized for being a little grumpy at the bell-ringing session, saying he became crotchety when tired. Al wasn't surprised he was tired with such an energetic, noisy doggie to walk every day.

Phoebe smirked. 'Poor Mr Bovis! That was bed linen too, I seem to remember.'

She was still helping her father with the system and now had a good understanding of what everyone in the village was ordering.

Al nodded gravely. 'Just as well the packaging was waterproof. But I do wonder how the parcel could've moved.'

He left Phoebe to have a nap and headed into the garden. He fetched a fork from the shed, wondering why life always left him so bemused. Nothing ever quite panned out as intended. How mortifying that Mr Bovis had complained about the package. If it hadn't been for the photo, he would have doubted his own memory. He set to work, dreaming of some magical day in the future when he'd have everything under control.

His wife had invariably had breakfast on the table at seven every morning, lunch at one and dinner at six thirty. She had organized sports clubs and ballet for the children. She had always ensured their shoes were polished. She had attended every parents' meeting at the school. She had known which days were bin days and when it was time to get the car MOT'd. She had been efficient, energetic and quite wonderful. And he had trailed in her magnificent wake, adoring her and agreeing with her because – let's face it – she was always right.

Ruth had been well liked and respected by everyone. She'd excelled in her job, which was in human resources at a hospital, until she had ended up with a brain tumour at the same hospital. Since her death, Al had grappled with even the tiny challenges of life, like changing Hoover bags and choosing which brand of toilet roll to buy.

Docks and chickweed surrounded him, usurping the vegetable bed in vigorous clumps. He dug them out and threw them into the wheelbarrow, handful by handful. Why couldn't Darleycombe's wretched slugs do something useful and feast on the weeds rather than his precious vegetables? He stuck the fork in the ground again to root out a stubborn thistle. When he drew it out again, a potato was impaled on the prongs.

A potato!

It was a thing of wonder and beauty.

He rummaged further in the soil and discovered that several more were ready. Some were as tiny as pebbles, but others would make a hearty side dish. He gathered them up in a plant pot, took them to the outside tap and rinsed off the earth until their creamy flesh was revealed. They were round parcels of pure nourishment. They were living orbs. They were knobby baubles of glory. They cheered him immensely. He had achieved something.

He took them in and displayed them on the kitchen table.

The minute his daughter came downstairs, he pointed at them with glee.

'Look, look, Phoebe! New pots! We did it!'

'*You* did it,' she said.

'And all organic! The slug runs paid off.' He broke into Kermit the Frog's song 'It's Not Easy Being Green'.

Phoebe smiled. Al was proud of his Kermit impression. He sometimes wondered if he'd missed his vocation as a Muppet. He did a good Miss Piggy too, and a great Swedish Chef, which he had occasionally come out with at school, to the delight of his pupils.

'Christina would be proud of you,' said Phoebe.

'Eh?' Was Christina a Muppet fan?

'She's a bit of an eco-warrior.'

'Ah.'

His mind produced an image of Christina wearing a green breastplate, wielding a sword in one hand and an anti-hunting placard in the other, somehow scaling the walls of Buckingham Palace. It was the type of militant behaviour that made him nervous.

'Please tell me she's never chained herself to a tree,' he said.

'Oh, I'm sure she hasn't. When I say eco-warrior, I mean it in a good way,' Phoebe assured him. 'Why don't you give her some of the new potatoes?' she suggested. 'Tell her they're organic and you removed all the slugs by hand.'

Al could see that Phoebe was angling at something,

and if he wasn't mistaken it was a romance between himself and her friend. She meant well, but it was ridiculous. Yes, Christina was single and attractive, but she was way too Bohemian for him.

'You'll be seeing her anyway,' he said. 'Why don't *you* give them to her?'

'No, I'll have my art stuff with me and I don't want to carry anything else,' Phoebe whined. 'It would be much, much easier for me if you could do it.'

Which convinced him, of course.

13

Nettles

PHOEBE TRIED TO get her daily crying done between nine and ten in the morning. If she got it over with early she could, with the help of cold water, tone down the tell-tale swollen-eyed, froggy look and be behaving like a real human being again by the time her father returned from work. He had enough to worry about without witnessing gallons of tears.

This meant she had to be exact about when she took her painkillers. The instructions on the packet only allowed her eight every twenty-four hours, so at certain times of day existence became hard to bear. Those were the times when any position was excruciating: standing upright, walking, sitting or lying in bed . . . She had discovered she could cope best by crouching on the floor with her head in her hands. Always horribly cold, even in summer, she huddled as close as she could to the electric heater. The warmth dried up the wet patch created by her tears so at least the carpet wasn't damaged. It helped if she moaned out loud as well, something she only permitted herself to do when nobody else was around.

She hadn't yet finished today's crying session when the phone rang. She rushed to the basin, gulped down some water and splashed her puffy eyes. The phone trilled insistently. She cleared her throat and went to pick up.

'Hello?'

'Hi, it's me, Jules.'

'Oh, hi. How are things?' Phoebe sank on to the floor again and sat cross-legged, not feeling strong enough to stand up for this conversation.

'I'm good, good,' said her sister. 'Stayed up half the night finishing an essay and got a party tonight. Big crisis. Do I wear my new cami top with jeans or my split-thigh black skirt? I'm fifty-fifty at the moment but leaning towards the jeans. Or is that just too predictable? I don't want to be a clone of everyone else, but I don't want to stick out too much either. Decisions, decisions! Anyway, how's the otter?'

'Coco's doing well, thanks.' Phoebe felt required to give more information. 'She's moved on from milk now and I feed her with a kind of fish gruel.'

Jules sighed loudly. 'You're so bloody lucky. I wish we were allowed pets here, but the landlord won't allow it. Although we're talking about getting a hamster anyway. I somehow don't think we could get away with an otter. I really must come and see your Coco soon. And see Higher Mead Cottage. And you and Dad, of course.'

Jules hadn't shown much interest in visiting them since

the move, but now she was latching on to the idea. Phoebe could sense it down the phone.

'I told you about my job, didn't I?'

'Yes.'

Jules would be working in a Plymouth hotel for most of the summer break.

'I'll come to Darleycombe before I get stuck in. How's Dad doing?'

'Oh, you know, happy on the surface.'

'I'm relying on you to keep an eye on him, Phoebe. By the way, you still haven't sent any photos or vids of Coco, even though I must have asked you dozens of times.'

'Ah, yes, sorry.'

The truth was that Jules would put cheesy music over them and plaster them all over TikTok. Phoebe, although she didn't have to look, balked at the idea of it. She disliked social media. And Coco was *her* baby.

'I'll have to keep on at you,' said Jules. 'Dad is just so forgetful and you're . . . I suppose you're just too tired.'

Phoebe could feel her hackles rising at the way Jules pronounced the word 'tired'. It was drawn out and heavy with insinuation.

'Yes, I *am* tired,' she answered. Her head was pounding. Her bones ached and seared.

Jules tutted. 'Don't give in to it. The way to deal with tiredness is to ignore it.'

'If I do any more ignoring, I'll explode.'

Now Jules would be rolling her eyes. She was one of those people who was relentlessly not-tired the whole time. Envy bubbled up inside Phoebe like soup in a pressure cooker.

They had been great friends as children. Phoebe used to tell stories to her older sister while Jules plaited her hair, which was long then. Then they had acted out the stories, making hideouts and time machines and spaceships, sometimes with Jack's help, out of the living-room armchairs.

These days, they always ended up snapping at each other. Part of the problem seemed to be Phoebe's 'condition', as Jules called it. Never having suffered a day's illness in her life, Jules appeared convinced that Phoebe was a self-pitying attention-seeker. If ever Phoebe mentioned her struggles, Jules doggedly changed the subject. It was almost as if by denying her sister's illness she thought she could rid her of it and help her start living like a sensible person again.

If she'd had a quick, fatal condition, like her mother's brain tumour, Jules might have understood better. It was the vague, invisible nature of the thing that was the problem. Or was she in denial because she couldn't face another family crisis? Maybe it was sheer bloody-mindedness.

Life being unfair, Phoebe had a dark need within herself to detest somebody. Jules, with her brightness and bossiness and complete sympathy bypass, made the ideal candidate. Phoebe loved her sister but couldn't help hating her too.

Now Jules launched into a description of some student prank that involved putting woolly cardigans on statues.

Jules required specific reactions to her anecdotes. If you didn't respond the required way, she tended to repeat them, in slightly different words, more dramatically. And louder.

Phoebe longed to lie down in silence. Her nerves were jangling by the time she heard the front door and was able to say, 'Ah, Dad's just back. I'm sure he'd like a word.'

Al sped towards her. She handed him the phone and tottered back to bed.

The bullying had started the year after Ruth died, when Phoebe was twelve. She'd missed her mother far more than she let on, but the rest of her family were so stricken there didn't seem to be room for any more grief in the house. Outside, Birmingham whizzed and whirred on. Phoebe had carried her bleeding heart dutifully to school. She had been given a few counselling session with a bland, round-faced woman who'd asked how she felt.

'Hungry,' she'd replied.

She never mentioned how much she also felt set apart from her peers by her gaping loss. She had crammed the inner black hole with doughnuts, biscuits and everything sweet she could find.

Once, approaching a group of boys in the school corridor, she had noticed that Tom Crawley had bundled his school bag under his jumper and was stroking it as if it was his belly. She heard the words 'Fatty Featherstone' as she passed, and when she glanced back, he was walking directly behind her with a comic waddle, accompanied by strident laughter from his friends.

Unfortunately, she had to pass them again later to fetch her books. They all had big bulges under their jumpers this time.

Hold your head up. Keep going.

She managed a degree of dignity until Tom had stuck his foot out and tripped her up, making her fall headlong.

'Oops, sorry!' he sneered.

Then on of his mates had 'accidentally' trodden on her hand. That was just the beginning.

School had previously provided an escape from the sadness of her motherless home, but now it became a place of terror. The only respite was the actual lessons. Phoebe had always deluged the teachers with questions in class (*How much does a cloud weigh? Is it true that the ancient Romans used urine as mouthwash? Do tadpoles have lungs?*) She asked because she was burning to know the answers, but unfortunately, her contemporaries saw it as showing off. After a while, she had learned to act stupid to protect herself from the playground beatings, but it was too late by then. The misery had sent her after comfort in the form of sugars and carbs, and she had piled on more weight, which only gave the gang more material to pick on. She knew all about vicious circles . . . but the fact remained: Jaffa Cakes were so much nicer than most people.

Somebody had then discovered that Phoebe was a vocal spoonerism for 'Beefy' and she became 'Beefy Featherstone' for a while. 'Hi, Beefy!' the children had chanted whenever they saw her. When nasty written messages were passed around the class, it was sometimes spelled Boephe, causing a hurricane of giggles.

Names, Phoebe realized, exerted way too much influence and altered the way everyone saw you. Even the way you saw yourself.

She would always remember *that* history lesson. The teacher had written up on the board things that typified life during the Second World War (words such as 'gas mask', 'powdered eggs' and 'Home Guard') and had asked for more suggestions. Tom Crawley had stuck up his hand and yelled 'Bully beef!' The teacher, oblivious to the significance of these two words, had added them to the list. As soon as he'd left at the end of the lesson, Tom had run up and drawn a ring around the 'Bully Beef', inciting the crowd. Phoebe had fled to the playground, gasping, pursued by her torturers. They had caught her, held her hands behind her back and thrust stinging nettles down her clothes.

Looking back, it was crazy that she hadn't told anyone. At the time, silence had seemed like the only option. Everyone knew that if you grassed, the bullying just got worse and you'd be more isolated than ever because anyone who spoke to you kindly would also be targeted.

Anyway, her father was so sad . . . how could she have inflicted any extra worry on him? The fact that she herself was also grieving (something her classmates didn't even know) hadn't factored into her choices. Perhaps it had manifested itself in other ways.

When she had started to get ill, the weight had suddenly dropped off. So had the nicknames. It was a trifling compensation. Given the choice, she would have welcomed back the layers of fat in a heartbeat rather than bear this relentless burden of pain.

She had become quieter and quieter. She had missed out on weeks of school because she was simply too ill to cope. She'd studied at home as much as she could. When it came to her A levels, she had gone in, braced with pain-killers and coffee. Teachers had predicted she would be a straight-A student, but she'd ended up with a B and a C in the mix. She knew that she could have done so much better. She had intended to read Biology and Anthropology at Durham University, but hadn't made the grades. In any case, by then she was in far too much pain to leave home.

She had been awarded a place at Durham University anyway. She never went. By then, she was in far too much pain to leave home.

14

Neighbourly Behaviour

WHEN AL GOT off the phone, Phoebe was chewing her nails and staring out of the window. He decided not to tell her that he'd forgotten to take the potatoes to Christina. She would only be cross with him, and the potatoes would happily last another day or two. Or he'd take some from the next batch. He cast about in his mind for some other topic of conversation. Something that would divert Phoebe and take her out of herself.

'Odd thing this morning.'

'What?' He had piqued her interest.

'Well, Mr Bovis has some magnificent hydrangea bushes that he's very proud of. I've been admiring them every time I go there. But a few days ago, I noticed they seemed to have abruptly stopped flowering. Then, when I knocked on his door today, I saw that every flower head had been neatly cut off.'

Phoebe sucked in her breath.

Al, now a little smug, put his theory to her. 'Mrs Bovis must be a keen flower-arranger, I guess. Perhaps she's one of the team who does flower-arranging for the church.'

'When you went bell-ringing, did you see arrangements with hydrangeas?' Phoebe asked.

He rubbed his chin. 'No, come to think of it, no. I didn't.'

'I have a different hypothesis.'

He glanced at the discarded painkiller packet and drained coffee mug by her bed. She had now slipped into her problem-solving (not to say nosy) mood. He fully expected a bout of caffeine-induced brilliance.

'Go on, then. Sock it to me.'

'Here's the thing. Mr Bovis and his neighbour, Spike Dobson, are in the middle of a feud. They totally hate each other's guts. It was your Viking-in-a-tracksuit Dobson who snipped off Mr Bovis's prized hydrangeas. And you told me you'd spotted George Bovis mowing his lawn very early the other day. He was deliberately making a racket to wake up Spike Dobson.'

'Oh, Spike did mention that he was particularly tired. I assumed it was because of his Jack Russell, but it could have been that, I suppose.'

'Then Spike moved Mr Bovis's package from the summerhouse to the front gate and ensured that the Jack Russell did the dirty on it.'

Al was stunned.

'Wow. If you're right, that is quite some feud they're waging.'

'I *am* right.' Phoebe seemed very much cheered by her own detective work. 'I wish I knew more, though. How the feud started, for example. Even though the whole thing's insanely childish, I'm rather looking forward to the next instalment.'

Phoebe pondered. Your health, like your moods or your finances or your love life, was in a constant state of flux. Either disintegrating or gathering strength. Either on the way up or on the way down.

At the moment, as she strolled around the sanctuary, she didn't feel too bad. It might be because of the codeine she had swallowed earlier. It might be due to the sunshine that had hazily lingered all afternoon and now intensified to a clear brilliance that gilded every leaf and twig. It might, of course, be the Otter Effect. Holly and Hawthorn were cruising along the surface of their pond, webbed toes stretched wide, radiating happiness.

Possibly it even had something to do with Carol, who walked by Phoebe's side. Phoebe had established a quiet bond with the grey-haired, thin-lipped sanctuary owner. Neither of them was outgoing but they'd developed a mutual respect which did not need to be fed by very much conversation.

Phoebe had discovered that Carol had never been married and had helped on her parents' farm for most of her life. She now lived alone, in one of the buildings adjacent to the sanctuary. With a few notable exceptions (Rupert, Christina, Dan Hollis and now, Phoebe hoped, the Featherstones), she had more time for otters than for humans. Although she enjoyed looking after the residents of the sanctuary, her real passion was helping otters in the wild.

'I've successfully reintroduced eleven otters to the area since I started,' she told Phoebe with pride. She pulled a tissue from her pocket, spat on it and used it to scrub some dirt off a sign. 'It's just such a shame the fish farm started up down the road at the same time. There's no love lost between us. Otters are avid fish-plunderers and the business had to spend a hell of a lot of extra money on barricading in their supplies.'

They paused to watch Twiggy and Willow, the devoted sisters.

Willow scurried into a corner and performed a wriggly dance with her tail in the air as she defecated. She yawned simultaneously, opening her mouth wide.

'Such sharp, pointy teeth she has,' Phoebe said.

'She has indeed,' Carol answered. 'Rev Lucy knows only too well.'

'Oh yes, Dad told me it was her son who got his finger bitten.'

'Terrible, it was. He was howling, and we were all panicking and there was blood everywhere and the ambulance took for ever to arrive. It wasn't Willow's fault – she thought she was being offered a nice chipolata sausage. But Rev Lucy was beside herself. Screamed at me.'

'Really?'

Quiet, sweet-natured Rev Lucy?

'Oh yes, she's got quite a temper on her when she's worked up.'

Phoebe didn't reply. She supposed that even vicars must need to vent their wrath occasionally.

'So many dramas we've had here.' Carol sighed.

'It does seem like it.' Phoebe thought of the incident with the Alsatian and gave a shudder. The scene replayed rapidly in her head, up to the moment when she was sitting trembling over her cup of tea.

'Carol, when Seth Hardwick's dog jumped into the otter pen, you mentioned something about it not being the first time?'

'It wasn't. Seth doesn't seem able to keep any dog under control. He's a bit of a loner, but he's always had a dog. He lives next to the sanctuary so he walks them along the path at the back by the fields. Unfortunately, his last dog also got into the enclosure nearest to the back gate – Rowan and Quercus's. Dogs go mad when they scent otters, and vice versa. When the spaniel attacked, the otter fought back. It was Quercus. That's how he got the injury in his back leg. The spaniel came off worse, though, because it was bitten in the jugular.' She mimed a slicing action with her hand. 'It was in agony and the wound was so bad the poor creature had to be put down in the end.'

Phoebe gasped. Carol had stated it as a plain fact, without any display of emotion, but now she added: 'It was another terrible day and we felt awful, but there was nothing we could do. I'm sure Seth has never forgiven us.'

Phoebe was very glad she hadn't witnessed that fight.

Naturally, Carol Blake was the first to meet Paddy, closely followed by Rupert Venn. Al and Phoebe were told to hold back for a day while he recovered from his journey from Wales. It was traumatic for an otter cub to be transported in a small box, accompanied by car engine noises and vibrations, so Carol had decided to give him a little quiet time and space on his own. In the evening, Phoebe, Al, and (because she was so insistent) Christina were allowed to be present when the two cubs met for the first time, with the usual conditions of respect, distance and strict silence. Otters were capable of inflicting horrific injuries on each other, so much would depend on this meeting.

When Al brought Phoebe in, the others had already gathered in the sanctuary's office. Carol gave them a formal greeting, but Rupert sprang forward, grasping Al by the hand and showering benign smiles on Phoebe. 'So glad you could both make it! This is an auspicious day. You're going to love our new resident.'

Christina threw up her hands. 'And they made me wait until you arrived, so I haven't met him yet. Can we go and see him now, *please*.'

'Yes, yes, all right,' said Carol. 'I'll go ahead and take him to Coco's enclosure. You follow in a few minutes. I'll let him out into the pen once you're gathered and quiet.'

But now Christina seized a handful of Carol's jumper and pulled her back. 'You understand otter language better than anyone, Carol. Could you give us a hand signal or something to show how it's going?'

'I'll give you a thumbs-up if it looks like friendly flirtation and a thumbs-down if it looks like aggression. Okay?'

'Okay,' said Christina. 'Go, go, go!'

Phoebe was disappointed to learn from Rupert that Paddy wouldn't need to be handled at all. He was past the bottle-feeding stage and already beginning to eat solids. Coco had some catching up to do, but she might learn from her new big brother, if they got on well.

When they arrived at the wild-otter pen Carol was at the gate, poised for action with the cat basket. Coco was invisible, inside the hutch.

'We can watch on video later if we don't get to see much,' Rupert whispered.

Carol glared at him and indicated that none of them was to move a muscle. They waited, breathless and obedient, as she placed the basket on the ground, slid open the door and retreated again. She stayed close, ready to leap in at the first hint of a fight.

Phoebe clutched the railing and prayed that the cubs would not hurt each other.

She fixed her eyes on the basket. Nothing happened for a long moment apart from the loud thumping of her heart. Then she saw a brown nose peeping out, sniffing the air. A paw and then another edging forward. Quite big paws for a small otter – Phoebe could see how he had got his name. He moved in a distinctive way, patting the ground with wide-spread toes as he trod. Within a beat, Phoebe knew that she had fallen in love with Paddy, just as she had with Coco.

Suddenly, taking fright, he darted towards a heap of twigs and small branches. He sped so fast that they could make out little more than a panicked arrow.

Next to Al, Phoebe raised a silent finger to point. Coco was emerging from the hutch. She had heard something and assumed, perhaps, that it was feeding time. She was leaning forward in an eager stance, ears alert. Spotting a tiny movement among the branches, she did what could only be described as a double-take. And suddenly she was all curiosity, all action. She launched herself forward, squeaking excitedly, quite fearless.

Now, Paddy, seeing this small, feisty otter hurtling towards him, scuttled out from the branches. He skirted around the edge of the enclosure, almost up to the feet of the still spectators. Then he slowed, as if recognizing her call. The two cubs faced each other. Coco opened her mouth and gave a warning hiss, followed by a series of higher notes.

Christina drew a question mark in the air at Carol.

Carol turned one hand with her thumb up, the other with her thumb down. Flirtation *and* aggression?

Paddy backed away respectfully. Coco edged forward again. She leaned in and touched her nose against his. The ground rules had been established. Carol withdrew her downward thumb and pointed the other thumb high in the air, giving one of her rare smiles. Phoebe started breathing again.

It would be easy to tell the young otters apart. Paddy, as well as his larger size and darker coat, didn't have Coco's distinctive white strands of fur around the mouth. Next to him, she still looked babyish, but she had already established herself as the boss.

Now the two otters were cavorting around together. The humans relished the scene, hardly able to contain their giddy relief.

'Well, that was a success,' declared Rupert, after they'd tiptoed back to the buildings.

'Yes. What a great little character,' said Al.

Phoebe sank into a chair. 'A friend for Coco at last,' she murmured.

'Such a joy to see the two of them together!' cried Christina.

'So now,' said Rupert, striding towards the fridge, 'a little celebratory fizz.' He pulled out a bottle with a flourish, opened his leather case and laid five champagne flutes on the table.

Christina gaped. 'Oh, you do spoil us, Rupert!'

'Hands over ears, ladies,' he said as he popped the cork.

Al wasn't sure whether the term 'ladies' was well advised, although none of the females present seemed bothered about it. 'Only a tiny tad for me,' he said as Rupert poured. 'Got to get Phoebe back home safely.'

Al disliked show-offs. But maybe he was just giving in to a touch of envy due to Rupert's great generosity. And height.

'To Paddy and Coco, and their eventual release into the wild!' cried Rupert, holding up his glass.

They followed suit. 'To Paddy and Coco!'

15

Otterly Unacceptable

Aʟ ɢᴀᴠᴇ ᴀ low whistle. 'Your otters are in the local paper.'

He held it out and Phoebe snatched it from him. It wasn't an article, it was a letter, but it was hard to miss. The page was dominated by a large photo of an otter – perhaps Rowan (Phoebe couldn't quite tell the bigger ones apart) – peering through the caged fencing of an enclosure. The picture was in close-up, so the large run behind the animal wasn't in view. The way the bars left shadows on the otter's face made it look sad, even pleading. The whole thing was a cleverly caught moment suggesting misery in captivity.

The letter had been sent in anonymously. As Phoebe read out a passage, her voice rose in indignation. ' "The sanctuary purports to save and release otters, but these creatures are hemmed in on all sides. Most of them will never know freedom." What?' she demanded. 'What's he on about?'

'Or she. It might be a woman,' Al said.

Phoebe read on, struggling to ignore the sharp pain that kept clawing into her cranium. ' "The otters in this establishment are used as entertainment for greedy human eyes. They are caged and live out their days in unnatural conditions, while all they want to do is to run free. These are shy and elusive creatures in the wild. When I visited the sanctuary I witnessed otters that were clearly suffering from boredom and maltreatment." What a load of bullshit!' she exclaimed. 'Whoever wrote this needs their eyes testing.' She read on, through gritted teeth. ' "Not only this, but they lack any proper protection. Last week, the owners failed to prevent a vicious dog from getting into one of the pens. Two otters were traumatized and might have been killed. One had previously been injured by a dog in a similar incident and is now maimed for life . . ." ' She threw down the paper in disgust. 'God, this is awful! I can't read any more. They've twisted everything!'

'Well, sometimes people only see what they decide they're going to see,' Al said grimly. He straightened his fingers one by one, making his knuckles crack.

'Carol and Rupert will be devastated.'

'It won't be good for business,' Al agreed.

'No, it'll be awful. Do you think I should write a letter in response, defending the sanctuary?'

'I think Carol will probably be on the case herself.'

'You're right, Dad. She will. But I'll check with her anyway, when you take me to meet Christina.'

145

She had been looking forward to their next drawing session. Even now she was calculating when to take her tablets so that at the sanctuary she'd hit her physical peak (which, admittedly, could hardly classify as a 'peak'; it was a mere molehill in a deep, deep valley of unhealthiness). Her whole life seemed to be measured out in painkillers.

At least she had fully harnessed the power of the smile. It was a vital tool now that she was getting out more. It was amazing how nobody detected the slightest whiff of suffering so long as you kept a smile glued to your face.

When they arrived a crowd had gathered in front of the entrance. There were at least twenty-five people, mostly young and, without exception, looking very aggressive. Some had placards with messages such as: THERE'S NO EXCUSE FOR ANIMAL ABUSE, CRUELTY IS NOT ENTERTAINMENT and OTTERLY UNACCEPTABLE.

Phoebe undid her seatbelt, but Al was reluctant to let her out of the car.

'Wait a moment, Phoebes. They're looking pretty angry.'

'Yes, but look. Carol has closed the gate early. Why would she do that? I think they may be threatening to force their way in.' She stared. 'Are they planning on trashing the place? Or breaking down the barriers to release the otters?'

Al surveyed the crowd with dismay. He should go and reason with them, but they looked as if they wouldn't be swayed easily. He needed to get his brain into gear first.

Christina was just pulling up in her Peugeot. She hadn't

seen the protesters yet. She gave Al and Phoebe a friendly wave as she stepped out into the car park. She was in an electric-blue poncho and her hair was tied into a high ponytail that bobbed and flowed in the breeze. She dipped her head back into her car to fish out her easel and woven bag which Al knew contained her art stuff. As she turned again, she noticed the throng of protesters.

The sanctuary gate opened and Carol now appeared on the other side, her face bleached white, her back to the wall. She took a step forwards, then a step backwards. Rupert was nowhere to be seen.

At once Christina dumped her things on the bonnet of her car and, head held high, aimed herself straight at the group. Al opened the door of his own car. It was looking as if he might be required in a protective role. Here was his cue to step up and be heroic.

'Stay there,' he urged Phoebe, but it was no good. She wanted to be in on the action too, wanted to help if she could.

Christina was remonstrating with the protesters, stirring the air vigorously with both hands.

As he came closer Al heard her words.

'. . . Not right at all. Listen, I love all animals, I'm a vegetarian – almost vegan – and I have protested like you in the past. I once set a load of white mice free from a lab and I'm always writing to my MP about live animal exports. I adopted a load of battery chickens once and gave them a new, free-range life. I completely get where you're coming from.'

At least she hadn't mentioned climbing the walls of Buckingham Palace. Or chaining herself to a tree.

'I am one of you!' she declared.

'Join us, then!' somebody shouted.

'No!' she called back. 'You've got it all wrong. This place *saves* otters. It takes care of them and releases them back into the wild.'

A few people lowered their placards, although others seemed determined to keep hold of their rage. They growled at her and murmured, 'Come on,' to each other. Their ranks closed around Christina and for a moment Al lost sight of her. He fumbled for his phone. He should ring the police . . . or at least Jeremy Crocker, who, with his contacts, might be quicker and more effective. Then he remembered it was useless. No blasted phone signal here.

He scanned the crowd and spotted Christina's ponytail bobbing aloft. He lingered, with one arm around Phoebe, ready to stop her if she tried to get involved. He willed Christina to look at him and see that he was prepared to step in and help. If she was aware of him, Christina didn't show it.

'Believe me, people, these otters are well looked after. I don't know where you've got the idea they're not, but you've been misinformed.'

A woman with a nose stud glowered at Christina.

'It's irrelevant!' she shouted, her voice splintering with fury. 'Otters are wild animals. They should never be locked up.'

'They should be free!' called another young woman, who had streaked blonde hair with frayed-looking ends. 'Free, free, free! Set them free!' she started chanting. The scrawny man next to her took up the chant, and the crowd followed.

'Free, free, free! Set them free!'

As one body, they moved towards Carol. Her face was whiter than ever. Her mouth opened, but Al couldn't hear what she was saying. The crowd swarmed around her, pushed her aside.

Al and Phoebe shouted at them to stop. Their voices were drowned.

'Wait!' Christina roared. Her voice boomed with improbable volume, rising above the chant. Heads turned. The noise ebbed a little, enough for her to belt out her message. 'These otters have been saved. *Saved*, do you hear me? They were injured or orphaned and, if they'd been left in the wild, they would have died.' She was in full swing now. 'They would be dead if it wasn't for Carol, here. *Dead*,' she repeated, even louder. She looked around, showing them the extent of her indignation. 'Would you want that for them?'

Uncertainty spread among the sea of faces. Once again, Al lost sight of Christina and started to fight his way through. Angry faces turned to him. Bodies smelled of sweat and rancour.

Then Christina reappeared, flushed and animated, a spot of electric-blue certainty amid a throng of doubt.

She pointed at Carol. 'This woman is a saint. She has sacrificed so much to look after these poor animals. She has given her own money and devoted her whole life to them. She loves these otters, I swear it on my heart.' She slapped herself on the chest. 'I swear it on anything you like. Go in and see for yourselves. The otters are healthy and happy. I know them personally: Twiggy, Willow, Holly, Hawthorn, Quercus and many more.'

'And Coco, and Paddy,' Phoebe said, but only Al could hear her.

'They have all been given life, and a very good life it is too!' yelled Christina.

A ripple of reaction spread through the group. A debate had started. Al, one arm still firmly around Phoebe, infiltrated them to try to back Christina up. 'She's right – she's quite right, you know,' he said, again and again.

Phoebe clung to him, facing outwards and saying to anyone who would listen, 'Yes, the otters are well. I'm looking after one of the cubs myself. She's going to be released when she's big enough.'

Christina had edged her way around to Carol and was clearly trying to persuade her to let everyone in. Carol looked as if this was the last thing she wanted to do. At last Al saw her throw up her hands as if she couldn't bear to argue any longer. She unlocked the gate and gestured to the crowd that they could come in. Christina beckoned to them.

The protesters seemed nonplussed. It was impossible for them to force an entrance now that they'd been issued an invitation. Several shuffled forward. A murmured agreement began to circulate: they should at least go and look at the otters before taking any further action. Only a few refused to be swayed. They stood gripping their placards, pounding them rhythmically into the tarmac and continuing with the chant. The blonde girl was among them. She eyeballed Al and Phoebe as they passed.

The more amenable protesters filed through, if only because it was hard to resist a free ticket to anything. Christina led the way, taking them through the gift shop and then outside, pointing to the spacious enclosures where Rowan and his friends were gambolling around. Carol followed. She sought out those who looked less convinced and tried to explain how the sanctuary worked. Al overheard the words 'difficult decisions' and 'short of funds' and 'as close to their natural habitat as I can'.

The otters themselves were now working their magic, too. They put on a fine display of antics, fit to charm even the crankiest visitor.

Al gazed around at the protesters, searching for signs that they were thawing. Phoebe whispered to her father, 'If they have eyes (and I think they all do), they must see that every animal here has plenty of space to run around in, and every animal is happy.'

He whispered back to her, 'True. But nobody likes to be proved wrong.'

Some of the humans, he guessed, were just fond of protesting for the sake of protesting. It made them feel virtuous and important.

Still, what Phoebe called the Otter Effect was starting to spread. Soon the sanctuary was filled with chatter. The woman with the nose stud had taken out her phone and was photographing Rowan, who was standing on his hind legs and examining her with his head on one side. And when she was shown Quercus, who was looking particularly active and cheeky, despite his limp, she started gushing down the phone. '. . . Just so cute . . . I'm about to send you the pics, Mum . . .'

Carol was now shepherding the group around. 'Come and look at our cubs,' she urged.

Al thought for a moment that she was going to lead

them to Coco in the flesh, but, of course, she wouldn't do that. Instead, she took them to the video screen in the office. They gathered round.

Onscreen, Coco was moving close to the ground paw by paw, stalking her friend. Paddy, oblivious, was nosing about in a patch of docks and buttercups. As they watched, Coco pounced – a balletic, high leap into the air – and landed right on top of him. He rolled over in shock, before springing to his feet and hurtling after her. She ran right up to the camera so that they could see her tufty face in close-up. She looked as if she was laughing hard.

'Aw, aw, how gorgeous!' spouted the protesters.

'Can we go and see them?' somebody asked.

Carol shook her head. 'I'm afraid not. They are due for release, you see, and human contact will mean they have to be kept here, and you don't want that, do you?' Her face was solemn, but a slight twitch played at the edges of her mouth.

After a while, the group departed in threes and fours, many of them putting donations in the collection box as they left.

Christina whispered to Al and Phoebe: 'Well, that was close, wasn't it? But I think we've saved the day.'

'*You*'ve saved the day,' Phoebe corrected her.

'I did all right, didn't I?'

'You were magnificent!' cried Al, unable to stop himself. He wondered whether it was appropriate to throw his arms around her. He settled for giving her a pat on the back.

He happened to glance at Phoebe, who was standing with her arms crossed and a rather ape-like grin on her face.

*

'Perhaps we'll leave off the drawing for today,' Christina suggested. 'Too many people now.'

'Agreed.' A persistent ache invaded Phoebe's neck and hovered behind her eyeballs. It was hard to keep holding her head up. She felt as if it might drop off at any moment. All the same, she craved the calming presence of the otter cubs. 'I'm just going to check on Coco and Paddy before we go, and give them a spot of supper.'

Battling the need to collapse, she set to work. She pulled on a pair of plastic gloves, helped herself from the tub of fishy bits and liquidized them with water. Paddy was able to feed himself and would lap up the mixture if she left it in a bowl. Coco was catching up with him fast. Phoebe would have to stop handling her very soon. It was vital to make the most of every available Coco-cuddling minute.

When she found them, the cubs were scampering about and nipping each other's tails. Coco rushed up and patted Phoebe's calf, eager for the bottle. Phoebe picked her up and stroked her as she drank.

'Well, Coco, you've no idea how close that was. It could have spelled the end of the sanctuary. And who knows what would have happened to you all?'

Phoebe listened. She could faintly hear the chant 'Free, free, free! Set them free!' from the stubborn activists who had stayed outside.

'That's exactly what we're going to do. But only when you're good and ready and we know you'll be safe. They don't get it at all, do they? I wish they'd just shut up and go home.'

Coco clutched the bottle with her paws. Her tail beat

against Phoebe's sleeve. Phoebe held her close, her mind whirring, her eyes drifting beyond the boundary to the public footpath and barbed-wire fence. Life, with all its complications, very much resembled that barbed wire. It went smoothly for a bit, but very soon you were guaranteed to come across a tight, jagged knot. Then another, then another, then another. A whole series of spiky lumps lined up, just waiting to snag you.

Phoebe frowned. 'Oh, Coco, Coco, baby, something's just occurred to me. And it's not good.'

Coco, intent on her meal, didn't seem that interested. As soon as she'd finished she struggled to be put down again. She ran straight over and joined Paddy at his food bowl. Phoebe left them with a full heart.

As she turned, she caught a glimpse of Seth Hardwick walking his Alsatian in the distance, a lone figure with a huge, leaping companion. She double-checked she had closed and padlocked the back gate.

Al helped Carol dole out mugs of tea. He wondered whether to make coffee for Phoebe instead, but tea was supposed to be good for shock. He had just sat down when she returned. She looked fragile and he leaped up to let her have his chair, since there weren't enough for everyone. As they sipped, Rupert came dashing in, alarm all over his face.

'My God, what happened? Carol rang to say there was a horde of violent-looking yobs outside. I set out straight away, but my car got stuck behind a load of wretched sheep on the road. I saw a couple of chaps with placards by the gate but couldn't see any damage. Is everything okay?'

They explained how Christina had sprung into action and defended their beloved sanctuary.

'She was fabulous,' said Phoebe.

Rupert focused his gaze on Christina. 'I'm very sorry to have missed that.'

'Oh, anyone would have done the same,' Christina said, glowing from her victory. 'I just wish I'd been able to convince all of them.'

Her eyes swivelled to the window. The blonde girl and the man who seemed to be her boyfriend could be seen arguing with a couple of tourists who had just arrived.

'I do wonder what's at the bottom of all this,' Phoebe mused. They all looked at her.

'What do you mean?' Rupert asked.

'Well, there just seems to be one disaster after another, doesn't there? The child with the bitten finger, the health-and-safety inspectors, the theft, Seth's dog, the newspaper article . . . and now the animal-rights protesters . . . It looks to me as if somebody is trying to sabotage the sanctuary.'

Nobody offered an opinion. Carol handed out some chocolate digestives. Phoebe declined. Christina took two. She deserved them, though, nobody could deny that.

Al felt illogically annoyed that Rupert hadn't been there during the emergency, even though it wasn't his fault. Sheep in the road were a common problem around here. He also felt cross with himself for not having done more, acted faster, shouted louder. Christina had put him to shame. He sensed that Phoebe hero-worshipped him a little bit less and her a little bit more.

Christina now pulled a package from her bag and presented it to his daughter.

'Just a little something for you, Phoebe.'

Phoebe pulled off the tissue paper. Inside was a beautiful little otter pendant in silver, one that Christina had made herself, similar to the one he'd seen Rev Lucy wearing.

Phoebe wasn't a jewellery person, but she was clearly touched. Al knew she would treasure it because of the giver. She might even go so far as to wear it sometimes.

16

Giving and Receiving

AL FEATHERSTONE DROVE through the lanes of Exmoor, alongside the bright meanders of the Darle and up over wild, heather-sprung moorland. He bumped over potholes, clanked across cattle grids and reversed into passing places to let tractors by. Sometimes he whistled, sometimes he listened to his radio, sometimes he enjoyed the silence. Often, he braked for pheasants that were sauntering about in the middle of the road. Even more often, he slowed down to admire the view. His mind drifted between thoughts of his family, past, present and future, his garden and the plumbing problems of Higher Mead Cottage. Now these thoughts were punctuated with images of the sanctuary, the protesters and Christina. Especially Christina.

Al stopped frequently, pulling up in driveways, farmyards, cul-de-sacs and closes. He gave out a cornucopia of packaged objects and exchanged endless comments about the weather with their recipients. He took photo after photo as proof of delivery. He hefted heavy boxes to front doors, he left parcels on steps or in porches or outhouses. He was growing leaner and fitter. His skin was darkening and the muscles on his arms stood out like thick, fibrous ropes.

When Al's car drew up at the vicarage gates, Rev Lucy spotted him from the kitchen window. She left the eggs she was beating for her home-made quiche and hurried to greet him at the front door. Her black Labrador, who was getting old, rose stiffly and joined her to ensure that Al's hands received a good licking. Rev Lucy accepted her packages with gratitude. One was a gym-kit bag her daughter needed for school and the other was a book on Christian unity that she hoped might help with sermon-writing. (Just occasionally, Rev Lucy allowed herself a new item of clothing, modest and inexpensive, carefully selected from online Marks & Spencer or the Cotton Club, but she hadn't ordered anything like that recently.) Al handed her a small box addressed to Mr Daws, who also liked to order from the Internet. She called to her husband after Al had left. He came downstairs to fetch the box, with a 'Thank you, darling. That'll be my shoe-laces.' He returned upstairs at once to unwrap them. With a small sigh, she went back to the quiche.

Jeremy Crocker heard Al's car engine outside his house, followed by a crescendo in the chicken cluckings that made up the soundtrack of his day. His pulse quickened. It wasn't so much because he was pleased to see Al (although it was always pleasant to have a conversation about bell-ringing) but because he was very much looking forward to seeing what Al had brought. Not that he would hurry over opening it. He might even tantalize himself by leaving it a while. He would take it up to his bedroom later and place it on the bed and, when he was good and ready (perhaps after a small snifter), he would wash his hands. Then he would snip the tape with scissors, hoping that what was inside lived up to the images that had propelled him to buy it.

Seth Hardwick did not know Al Featherstone by name but knew him as the delivery man who sometimes rang to say he was running late and would be there in another fifteen minutes. Seth shut his Alsatian in the kitchen (Boz could be a bit over-enthusiastic at times) then went to answer the door. He took the packages without much interest. They weren't joy-givers, they were practical things: a torch, a packet of screws, a phone charger. He'd open them after he got back from work. Work. Even the thought of his job in payroll for the local planning authorities depressed him. It was just as well he had his motorbike and Boz. He didn't know what he'd do without them. He had been utterly panicked when Boz had somehow launched himself into the sanctuary and over the wall of the otters' pen. He knew from bitter experience not to let a dog off the lead anywhere near the place . . . but Boz had galloped miles through the fields and ignored his calls. He was a crazy dog – but much loved, like his predecessor. Seth couldn't bear to think of him meeting a similar fate.

Al had a package for his fellow bell-ringer, Spike Dobson. He wanted to ask him about whether they were practising this week, as Rev Lucy had muttered something about a PCC meeting. But neither Spike nor his wife was in. Al heard the Jack Russell barking from within the house as usual, though. He duly left the parcel on the doorstep, giving George Bovis (who was out watering his delphiniums in the next-door garden) a wave as he did so.

Al switched on the radio. It blared out loud, punchy music, manufactured sounds with a pounding bass; the sort of thing his son, Jack, listened to and not to his own taste at all. He slowed down to twiddle with the channels and find something more relaxing.

At the same time he glanced in his rear-view mirror. *What the . . .*

George Bovis had angled the hosepipe upwards so that the jet of water arced over the hedge, right on to the parcel that sat on Spike's doorstep.

He blinked, and the hosepipe was back where it should be, aimed at the delphiniums again. It had happened in the space of two seconds, and Al wasn't sure it had happened at all. Should he go back to check if the parcel really had received a soaking? Was Spike likely to complain to head office? Al thought not, bearing in mind they were acquainted, and he certainly didn't want to snitch on George Bovis.

He decided to leave it for now and call Spike about the bell-ringing later. If he brought up the matter and the delivery did turn out to be damaged, he would mention that a certain hosepipe had been seen in the vicinity. It looked as if Phoebe's theory about the feud was right.

Al Featherstone put his foot on the accelerator. There was one more delivery to go, and he mustn't forget about the potatoes.

Miaow and Christina answered the door together. Christina had a glint in her eye, as if she'd seen him coming from the window and hatched a little plan. Miaow had a disgruntled, ruffled look, as if she'd just been ousted from a comfy chair and placed on the doormat to greet him. Still, when he stooped and gave her a stroke she purred softly and wound around his legs.

Christina, who was dressed in a flowery tunic, gave him a peck on both cheeks. He pecked back and presented her with the bag.

'Phoebe thought you'd like these new potatoes.'

Christina accepted the bag. 'How very lovely!'

He twisted his hands together. 'All grown in the garden of Higher Mead Cottage despite the best attempts of an evil community of sniggering slugs.'

'Sniggering slugs. Well I never,' said Christina.

'Organic. No slug pellets. Phoebe said to tell you. Every slug removed by hand. Escorted politely to new slug-friendly quarters. Every night. In a pot.' For some reason, his sentences had become very short and clipped.

She took a peek inside the bag. 'These look delish. Thanks so much. I'll have them with nut cutlets and baby carrots tonight.'

'Great,' he said, unable to muster much enthusiasm for the nut cutlets but pleased that she was pleased.

She beamed at him. 'Come in, come in. I've just made flapjacks.'

He dithered on the doorstep. Today's circuit had taken a long time. He should get back to Phoebe. But he found himself stepping inside and accepting Christina's hospitality again.

The flapjacks were delicious, crumbly and still warm.

He cast about for a topic of conversation. 'Potatoes are quite miraculous, don't you think?' he blurted out.

'I agree,' she said, surprising him. 'But miracles are pretty common, if you ask me. The chances of life existing at all are infinitesimal, but it somehow keeps popping up all over the place. Then there's the fact that this planet is precisely the right distance from the sun so that we don't frazzle or freeze.'

He nodded manically. 'Yes, it's mind-boggling. And amazing that you're you and I'm me. I mean, I only exist because my parents just happened to coincide on a damp Thursday night, queuing for chips in Carmarthen. And their parents just happened to meet in some equally random way . . . And their parents before them. A long line of chance going back in time, hanging from threads.'

She smiled. 'And every moment that has the cheek to happen is carelessly shedding millions of alternative possibilities. Yet here we are, defying all odds, sitting at my kitchen table in Darleycombe, sipping tea and eating flapjacks.'

Al reeled slightly when he thought of all the parallel universes in which he might be doing other things.

Christina brought him back to earth. 'Al, I'm going to have a barbecue to celebrate Miaow's return. You Featherstones will be the guests of honour.'

'Cool,' he said, instantly regretting his (probably very uncool) choice of vocabulary.

'Does next Saturday suit you?'

'That would be perfect.' Although he could never be sure about Phoebe. 'I'm really grateful to you for taking

Phoebe drawing at the sanctuary,' he said. 'It's given her a great focus, great therapy.'

'She's a little star, and I'm glad she's enjoying it.'

'She is. She's completely fallen in love with the otters.'

Christina gave him a full, frank smile. 'It's hard not to.'

'Yes. No. Quite.'

He gulped down the remainder of his tea. 'Still, it's good of you to take her under your wing like this,' he said. 'You must have plenty of other things to do.'

'Not really. My shop in Porlock only opens three days a week. My son lives far, far away, and I don't get to see much of my best friend, Ellie, these days. I'd be going to the sanctuary to draw anyway, and it's great to have Phoebe there too. Rupert and Carol are always so busy, and Carol's not exactly a socialite, is she? Phoebe may be a lot younger than me, but she has a wise head on her shoulders, and a true heart. Like you.'

'Like me?' It sounded like a compliment. It *was* a compliment.

'Yes. I love her company. I just hope those animal-rights activists don't put her off coming again.'

'Oh, nothing will put her off coming again. You can be sure of that.'

17

Conjectures

SOMETHING'S GOING ON, Coco. I'm sure of it. Somebody is trying to jeopardize the work of the sanctuary. There have just been too many disasters for it to be a coincidence. But who? And why?'

The otter shuffled against her. Phoebe stroked the thick fur on the nape of her neck and tilted the bottle of fish soup a little so that Coco could guzzle while she was listening.

'I can think of only three reasons. First, certain people don't believe in animals being in captivity, under any circumstances.'

The girl with the streaky hair and her boyfriend were still posted outside, along with three other protesters. They waved their placards and snarled at any tourist who came in. They refused to listen to arguments and made for a sinister presence. At least they had not done any physical damage. Not yet, anyway.

'Another reason might be because otters are fish guzzlers. Carol has reintroduced quite a few otters into the wild since she started up. Maybe the guilty party is somebody connected to the fish farm? Or somebody who has a fish pond?'

Coco didn't comment, but then she had other things to think about. She was nearing the end of the bottle. 'And third, somebody might have an issue with this place if an otter had hurt them or one of their loved ones. Otters have been known to bite, after all. Even kill.'

Phoebe mused on the less cute side of otters. Earlier, she had witnessed Holly and Hawthorn using a frog as a tug-of-war rope. Evidently fun for them, it had been a lot less fun for the frog. 'I sincerely hope you would never do such a thing, Coco,' Phoebe added, stroking the tiny, round ears of the cub. 'Nor you, Paddy,' she added to the other cub, who was near her feet, busily batting at a moth with alternate paws.

With a jolt, she became aware that a figure was standing in the shadow beside the enclosure.

She blinked. 'Oh, I had no idea you were there!'

It was Rupert, his head to one side, a quizzical look on his face.

She attempted a charming, Rev-Lucy-style smile. 'Silly me, chatting away to Coco!'

He chortled. 'Don't worry yourself about it, Phoebe. She's such a sweetie-pie, isn't she? I'll confess I do sometimes' – he lowered his voice to a whisper – 'talk to her myself. Don't tell Carol, though, will you? She'll think I've gone soft.'

Phoebe watched his Adam's apple move down his long

throat. Much as she liked Rupert, she felt defensive and slightly put out. She had presumed that only she and Carol had close contact with Coco. Although, thinking about it, it made sense that Rupert filled in sometimes.

'Between you and me, Phoebe, I *am* actually a big softy. With her farming background – killing pigs and wringing the necks of chickens, and so forth – Carol doesn't really comprehend us tender-hearted people. The cubs are so endearing, with their mischievous little ways, people like us can't help falling in love with them. Your Coco is particularly delightful. Such a shame we'll be losing her in the spring.'

'Not from her point of view,' said Phoebe. She set down Coco, who scampered off happily and joined Paddy. Rupert accompanied Phoebe back to the main building, slowing his pace to match hers and extolling the virtues of the cubs all the way. He really was a lovely man, even if he did go on a bit.

'Rupert,' she said.

'Yes, Phoebe?'

'I want to get a present for Christina. Have you any ideas what she might like?' Her friend had been so very generous, first with the easel and more recently the pretty otter pendant.

Rupert stroked his chin, thinking. 'She likes arty-crafty things. And otter-related things, obviously. There may be something suitable in the gift shop.'

It was certainly worth a look.

'I'll be out the back, counting today's takings, but let me know if I can help with anything,' he said.

Phoebe wandered listlessly around the sanctuary's

shop, picking a few things up and putting them down again. In addition to Christina's jewellery and Dan's oak leaves, the shelves were crowded with cuddly toy otters, tea towels, coasters and tote bags. But nothing seemed quite right.

As she pondered, the back door opened and in came a familiar-looking figure, carrying a box. She remembered those finely chiselled features and penetrating dark eyes.

'Hello,' she said. 'You're Dan Hollis, aren't you? We never actually introduced ourselves last time. I'm Phoebe Featherstone. I help look after the wild cubs.'

He stuck out his hand. 'Very pleased to meet you, Phoebe-Featherstone-the-Wild-Cub-Carer. I am Dan Hollis, the Exmoor harp-maker.'

He was full of surprises, this man. Phoebe wasn't sure if she had heard him right. Had he said 'harp-maker'? Ah, no. What he must have said was 'heart-maker'. He probably made little wooden hearts, like he made little wooden oak leaves. They'd be intended for table decorations at weddings or as gifts on Valentine's Day.

'Have you brought some more things for the shop?' she asked.

'Indeed I have,' he said. 'Eighteen leaves.' He placed the box on the floor, perfectly parallel with the wall and in exactly the position where he had placed it last time.

It occurred to Phoebe that Dan might be able to help her.

'I'm looking for a gift for Christina. I love your leaves, but I expect she has one of them already?'

'She does have an oak leaf already. Ellie gave it to her on the seventeenth of February last year as an unbirthday present. Most days of the year are her unbirthday, as a

167

matter of fact, but Ellie chose that unbirthday in particular because Christina was feeling a bit down. It used to happen a lot, but the leaf helped cheer her up. I was glad about that. Very.'

'I'm wondering if I could commission you to make something else?'

He stopped to think for a minute. 'There's not much else I can make, I'm afraid. Only harps.'

Harps again? She was sure that was what he'd said this time. He must mean miniature wooden harps, perhaps designed for hanging on Christmas trees. That wasn't quite what she was looking for.

'And I once upon a time made a candlestick,' Dan added helpfully.

Candlesticks were an idea. Christina was the sort of person who had lots of candles (probably scented) and took baths by candlelight.

'I bet Christina would love a hand-made candlestick,' she said. 'Do you think you'd be able to make one that's a bit quirky . . . Maybe with a carved figure of a cat coiled around it? Is that asking rather a lot? Could you do that for me? And if so, how much would it cost?'

Dan considered. 'She *would* like that. And yes, a quirky one. A Miaow candlestick. And no, it isn't asking a lot. And yes, I could do that for you. As for your fourth question, that is more difficult to answer.'

It sounded as if Dan knew Christina pretty well. The candlestick would be very special. He seemed reticent about money, though. Phoebe was unable to earn anything, but she hardly ever spent anything either and her father insisted on giving her a monthly allowance.

'What sort of wood would you like?' he asked.

Phoebe made a mental note to google types of wood later. 'Ummm . . . I think she'd like something grainy.'

'I have some walnut, cherry, lime and oak. The oak is nicely grained and might do?'

'It sounds perfect. But how much would I owe you?'

He blinked several times as if he couldn't cope with the question.

'Your leaves are £11.99 each,' she said, thinking aloud. 'But I imagine a candlestick would be more complicated to create.'

Dan nodded. He wasn't helping much.

'Do you think twenty-five pounds might cover the cost of wood and your time and talent?' she hazarded.

'Yes,' he answered. 'Probably. Maybe. I think so.'

'Hooray, that's settled, then. Please will you make one for me out of the oak, and drop it off here as soon as it's ready? I can pay you a deposit now.'

She dug around in her pockets, found a £10 note and thrust it into his hand. He stared down at it.

'I will do as you ask,' he said. 'It is an absolute pleasure to be working for you, Phoebe-Featherstone-the-Wild-Cub-Carer.'

The last four words were uttered as if they were her surname. It gave her a warm glow that he had acknowledged her in this role. It was a long time since she'd possessed a proper *raison d'être*, and this was rather a fine one.

Al walked through the village, past the green, the duck pond and the shop, up the footpath that took him to the weir. He stopped and leaned against the gate to admire the water. It was soothing to watch it glide elegantly towards its destiny, then suddenly a little shocking as it changed from horizontal to vertical and spilled over the edge of the rocks. Hart's tongue ferns clung to the sides of the torrent. Between the recesses and deep hollows the cascade caught thousands of sparks, tossed them about and hurled them downstream.

Al let his mind meander. It drifted hither and thither, but kept pinging back to Christina.

How fantastic it was that she'd forged this unlikely friendship with his daughter in spite of the age difference. He could see she had made quite an impact on Phoebe. A mother figure? Hardly. He smiled. It was Phoebe who came across as the more mature of the two. Yet Christina had done something he had failed to do. She had reanimated his daughter, brought her out of herself.

The green reflections jiggled and merged before streaking down and away. Darts of light speared the froth below. The waterfall reminded him of the importance of exuberance and enthusiasm, qualities he'd almost forgotten about until the advent of Christina and the otters in his life.

He must not forget to restock Phoebe's painkillers. She had called out to remind him just as he was setting out. He would pop into the shop on his way back home.

Christina was incredible. Her actions at the sanctuary had been so emphatic and effective, in marked contrast to his own. The line between brave and foolhardy was a thin one, yet while he was pussyfooting around, Christina hadn't hesitated for a moment. You had to admire that kind of courage. Then there was her kindness to

Phoebe, which, in his mind, counted as the most endearing of her qualities.

A thought was tugging away at him, an invisible fibre, too subtle to identify.

He watched as eddies swirled around the jutting roots, scouring them clean. Bracken and brambles overhung the strands of water. They annoyed him somewhat. They obscured his view.

He would like to get to know Christina better. He would like to spend more time in her company. And she had said – or implied at least – that he had 'a true heart'.

He should be careful, though. She had been hurt a lot and was possibly needy. He remembered how she'd talked about her son living far, far away and the fact she didn't see her best friend very much these days. *Definitely* needy. And he couldn't manage being needed by anyone else apart from Phoebe. He felt inadequate even to that task. He had to put Phoebe first.

What was he thinking, anyway? There was no way Christina would think of him like that, or even be interested in him at all. He felt vulnerable and small. And dull, far too dull, for someone like her to consider as a friend. She'd laugh at the idea of anything more.

Every way he looked at it, he came to the same conclusion. It would be better to keep his distance.

18

Trying

AL HAD FORGOTTEN to buy the painkillers. When she pointed it out, he'd immediately driven back to the shop for some, but Phoebe wasn't sure she would be able to survive the next fifteen minutes. Pain beat through her blood, flared in her joints, grated in her head. Even the slightest movement hurt like hell. She tried to breathe shallowly so that her ribcage wouldn't move at all. Unfortunately, staying still hurt too.

Horizontal wasn't working. Wincing, she got to her feet and tried vertical. No, it was agony. She forced herself to take a step, then another. Sometimes, walking was the best way. She stopped again. No good.

She screwed up her eyes and tried to focus on lovely things. Daffodils. Strawberries. Otters. Surely the otters would help? Much as she tried to conjure them, her mind wasn't up to it. It kept yelling '*ouch, ouch, ouch,*' instead, along with a range of expletives and profanities.

She tried music. In her head she listened to uplifting tracks: the ones that didn't stop believing and walked on sunshine and always looked on the bright side of life . . .

The pain was too noisy and drowned them out.

She'd read somewhere that if you put a pen into your mouth, propping up your lips, it made you smile, and that tricked your system into actually being happy. She grabbed a pen from the bedside table and put it in her mouth.

No difference.

She even tried fake laughter. 'Ha ha!'

The pen dropped to the floor and rolled across the carpet.

'Hahahahahaha.'

The jolting made her muscles scream in protest.

She dug her nails into the soft flesh of her arm to try to give herself another shock to think about. It worked momentarily but then the pain flooded back, strong as ever.

Her eyes pricked with tears.

Dad, please hurry.

She sank into the armchair and crouched, hugging her arms around her body. She was out of ideas. It was clear the torture was going to go on, no matter what she did. She clenched her teeth, her fists, her forehead. She would just have to weather it.

The pain bloomed until it filled her like a pit of scalding lava. It reached right down to the roots of her teeth and made them jangle. It dug into the back of her brain. It drove out the awareness of everything else in the world.

She was in the same crouched position when the key turned in the front door and Al's voice called, 'I'm back!'

Thank God.

She heard him come into the bedroom.

'Phoebes?'

She lifted her head, slowly, creakily, hating that he saw her tears.

'Have you got them?' she managed to say.

'Here. Here they are.'

He fumbled with the box as he handed it to her. But she needed water.

'Hang on. Won't be a tick.'

She swallowed two tablets anyway. They stuck in her throat, coating it with bitter sediment. She gagged and spluttered. When her father returned with the water she gulped it quickly and the disintegrating pills washed down through her.

'Sorry,' Al murmured. 'Sorry, sorry, sorry.'

He wrapped her in his arms, holding her against his heart. It hurt her physically, but she wasn't going to hurt him back by saying so.

However did people manage in the days before painkillers?

Sooner or later, they would start working. Then she would find something positive to think, and to say.

19

Holding On

'Just got an email from Jules. She's coming to stay.'

Al's voice contained only delight, but in his eyes there was a flash of concern.

'Oh, that's great,' Phoebe responded insincerely. 'When?'

'Next week.'

'Amazing.'

The prospect of anyone coming to stay, even (or perhaps especially) her own family, alarmed her. Phoebe would need to pace herself carefully. After Jules's last visit it had taken her three weeks to recover. She had overdosed on painkillers because she'd been so exhausted she had lost track of how many she'd swallowed. She'd narrowly avoided ending up in hospital.

Al knew this, but Jules didn't. Sometimes it was better not to tell Jules things.

In her own eyes, Jules was a bringer of fun and

laughter. Her ideal life consisted of endless socializing, and she assumed everyone else felt the same. Peace, quiet and rest were concepts that didn't interest her. But these things were essential for Phoebe.

'I'll take her out as much as possible,' Al promised.

'Do you think we could persuade Jack to come down too?'

'He seems to like his northern bachelor pad, but I'll try my damnedest.'

It was always easier if both her siblings were there. Although Jack possessed similar energy levels to Jules, he got on well with both his sisters and was good at defusing any confrontations that arose. Jack also stopped them all from taking themselves too seriously.

A quick phone call established that Jack was able to coincide with Jules.

'He asked if he could bring the current girlfriend.'

'And?' asked Phoebe, a smile plastered over her anxiety.

'I said no. Higher Mead Cottage will already be bursting at the seams, the hot-water tank wouldn't be big enough for all those morning showers and, this time round, at least, I'd prefer it to be just family.'

In the event, it was just as well because Jack split up with his girlfriend shortly before the visit. He got through girlfriends fast. He tended to follow the same pattern whenever it happened: immediately heartbroken but quickly rallying again.

Phoebe hadn't been to the sanctuary for several days, and the Otter Effect was beginning to wear off. Sore neck muscles and worries for the future were getting to her.

'I have to see Coco,' she told Al.

'I'll take you,' he said. 'I could do with a bit of otter therapy myself.'

When they arrived, the sun was low in the sky, lolling on a bank of burnished cloud. The group of protesters had left for the evening. Phoebe let out a sigh of relief. Even though Al always saw her inside safely, she hated the threatening looks they aimed at her every time she passed. The girl with the feathered blonde hair and her greasy-looking boyfriend seemed to be the ringleaders. They had gathered more support again and there was now a daily knot of zealots posted outside. So far, they had just put off the tourists and deprived the sanctuary of some entrance-ticket fees. Phoebe fretted that any day soon they would take more violent action.

In the shop, Rupert had started to cash up. He looked up, pleased to see Al and Phoebe, but something uncomfortable lurked behind his smile.

'I wish they'd leave us alone,' he growled, with a nod towards the door as he swept a heap of fifty-pence pieces into a coin bag. 'The takings are peanuts these days. I've nearly finished counting already. I think those otters are going to have to tighten their belts. Just as well the chippy provides free fish.'

With a sinking feeling, Phoebe realized this was an attempt at optimism. If things didn't change soon, the sanctuary might be forced to close.

'Is there anything we can do to help?' Al asked.

'No. The stupid oafs won't leave us alone. I've reasoned with them, Carol's reasoned with them, Christina's reasoned with them. They won't budge. And they refuse to come inside to look at the otters and see the conditions for themselves, always harping on that wild animals should be *in the wild*. Anyway, you don't want to listen to me ranting on. Carol's outside, hosing down the pens. She says she wants a word with you.'

Phoebe's heart took another downward plunge. She thought she knew what this would be about.

They found Carol in the far enclosure, a solid presence with a bucket and hose, lit by streaming summer-evening sunshine. She was knee deep in vegetation and seemed surrounded by leaping otters. Willow darted forward to nibble at the strap of her right welly. Twiggy skipped in and out of the jet of spray as it came out of the hosepipe nozzle, chasing the rainbows that danced in the refracted light.

When she saw them, Carol strode to the tap and turned off the water. She spoke over the fencing.

'Ah, Phoebe, Al. I was wondering if you'd come. Coco and Paddy have already been fed. And I'm afraid the time has come. Coco doesn't need the bottle any more.'

Phoebe swallowed. She told herself to be strong. This was a good thing, even though it might not feel like it right now.

'You can pick her up today,' said Carol, 'but it will have to be the last time.'

'Right,' Phoebe murmured.

'Can I pick her up, too?' asked Al.

Carol screwed her face into a frown. 'Well, I suppose I'm going to have to let you. But only very briefly, please. You know why. If she becomes imprinted, she will never be released.'

178

'Yes, yes, of course,' Phoebe said, steeling herself. She had known this was coming. She just wished it didn't have to be today.

When they reached the enclosure they hung back and watched for a while. Coco and Paddy had discovered a patch of bright-green moss. They were rolling about in it, tearing out tufts with their teeth, tossing them into the air and catching them again. It was a great game. Every so often they stopped to wrestle with each other. Phoebe stepped into the pen and gathered Coco in her arms.

She treasured these last moments of physical contact, sinking her face into Coco's warm fur. Coco wriggled and snuffled wet kisses into her neck.

'Well, little Floof, it's time for you to learn how to be wild again,' Phoebe whispered to her, gazing down into her chocolate-brown eyes. 'We'll still look in on you, still care for you, but you must get on with your otter life if you want to be free. That's what you really want, don't you?'

As if in answer, Coco twitched her nose and patted Phoebe's arm with one paw. Phoebe ran a finger along the ridges of her snout where the whiskers sprang out, then held Coco against her chest, feeling the tiny otter heart-beats against her own. She never wanted to let go.

At last she handed Coco to Al, tears welling up. Al accepted her gently, just as he'd done that first day by the river. He stroked her all the way down from her nose to her tail and took a deep breath.

Then he set her down again. Without hesitation, she whisked off to join Paddy and claim the moss ball.

'It's for the best, you know,' Al murmured.

Phoebe turned her face away for a moment, cleared her throat.

'Yes,' was all she could say.

They walked back down the path in silence.

20

All the Featherstones

AL WAS IN a flurry of tidying, dusting and hoovering.

Phoebe couldn't manage the vacuum cleaner at all, but she joined in with flicking some dust around until Al begged her to stop. He knew she needed to reserve her energy for when the rest of the family arrived.

'Is it really necessary to do all that?' Phoebe asked, looking distressed.

'Yes. Don't want them to think I'm not coping.'

It was just as well he hadn't unpacked all the boxes, otherwise there would be triple quantities of stuff to dust. In fact, he was beginning to ask himself if it was necessary to *ever* unpack. He and Phoebe seemed to be managing fine without most of their possessions.

He fetched Jules and Jack at the same time from the station in Exeter. How good it was to see them again!

In Al's eyes all his children were beautiful, but by

society's standards Jack was arguably the best-looking of the three. It was a shame about that ear stud he insisted on wearing. Jack had the sort of firm jawline, flashy eyes and rakish charm that girls loved. Al was sure he also classified as 'cool' (or whatever the equivalent was these days. Even words were at the mercy of fashion's whims, and Al had little hope of keeping up).

Jules, despite her regular features and nice, shiny hair, had nothing that particularly made her stand out, although she was skilled in the art of make-up and always well dressed. She had been using a fake tan which gave her face a slightly orange sheen.

She was very chatty on the drive to Darleycombe, but it was Jack who asked after Phoebe. Al was pleased to relate that their sister had found at least one good friend in the village, old enough to be her mother but nevertheless a big hit. He also told them that Phoebe was prying into the affairs of many other locals and was extremely involved in otters. All these things suggested a huge improvement on life in Birmingham. However, she was still nowhere near what you might call 'well'.

'I'm dying to see the otters,' said Jules.

When they arrivedat Higher Mead Cottage, Phoebe had made it downstairs and was sitting in the kitchen. She had intended to put the kettle on, but it was too painful for her to pick it up. She had managed to get out some biscuits, though.

'Hi there, sis!' shrieked Jules, throwing her arms around her.

'Yay, Phoebes, great to see you!' cried Jack, adding his arms to the mix.

Phoebe hugged them both, inhaling their warm presence. This was going to be fun. She just needed to accept that she wouldn't be able to keep up with them. She needed them to accept it, too.

'Where's Coco?' asked Jules, looking around.

'Er . . . at the otter sanctuary. Down the road.'

'What?' There was a beat while she took it in. 'Oh, I thought you had adopted her. I thought she was here.'

The otter sanctuary had been mentioned several times during phone calls. Jules had only listened to what she wanted to hear and therefore had fully expected to find Coco curled up by the fire or trotting about the sitting room. Phoebe sensed her sister's disappointment, which would quickly fester. Already the atmosphere had been tainted.

Pulling her mouth down, Jules laid a package on the kitchen table. 'I have a gift for you both, for the house. Hope you like it.'

'A gift? How lovely of you,' Al said.

He unwrapped the little parcel. 'How beautiful is this?' He drew out a china butter dish decorated with ornate pink-and-gold roses.

'I absolutely fell in love with it,' declared Jules, her peevishness melting a little in the warmth of her father's praise.

Al walked over to the fridge, extracted a slab of butter and slid it into the dish, making noises of appreciation. Phoebe knew that the minute Jules had gone, the dish would be put at the back of the cupboard. It wasn't the sort of thing they would ever use.

'I'm afraid I didn't bring you anything,' Jack said, frowning.

'For goodness' sake, we wouldn't expect it,' Al told him.

It was time for them both to tour the house.

'Oh my God!' Jules cried, as they followed him round. 'How can you live like this? You've been here weeks and everything's still in boxes.' Her voice was shrill and her presence seemed to fill the entire building.

Al hung his head. 'I know. It's terrible. But I got the job as soon as we moved, and there hasn't been much time.'

Phoebe sighed quietly. Most of his time was spent looking after her.

'Not to worry. I'll unpack everything for you.'

This was not so much an offer as a right that Jules had claimed. She had inherited her mother's ability to organize and get things done. Al knew she would enjoy it.

'If you insist,' he said.

Jules spent most of the afternoon extracting their possessions from the boxes and arranging them around the house.

While she was occupied, Phoebe took advantage of having a little time with her brother. They sat together on her bed.

'Loving the boudoir,' he said.

'Thank you. All Dad's handiwork.'

His eyes fixed on Ruth's ukulele, which was on Phoebe's wall, garlanded with fairy lights.

'I remember Mum playing that, sitting cross-legged on a cushion on the floor. She used to play "Sailing". And Dad joined in with his air guitar and his Rod Stewart impression.'

'Oh, I'd forgotten that. But I do remember her doing "Smile".'

They paused, each running through their own memories. If Phoebe listened hard, she could still hear the echo of Ruth's reedy singing voice, gently advising her to 'smile, though her heart was aching' and to 'hide every trace of sadness'. She blinked a tear away. She hoped her mother wouldn't have been disappointed in her.

She decided to take Jack into her confidence about her current project.

'Jack, I'm hoping to pair up Dad with the friend I told you about, Christina.'

Jack raised his eyebrows. 'Interesting. I'm sure she's very nice, but, to be honest, Phoebe, I'm not convinced Dad wants another woman. He loved Mum so much. I'm not sure he's ever going to get over it.'

'I know. He did love her so, so much, and of course she can never, ever be replaced in his heart. But Mum would have wanted him to be happy. And he needs someone like Christina to take him out of himself. She's really good at that sort of thing.'

'Is she? Well, she certainly seems to have got *you* out and about.'

'True. Dad's fine getting out and about physically, of course . . . maybe not so much emotionally.'

'He's got friends here, though, hasn't he? The bell-ringing bunch?'

'Yes, but he's not that close to any of them. He acts happy, but I can't help feeling he doesn't really enjoy anything deep down, except, perhaps, the garden and the Exmoor countryside. I'd love him to be more fulfilled. There's a kind of hollowness, as if he's only carrying on because of . . . well, us. Me, in particular.'

'I know what you mean. He seems to be operating mainly on autopilot.'

185

'Yes, and he goes vague on me a lot. He needs to be shaken up. Shaken and stirred.'

'Like a James Bond Martini cocktail?'

'No. That was—'

'I know. Shaken, *not* stirred.'

'Dad needs both the shaking and the stirring. And I honestly think Christina is the person to do it.'

Jack considered. As someone who led a life full of girl-friends, he should understand.

'You might be right,' he said at last. 'It would be brilliant if he found true love again.'

'I knew you'd agree.'

She made him promise to get to know Christina at the barbecue and report back what he thought of her.

'But please make sure she gets plenty of time with Dad,' she added. 'And please like her. I really want you to like her.'

'I'll do what I can.'

'Hey, guys!' It was Jules's voice calling up to them. 'Come down here. You'll never guess what I found.'

Jack and Phoebe exchanged glances.

Jack grinned. 'Best do as she says.'

They went downstairs and found Jules on the sitting-room sofa, poring over an old scrapbook.

She looked up at them, her eyes bright. 'It was Mum's. She pasted our drawings in here when we were kids. And do you remember how she got us to tell each other stories and she wrote them all down? They're in here too.'

Jack and Phoebe drew closer and sat on either side of her. Their three heads bent over the faded, multicoloured pages of the scrapbook. In between the childish, cray-oned drawings, numerous sheets of lined paper were glued in, covered with their mother's neat handwriting in blue ink. A warm glow expanded in Phoebe's ribcage.

'Your stories all seem to be about space aliens,' Jules said to her brother.

'And yours were about princesses,' he returned, laughing.

Phoebe noticed that, although she was the youngest, her own stories tended to be the longest and the most detailed. Jules turned a smiling face towards her and nudged her with an elbow. 'And yours were all about goblins.'

Phoebe nodded, remembering.

Sometimes Ruth had drawn a little picture too, and she'd always written 'by Jack', 'by Jules', 'by Phoebe' in large, proud letters beside the titles.

The Martian and the Tractor, by Jack.

The Princess Who Needed a New Tiara, by Jules.

The Goblin Who Was Always Gobblin', by Phoebe.

They read the stories together, pointing at sections and giggling, trying to recall what had been going on in their lives at the time. Phoebe pictured her mother as she sat with her pen moving swiftly over the paper, completely with them in their wild imaginings, encompassing them all in her smiles whenever she looked up.

Near the end of the book, they found a story anonymously penned, still in their mother's hand. It was entitled *The Space Alien, the Princess and the Goblin.*

'It's the one Mum wrote for us. Shall I read it aloud?'

'Yes, do,' said Phoebe.

Jules read clearly, imbuing each scene with high drama and putting on the voices of the characters: a disjointed monotone for the space alien, a dainty lisp for the princess and a gabbling West Country accent for the goblin. The story told how each of them had fallen into trouble but was saved by the others. The alien had tumbled out of his spaceship and desperately tried to clutch at the stars for help, but failed to reach them. Then, as he crashed to earth, he was caught safely by the princess and the goblin. The princess, though, was panicking because she had forgotten where she'd left the Crown jewels. The others helped her find them; they were hanging in an apple tree in the Royal garden. But that evening, tired from the celebrations, the goblin tripped and fell into a dark pit. It was only when morning came that the other two found him and pulled him out.

As Jules finished reading, her voice quivered. Phoebe glanced up and noticed that their father was standing in the doorway. His eyes were screwed tight shut and his brow was furiously furrowed. He looked as if a huge weight was pressing down on him. And she knew these moments of intense loss would recur from time to time, probably for the rest of their lives. Al bowed his head and silently backed out. Her brother and sister hadn't seen him.

'It's a lovely story,' said Jack.

Jules sniffed. 'It is.'

'Dear, dear Mum,' whispered Phoebe.

It was important that they witnessed the beauty of the local countryside, so Al proposed a walk. Phoebe declined, saying she really didn't feel up to it. Her siblings made up for her lack of enthusiasm.

Al had forgotten how very physical they were compared with Phoebe. They seemed to be always pouncing on each other in ambush and giving each other piggy-backs. He remembered now that it was a youth thing. The sort of thing Phoebe had done too, before she got ill.

Still, it was wonderful to see Jack and Jules striding through the bracken, fully able to appreciate the sights and sounds offered by a strenuous hike in the hills. How great it was to share at last his appreciation of this part of the country; to point out the slim ribbon of the Darle and the farms and villages he visited on his rounds, small dots in the land spread out before them; to admire the round tufts of heather and yellow flames of gorse flowers, the oak trunks festooned in woolly lichen, the young beeches twisting out of old stone walls. A couple of deer bounded on prong-like legs into a thicket, startled by their approach. Sheep bleated in the fields, a distant trac-tor hummed, a buzzard wheeled overhead.

While Jules was ahead, Jack confided in Al the details of the break-up with his girlfriend. Al listened and sym-pathized. He was surprised when Jack asked if there was a special lady in his own life.

'Only your mother,' he answered quickly. It was true, wasn't it? And it was surely the answer Jack wanted to hear.

Jules, rushing back to them, made Al take dozens of photos of her – posing by an old wooden gate, standing on top of a cairn, pretending to have a bath in a sheep trough, wobbling dramatically at the edge of a steep slope. Jack was more interested in following their route on an Ordnance Survey map.

The three of them came back windswept, with colour in their cheeks and mud on their boots. The house was quiet. Al couldn't stop Jules from bursting in on Phoebe, who had the curtains drawn around her bed.

'Woohoo. We went miles! We saw the sea in the distance, and so much wildlife on the moors, and a view that just went on and on. It was glorious. But my blisters are bloody killing me.'

She was keen to show her photos to her sister. Phoebe politely looked at them and said, 'Wow.' Jules would be showing them to all her friends later to illustrate the craziness of country life. Most would be shared on social media as well. Jules even took a photo of the blister on the sole of her foot and digitally enhanced it, making it larger and more purple.

'My fifteen thousand followers will be horrified,' she said gleefully.

Jules and Jack gave Al a hand cooking the dinner, which was very welcome. Al was competent in the kitchen, but only ever made simple fare. Tonight's would be roast chicken with green beans, his own new potatoes and the first of the courgettes from the garden. He put a heap of sausages in the oven as well, because he worried it wouldn't quite be enough otherwise. Jack had one of those metabolisms that demanded vast quantities of food.

'So unfair!' said Jules to her brother. 'You don't know the meaning of self-discipline, but you get to be ridiculously thin anyway.'

It was a shame she felt it necessary to count the calories in everything, because she was extremely helpful otherwise and knew just what to add to make a dish extra special. ('A sprinkling of toasted pine kernels, Dad', 'A knob of garlic butter', 'One more twist of pepper, please, Dad'.)

Phoebe never cooked. The only thing she could make was an omelette, and the last time she'd made one of those had been two years ago.

It was about halfway through dinner that Phoebe began to feel it under her skin: the discomfort that her sister's presence always seemed to instigate. Jules was holding forth with a story her flatmate had told her.

'And she stood up in the middle of this lecture and started declaring her undying love. Just when the lecturer was discussing the finer points of Palladian architecture, too.'

'What did he do?' asked Jack, who was more tolerant than Phoebe.

Jules held her fork in the air to illustrate her narrative. 'Apparently, he stopped in his tracks, totally thrown. Everyone just sat there, gawping.' She grabbed her spoon from the table and faced it towards the fork, both of them suspended over her plate. 'And he was looking at her and she was looking at him. Then she got off her seat and starting coming towards him.' The spoon approached the fork, swaying sexily. 'He looked like a rabbit in the headlights. I think he was afraid she was going to try and kiss him, right there. He shrank back' – the fork leaned away – 'and said something about it not being the time or the place. And she looked him in the eye, sticking her bust out at him, and said in her sultriest voice: "Tell me the time. Tell me the place. I will be there." And everyone cheered.'

She made the spoon bow. Jack and Al burst into applause.

Phoebe looked down at her plate and shuffled her sausage around on it. Pain was drilling into her head, just behind the eyes, despite the extra tablets she had taken. She had no appetite, and the anecdote just made her feel annoyed, resentful and jealous. For a brief moment, during the reading of their mother's story, she had felt close to Jules. Now she was shrinking from her presence again. What was it about her sister that always seemed to embitter her, bring out the worst in her? She didn't like herself much at the moment. This family time should be happy. She must try harder, must pretend harder, so that at least she wasn't spoiling it for the rest of them.

She stretched the muscles of her mouth and produced a grin worthy of the Cheshire cat.

Jules, however, had moved on and was now commenting about the bad plumbing at Higher Mead Cottage.

'Tell me about it,' said Al.

'Jack, you're practical. Can't you fix it?' she asked.

Her brother guffawed. 'Nope. Of course I can't. You know I haven't a clue about that sort of thing.'

As soon as the meal was finished, Jules directed her energies towards contacting local plumbers via email and phone.

'She is incredible, isn't she?' said Jack over coffee, as her voice was heard leaving her fourteenth answerphone message. Al and Phoebe had to agree. Jules would never give up once she'd set her mind on something. She always got what she wanted, in the end.

Two days later, Higher Mead Cottage had a tap that didn't drip and a water heating system that actually worked.

21

Twisting and Turning

CAROL HAD AGREED to let the Featherstones call in *en masse* to see the otters. She had even said they could pop in for a few minutes to see Coco and Paddy, always providing they were extremely quiet and stayed downwind.

Phoebe impressed on her brother and sister every way she could how important this was.

'They won't even know we're there, will they, Jules?' Jack said.

Jules was not used to being invisible and the idea of it clearly didn't appeal much, but she agreed anyway. It wasn't every day you got to see otter cubs.

The protesters were sitting around the entrance in a huddle, interspersed with their backpacks, eating sandwiches. The girl with the blonde hair (who today had painted black bars over her face) and her boyfriend both hissed as the family approached. Jack stared and Jules giggled. Al marched them on.

Inside, Phoebe caught sight of Dan Hollis deep in conversation with Carol. He waved and hailed her as 'Phoebe-the-Wild-Cub-Carer' once again but seemed alarmed to see such a large quantity of Featherstones all at once. When she hung back, he sidled up and whispered in her ear.

'I've nearly finished the Miaow candlestick.'

Curious as she was, Phoebe just nodded and smiled, worried that Jules would take over the conversation and make a big scene over it. She sensed that Dan wouldn't cope well with a big scene.

'Who was that?' enquired Jules as they went through, her eyes flashing admiration for Dan's good looks.

'Just a nice, sweet man. He makes wooden oak leaves. And miniature harp decorations. And sometimes candlesticks.'

'I was tempted to flirt,' her sister admitted.

'You'd have been wasting your time,' said Phoebe. 'Not only is he way too old for you, but he is utterly devoted to somebody called Ellie.'

Jules groaned. 'Why is there always an Ellie?'

They trooped round the public enclosures first. Quercus, Rowan and the others were in fine form. They swished through the pond and clambered out, their fur slicked back and water-polished. They disappeared down tunnels and popped out again. They lolloped round the inside of the fences, just as interested in the Featherstones as the Featherstones were in them.

'My God, they're crazy!' cried Jules. 'I can't believe

how super-cute they are. Let's have a group picture with the otters behind us.'

She thrust her phone at an unsuspecting tourist in a baseball cap, who obligingly photographed several combinations of otters and Featherstones, complete with cheesy smiles.

While Al and Jules were ahead, Phoebe told Jack about the recent events at the sanctuary and her suspicions.

'I've been mulling it over. There are a few possibilities in my head, people who would have some reason to want this place shut down.'

'Like who?' he asked.

'Like the vicar of Darleycombe, Rev Lucy.'

He turned to her with a face full of scepticism. 'A lady vicar? Surely not.'

'It's just a hunch. Nobody is above suspicion.'

'C'mon, Phoebe. In detective dramas it's always the least obvious suspect who is guilty, but I somehow don't think it works like that in real life.'

'But wait till you hear Rev Lucy's motive: the end of her son's finger was bitten off by an otter.'

He gave a low whistle. 'No way?'

'Yup! In any case, I'd value your opinion of her. Would you be able to check her out at the barbecue? Maybe mention the otter bite and watch her reaction.'

He shrugged. 'If it makes you happy. And you want my opinion on Christina as well, as a potential girlfriend for Dad?'

Phoebe nodded, then held a finger to her lips since they were getting closer to Al and Jules.

It was time to visit Coco and Paddy.

'I'll stay back at reception,' said Al. 'I want to ask Rupert about grandsire triples. It's a complicated bell-ringing sequence that I'm hoping to master one day. You guys go on.'

Phoebe threw him a grateful look. He understood that four people at once would be too much for the cubs. She led her siblings up the pathway.

Jules hopped on one leg. 'Ouch. My blisters are giving me hell. I hope it's not too far.'

'It's not,' said Phoebe. 'Remember to be quiet, won't you?'

'We'll be good, I promise,' said Jack.

'Will you take a vid of me holding Coco?' Jules asked him.

'You can't hold her,' said Phoebe quickly.

'Well then, in that case, Jack can film me stroking her while *you* hold her.'

Phoebe shook her head. 'I can't hold her either.'

Jules stopped. Her face had dropped into a scowl. 'Since when? I thought you were bottle-feeding her?'

'That finished a few days ago. Nobody's allowed to touch her now.'

'Oh, really? That's very convenient.'

'What do you mean, "convenient"?' asked Phoebe.

'Suddenly, like, the day Jack and I arrive in Darley-combe, there's no handling of Coco allowed any more. Funny, that.'

'It wasn't my decision, Jules.'

'Yeah, right.'

Breathe, relax, count to ten, Phoebe told herself.

She took them to the wild otters' enclosure, put a finger

against her lips, and pointed. Coco was playing with a feather, running with it in her mouth then letting it go, watching it drift in the breeze and catching it again in both paws. After a moment, Paddy emerged from the hutch and joined her. They jostled each other, galloping along side by side after the feather and competing for it.

'Unreal!' whispered Jack.

'Wow, total cuteness overload,' Jules agreed, momentarily forgetting her grievances. 'I deffo need a vid of this one!' She started filming Coco. But when the little otter gave a leap into the air to catch the feather and it stuck to her mouth like a moustache, she couldn't help squealing with delight. Coco froze for a millisecond then darted to the cover of her holt.

Phoebe felt a strobe of anger flash through her. She swore at her sister. 'What part of "quiet" don't you understand?'

'Okay, okay, sorry, sorry! Sorry for existing. Sorry for enjoying myself! Phoebe Featherstone has spoken. Must remember: Fun is not permitted here.'

As they walked back down the path, Jack tried to reason with them both, but the air was stiff with resentment. Phoebe felt drained, knotted up inside. Her nerve endings bristled with pain.

'I need a lie-down. Can we go home now?' she said to Al as soon as they'd reached the office.

'Of course,' he said, rummaging for his car keys.

By the gate, the activists were on their feet again, brandishing their placards. The blonde girl, as if emboldened by the bars she'd painted on her face, took a step forward, blocking their way.

'You should be ashamed of yourselves,' she said with contempt.

'No, we shouldn't,' said Jack.

'Don't bother arguing. We've tried,' Al told him.

'You're sick in the head, the whole lot of you,' she retorted. The other protesters gathered round, every face tight with hostility.

Oh God, I don't have the strength for this, thought Phoebe.

Jules was getting out her phone.

'Don't film them. It will make them angrier,' warned Al in a low voice.

Ignoring him, she held the phone up directly in the face of the girl. Shock and fury registered behind the black bars. 'Don't you dare—'

'Look,' Jules interrupted. She was playing the footage she'd taken of Coco and Paddy romping after the feather.

The girl couldn't help looking. Her boyfriend took a look too, as did several of the protesters over her shoulder.

'Happy otter cubs,' Jules said. 'Zoomed in because I wasn't allowed to go near these ones. They're due for release as soon as they're ready. Too young at the moment. They'd die in the wild.'

Despite their refusal to enter the sanctuary, the protesters had finally got to see the truth.

Al took advantage of their surprise and ushered his family swiftly back to the car.

Phoebe set her teeth and grappled with her grudge. Infuriating though she was, Jules certainly got results.

*

In the afternoon, Al suggested a stroll by the river. Phoebe said she couldn't manage it. In spite of their argument, Jules attempted to persuade her to come too.

'I'm just too tired and achey, Jules.'

'Oh, come on, you used to be a laugh . . . Still, that was a seriously long time ago.'

Her words cut Phoebe. Suddenly, she wanted to cry. 'I thought your blisters were killing you,' she pointed out.

Jules put on a superior expression. 'Yes, they are *horrendous*, but I'm going to ignore them.'

Phoebe did not even attempt to muster any sympathy.

Jack pulled a face. 'Let her be, Jules. We have a busy day tomorrow if we're going to this barbecue, so she probably needs some quiet time. Am I right, Phoebes?'

Phoebe nodded gratefully.

She went to bed early that evening. Al put his head round the door of her bedroom just as she was settling down and about to draw the curtains around herself.

'You haven't fallen out with your sister again, have you?' he said mournfully.

'Sorry, Dad. I can't seem to help it.'

'What's the problem?'

'Oh, not a lot. When she was boasting about going out despite her blisters, I wanted to throw the stupid butter dish at her smug face. She just has no inkling of what I've been going through for the past three years. And if there is any available molehill anywhere, Jules will make a mountain out of it.' She ground her fists into the pillow.

Al frowned. It was hard to navigate the shifting sands of family politics. 'She doesn't mean anything by it. It's just her way. And you have to admit she was brilliant with those protesters today.'

Her father would never admit there was anything wrong with Jules.

'But you have to be so bloody careful. Anything you say might be twisted and used in evidence against you.'

Al didn't respond.

'And I'm not good at being careful what I say these days,' Phoebe continued. 'It takes a humongous effort and I'm just way too knackered. Way. Too. Knackered.'

22

Party Animals

Jack had shaved specially and Al had removed his holey jumper in favour of a crisp new shirt. Jules was looking festive in a slinky dress and expensive-looking sunglasses, so Phoebe felt obliged to put on a dress too. It was months since she'd worn one. At home she was nearly always in pyjamas and only ever wore jeans and T-shirts on her visits to the otter sanctuary. Now she pulled on the high-waisted turquoise cotton number that she'd once loved. She grimaced at herself in the mirror. The dress was hanging in loose folds around her. She must have lost even more weight. Her arms looked like Twiglets poking out of the short sleeves. She pulled on a padded jacket to cover them up and felt slightly better about it.

'Aren't you hot in that jacket?' asked Jules, when she came down.

'No,' said Phoebe.

Her stomach clenched at the prospect of an actual social event, after all these years. She hoped she'd manage to hold her head up and look well, hoped she'd manage to talk to people, hoped she wouldn't let her father down.

Christina's garden was already milling with people and humming with chatter when they arrived. The scent of herbs and roasted nuts wafted on the breeze, along with soft wraiths of smoke lit by the afternoon sunshine.

Phoebe had suggested that Al present their hostess with a box of home-grown courgettes as well as some nice bubbly and snacks, and – a last-minute stroke of genius – they had brought some expensive cat food for Miaow, too.

Christina, decked out in magenta dungarees and an excess of bangles, was delighted with these gifts.

'Hey, Featherstones! Great to see you!' she cried. 'Gosh, Phoebe, you look lovely. But aren't you hot in that jacket?'

Phoebe, unused to compliments, was a little thrown. 'Thank you. And no.'

'How are the sniggering slugs, Al?'

'Rehomed,' he answered. 'By the river. And not so sniggery now.'

Christina flitted around, forcing veggie burgers on to people and making introductions. Jules and Jack were quite at home talking to strangers.

Being among all these people brought Phoebe mixed feelings. Her system was swilling with painkillers, coffee and stress, yet it was stimulating to have so many things to observe, so many little nuances to take in. She was startled at the heady challenge and dazzle of it all. Thrilled, even.

Christina ushered her to the barbecue. 'Let me introduce you,' she said, indicating a man who was not much older than Phoebe. His eyes were steely grey and his low forehead was dominated by heavy, dark eyebrows, which gave the impression of grumpiness. She recognized him immediately. Christina acted as though they'd never set eyes on each other before.

'This is dear Phoebe Featherstone, who is new to the village. Phoebe, this is Seth Hardwick. He lives next to the otter sanctuary.'

'Hello,' Seth said rather blankly. He clearly didn't remember her. She wondered if she should ask after his Alsatian, but the fact that his other dog had died because of an otter made it too delicate a subject. Phoebe considered herself to be an otter mother, and presumed this made them enemies. Fortunately, Christina vetoed any conversation with Seth by dragging another man towards her.

'And this is Dan Hollis, who you've already met, I believe.'

'Hello, Phoebe-Featherstone-the-Wild-Cub-Carer.'

He stuck out his hand to be shaken anyway. Phoebe shook it up and down, pleased to see him. Dan was hewn from substances such as sensitivity and creativity and honesty. He had no comprehension of the underhand ways of the rest of the human race. She felt the tension drop from her shoulders in his company. She noticed him looking at her clothes.

'Before you ask,' she said, 'no, I'm not hot in this jacket.'

He blinked. 'I wasn't going to ask.'

'Oh, sorry.'

'You have all your buttons. Six,' he told her.

She glanced down at her jacket. 'Er . . . Yes.'

'Seth has eleven on his shirt. Not twelve.' Dan pointed to the other man, who was helping himself to a burger.

Phoebe took a quick glance at Seth's black shirt and noticed that, yes, one of his buttons was missing. Dan had now started scrutinizing Rupert, who was striding up to talk with Christina. 'Only zips,' he remarked in a tone of disappointment. 'Nothing to count.'

Rupert was indeed wearing a leather jacket with zipped pockets.

Dan took a few steps away from the group, suddenly perturbed. 'I might need to escape from all the jangle of humans,' he muttered to Phoebe. She knew what he meant.

She cast around, looking for anybody else she might recognize. She spotted the two older yoga ladies, the ones she had dubbed 'Serene' and 'Melancholy'. She had learned from Christina that their actual names were Felicity and Marge. Serene aka Felicity was clutching on to the arm of a man with a flat nose and a ginger-grey beard, who, if only he would wear a horned helmet, would definitely resemble a Viking: he could only be Spike Dobson. Melancholy Marge was hanging about with a florid, round man in a waistcoat who must be George Bovis. Mr Dobson and Mr Bovis glared and smouldered if they happened to catch each other's eye. Interesting, Phoebe thought, that the two women were such friends while their husbands were at war.

How useful it was to have absorbed Al's descriptions

of everyone. The balding guy with protruding eyes must be Mr Crocker, the ex-policeman. And she already knew the frizzy-haired lady in the dog collar. Reverend Lucy Daws was clutching a glass of wine and looking rather desperate. She switched her expression to one of amicable warmth when they approached, shook hands with Jules and Jack, and produced a flow of small talk.

Phoebe exchanged glances with Jack, and he winked at her to show he had not forgotten her request. He was just beginning to manoeuvre the conversation round to the otter-biting incident when Al wandered over.

'No husband and children today, Rev Lucy?'

She shook her head quickly. 'He's gone to an old boys' reunion of his school, and I didn't think I should bring the children. They get a bit rowdy, so I've left them in Kandisha's capable hands.'

'Kandisha? Your babysitter?'

'Yes,' she said. She produced a smile. It was a well-practised and sweet one, but, if you looked carefully (and Phoebe did), you could see there was no hint of it in her eyes. 'Kandisha's a lovely girl. You should meet her, Phoebe. She's about your age.'

Phoebe had no particular wish to meet this Kandisha, especially just on the basis of a shared age group.

'Oh look, Dad. Christina could do with some help setting up the croquet.'

She pulled Al away, then glanced back. Jack was still talking to Rev Lucy, who was gesticulating. The smile had vanished from her face.

The croquet had started up, and the people who weren't involved drifted to the edges of the garden. Phoebe remembered how, at school, she had won an award for putting the shot. Now she couldn't even lift a croquet mallet. Envy rose up in her like a cold vapour. Struggling to suppress it, she shrank towards the hedge to avoid a scudding ball. She found that she had ended up next to Marge Bovis.

'Hello, dear. I haven't seen you in yoga for a while,' she said with a baleful air that would be at home in a Greek tragedy.

'No, been a bit busy.' To back up her untruth, Phoebe added, 'My brother and sister have been staying with us, and I've been doing voluntary work at the otter sanctuary.'

'The otter sanctuary?' Marge lifted her sparse grey eyebrows. 'Don't mention that to my husband, will you? He's not a fan of otters. Our fishpond was raided by a gang of them last year, and they banqueted on our koi carp. We'd put down nets and everything, but those otters were so clever they got in anyway. They wreaked utter havoc and guzzled every single fish. They were very valuable specimens, too. Some of them we'd had for over sixteen years.'

'Oh dear,' said Phoebe. 'Naughty otters.'

'I don't hold it against them,' Mrs Bovis assured her with a deep sigh. 'They're wild creatures, and are bound to make the most of food wherever they find it. Still, I don't think George has ever quite forgiven them.'

Phoebe uttered a faint 'So sorry' on the otters' behalf.

Marge sniffed. 'We've replaced the carp now. My goodness, they cost a bomb! George goes and counts them every day to make sure they're all still there.'

She drifted off to join another posse of people.

Phoebe's brain started prickling. She shook her head, trying to order the thought waves that were now lapping in contradictory directions. She scanned the garden for her ally, Jack, who had joined in the croquet game. He gave an almighty thwack to the ball, which went spinning through a hoop. Cheers went up.

She walked over and congratulated him, then whispered in his ear. 'Jack, I have a new suspect. Could you engage him in conversation and throw in a reference to the otters, please?'

'Chrissake, Phoebe. I'm not your spy. Why don't you do it yourself?'

'But I'm not good at talking to people I don't know. These things come so much easier to you than to me. Pretty please.'

'Oh, all right, then. You win. Who is it this time?'

She pointed at George Bovis, whose head was shining like an egg in the sunshine.

'The fat guy in the waistcoat? Okay. I'll go over and suss him out once this game is finished.'

Phoebe was already flagging and beginning to wish she hadn't come. She spotted her father across the other side of the garden, conducting a stilted conversation with Carol, Rupert and Christina while eating a veggie sausage. Somehow, he had managed to slop tomato ketchup down his front. Perhaps noticing her lost expression, Christina swooped on Phoebe and took her arm.

'Come on, Phoebe! Come and meet Miaow, the Queen of the Day.'

It was the first time Phoebe had been inside her friend's

home, but she scarcely had time to register the colourful throws and fittings before finding herself in Miaow's presence. To please Christina, she curtseyed before the cat. Miaow had been provided with a crimson velvet cushion but had chosen instead to squeeze herself into a tiny shoebox.

'Utterly gorgeous, isn't she? Aren't you, my gorgeous porgeous smorgeous ladyship?' Christina said, chucking Miaow under the chin. She took another swig of her drink, which she had described as 'fruity punch', but it presumably contained alcohol because she was becoming gigglier and gigglier. Miaow poked her head out and butted Phoebe's outstretched hand. The purr volume increased.

'She's scoring well on the purrometer,' said Phoebe.

Her friend hooted with laughter. 'What unit does that measure in?'

'Purrz?'

Christina snorted her drink up her nose.

As they stepped out again, she stumbled into Al, who was now engaged in conversation with Mr Crocker.

'Officer, arrest this gentleman!' she declared in mock outrage, pointing at Al's chest. The ketchup did look very like a bloodstain.

Al chuckled politely. Mr Crocker hastened to tell Christina that he was no longer able to make arrests, he was retired now, although he still had contacts in the police force. His words had little effect. Now that she'd discovered the phrase, Christina reeled it out again and again. She pulled Mr Crocker around with her, pointing at various men who were engaged in innocent activities such as getting out deckchairs or collecting croquet balls,

'Never mind, we'll catch up soon,' said Christina, and waved away all her friend's thank-yous, crushing her in a hug.

After they'd gone, Christina turned to Phoebe. 'She's been through a lot, that one. Ellie is one of the strongest people I've ever known in my entire life. Not strong in a hard, brash way, but . . . what's the word? . . . resililident . . .'

'Resilient?' Phoebe prompted.

'Yes, clever you. That's the one. Nearly her whole life, she's been undermined' – Christina was getting emotional now, almost tearful – 'by people who should have loved and looked out for her, but they were horrid – just horrid – to her.'

'Surely not Dan?'

Christina shook her head vehemently. 'Oh no, not Dan. He was the one who changed everything. Dan is a miracle-worker and has brought out the best in her. Such a shame he doesn't like parties.'

'He told me earlier that he might flee from the jangle of humans.'

'Haha, yes, that sounds like him. I'm completely adoring the jangle myself!'

After she'd had her recovery rest, Jack, Jules and Al came into Phoebe's bedroom with coffees. Everyone seemed to be hanging around the bed, discussing the barbecue. Jules, who had forgotten her issues with Phoebe, had really enjoyed herself. 'And Christina's a real laugh,' she said.

Jack nodded. 'What do *you* make of Christina?' he asked his father.

Al pulled a face. 'I know she's been good to you, Phoebe, and she was great with the protesters. But let's face it, she is truly *awful*.'

Jack threw a glance at Phoebe. Christina's behaviour at the barbecue had been rather feral, admittedly, but she was amazed at Al's reaction. He normally saw the best in everyone.

When Al and Jules went downstairs, Jack lingered on with Phoebe.

'So . . .' she said. 'Did you get a chance to talk with Mr Bovis?'

'Yes, ma'am, I did. Unpleasant kind of man. Likes to think he's important. He's in with all the local bigwigs and was continually dropping names that meant nothing to me. It was hard not to laugh. He clammed up as soon as I mentioned otters, though. A definite sore point, I'd say.'

'Thank you, Jack. That's so useful. How about Rev Lucy? Did you talk to her about her son's otter injury?'

'Not exactly. I mentioned our visit to the sanctuary and tried to find a way in, but she didn't volunteer any information and it seemed unnatural to ask.'

This was disappointing. 'Do you think she's the sort of person who might operate in underhand ways to get revenge on behalf of her son?'

He considered. 'She's definitely a neurotic type under that calm exterior. I wouldn't put it beyond her. Dad seems to like her a lot, though.'

Phoebe didn't like the way he'd said that. 'Dad is not the least bit interested in Rev Lucy, and anyway, she's married. What did you make of Christina?'

'She seemed very lovely and lively.' He scratched his

head. 'But somehow I don't think you're going to get her together with Dad.'

'He will change his mind,' Phoebe asserted. 'He was just put off by the "Officer, arrest this gentleman" business.'

'I don't think he'll have the chance to change his mind,' Jack replied. 'When I went round the back hunting for a loo, I saw Christina looking very involved with the posh guy.'

Phoebe gasped. 'Rupert Venn?'

Surely not?

'Yes, I think that was his name. The tall one with a long neck and a jolly manner?'

'Posh but nice? Yes, that's him. That's Rupert.'

'She and he were welded together.'

Phoebe was stunned. 'Were they actually kissing?'

'Passionately.'

'Are you sure?'

Jack nodded. 'Totally. Sorry, Phoebes.'

23

Smaller Passions

Two outings in two days. How very reckless. And how very exhausting. She had measured out her painkillers with care and swallowed the maximum dose, but her joints still ached and groaned. The yoga class (moved to a Sunday to make room for Thursday's Parish Council meeting) was a chance to see Christina, though, and to check up exactly what was going on with her and Rupert. Besides, yoga would be quieter than staying at Higher Mead Cottage with the rest of her family. Jules had nearly decided to accompany her to the class, but the allure of Monopoly, wine and nachos with Al and Jack had proved stronger.

When Phoebe stepped into the village hall, Rev Lucy turned to her, sweet smile in place. Phoebe suspected that she smiled sweetly at everyone and everything, even at the quiche Lorraine she imagined her so beautifully making; a smile that stretched over her face as she shaped pastry, whisked eggs and grated cheese, all the while plotting the demise of the otter sanctuary.

'Nice to see you here again, Phoebe. It was fun at Christina's yesterday, wasn't it?'

'Yes. Great fun.' Phoebe couldn't quite meet her eye.

'It's unlike Christina to be late, but I think we know why.'

Rupert? Or just the hangover?

The only others in the hall were Serene and Melancholy aka Felicity Dobson and Marge Bovis. With so few attendees, Phoebe wondered why Christina bothered.

Felicity and Marge were chatting.

'I'd like to knock their heads together,' said Marge.

Phoebe's attention homed in like a hawk after its prey.

'Who are you talking about?' she asked, feigning ignorance.

Marge rolled her eyes and snorted the word 'Husbands!'

'Really?' said Phoebe. Taking it in turns, they disclosed the details she was longing to hear about the feud. Rev Lucy drew closer, her smile converting to an expression of sympathy.

It had apparently all started two years ago, when Spike Dobson, who didn't possess a bird table, decided to put bread crusts down on the grass bank outside his house for the sparrows. However, the crusts attracted rats, which were an anathema to George Bovis. He indignantly told Spike to curb his habit. Spike took an aversion to his neighbour's way of asking and put out yet greater quantities of bread over the following week. This was appreciated by both the sparrows and the rats, but not by George. George, who saw himself as one of the more righteous and responsible of Darleycombe's residents, invested in some rat poison and put it down on the bank alongside the crusts. This drove Spike incandescent with rage. Not only was it a personal snub to him, he believed that other creatures, not least the sparrows, would ingest it.

At this point, the two men had reached a temporary impasse. Their wives hoped that the bad atmosphere would disperse if they were patient, but it was not to be.

A few weeks later, George Bovis had put in for planning permission to build a new summerhouse in his garden, in a position where it would block the view from Spike Dobson's study. Spike immediately filled out every available form to register an official complaint against this. However, George had a friend on the planning committee and, using his influence, was able to put up the summerhouse anyway. It had all escalated from there, with one petty act of revenge after another. Hydrangea-snipping fury, mowing madness, dog wee on deliveries . . .

'I don't know where it will end!' cried Felicity.

'We've both tried to reason with them, but they won't have it,' added Marge. 'I've never known anybody who holds a grudge the way that George does. He just lets it fester and fester, and I have no idea what nasty act of revenge he's planning next.'

'Oh, my Spike is just as bad,' said Felicity. 'Never marry,' she added to Phoebe.

'I don't think I'm ever likely to,' said Phoebe. No wonder Marge Bovis was always so melancholy. It was a miracle that Felicity Dobson managed to conjure up such serenity.

The koi carp had not been mentioned in the conversation but nonetheless, they persisted in splashing about in Phoebe's mind.

Rev Lucy, she decided, was her number-one suspect, but George Bovis was a very close second.

They had been talking for a good ten minutes when Christina dashed in, full of apologies, her hair loose and wild. She flung down her mat and exchanged a hello with her yoga students. 'Hey, Phoebe! Thought you'd given up on yoga. Good to see you here!'

Phoebe, unable to wait for a more appropriate moment, sidled up and whispered, 'So you're going out with Rupert?'

Christina's eyes widened. She hesitated. 'Phoebe, it might be an idea sometimes to mind your own bloody business.'

Phoebe had no intention of minding her own bloody business – mainly because her own bloody business was so wretched and dull.

A little guilt-tripping might be more effective than further questions. 'Sorry I spoke,' she said in a wounded voice, turned and went back to her own mat. The other three were all poised and ready to start.

'Right, let's just stand and breathe for a few moments,' said Christina, facing the class. 'Empty your minds. Think of nothing. Absolutely nothing. Nothing at all.'

Phoebe obeyed. How lovely it was to think of nothing, absolutely nothing, nothing at all. Hard to maintain, though. As fast as she forced them out, the thoughts swarmed back in again.

Gradually, Christina introduced the exercises.

Yoga reminded Phoebe how much better it was to do things well than to do them fast. The calm of the room soothed her. However, the moves and stretches had somehow become trickier than last time.

Christina seemed seriously hung-over. She moaned to herself as she bent into downward dog. Phoebe, also engaged in a downward dog, echoed the moan. During the supine spinal twist she caught Christina looking at her, and the two of them eyeballed each other.

Christina ignored her over the next sequence of stretches and seemed to be processing her own thoughts.

At the end of the lesson, as they were rolling up their mats, she stalked over. She said, as much to herself as to Phoebe, 'Okay. Yes, then. I *am* going out with Rupert. Is there anything wrong with that?'

Yes. Yes, there is. Because my dad is ten billion times nicer, and he's lonely and he needs someone like you.

'Of course not,' Phoebe answered out loud. 'Only, I thought you said your man-eating days were done.'

Christina laughed. 'To be honest, that could've been sour grapes. I thought I was way beyond my sell-by date. And I never thought anyone as lovely as Rupert would look at me twice, let alone want to be with me.'

And there it was. Contrary to all appearances, even attractive, bubbly extroverts like Christina lacked any real confidence in themselves.

'Rupert *is* lovely,' Phoebe admitted. 'But not as lovely as you.'

'Why, thank you, my friend, but I beg to differ.'

Phoebe dawdled, in no hurry to get home to the nachos, wine and Monopoly. Al had asked her to ring him when she was ready so he could come and collect her. She decided to wander beside the river for a while first to clear her head.

The evening was full of mild breezes and muted birdsong and issues to think about. It was hard to believe that Christina was going out with Rupert Venn. She supposed Christina and Rupert had quite a bit in common. Carol had once mentioned that Rupert was a divorcee, and they were both otter fans. It had been clear from the outset that Rupert was charmed by Christina's vivacity and good looks. Phoebe hadn't detected any romantic interest on Christina's side, however. Otherwise, she would never have latched on to the idea of getting her together with her father. She had convinced herself that nobody else in the village would be right for Al. Nobody else she knew, anyway. Disappointment weighed down on her.

Al had described Christina as 'awful', too, although that could be a case of psychological game-playing, of denigrating her to try and prevent himself falling for her. To protect himself from hurt? Because he didn't think he had a chance? Because he felt he should put his children first?

And what of Jack's comment about Al liking Rev Lucy *a lot*? Rev Lucy, her number-one suspect, who was possibly even now cooking up a new way of undermining the otter sanctuary. Phoebe could only hope that Jack was wrong.

She leaned her back against an oak and gazed at the restless currents of the Darle. The water was neatly combed in some places and viciously clawed in others. A single leaf was caught up in the swirls. It seemed desperate to reach land, straining towards the banks and floundering on the rocks. It clung to a stone for a split second before it was swept mercilessly onwards. It looked so helpless. So despairing.

She wondered if she'd been mistaken in her notion that her father was in need of a romantic relationship. Books, the media and TV all pushed you towards a belief that, if you wanted to be whole and happy, you had to find a partner, but maybe that was a lie. Maybe friends and family mattered more. Or maybe you should just learn to be content with whatever brand of emptiness you were given.

She thought of the stupid, pointless feud between George Bovis and Spike Dobson, and the distress of their wives, who only wanted peace. Then she thought of their advice: never marry.

In her mid-teens, Phoebe had fallen in love at regular intervals. It had made her blood beat hot and her mouth go dry. It had made her google how to kiss well and made her listen to soppy music. It had made her buy underwear that was supposed to snip her waist in but which only spread the bulges upwards. As 'Fatty Featherstone', she had assumed that the boys she fell for were out of her league. She had built each of them up in her imagination as superlatively brave, kind and clever. Then, one by one, without knowing it, they toppled from the pedestal she'd set up for them. What was this strange, naughty little sprite that kept messing about with her hormones?

She had only had one boyfriend, Aiden, and she wasn't sure he even counted. They had gone out for about three months when she was sixteen, and it was hardly the great, transcendent love story she had dreamed of. The main reason they had got together was that they were sorry for each other, she because of his chronic shyness (he crumbled if anyone so much as looked at him) and he because of her podginess. They were both outcasts. This might have been a good basis for a friendship, but pity made a very poor aphrodisiac. Things had changed as soon as they started experimenting. Sex (if you could call it that) led to sky-rocketing self-consciousness and a stack of white lies. She cringed to think of their strained conversations now. And she still remembered the effort of sucking in her stomach while straddling him and pretending to enjoy herself. She'd felt sapped, trapped, disillusioned. And ugly, inside and out.

She had been too ill since then to contemplate romantic relationships. She did not see herself as a sexual being at all. It was normal, wasn't it, for teenagers to hate their own bodies? She certainly did. Although if sex had been on the agenda now, she wouldn't have had to suck her stomach in at all because it had become virtually concave . . . but the whole concept was out of the question. It would require far too much energy.

The surface of the water, where it caught the evening sun, had become a rippling sheet of golden silk. The silhouetted rocks looked as if somebody had taken a pair of scissors to it and cut pieces out, leaving a mass of jagged holes. Phoebe stared at the black shapes. As the old, cruel pain pincered her neck, she let out a sigh. A strange sensation crept over her; a sharp, unidentifiable longing.

She shifted her focus from the gaping blacks to the sheer expanse of gold. As it shone and shone, she gazed and gazed until at last she felt she'd absorbed something of its brightness.

At least she was getting out these days, far more than she would have believed possible. She had Coco to thank for that. And her father, and Christina. And her own will-power. She had been fighting her silent war against pain for so, so long . . . but she'd fought hard, and the pain hadn't won every battle.

It wasn't impossible, was it, that she might be cured one day? It would take a miracle, but miracles did occasionally happen. There might be a time, perhaps years and years in the future, when she could function like a normal human being. One day, she might even be well enough for a relationship. And if that ever happened, she would not hold back. She would throw herself headlong into an irrepressible torrent of love. She would give everything she had.

In the meantime, she would have to content herself with smaller passions, such as detective dramas and otters.

24

Button, Candlestick, Pickles and Poison

JULES AND JACK had gone. Phoebe was spending a good deal of time in bed, recovering. Al tiptoed around the house, understanding how badly she needed rest. He also realized that something was on her mind but didn't press her about it.

She was finding it hard to concentrate on anything, even her Sherlock Holmes audiobooks. She couldn't shake off this vague feeling she should be working something out, but her brain wouldn't function. Hopefully, if she unplugged it and plugged it in again later, it might begin to work again.

She had unwillingly left the care of Coco and Paddy to Carol for a week. Now she was itching to get back to them. So when Christina rang to suggest another late-afternoon otter-drawing session, Phoebe accepted, even though she feared she would be playing gooseberry. She was missing all the otters and wanted to get beyond just drawing the lines of their backs. It would be a fine thing to get on to ears, eyes and noses. There was good news, too. Apparently, the protesters had not been seen for the last few days and it didn't look as if they were coming back. This might have had something to do with Jules's video, Phoebe reflected. She was beginning to feel charitable towards her sister again.

Al dropped her at the sanctuary and took himself off to the village shop to stock up.

The first thing Phoebe did was to check out Coco and Paddy on the video screen.

'Aha.'

The voice seemed to come out of nowhere. He had come in so quietly she hadn't noticed him at all. But there he was, standing beside her. She had no idea how long he'd been there.

'Hello, Dan!' she said.

'Hello, Phoebe-the-Wild-Cub-Carer.'

He handed her a long package, perfectly wrapped in brown paper. 'Here it is. I hope you like it, and I hope Christina likes it. I asked Ellie about it, and Ellie definitely likes it. So that's a good sign.'

Phoebe undid the string and pulled out the candlestick. It was fashioned out of dark oak with clear graining, and curled around the body of the stick was an exact likeness of Miaow. Her posture was perfectly catlike. Her little paws were dainty and her eyes had a lovely, affectionate expression as if she were purring. There were fine cuts in the wood to give a suggestion of fur, and even her whiskers were full of character.

'Wow. It's amazing. You're a genius!'

Dan shrugged his shoulders.

'I can't do a lot of things that other people do very well, such as skiing or making jam or saying the right things at the right times. But the thing I *can* do is carve wood.'

'You certainly can!'

As she was admiring his handiwork, Carol stepped in.

'Look, Carol. Look what Dan has made for me, as a present for Christina. She's going to adore it, isn't she?'

Carol rubbed her hands on her jeans before taking the candlestick to examine it. 'It really is very special, Dan. The life in that cat . . . it's incredible. I wonder . . . The oak leaves do very well, but we could charge a lot of money for this sort of thing. Do you think you might be able to make some similar ones, but with otters, for us to sell in the shop?'

'Oh, you definitely should!' declared Phoebe.

'I really otter,' said Dan, and gave an abrupt puff of laughter as if he'd surprised himself. They both laughed too. 'I'll give it a go,' he said. 'And I'll bring in a prototype next week.'

Phoebe hadn't quite forgiven Christina for going out with Rupert, so she decided to defer giving her the Miaow candlestick for now. She put it in her bag, with profuse thanks to Dan.

Desperate to see the cubs now, she hurried outside and crashed into Rupert, who was brandishing a broom and dustpan.

'Hullo, Phoebe!'

It wasn't surprising he was looking extra smiley and sprightly. Love (or sex or romance or whatever it was) had that effect on people, Phoebe had observed.

'Beautiful afternoon, isn't it?'

Was it? She hadn't noticed. She glanced up at the sky, which was the colour of mould.

'I'm just off to sweep the area by the young otters' enclosure,' Rupert told her. 'It's getting rather filthy. I think it's best to keep things clean, bearing in mind we never know when those blasted health-and-safety inspectors will take it upon themselves to come round.'

'Good point,' said Phoebe. 'I'll do it if you like. I'm going down there anyway.'

'That's very sweet of you, Phoebe. Thank you. I'll get back to the accounts, then.'

She accepted the broom and dustpan from him, suspecting he knew Christina was on her way.

Coco and Paddy were both fast asleep in their hutch when she arrived at their pen. Disappointed, she started sweeping around the front area. It wasn't too bad: there were a few twigs and a bit of dried mud, and a small black button. She wondered how it had got there, since this area was out of bounds to the public. She slipped it into her pocket. She would analyse it sometime later, when she had more energy. She had forgotten how an action like sweeping aggravated her shoulders. Why had she been so stupid as to offer? It only took five minutes to finish the area, but she was beset with twanging pain by the time she was done.

The otters were still asleep. Never mind. She'd call on them again later, after the drawing session.

Returning to the public area, she found Christina in conversation with Quercus and Rowan, her easel already set up by their enclosure. Christina threw her arms around her. She had an orange felt flower in her hair and a sunny grin on her face; again, the effects of new-found love, Phoebe presumed. Not that she wanted to think about it. She set up quickly, selected a pencil and focused on the otters.

As always, she was transfixed by the antics of her models. Quercus and Rowan scooted through the pond together then shot out again, their fur sticking up in damp spikes. They rolled over on their backs and, side by side, gave themselves a thorough rub, using the dry grass as a towel. Their limbs were in constant movement. Phoebe's pencil couldn't keep up with them at all.

Christina kept making excuses to leave her easel and disappear inside. Carol had gone home to take a rare evening off, she said, so Rupert had to shut up shop by himself.

Poor, lonely Rupert, Phoebe muttered under her breath in her most sarcastic voice.

'What took you so long?' she asked Christina pointedly after her third long absence.

'Oh, I just got chatting with Rupert.'

'Chatting?' And the rest, no doubt.

Christina prodded the flower in her hair. 'Yes, just gossip, really. I'd mentioned to him the stuff you told me about Spike Dobson and George Bovis and their mutual hatred. And Rupert said he coincided with them both at the village shop yesterday and they were looking daggers at each other. It's so funny!'

227

'Hmmm.' In Phoebe's opinion, it was rather tragic, especially bearing in mind what their wives had to put up with.

'And Rupert was telling Spike about our otter cubs who will be released next spring and then George Bovis was looking daggers at *him*, too.'

'Worried about his fishpond, I suppose.'

'I expect so. He's always *carping* on about it.'

'Haha,' said Phoebe, mentally promoting George Bovis to number-one suspect status.

It wasn't long before Christina disappeared yet again.

Quercus and Rowan were still defying any artist to capture them on paper, and Phoebe was getting nowhere with her drawing. She decided to leave her easel for a while and go to see Coco and Paddy again.

When she reached the enclosure, she was pleased to see that Coco was up and snuffling about. She watched as the young otter yawned, stretched and bent her head back to scratch an ear with her hind foot, balanced brilliantly and showing off her whiskers. Scratching finished, she trotted to the side of the pond. She dipped herself down to the water, sucking and gurgling as she drank. When she'd had her fill, she lifted her head up again and blew a fine spray of water through her teeth and into the air, just for fun. There seemed to be no purpose to this apart from fun.

Coco had not yet learned to swim. 'They'll enter the water in their own sweet time,' Carol had said. 'They'll suddenly realize how buoyant they are and work out a swimming technique for themselves.'

Now Paddy's face appeared at the entrance of the

hutch. He came out, crawling on his front in an odd, sluggish way. His eyeballs were rolling. Phoebe gasped. She'd never seen him like this before. As she watched, his legs gave way and he toppled to one side.

Phoebe felt a swift, fierce arrow, plunging deep into the back of her neck. Alarm had triggered it; she knew that. This was an emergency, though. She mustn't let pain make her useless, as it had done when Seth's dog had invaded the sanctuary. She bit her lip hard, opened the gate and crept in towards Paddy, as quietly as she could so as not to scare him. Coco skipped away as soon as she approached, but Paddy just wobbled on the spot, ignoring her. She bent down and picked him up. Maybe it was wrong to touch him, but what else could she do? He was in need of medical help, and quickly.

'Be careful!' she whispered to herself, worried for her fingers. Paddy thrashed about in her arms. She grasped him by the scruff of the neck and held him tight to her ribcage. With an agonizing twist, she managed to pull off her jacket and wrap it around him.

'Calm down, my darling, calm down. We'll fix you. Everything's going to be okay.'

Her words seemed to soothe him, and he was exhausting himself anyway. His eyes were half closed and his legs gradually stopped kicking. He lay flaccid in her arms now.

She was about to carry him out when she noticed that Coco was crouched in the corner, looking unsteady on her legs too. She looked up at Phoebe, her eyes unfocused. Then she collapsed.

'Oh no. Oh God, oh God. Not you as well, Coco. What the hell is wrong with you two?'

She swooped down and gathered Coco up in her other arm, her heart clunking wildly in her chest. She had been longing to hold these sweet little otters, but now their warm bodies felt horribly limp and helpless. Cradling them both, she dashed down the path.

Christina and Rupert were intertwined in a passionate kiss, which broke apart as soon as they saw her charging at them. Her voice came out squeaky and shrill.

'Christina, Rupert, help! There's something wrong with these two!'

'What? What are you talking about?' cried Rupert, riled by this rude interruption. 'You're not supposed to pick them up.'

'I think they're dying,' Phoebe gasped. Hot tears sprang from her eyes and splashed down on to the heads of the cubs.

Christina came close and put her hand on Coco's side. 'She's right, Rupert. They're not well at all.'

He looked at her, then at the otters, his face aghast.

'I'll call the vet,' he cried, sprinting towards the phone. 'Do anything you can,' he called back to them.

Christina threw a *my hero* look after him.

'We need to put them somewhere warm.' She started rifling around, clumsy in her panic.

'There are some boxes in the storeroom.'

'I'll find one.'

Phoebe stood, waiting, gazing down at the otters in her arms. Their tiny, soft faces were so dear to her it was almost unbearable. Pain flowed and ebbed around the channels of her body, but it was nothing compared to the agony of her emotions. Her blood drummed in her ears.

She wondered if this was what it was like to be a parent, seeing your child suffer. Was this how Al felt about *her*?

Moments flashed by, cramming themselves in frantically one after the other but seeming to add up to an eternity. At last, Christina reappeared with a cardboard box lined with fresh, sweet-smelling hay.

Reluctant to let go of them, Phoebe made herself lay the otters inside.

Rupert was back. He told them he had rung both the vet and Carol, both of whom should be arriving soon.

Christina seized his hand. 'Thank you, thank you, Rupert!' She turned to Phoebe. 'My God, Phoebe, you're white as a sheet. I don't want to leave Coco and Paddy, otherwise I'd take you home, but I'll ring Al, if I may. He can come and fetch you.'

Phoebe was about to protest because no way was she going to leave the otters, but then it struck her how good it would be to have her father's calming presence here too. It might be a long night. And it wouldn't be much fun sitting here stressing, with Christina and Rupert mooning over each other. So the phone call was made, then all they could do was wait.

It was only five minutes before Carol arrived. She took a look at the otters, tutted and went at once to fetch a bowl of water for them. Why hadn't Phoebe thought of that? As soon as they were aware of the water, both cubs put out weak tongues and lapped. Paddy was promptly sick twice, his lithe body coiling and jolting as a jet of brown, pulpy liquid spewed out.

He seemed to rally a little and blinked blearily but showed no signs of getting up.

Mr Pickles, a middle-aged man with thick glasses and vigorous hair, arrived to examine the otters within the next fifteen minutes. Al arrived at the same time. He went over at once to his daughter.

'Are you all right?' he whispered in her ear.

'Rather contrapuntal, if truth be told,' she whispered back. 'You?'

'Reasonably archaic, thank you.'

It was reassuring to engage in the familiar, illogical interchange.

Mr Pickles pulled on plastic gloves and took a blood sample. He pushed his glasses up his nose and told them the problem was probably due to something the otters had eaten, bearing in mind the sickness. Which Phoebe had already worked out for herself.

'Have they been fed on anything different recently?' Mr Pickles asked.

Carol assured him that Coco and Paddy had only eaten the standard fishy mix and day-old chicks that they were fed every day.

Mr Pickles advised them to keep the otters hydrated and warm. There was little else he could do, so he left soon after. Carol, Christina, Rupert, Al and Phoebe were left drinking cups of tea and speculating. The otters lay still and quiet.

'We're so grateful, Phoebe,' Carol said. She turned to Al. 'She acted incredibly quickly to save these two. Otherwise, they might already be dead.'

Al leaned over and whispered in Phoebe's ear again. 'Your mum would've been proud of you.'

It was something he only said very occasionally. It meant a lot.

Desperate as she was to stay, pain was sinking its teeth into Phoebe's spine, and before long she had to ask her father to take her home after all.

25

Something in the Water?

'Try not to worry,' Al told his daughter. He hated seeing her so agitated. She had an odd quiff of hair on one side where she'd been tugging at it and her eyes were wide and wild.

'Is it too early to ring, do you think?'

Dull, blueish light seeped through the curtains. He pulled them back and consulted his watch. It was seven in the morning, a time of day Phoebe would never normally be awake, let alone fully dressed and pacing around the kitchen. Every so often she sank into a chair, only to get up and start pacing again a few minutes later.

'I'm sure Carol won't mind, considering the situation. Shows you care,' he said. He cared about those otter cubs as well; far, far more than he was prepared to let on. Especially Coco.

At once Phoebe aimed her steps towards the phone. He

listened in, heard her apologies and the tightness in her voice. He felt the tension drop from his own shoulders when she said: 'Oh phew!' and then, 'Thank you so much, Carol. Thank God.'

'Are they all right, then?' he asked the minute she'd finished the call.

'They're both still with us, both holding on. Coco has picked up a bit, apparently. But Paddy still seems pretty ill. Can we go there as soon as you're back from work? I need to see them.'

'Of course.'

She headed back upstairs. He hoped she'd be able to relax, maybe even sleep until the time came.

Light rain was falling when Al went out to the car. The hills were absorbed in a silvery mist. The river hissed violently, as if angered. The trees creaked in the wind.

Al felt fuzzy and distracted as he drove to the car park where he was to collect the day's deliveries. Phoebe had told him about her suspicions that somebody was trying to get the sanctuary shut down. He had put that down to her bored, under-used brain needing some spice. It was true, though, that everything had been going very awry there recently. All the mishaps must surely just be a string of coincidences . . . yet now he was beginning to wonder if her theory might be correct. But what kind of human being would deliberately poison otters? No, no, it was impossible.

He loaded the car as quickly as he could, trying to shield the packages from the damp. The process of calculating his route was much faster these days. The morning rounds dragged on, though. He had to reverse several times to let cars pass on the narrow lanes and he was late for a big delivery of animal feed at one of the farms. He was waylaid further at Jeremy Crocker's house due to an unavoidable doorstep conversation about coddled eggs and the history of Darleycombe church's spire. Once Mr Crocker got started, it was hard to stop him.

Finally, the morning's work was done and Al sped back towards Higher Mead Cottage. Phoebe stood waiting in the porch. She dashed out through the drizzle and leaped into the passenger seat beside him. She had even made him a sandwich.

'I'll feed you this on the way. We need to get to the otters asap.'

'No rest for the wicked, then,' he said, not really minding.

Phoebe posted the sandwich into his mouth as he drove. Cheddar and chutney, the cheese in thick slabs, the chutney in spadefuls. She knew exactly what he liked.

'Have *you* eaten?' he asked, as he gulped it down.

She shook her head. 'Couldn't.'

'What, nothing at all?'

'Just two painkillers.'

He sighed. He had tried every tactic in the past, but perhaps it was time to make use of those otters. 'You'll be no good to Coco or Paddy if you're too weak to function.'

She took a token bite out of his sandwich then fed him the rest. Her eyes were fixed ahead. He noticed the bags under them, and the puffy grey circles of skin. She had been crying. Pain? Or worry? Probably both.

'Dad?' she said, struggling to get something out of her jeans pocket.

'Yes, Phoebes?'

'Do you recognize this?' Lying in her palm was a small black button that looked as if it had come off a shirt.

'Nope,' he said. 'Not mine.'

She frowned, put it back in her pocket and stared out of the window at the rolling clouds.

There were very few cars in the sanctuary car park, and the wet grey tarmac reflected the grey sky. Al had seldom seen Phoebe move as fast as she did when she propelled herself from the car and towards the entrance. He strode after her. The front gate was open, but nobody was at reception. A bell was at the desk, with a sign that read: *Please ring for attention*.

Phoebe ignored it and knocked on the door of the office. No answer. She pushed it open. The box of hay was still there, sitting on the table, with some chicken wire stretched over it. They rushed in to look. Inside the box lay a single small otter, motionless, curved like a comma. Its nostrils were flared. Its tiny paws curled and uncurled very slightly as it slept.

Phoebe bent over to examine it. 'It's Paddy.'

She looked around desperately. 'What does this mean? Where's Coco?'

'Yes, it was poison. Mr Pickles has confirmed it. We need to work out where on earth it could've come from.'

Carol's voice was low and steady, almost monotone. Her grey bunches of hair lay slackly on her shoulders.

Her face displayed no emotion at all. Anyone who didn't know her would think she wasn't bothered. But Phoebe knew she was.

She had found them walking back up the path from the pen, deep in discussion.

'Could it be that something has got into the water?' asked Rupert. He stretched his neck to one side then the other. 'The Darle is normally so pure, but some idiot might have put something into the river upstream. Harmful chemicals, perhaps?'

'I certainly hope not,' said Carol. 'Otherwise we've got huge problems on our hands. I really think it can't be that, though. We use the river water to clean out the otters' pens and they all drink and swim in it every day . . . but it's just those two that were affected.'

Rupert nodded. 'You're right,' he said, perplexed. 'Christina and I were discussing what might have happened last night, and that was just one possibility. We wondered about poisonous plants, too, and spent ages looking them up. We've checked every spot of vegetation in the enclosures with a fine-toothed comb but there's nothing that could have harmed them.'

Phoebe cringed slightly at the 'Christina and I', but at least they had been doing something useful. Christina, she had learned, was working in her jewellery shop in Porlock this morning. Phoebe had her own theories but wasn't ready to share them yet. She silently resolved to check out the recent footage of Coco and Paddy's enclosure on the video camera.

Carol took her aside. Her eyebrows were drawn together and her lips looked pale and bloodless.

'Phoebe, I have to tell you. Mr Pickles asked if we wanted to put Paddy down, to end his suffering.'

'No!' cried Phoebe, anguished. 'I mean, we don't want him to suffer any more, of course we don't. But we need to give him longer. He's going to get better, I'm sure of it. He's going to have a good life, a long life. And a happy one.'

'We can't know that, Phoebe.'

We can't know that about me either, she thought, *but nobody talks about putting me down.*

'*Please.*' Her voice was almost a squeal. 'Please,' she repeated, aiming for a rational, less neurotic tone.

Carol crossed her arms.

'All right. We'll give him a little longer. He's going to need a lot of extra care and attention for at least a week. He is scarcely able to lift his head, so he'll have to be fed by syringe. And the chances are that, even if he survives, he will never be free now. He'll become too dependent to be released.'

'Even so, a life in captivity – so long as you are loved and cared for – is worthwhile, isn't it?'

'I believe so,' said Carol, nodding slowly. 'I wouldn't be running the sanctuary if I didn't. Well, *que sera sera*. We can only do our best.'

'I'll help all I can.'

Carol looked at her; a sad, slow gaze. Phoebe had done her utmost to hide all her pain, but Carol had seen quite a lot of her and might have guessed that something wasn't right.

Al had been hanging about awkwardly during the whole conversation, hands stuck in pockets, his attention divided between what they were saying and heightened concern for Phoebe. They went back to the office together.

Paddy was awake now, his mouth slightly open, his pink tongue resting delicately against his teeth. His eyes were closed.

Following Carol's instructions, Phoebe made up a solution with water, liquidized fish and the electrolytes prescribed by the vet. She gently lifted his head up to squirt the mixture into his mouth and stroked his throat to help it down. He opened his eyes, moved feebly and gulped. His head sank back on to the hay. Phoebe spoke to him softly, caressing the fur on his face and his neck and all the way down to his tail, willing him to be well. A tear fell on to his fur. 'I'm not going to let them end your life. Fate has been cruel to you, but you're a fighter, and a survivor, like me, aren't you, Paddy?'

He snuffled into her hand, and she took that to be a yes.

Phoebe and Al sat with him for a while, but there was little else they could do.

They walked back one more time to the wild otters' pen. Coco, who had been returned there earlier in the morning, was pottering about in circles. Her behaviour seemed stress-related rather than playful. She was physically much better than the last time they'd seen her but lacked her usual verve and interest in everything. She already seemed to be missing her companion.

Al pulled out his handkerchief and blew his nose loudly, then said, 'Ooops, sorry,' when Coco turned her head to look. She fixed her eyes on him, and Phoebe wondered what was going on in her little furry head. She wished she could still talk to the otter. If only Coco could tell them what had happened, who had been here.

'She's going to be fine,' Al whispered. 'And Paddy will slowly pick up too, I'm sure he will. Come on. It's time we went back home.'

Phoebe agreed. She had thinking to do. As they crossed the reception area, a group of tourists in macs came in, a family with clamorous children who were completely unaware of the dramas that had been going on behind the scenes. Al made Carol promise to ring him if Paddy showed any signs of getting worse or if Coco relapsed.

The rain had eased off, but the air was still chilly and dank. In the car park, Dan Hollis was climbing out of a battered old Land Rover with a carrier bag.

'Hey, Dan!' called Phoebe.

'Hello, Phoebe-Featherstone-the-Wild-Cub-Carer,' he said as they approached. 'Hello, Phoebe's-father-Al-Featherstone.'

'Is that the new candlestick you've got there?' she asked.

'Yes,' he said. 'The otter-stick prototype. Just finished it.'

'Can I look?'

He pulled an irregular shape from one of the bags and unwrapped the paper around it. The candlestick was every bit as beautiful as the cat one. The otter seemed to be romping around the glossy wood; its nose seemed to twitch, its tail seemed to flick.

'I might try and carve one with two otters as well,' he said. 'This was just an experiment.'

'That is a complete and utter masterpiece!' declared Al. 'You are wasted on harps, young Hollis.'

He was speaking in his jovial-maths-teacher tone of voice, which Phoebe thought was not appropriate at this time. Also, Dan Hollis hardly classified as young. Also, it was extremely annoying that her father knew something about him that she didn't.

She looked at her father then at Dan, whose expression was slightly indignant.

'You really do make harps, then, Dan?' she asked. 'Actual harps? As in musical instruments? Not just decorations?'

'I already told you, I am the Harp-Maker of Exmoor. And I do not believe I am wasted on harps. Not at all.'

'Dad was only joking,' she explained. 'He has a very poor sense of humour.'

'Ah,' said Dan. 'That explains it.' The cloud passed from his face and he beamed at Al.

'Anyone who can make actual harps must be pretty amazing,' Phoebe added, impressed at this new revelation.

'Agreed,' said Al. 'I only meant that the candlestick is superbly crafted and, well, breathtakingly brilliant.'

'Do you recognize the otter?' asked Dan.

Phoebe hazarded a guess. 'It's not Coco, is it?'

'It is.'

Dan had only ever seen Coco on video yet had expressed something of her individual personality. Phoebe felt her eyes prickling.

'Have you heard about the two cubs falling ill?' she asked.

'Yes,' he replied dolefully. 'Christina rang Ellie last

242

night and told her all about it, and Ellie told me all about it, and then I felt sad. Very. Are they any better today?'

'Coco has recovered enough to be returned to the pen, but Paddy is still in danger.'

Dan's hands started twitching in agitation.

Phoebe put her own hand in her pocket and took out the button. 'I wonder if you could tell me, Dan, whose this is? Do you recognize it?'

'Yes,' he said at once, pleased to be consulted on the matter. 'He had one missing. He only had eleven of them, not twelve. At the barbecue. Seth Hardwick.'

'Thank you. I thought as much.'

'What was that all about?' Al asked as they got into the car.

'Dad, can you lend me your phone, please?'

He handed it over. She scrolled through his photos. He watched her face curiously. She looked utterly wiped out but it was clear she was not going to let go of her train of thought, no matter how much effort it cost her. She chewed her lip as she viewed all the packages and their settings, scanning for details. She enlarged several.

'I see Felicity Dobson has ordered a lot of books. That might account for her unwavering serenity.'

'I suppose.'

She tutted under her breath, unable to find what she was looking for.

'Can you find me the photos of all the parcels you've delivered to Seth?' she asked, handing the phone back.

He flicked through the numerous photos and book-marked them for her. Whatever made her happy. Not that she was looking happy at all.

'Make of it what you will,' he said, tossing the phone into her lap before starting up the engine.

Seth hadn't ordered much in the last month apart from something from a hardware shop that looked like a drill, some weedkiller and a packet of biros. Then there was that one time he had ordered cat food.

Phoebe's eyes had opened even wider. 'You couldn't do me a favour and take some photos of his garden next time you're there, could you?'

'No, Phoebe! I draw the line there. I have to take photos of the deliveries, but I'm not going to snoop any further. That would be dishonourable and not on at all.'

'Oh, you're such a goody-two-shoes,' she replied crossly. 'Well, can you at least describe Seth's garden to me?'

Al screwed up his eyes and tried to picture it. It was a while since he'd been there. He recalled that there wasn't much of it, just a small patch of lawn with a limp, uninspired flowerbed and a raised concrete area to one side with a few plant pots. Phoebe was fascinated by the fact that nothing was growing in the pots except tufts of grass and bindweed.

'Have you ever actually seen Seth gardening?'

Al shook his head.

She raised her eyebrows as if she was waiting for him to react in some dramatic way, but he couldn't see why on earth it was so important.

26

Means, Motive and Opportunity

Phoebe's List of Suspects

Phoebe Featherstone – Unless I was operating in my sleep, highly unlikely.

Al Featherstone – I think I know him well enough to rule this out.

Christina Penrose, Carol Blake, Rupert Venn, Dan Hollis (harp-maker) – Invested in the sanctuary and fond of otters, so very unlikely too.

Rev Lucy – Revenge for injury to her son? Is she embittered and vindictive underneath that niceness? (NB DO NOT let Dad get fond of her.)

George Bovis – Revenge for koi carp massacre. Holds grudges and hates otters.

Seth Hardwick – Big motive of revenge and recent reminder of it.

Animal rights activists – Upside-down & misplace morality.

Person X – Somebody I haven't thought of yet.

Phoebe sucked in her breath as her muscles protested at the act of writing, even though she'd tried to do it quickly and lightly, before the pain overwhelmed her. Writing did help concentrate her thoughts, which had a habit of tying themselves in terrible knots. She read the list back to herself, picked up the pencil again and ringed the name 'Seth Hardwick' several times.

What an odd, quiet guy that Seth was. Phoebe's impression of him, both at the sanctuary and at the barbecue, had been largely negative. She wondered if he was always that grumpy. Or maybe grumpy wasn't really how he was. Maybe it was just the way his face settled, his default expression, like it was with Carol. The adage about books and covers came to mind, and Phoebe warned herself not to judge. She must look at the facts, only the facts.

She knew that Sherlock and most other detectives worked things out using three criteria: means, motive and opportunity.

She scribbled these down as headings. Under *Means*, she wrote:

Weedkiller. Most likely added to cat food and placed in otter enclosure after dark.

Under *Motive*, she wrote:

Grudge against otters because former dog (spaniel) died from otter bite.

Worried current dog (Alsatian) will also be injured?

Under *Opportunity*, she wrote:

Lives next to sanctuary, knows back path and could access via back gate.

Crime might have been committed any time during closing hours.

She sucked the end of her pen. Then wrote:

Evidence: One black button, belonging to his shirt, found outside Coco and Paddy's enclosure.
Question: Would otters eat cat food?
Thought: Black shirt buttons are not uncommon.

It would be good to have further evidence to back up her theory. She had already checked the videos and found nothing unusual. That did not mean to say there hadn't been an intruder, though. A section of the enclosure, including the back gate, was not covered by the camera. She had mooted with Carol and Rupert the possibility of getting a second camera set up, but neither of them had thought it was worth the expense. Of course, they neither knew about the button nor shared her suspicions. She didn't want to throw accusations around. But where should she go from here?

Al took Phoebe to the sanctuary every day to help care for Coco and the sickly Paddy. Coco was still grieving for her friend's company. Although she entertained herself with sticks, stones, her old teddy bear and anything else she could find, she often seemed to be searching for him. Perhaps as a distraction, she had now ventured into the pool on her own and started to swim. She didn't yet move in the water with the grace and ease of the adult otters. Instead, she bobbed up and down, kicking her back legs to stay afloat. But it was a start.

Paddy was slowly gaining strength. Phoebe was glad to be doing something to help, even if she wasn't well enough to stay for long. Al, Carol, Rupert and Christina also partook in the feeding and cleaning duties. Paddy was inevitably getting too fond of the humans, just as they were of him.

Christina and Phoebe had both taken advantage of being able to sketch him at close quarters. It was so much easier with an otter who wasn't constantly partying. Even though Phoebe still struggled with drawing, she knew she was improving. She enjoyed it, too. A drawing was an achievement once it was done, something you could keep; unlike, say, tidying your bedroom or washing your hair, which reverted almost immediately back to the same old mess and shouted at you to do it again. Phoebe quite liked her most recent study of Paddy. She might gift it to Al.

If only it didn't hurt so much to hold the pencil, to look down at Paddy, to look up at the paper.

She winced as she laid down her pencil. She didn't think it was that obvious, but Christina noticed.

'I know you don't like talking about it, but are you hurting a lot, Phoebe?'

Phoebe had trained herself so well that her first impulse was to deny it, even though barbs of pain were spiking into her vertebrae and a thousand wasps were stinging the tender tissues of her brain. But the compassion in Christina's voice disarmed her. Was it so very bad to accept a little sympathy from her friend? It wouldn't really be tantamount to defeat, would it? So long as she didn't make a habit of it.

Could she be honest without dissolving into tears, though?

As a compromise, she gave a minimalist nod (a whole-hearted nod would aggravate her neck too much). 'Your easel really helps, but yes. Drawing is uncomfortable.'

Christina put a hand on her arm.

'Come round to mine tomorrow afternoon,' she said. 'I may be able to help.'

Phoebe lay face down on a massage couch, looking through a padded hole at Christina's feet. Christina was in flip-flops. Her toenails were painted a rich, iridescent green.

'Try to breathe very deep and steady, from your abdomen,' she advised. 'It will slow the heart rate and boost your energy.'

Phoebe did as she was told, inhaling the scent of lavender oil. Christina's hands slid across her naked shoulders, kneaded her sore muscles. Her touch was assured, both strong and sensitive. It made Phoebe want to cry.

She kept breathing and closed her eyes to stem the tears. She didn't want any of them falling through the hole.

An inquisitive mew came from the direction of the chair. Miaow was evidently viewing proceedings.

'Your muscles are like concrete,' Christina said. 'You haven't been to a doctor at all about this?'

'So many times you wouldn't believe it,' replied Phoebe, her voice muffled.

'And no diagnosis.'

'None.'

Christina pushed gently into her shoulder blades. 'People do sometimes feel pain when there's no medically identifiable damage to trigger it.'

Oh God. Here we go. She thinks I'm making it all up.

Christina carried on. 'Your neural pathways can start interpreting all sorts of things as pain. Or exaggerating it. It's a funny old thing, is pain. The smallest paper cut can be agony, but soldiers losing limbs on a battlefield can feel nothing at all until much later.'

Phoebe gave another little grunt in reply.

Christina didn't get the hint. 'I do remember one time when I was a child, lacerating my leg on some barbed wire. The cut was really deep, but I didn't actually notice it for a good ten minutes. I didn't feel a thing until I actually saw it . . . *then* it hurt like hell.'

'Can we talk about something else, please?'

'Oh. Oh, yes, of course. What do you want to talk about? Otters? Are you still thinking somebody might have poisoned Paddy and Coco deliberately?'

'Yes.'

'I mentioned your suspicions to Rupert,' Christina said. 'He just laughed.'

Phoebe frowned into the hole. Christina meant well, but a lot of what Phoebe said now seemed to get passed on to Rupert. She would have to review Christina's role as confidante and watch her mouth from now on.

She still had doubts about Seth. Should she go and visit him herself? But how would it be possible to muster up the energy for such a thing? And what excuse did she have to knock on his door?

She wondered again if George Bovis was the guilty one. He was an intense, obsessive man, and the argument with Spike Dobson proved he was a vengeful type. But would he go so far as to poison an otter? Even if koi carp *were* astronomically expensive.

She was not going to let Rev Lucy off the hook either. In one of the detective dramas (she couldn't remember which), somebody had said that poison was the chosen weapon of women. And there were hundreds of stories that illustrated the violence of a mother whose child had been harmed.

Phoebe's thoughts were interrupted by a soft padding sound. A small, fluffy head pressed into her dangling fingers, as if to say, *Stroke me!* She stroked. The sound of purring filled the room.

'How much is that on your purrometer?' asked Christina.

'At least five hundred purrz.'

Phoebe remembered that she still hadn't given Christina the Miaow candlestick made by Dan Hollis. Another time.

'You'll do,' said Christina finally, giving her a soft slap on the back. 'I hope you're a bit more relaxed now.'

'Thank you. I am,' said Phoebe. She was certainly feeling floppy and uncoordinated. She unpeeled herself from the couch.

Christina crossed her arms. 'I get that life can be grim for you, Phoebe. I've been through grimness, too. Not physically, but oh so much self-loathing and desperation and darkness . . . Darkness multiplied by darkness, so thick that I thought some evil god had snuffed out the sun for ever . . .' She paused and gulped. 'And I've coped badly and let myself get swallowed up in misery. But there's one thing I've learned. There are days – many days – when all you can really do is to tread water. It's okay. Just keep treading that water. Because it's quite possible that one day, you'll learn to walk on it.'

Phoebe accepted the advice with silent scepticism. But she would remember it.

As she was pulling her shirt back on, she was startled by a knock at the front door. Christina scuttled off to open it.

Phoebe heard a shriek of delight, followed by Rupert's voice, saying, 'Hello, dear thing.'

They would be kissing now. Ugh.

She had to pass them to get to the door. Miaow requested another stroke, uttering her name several times in a voice so loud it couldn't be ignored. Phoebe obliged and then shuffled into the hall. Christina and Rupert were whispering together. 'Hello, Phoebe!' cried Rupert, who, if he was sorry to see her here, didn't show it. 'I gather you've been having a lovely massage?'

'Yes.'

'Jolly good.' He gave Christina an affectionate poke in the ribs. 'Is it my turn now, old bean?'

Since when had he been calling her that? Phoebe presumed he was taking the mickey out of his own poshness.

'Got to go,' she said. 'See you at the sanctuary sometime.'

Al was coming to fetch her, but she'd told him to pick her up at the village shop. She had read online about exercise being the best medicine so thought she'd better give her legs something to do.

She ambled alongside the river, her thoughts swirling like the currents. The village ducks were sailing along, following their beaks. Under the surface, their feet would be paddling like mad.

She paused on the bridge and looked over. The river seemed full of jewels. Ripples weaved and twisted and threw fluctuating patterns of light on to the underside of the arched brickwork. It was beautiful – she knew it was beautiful – but somehow she couldn't catch hold of the beauty or enjoy it in any way.

The water was deep here, and she couldn't see the bottom. A skein of speckled fish hung just under the surface. She waited for them to flick away, then picked up a stick from the bank. She threw it in and crossed over to see it float out the other side. It twisted slowly, angling itself different ways and then, caught in a sudden violent current, sped on downstream.

What should I do about my suspicions? she thought. *Should I do anything? Say anything?*

The river shouted a million different answers at her.

A distant buzz sounded from up the valley. It crescendoed into a roar and, taking her breath with it, a motorbike zoomed past her. It screeched to a halt just outside the shop. A figure in leathers got off and went in, unstrapping his helmet. The very person who had been plaguing her thoughts. Seth Hardwick.

Mesmerized, she followed. A bell rang as she pushed open the door. She needed to look into Seth's face, but at the moment she could only see his back. He was gathering items from the shelves and putting them into a basket: a pizza, a bottle of ginger beer, sliced bread, Cheddar cheese, two tins of Pedigree Chum. As he reached up to a high shelf he twisted and saw her.

'Hello,' he said, his thick eyebrows pulling together as he tried to place her.

'Hello.'

She wouldn't and couldn't smile. She scrutinized him. Was he looking shifty at all? Was he looking like an otter poisoner? What did an otter poisoner look like anyway? Even Google probably couldn't help with that one.

She pictured her beloved Coco and Paddy lying sick in her arms and a queasy kind of rage formed in the pit of her stomach. If only she'd had time to compose herself, to prepare, to arrange her words into some clever sentence (a reference to buttons, perhaps) that would make Seth confess. But the conversation went no further. Against her will, Phoebe's feet turned her round and walked her into the other aisle.

She put out a hand to steady herself and found she had grabbed a packet of Jaffa Cakes by mistake. She stared down at them with revulsion. How had she ever liked them?

As she replaced the packet on the shelf she became aware of another presence in the aisle. In front of her was an athletic-looking girl with strawberry-blonde hair and flashy jewellery who stood surveying the meatballs. *That'll be Kandisha, Rev Lucy's babysitter*, Phoebe said to herself. *And if I'm not mistaken, those are Smelders earrings she's wearing.*

27

Cake and Confidences

THINKING WAS SO hard. Even when painkillered and caffeinated, her brain just kept drifting off on its own course instead of sticking to the path Phoebe so badly wanted it to pursue. Sherlock Holmes never had this problem, did he? But then Sherlock had cannabis. And his violin.

She decided to try yoga again. It just might soothe things, get her energy (or 'chi', as Christina called it) flowing in the right direction. It would be stimulating to see the other yoga students again, too. There might be more news of the Bovis–Dobson feud, or hints about what was going on with Rev Lucy.

Al dropped her off early. She was about to step into the village hall when she spotted Christina approaching along the road, so she waited by the door. Even from a distance, it was clear that something was wrong. Christina normally walked briskly with her head held high.

Now her posture drooped and her feet dragged along the road.

When she caught sight of Phoebe she waved and called out, 'Hello, stranger!' but her smile was fake. Phoebe knew all about fake smiles, being such an expert at them herself.

'What's up?' she asked.

'What makes you think something's up?'

'You look . . . you just haven't got your normal Christina spark.'

The smile dropped. She didn't answer, just shrugged and went on in. Phoebe had a very specific question to ask, but it didn't seem to be the right time. Inside, Christina spent ages fumbling with her shoes to take them off. Her face was hidden by her hair, but Phoebe suspected there were tears coursing down it. Much as she wanted to put her arms around her and comfort her, she didn't feel she could until Christina acknowledged her upset. If she was patient, the information would manifest itself before long. Yoga had a way of loosening muscles, and the tongue was made of muscle, wasn't it?

They worked through the series of stretches. After the plank and the bridge and the cobra poses (all of which hurt), Christina suggested they should have a break and lie in complete silence. Quietness descended like a soft blanket, wrapping itself around the other sounds: a bird tweeting outside, a gurgle in the plumbing, the bleat of a distant sheep. Marge Bovis's laboured breath hissed in and out and at one point turned into a gentle, rhythmic snore.

Phoebe tried to ignore it and instead tuned in to Christina's breathing. It became short and jerky for a while and then gradually elongated and smoothed out.

When the lesson finished, Phoebe's patience was rewarded. Christina leaned in towards her. 'I've split up with Rupert,' she said in a hoarse whisper.

'Oh no, have you? Why?'

'Silly argument.'

'I'm so sorry.' It had to be said, even if it wasn't strictly true.

Posh-but-nice Rupert was all very well, but now he was out of the picture other possibilities opened up again. Al could provide comfort, could be a shoulder to cry on, and that might, given time, lead to a more intimate relationship. He was good at being a shoulder.

'I won't be going to the sanctuary for a while,' Christina said.

'No, I can see why,' Phoebe answered.

After allowing Christina a little grieving space, she would send her father round with some more home-grown vegetables. The potatoes had gone down well, and the courgettes were still cropping prolifically. She'd never say it to Al's face, but she was getting tired of having runner beans with every meal, too.

Her father was waiting outside the hall. He said a stiff hello to Christina, evidently still remembering her tipsy behaviour at the barbecue. Maybe he also resented her relationship with Rupert, which he had no idea was now at an end. Phoebe wished he would muster up a more genial facial expression. He looked so much more handsome when he was being his usual kind self.

He seemed happy enough to see the vicar, though. He called her 'Lucy' and gave her a peck on the cheek and she awarded him one of her saccharine smiles. Her husband's infidelity was a proven fact in Phoebe's mind, but was she aware of it herself? If so, she seemed to be taking it incredibly well. Phoebe felt a prickle of concern. Al's shoulder must be used only to comfort Christina. It must not get hijacked by a needy Rev Lucy.

On impulse, Phoebe invited her friend round to Higher Mead Cottage for coffee the following afternoon.

'We have cake, don't we?' she added to Al with a *please say yes* look.

'Er, yes,' he said. He wasn't the world's best cake-maker, but she knew he'd gladly pop into the shop for some.

Christina hesitated. She glanced from Phoebe to Al and back again.

'Well, if there's cake . . .'

Al had decided to stay for the service after Sunday's bell-ringing. He had never done this before, and the other ringers didn't normally either, except for Rev Lucy. He guessed that Rupert Venn would be lunching with Christina, and Jeremy Crocker would likewise be spending time with his mysterious girlfriend, while Spike Dobson always had the excuse of needing to take his dog for a walk. Usually, Al rushed off as well, to look after Phoebe, but there really wasn't much he could do apart from provide her with company. By now she had her otters-sleep-painkillers schedule well sorted. And as for company, she had Christina coming round later anyway, which would be ample for one day.

Rev Lucy had seemed very tired and uncoordinated on the treble bell. At one point she had dragged it in a very skewed direction and then let go of it altogether, causing it to lash out frantically. She had apologized, but it was very unlike her. Al was concerned.

There were very few people in the congregation. Rev Lucy read out her words in a fast flurry, but with long pauses between each paragraph, as if trying to get her bearings. Her sermon was on the topic of forgiveness and quite thought-provoking, although she did repeat several times how extremely difficult it could be to forgive, especially when families or loved ones were involved. The hymns had too many verses, Al thought. He only knew one of them and it was pitched far too high for him to be able to join in.

As they filed out of the church, blinking in the bright light, Rev Lucy stood by the door to greet the parishioners and shake their hands. Al heard one of them asking her if she'd had a good birthday. Al hadn't realized it had been her birthday. He would have posted a card if he'd known.

'Did you get anything nice?' he asked when it was his turn for a handshake.

'Oh yes, my dear husband gave me a lovely book on Jerusalem. The photographs are fantastic!'

Al noticed that one of her hairclips was dislodged and flapping outwards instead of holding her hair in place as it should. He wondered if, when she arrived home, she'd look in the mirror and fret about how long it had been like that and feel annoyed that everyone had been too tactful to mention it.

On the way home, he bought a coffee-and-walnut cake from the shop. He wasn't sure whether coffee with coffee cake was overkill on the coffee front, but Phoebe had been vague about what flavour she wanted and had just said, 'Whatever you think Christina would like.' He had no idea what Christina would like, but Phoebe found caffeine helpful. And, he reminded himself, his main aim was to please Phoebe, not Christina.

Their guest arrived at three o'clock. Her hair was bundled untidily on top of her head and she wore a kind of brown wrap that was reminiscent of sackcloth and ashes. Al called Phoebe, who shouted back from her bedroom that she'd be with them in two ticks. She took an inordinately long time to get dressed and come downstairs, however. He managed to make small talk with Christina while putting two slices of cake on plates and pairing them with two mugs of freshly filtered coffee. He pushed a mug towards her. Her face looked a bit blotchy. She was very jolly, though, in a forced kind of way.

'Real coffee,' she raved, wafting the aroma towards her nose. 'Stupendous!'

'Yup. Bought it specially for you,' he said.

She took a sip. 'That's big of you, Al. Hey,' she added, 'we could call you Big Al!'

He frowned. 'Please don't.'

He stood up and moved towards the door as soon as Phoebe appeared.

'You're not joining us, then?' his daughter asked him.

He shook his head. 'I'll leave you two to chat. Strimming to do.' He disappeared outside quickly.

Phoebe took a bite out of her cake and sat down. She explained to Christina that Al worked so hard at his job and at being a caring dad that there was little time for him to squeeze in all the other demands of life. Christina nodded absently.

The moan of the strimmer started up outside. Phoebe put her slice of cake back on the plate. The question would not wait any longer. 'Christina, you once mentioned that Miaow was the only cat in the village. But that's not true, is it? Seth has a cat, doesn't he?'

'Not as far as I know,' she replied. 'No, I'm sure he doesn't. Just the Alsatian. Why?'

Phoebe explained her theory, itemizing the points on her fingers. Christina looked incredulous, then pensive.

'I don't know,' she said. 'No, I'm sure Seth couldn't . . . wouldn't do a thing like that. But it's odd about the button, and odd that he ordered cat food. And weedkiller. I see where you're coming from. I suppose . . . if he was feeling upset about the dog (and I'd understand that) and very, very bitter . . . no . . . yes . . . no . . . Well, at a stretch, it might just be possible.'

Phoebe, relieved to have a second opinion, decided not to press her any further. Not about that, anyway.

Now would be a good time to cheer Christina up by giving her the candlestick. She fetched it from the drawer and put it into her friend's hands. Christina, animated again at the prospect of a parcel to open, ripped off the paper and let out a crow of delight. She turned the candlestick over and over in her hands, marvelling at the fine carving, especially Miaow's likeness. Phoebe glowed, glad that something had turned out right.

'So how are Coco and Paddy?' Christina asked.

'They're both all right. Coco is swimming now. Paddy

is still weak but gaining weight again. They're missing each other, though.'

'I'm missing them too,' said Christina woefully.

Phoebe pressed her fingertip into a cake crumb on the plate, making it stick. She raised it to her lips and licked it off. 'What happened with Rupert?' she said, trying to sound nonchalant.

'All right. I know you're desperate to know, so I'll tell you. But can we go into your garden, please. It's so lovely out there.'

Phoebe agreed. But as soon as they were outside Christina wanted to walk down to the river, and as soon as they'd reached the riverbank she wanted to paddle. She took off her shoes and socks and rolled her trousers up to her knees and waded in.

'Careful,' said Phoebe. 'There may be sharks.'

'No sharks, I promise,' Christina chuckled, wobbling about. 'It's delicious. Come and join me.'

'No thanks.'

'Oh, come on, Phoebe. Live a little!'

Reluctantly, Phoebe shed her shoes and socks and dipped in a foot. The cool water licked her toes. She lowered herself on to a pad of grass, leaving her soles under the surface of the Darle.

Her patience wouldn't last out much longer. 'So . . . Rupert?'

Christina continued paddling among the trailing fronds as she related what had happened.

She had apparently been looking forward to a do at Rupert's house, a 'soirée', as he called it, a little get-together with some of his friends. She had assumed this might mean Carol, possibly even Phoebe, but it had turned out to be a group of people she had never met before. It was also the first time she'd been to his house, which was in a neighbouring village. The house was nice enough, spacious and neatly furnished, and Rupert had proudly shown the guests his collection of train sets that had taken up his whole garage for the last eight years. He also introduced her to his brother. The people had been pleasant, but she didn't feel she had a thing in common with anybody there.

'They were all hunting, shooting, fishing types, not veggie lefties like me,' she said, kicking at a dense mat of waterweed. 'To console myself, I ate a ton of canapés, assuming they were vegetarian, but then I suddenly realized they had fish pâté in them. Rupert's excuse was that his brother had done the catering, and he wasn't aware of what they were exactly. He did apologize, but not enough.'

She frowned, remembering. 'Then there was all this wine-tasting ponceyness going on,' she continued. 'I don't know my Premier Cru from my Irn-Bru and I'm sure I was being laughed at. Even Rupert's brother, who seemed quite nice at the beginning, was smirking. Rupert had invited me to stay over, and that's what I'd been intending to do, but at the end of the night I was hardly in the mood. The flaming row happened instead, and that was that. I dumped him.'

'At least it was you who did the dumping,' Phoebe said.

'That doesn't make it any better. Because now I just feel like an evil bitch for wounding him. As well as being miserable for myself. I miss him tons already. I'd really thought he was The One.'

Phoebe grimaced. 'Do people still believe that there is a "One" destined for them? A single one? Out of the whole human population? Isn't that rather naive?'

Christina stooped down and sent a splash of river water flying towards Phoebe. 'How can you be so young, Phoebe, and yet so blooming cynical and unromantic?'

Al had seldom felt so awkward. Mr Crocker had offered help and mentioned his police contacts many times now, but it was still going to be cringeworthy taking him up on his offer. Especially when the matter was so very unorthodox. He'd promised Phoebe, though, and he always kept his promises.

Fatherhood was a joy, but it was also a puzzle. And he was never quite convinced he possessed all the pieces, and the ones he did have he kept wedging into the wrong places or dropping on the floor. Did he pander too much to Phoebe's whims? Or did he cramp her style? He had no idea.

Either way, he had invited Mr Crocker for a drink at the Quarrymans Arms in the hope that beer would help the conversation flow. But Mr Crocker had uncharacteristically ordered only orange juice. Al bought himself a beer for Dutch courage.

He ushered Mr Crocker to a cosy corner by the fire, where they wouldn't be overheard. He took a gulp of beer and enquired politely after the chickens.

'The girls? Oh, they're well, thank you. Clucking loudly and laying beautifully.'

That was done. Now for the main aim of the conversation. Al took a deep breath. He must remember to use Mr Crocker's Christian name.

'Jeremy, I hope you don't mind if I'm straight with you. I'd like to run something by you. It's about my daughter, Phoebe. Well, not about her exactly. It's a suspicion she has about somebody in the village.'

He paused, hoping that Mr Crocker would give him some sign of encouragement, but none came. Mr Crocker seemed fascinated by the colour of his juice.

Al forged on. 'Phoebe has a . . . she is very . . . that is to say, she is quite astute . . . quite good at putting two and two together. I don't say this just as a besotted father, but as a matter of fact. She got it from her mother, not me.'

Mr Crocker rubbed his nose.

'She worked out that Christina's cat was in your hen-house back in June, through a clever process of elimination. And she's been doing some more amateur detective work.'

Al noticed that his companion's hand was shaking a little as he raised his glass to his lips. He wasn't sure if Mr Crocker was laughing at him. Or maybe he was worried that Phoebe had sniffed out who was his elusive girl-friend. Was it possible that Jeremy Crocker was carrying on with a married woman?

'It's a matter involving the otter sanctuary,' he said.

'Ah, the otter sanctuary!'

Was it Al's imagination, or was there a note of relief in the response? It was as if the frisson had burst like a bubble and evaporated from the atmosphere. Mr Crocker was finally looking at him, an expression of interest in his goggly eyes. It was a little like being scrutinized by a fish. Still, for whatever reason, Al now felt more relaxed and able to explain.

266

He related everything, as Phoebe had instructed: Seth's Alsatian attacking the otter. The loss of his last dog after a similar incident. The missing button that she had found at the sanctuary. The deliveries of cat food and weed-killer to Seth's house. He pointed out the strangeness of these deliveries, considering that Seth had no cat and did not appear to be remotely interested in the destruction of his plentiful weeds.

'I wouldn't have considered any of these things signifi-cant myself,' he continued, 'at least, not when you take them individually. Lots of people order weedkiller. Rev Lucy orders weedkiller too, but that doesn't mean she's an otter poisoner, does it?' He laughed nervously. 'But when you add them up, I wonder if my daughter might be on to something? She's convinced that Seth planted poi-soned cat food in the sanctuary. A malicious act that has caused damage to two otters. Do you think there's any possibility she might be right? And, if so, can anything be done about it?'

Mr Crocker blinked. 'Dogs aside, Seth has never been any trouble in this village. It seems far-fetched, I must say.'

It did. Al knew it did. He had no idea how Phoebe had made it sound so plausible. At least Mr Crocker wasn't treating him like a complete idiot.

'I'm sorry. My daughter is particularly attached to those otters, and concerned about them. And there seems no other possible explanation.'

'Seth is certainly not quite normal for the youth of today, living by himself like that with only his dog for company,' Jeremy Crocker went on, thinking aloud. 'If, as you say, he has good reason to despise the otter sanctuary, an act of revenge isn't wholly out of the question. If there's one thing I've learned in my years as a police officer, it is that once a person starts obsessing about something, they're capable of the most bizarre criminal acts.'

'Ah, indeed?' Al wondered whether to leave the subject there or to push it further. Mr Crocker swilled his juice around in the glass and ruminated a little longer. Then, to Al's astonishment, he promised that he would go round to Seth Hardwick's house and ask a few questions.

Phoebe would be pleased. She was terrified that another act of revenge might be attempted, one that would hurt Coco. And her concerns were contagious.

Both men were relieved to move the conversation on and to discuss Bob Minimus, another sequence in the complicated art of bell-ringing. Which, having been thoroughly explored, progressed to a homely chat about cricket.

On his way home, Al reflected that Mr Crocker could probably now classify as a friend. *Jeremy, I must think of him as Jeremy*, he told himself firmly. It was interesting that Jeremy had talked about his chickens and his bell-ringing with passion but had not yet mentioned his lady friend. Al had never seen the lady in question and wondered if she was living locally or if it was a long-distance relationship. Jeremy had certainly been lavishing her with plentiful gifts, judging by his deliveries.

28

Innocent Until Proven Guilty

THE BELL-RINGING SESSION had progressed well, but Al wanted to get back to Phoebe quickly. She had been looking even paler than usual, and he feared she was going through a particularly painful phase. So he excused himself from the drinks session. Thankfully, he had managed to catch Mr Crocker in the churchyard for five minutes while the others went on down to the pub.

Now he had to report back to his daughter.

All was quiet when he arrived back at Higher Mead Cottage, and he crept upstairs to see if Phoebe was awake. The curtains were drawn around her bed, but a quiet voice called, 'Dad?' Her hand pulled the curtains back and her face appeared between them. She was wearing a hot wheat pack around her shoulders.

'Phoebes, are you okay?'

'I'm mainly polyphonic, thank you,' she replied promptly. 'And you?'

'Oh, I'm pretty umbelliferous, thanks for asking.'

'Did you talk to Mr Crocker?'

'I did. He told me he's been over, as he promised, and asked Seth a few questions.'

'And?'

'I'm sorry, but he came to the conclusion your theory is wrong.'

Phoebe frowned. 'What? Why?'

' "Unsubstantiated evidence" were his exact words.'

'More details, please, Dad.'

'For starters, the cat food. Seth claimed that he'd read an article saying dogs like cat food . . . and cat food is cheaper than dog food, so he thought he'd give it a go. That's why he only ordered it once. Boz, the Alsatian, was not impressed.'

Phoebe groaned. 'I did wonder if something like that might have happened,' she muttered.

'Secondly, the weedkiller. Seth admitted he wasn't much bothered about getting rid of his weeds. He said he'd ordered it not for himself, but for his mother. Unlike him, she's a keen gardener. She normally buys her stuff at the local garden centre but nearly always bumps into her two friends there, both of whom are . . . like your Christina.'

'How do you mean, like *my* Christina?'

'You know – always wearing her hippie halo. Into all things eco and unable to accept that others might not be. Seth's mother, according to him, doesn't want her organic-obsessive friends to know that she's using potent poison on her tarmac.'

'How about his button, then?' Phoebe demanded. 'How did it get to be by Coco's enclosure, which isn't ever open to the public?'

Al shrugged his shoulders. 'It seems he was at a loss to explain that one. But Mr Crocker couldn't pursue it any further. Seth was pretty narked to be questioned, apparently. He'd produced plausible explanations for the cat food and the weedkiller, and Mr Crocker felt he wouldn't be justified in contacting his ex-colleagues in the police force on this matter.'

Phoebe wrinkled her nose. 'I still don't trust that Seth.'

Her voice sounded thin and strained. She shuddered and sank back on her pillows.

In a bid to cheer her up, Al resorted to gossip.

'I was thinking about Jeremy Crocker, actually. Wondering what his girlfriend is like.'

Phoebe was silent for a while. Then she said, slowly: 'He's ordered a lot of fine clothes, hasn't he? All sorts. Funny, isn't it? Men don't usually order fancy shoes for their girlfriends. Floaty scarves and jewellery and maybe dresses, but not shoes. And these shoes were in such a big box. Too big to be a normal size.'

Al knew she was getting at something. He folded his hands together, unfolded them again and cracked his knuckles.

Phoebe continued, in her swing now. 'Then there's the fact that you've never seen this woman, and he's never mentioned her. Do you know why, Dad? Because she doesn't exist.'

A pause.

'Why all the gifts, then?'

'They are not gifts for her. They are for himself.'

'You're not saying . . .'

'Yes. When Mr Crocker closes his curtains in the evenings he slips into silks and satins and high heels. He puts on glittering earrings and takes a handbag around the house with him.'

'Wow. Gosh . . . wow. Do you really think so? That had never occurred to me.'

'I've known for ages,' said Phoebe, not bothering with modesty. 'In one of the first photos of his hands receiving a parcel, I noticed he hadn't quite removed the last traces of pink nail varnish. He'd tried, though. He's very private about it, so please don't let on that you know.'

'I certainly won't,' said Al.

The chick's head hung down between her fingers. Its eyes and beak were closed, its feathers no more than flimsy yellow fibres. It would be a male, not usable for egg production or meat for humans, born in a local hatchery. What a very short life it had lived. Unlike Mr Crocker's birds, it would never have enjoyed any freedom, but Phoebe hoped that, within its single day of existence, it had felt sunshine and warmth and some kind of happiness in its tiny bones.

She wasn't allowed to talk to Coco any more, so she talked to the dead chick instead. 'You're going to give life to someone else now. Coco needs your protein and your vitamins and your roughage. Together with lots of trout, roach and oatmeal, you are going to be transformed into something better than the sum of its parts. You are going to be otter.'

She could see Coco now, weaving in and out of the sprouting plantains in her pen. It was a huge relief these days to find her still alive.

As well as the chick and some fresh hay, Phoebe had brought along a present for her: a bouncy ball. She had consulted with Carol, who had agreed, under the circumstances. She hoped the ball would help ease Coco's loneliness.

As she approached, Phoebe was filled with a sense of foreboding. 'I swear there are dodgy dealings going on here,' she whispered to the chick. 'Somebody is trying to stymie the whole operation, and no matter what Mr Crocker thinks, I'm dead certain that person is Seth Hardwick.'

She waited until Coco was at the far end of the pen and then quietly let herself in. She thrust the bundle of hay under a rock and looked about for a place to conceal the chick. It was important now that Coco learned how to find her own bedding and food.

Phoebe deposited the chick out of sight behind a squat clump of willow then floated the ball on to the water of the pond. It bobbed up and down enticingly and, by the time she'd retreated, Coco had already swum out to fetch it. Overjoyed with her new toy, she chased it round in circles, pushing it through the water with her nose and patting it with one front paw then the next.

How Phoebe longed to pick her up and wrap her arms around that soft, wet, fishy-smelling fur!

Instead, she could only watch from a distance as Coco played with the ball, manoeuvred it out of the water, caught a scent in the air and trotted around in search of her food. Her senses perfectly attuned, the little otter plunged towards the willow and, in moments, the chick was travelling down her gullet, already on its pathway of transformation.

Phoebe shivered. Summer was already growing old, and it wouldn't be many more months before Coco was due to be released back into the arms of the Darle. It was a spot of time in the future that reached back to disturb the present with a whole gamut of emotions. Dread was one, because the goodbye would be an ache that no painkiller could ever ease. But there was also a kick of thrill. Coco would be free to be her real self at last, to lead a true otter life . . .

Phoebe had once read an article that praised well-kept zoos and wildlife parks. It said these were like five-star hotels for animals. The animals, it claimed, were lucky to receive round-the-clock care, entertainment, a regular diet and medical help whenever they needed it, not to mention protection from predators. Most creatures – including otters – lived much longer in captivity than in the wild. The article writer argued that animals are every bit as lazy as people. Given the choice, they would certainly opt for this life rather than having to find food themselves – a job that was full-time, tough, tiring and dangerous in the extreme.

Much as she respected the work of wildlife parks, Phoebe wasn't convinced by the argument. Yes, she longed for Coco to stay at the sanctuary, where they would see her and know she was safe. Yet for her own sake she wanted her to be free. To run with the wind, to ride the wild waters, to take her chances. To face the perils of cars, dogs, cold, hunger or whatever else nature might throw at her. Phoebe knew that, if she were an otter, she would still choose freedom. Every time.

She couldn't stop herself saying it out loud. 'Coco, I promise you that, no matter what happens, we will give you that life. You are going to be free.'

Coco swivelled her head and the two of them exchanged a long gaze. Phoebe was aware that she loved Coco in an extreme, illogical way, a soft, human way that Coco could not return, and that was just as it should be. Nevertheless, she and the otter were inextricably linked, linked for life.

A little overwhelmed by it all, she retraced her steps to the sanctuary buildings.

Voices were murmuring in the back room. She was about to push open the door when it opened of its own accord and she was surprised to find Christina in front of her.

'Oh, hi there. Are you here to drop off jewellery?'

'No, Phoebe. Not this time. I've come to see my man.'

For a split second, Phoebe thought she meant Al. Her imagination had painted such a vivid picture of her father and her friend as an item, walking romantically entwined around each other beside the river. But it seemed this was not to be. Because Rupert Venn stepped up and slipped his arm around Christina's waist. Phoebe's heart plummeted.

'We made up,' Christina explained. 'Rupert came round with red roses last night, and we talked for ages, and I realized how rude and judgemental I'd been about his friends.'

'It was quite understandable. They're a mixed bunch,

and can be a bit set in their ways,' Rupert said, still holding her close.

'And we realized how much we need each other,' she said, more to him than to Phoebe.

'I am so glad you accepted my apology, my dear little thing,' he answered, bending to kiss her.

Phoebe turned away to conceal the disappointment on her face. If she ever grew as old as Christina and ever experienced real romantic relationships (two concepts which were equally inconceivable), she would not be so fickle.

'Well done, that's great,' she muttered, feeling the opposite.

Her bones ached, her brain ached, and now her heart also ached for her father. The plan had floundered once again. And now Christina and Rupert would be doubly lovey-dovey and she'd be seeing a lot less of her friend.

She left them to their canoodling and walked outside to draw comfort from the otters. In the public area, Quercus was racing about in his lopsided way, and Twiggy and Rowan were taking a dip. She recognized them all now. She wandered on to the short-clawed Asian otters. Her eyes tracked their movements, but she was distracted.

Assailed by a sudden need for home, she returned to the office. There was no sign of the lovebirds, but Al was there, chatting to Carol. He indicated he would be with her in a moment, so she wandered out to the car on her own. Her head was a vice crammed with issues and her body was a sack of rotten logs. She needed coffee or bed . . . probably both.

She had just reached halfway across the car park when

she became aware of him: Seth Hardwick. He was wearing a hoodie and walking his Alsatian, coming towards her. Her impulse was to veer off track and pretend she hadn't seen him, but it was too late. They'd caught each other's eye. *Oh, please let him not know it was me who was behind Mr Crocker's visit.* She swallowed hard.

Seth's face was getting redder by the minute and his mouth was a downward curve. The dog was straining at the leash.

Calm down, keep walking, just act like a normal, sensible person and say hello briefly. And try to smile.

Her heart was thudding, though. 'Hello!' she called in a falsely bright voice.

Before Seth could reply, the Alsatian jerked himself loose and bounded towards Phoebe. The dog was huge, and its teeth were bared.

She turned and fled.

'Oy, Boz, come back!' roared Seth.

She couldn't run very fast. She stumbled, jolted and fell headlong on to the hard tarmac. The dog was upon her. She felt its hot breath on the back of her bare legs, braced herself for the pain of fangs sinking into her flesh. A faint scream came from her lips.

But instead of biting, the creature just nuzzled her with a very wet nose and patted her with giant paws before jumping backwards and forwards as if they were engaged in a kind of game.

Seth caught up, panting, and shouting, 'Stop it, Boz! Stop that now!'

Phoebe felt her breath returning, bringing with it a flood of relief and anger.

'Don't worry. He won't hurt you.'

It was all very well saying that now.

He pulled the dog away and offered Phoebe a hand, which she didn't take.

With what she hoped was great dignity, she managed to get back on to her feet and dusted herself off. Her knees were bruised, but she was more shocked than hurt. She glared at Seth.

He pulled a face. 'Sorry about that. He must have smelled otters on you. Are you all right?'

'Well . . . I'm . . . I suppose so.'

'Phoebe, isn't it? You were at Christina's barbecue.'

'Mmm.'

Phoebe turned away from him. She was too shaken to think straight, and she certainly wasn't going to forgive him that easily. He was still her number-one suspect.

In fact, as she got into the car, she wondered if he hadn't let go of the dog's lead deliberately.

29

Learning to Live with it

BERRIES BLUSHED IN the hedgerows. The fields thickened with barley and ripe wheat. On the verges, grasses grew tall, sprouting in varied formations: tufted green bracts; long, burnished plumes that bent in the breeze; tiny seeds suspended on invisible stems like quivering dots of rose-gold.

Al Featherstone's door-to-door visits continued and left a trail of different emotions around Darleycombe. Jeremy Crocker took his package inside with trembling hands. Having closed the door firmly, he carried it upstairs. He glanced out of the window at the chickens pecking around the front, before laying the parcel on the bed and feeling in his pocket for the familiar hard edge of his penknife. He flicked the knife open and slid it gently under the tabs on the box, then lifted the lid. He unwrapped the tissue paper inside, his eyes bulging with expectation, and ran a finger along the edge of the silky fabric. He gently drew the garment out, held it against his body and kissed its soft folds, inhaling its fresh new scent.

Felicity Dobson thanked Al profusely. She would have liked to chat to him about the weather, but the dog was making such a racket it was impossible. She shut him up with a Bonio, took her parcel into the kitchen, switched on the kettle and listened to the water bubbling with excitement as she neatly snipped the tape and unwrapped her two new novels. She completely ignored her husband, who was standing there in his tracksuit, first berating her because he had wanted a word with Al about bell-ringing and then launching into a tirade against their neighbour, George Bovis. She knew that all their troubles would fade away as soon as she became immersed in her reading.

Marge Bovis despaired. Why did Al Featherstone always arrive just when she was trying to focus on a yoga move? She got up from her mat to answer the door. She called up to her husband to tell him a large parcel had arrived. He pottered downstairs, pushed his thumbs into the plastic packaging and tore it open. She sighed as he pulled out a dehumidifier, another household item that they didn't really need and she didn't really like. She told him (loudly) how lovely it was, and told herself (quietly) to be more tolerant.

Christina Penrose was always excited to receive parcels, and pleased to see Al too. As Miaow twisted around her ankles, she asked after Phoebe. Al invariably paused before answering and then came out with some cliché. She presumed Phoebe was putting on a brave face, but her underlying health issues were still causing problems. Such a shame! What a lovely girl she was – so thoughtful and original. Christina hadn't invited Al in again, as he'd been a bit frosty towards her since the barbecue. But she was grateful for her parcel. She could never find her scissors when she wanted them, so she just ripped open the packaging. It was always good to receive the little jewels, beads and chains that she would assemble into beautiful jewellery to sell, mostly in her Porlock shop but some in the otter sanctuary.

Rev Lucy's heart sagged as she watched Al come up the driveway. There was no doubt in her mind that this would not be a delivery for her but for her husband. At the beginning, he had rushed down to collect the parcels himself. Now he didn't even bother to pretend. For months, she had been too distracted to notice where his orders were coming from and what the packets might contain, but it had gradually dawned on her. Especially that time she'd been hurrying off to a church meeting and Kandisha had arrived at the house bedecked with a twisty gold necklace. Before involving herself in the evening's babysitting duties, Kandisha had fingered the necklace while shooting a meaningful look at Rev Lucy's husband. That small action had made Rev Lucy's life just a little bit less worth living.

Rev Lucy dug her hairclips firmly in to hold the frizz off her forehead and presented Al with a smile in the porch. She made sure she complimented him on his progress with change-ringing before she accepted the package. She placed it on the hall table for her husband, then shut herself in her study, closing the door behind her. How could she possibly concentrate on writing this week's sermon? She hunched over her desk, her head in her hands.

'Is Al avoiding me?'

'What?'

'Is Al avoiding me?' Christina repeated as they came out of the sanctuary together. 'I just get the feeling he closes off from me whenever I'm around.'

Phoebe speculated. Why would her father do that?

'I'm sure you're imagining it,' she said.

Christina shook her head sadly. 'I expect I opened my big mouth and went and said something offensive without even realizing it.'

Phoebe hastened to reassure her. 'No, no. Dad wouldn't take offence. He's not like that.'

'I didn't think so, really.' She continued walking, the easels tucked under her arm, thinking aloud. 'He's always been the sort of person I feel I can relate to, who will understand what I mean even if it comes out all wrong. And he's been staggeringly generous with his vegetables. And I know he has a soft spot for Miaow, which means we must be kindred spirits. It's just that recently . . .'

Phoebe would have liked to hear more, but at that point Christina spotted Seth Hardwick walking along the back path and hailed him.

Please don't come over, Phoebe thought. To her dismay, he pushed open the car park gate and made his way towards them. He was very red in the face again, and it made the steely grey of his eyes look even steelier. At least the dog was on a tight leash this time.

Christina chatted away to him, pleasantries about the weather and local walks and his motorbike, then she left a gap and looked at Phoebe, prompting her to say something.

Phoebe rifled through her brain. There must be a subtle way she could hint that she knew what he was up to and induce a reaction that would give him away. Then she would know for sure that he was the culprit.

'Did you hear our otters have been poisoned?' she blurted out. 'Deliberately.'

Christina raised her eyebrows. 'Well, we don't know that, Phoebe.'

Seth had bent down to stroke the dog, so his face was hidden.

'I'm compiling a list of suspects,' Phoebe added sharply. Far from subtle, but her head was too mangled to come up with anything more devious.

'Phoebe is a huge fan of Sherlock Holmes,' Christina explained.

'Are you?' Seth straightened, interested now. 'I like detective dramas too, but I'm more a Morse man myself.'

'Oh, he's good, yes,' Phoebe couldn't help saying. 'And Lewis, and Endeavour.'

'I agree. They've all got something. But I like the curmudgeonliness of Morse best. And, of course, the setting. My job is so mindless I like to keep my brain alive by trying to work out the answers to the mysteries.' The

Alsatian pulled at the lead. 'Anyway, I'd better be off. Boz is wanting his beefy bites. See you around.'

With that he strode away, Boz trotting at his side.

More of a Morse man . . . I like to keep my brain alive by trying to work out the answers . . . Phoebe was shocked and disgusted that she had something in common with Seth. Still, if he liked detective dramas, he'd be much more aware of ways to commit a crime and cover his tracks.

Even so, regarding the curious case of the otters, she believed she had outsmarted him.

In time, Paddy was released back into the enclosure with Coco. It was evident that he had become imprinted, since he always came up to the fence to meet Phoebe when she approached. He stood on his hind legs and performed acrobatics and comic dances for his food. Coco hung back, shyer, not sure what had happened to him. She had always been the gregarious one in the presence of humans, but now their roles were reversed.

'She will be all right for release next year,' Carol said. 'He'll be staying here with us, though.'

Phoebe was sad for Paddy, glad for Coco, and tried not to think of herself. She would take one day at a time.

'A word in your ear, if I may, Phoebe,' Rupert said as she was grabbing the Tupperware tub of fish from the sanctuary fridge.

She wondered what was coming. Did he want to know something about Christina? Or was he going to tell her off about talking to Coco? No, he looked friendly . . . but concerned.

'What is it?' she asked.

'Christina's mentioned that you've got certain issues with your health,' he began.

Phoebe felt a flash of annoyance. She had trusted Christina not to tell anyone else about this.

'I promise it won't go any further,' Rupert said, bowing his head slightly.

On second thoughts, she supposed it was inevitable the news would spread to Rupert, seeing as Christina was an open type of person and spent a huge amount of time in his company. At least Rupert would be discreet and not let it go any further.

'Don't blame her,' he went on. 'She told me because she thought that maybe I could help. Please don't take offence, but I understand the fish preparation might be causing you some . . . ah, problems? So I thought I'd offer to do it for you. When Carol isn't looking, of course.'

'Oh.'

It was true. If she still wanted to see Paddy and Coco, fish-chopping was part of Phoebe's duty since both were now on a diet of solids. And the task was increasingly painful for her. Even her own father had no idea how much, or he would have been the one offering help. But she was too proud to ask. Or too worried about upsetting him. Perhaps it was the same thing.

She gazed at the fish; bruised grey corpses, their hopeless, dead eyes staring up at her.

She didn't like to admit defeat, but since the offer was there . . .

'Thank you, Rupert,' she said, handing him the knife.

He accepted it with a courteous nod. 'Glad to help.'

*

She was woken up by the front door and Al's voice calling. It was nearly noon and she'd slept for ages. She sat up and pulled back the curtain of her four-poster bed. Light sprang in on her. Clouds were gusting across the sky and the rowan tree just outside the window was jiggling in the wind. She recalled that she wasn't due at the sanctuary today, but she had an appointment at Christina's house later, for a massage (how kind she was to offer her beautifully pummelling hands for free again).

Al would be up here in a minute. She picked up the book by her bedside. She could pretend she'd been reading.

When Al came into the bedroom he was carrying a plate of toast and Marmite. He nudged it towards her.

'Thanks, Dad.'

She must try to eat it to please him, even though she had no appetite at all. She put the book to one side, gingerly picked up a slice of toast and nibbled at a corner.

Al asked how she was and she answered that she was panegyrical and enquired after his own health. He returned that he was feeling quite sanctimonious, thank you, so that was that.

Forcing more mouthfuls down her dry throat, she asked how the morning's rounds had been.

'Oh, same old, same old,' he said. 'I bumped into Dan Hollis on my trek back to Darleycombe, though. He was in his Land Rover and we stopped for a chat out of our car windows. He said the otter candlesticks were selling well, and he specifically asked me to pass on his regards to Phoebe-the-Wild-Cub-Carer.'

'That's nice.'

Al waited until she'd eaten the toast, then took

something out of his pocket and passed it to her. It was a squarish plastic button designed to look as if it was made from wood. It possibly came from a woman's jacket.

'I mentioned that you'd be seeing Christina later, and Dan promptly gave me this button. He said you should give it to her. To be honest, I wasn't very clear why.'

She gazed at the button in the palm of her hand. 'How odd.'

'Yes, but Dan is odd, isn't he? Incredibly charming, but definitely odd.'

'Well, I expect Christina will know what it's all about.'

However, when she met Christina later, her friend seemed as bemused by the button as she was.

'I've no idea why he wants me to have it.' She shrugged her shoulders dismissively, then grinned. 'Tell me, Phoebe, do you notice anything different about me?'

They were in her sitting-room, side by side on the sofa, having a preliminary drink of elderflower cordial. Miaow was seated in the armchair opposite, washing her paws.

'Something different?' Phoebe inspected her friend. 'Well, let me see. Yes, there is something. You have an indecently smug expression on your face.'

Christina cackled. 'Apart from that?' She put down her glass of cordial, lifted her hands and waved them nonchalantly around in the air. That's when Phoebe noticed it. The ring. A great big flashy diamond, declaring its victorious news from the significant finger of the left hand.

Congratulations were in order.

'Congratulations!'

She produced a smile which felt like a rictus and instantly disappeared once she was hugging Christina and her face was hidden in her friend's shoulder. She grasped her for a long time and felt the beating of her heart. Rupert was a kind, thoughtful man, and he'd recently gone up in her opinion. She just couldn't see him and Christina as husband and wife.

Christina seemed to need to justify herself.

'I have a laugh with Rupert, and laughter is pretty important in this life.'

'Yes, true. Very true. And you love him?' She had to check.

'Of course I do!'

'That's good. It all seems very quick, though.'

Christina shrugged and tossed her hair. 'Oh, quick schmick! You have no idea how desperately lonely I've been this last decade. Maybe you don't realize it because you haven't experienced it, but living alone can send you crazy. The emptiness, the meaninglessness of it all. Of having nobody to share those special moments with – gazing at sunsets, picking strawberries, watching TV by the fire. Of getting up every morning on your own, and having meals on your own and going to bed on your own. I honestly don't know how I would've coped all these years without Miaow. But even Miaow has her limitations.' She indicated Miaow, who now had one back leg rigidly stuck up and pointing ceilingwards while she washed her bottom. 'I can't marry her. She's a cat, isn't she?'

Phoebe chuckled at the idea.

Christina went on. 'Rupert and I are no spring chickens. We've lived a lot longer than you, Phoebe, and we know what we're doing. We don't expect perfection. We know that at times we'll drive each other completely bonkers. But it will be worth it. Together, we have things we don't have individually. Passion and friendship and sharing – some of the most important things in life. Now, at last, I have a chance of happiness, and I'm going to bloody well grab it with both hands.'

She mimed snatching something from the air, as if her happiness were a moth that might flit away at any moment.

Phoebe inwardly scolded herself for not being gladder.

'I still don't get why it has to be marriage, though?' she asked. 'You could just live together and try things out for a while.'

'God, Phoebe, where's your sense of romance? At your age, I firmly believed in Romeo and Juliet.'

'Romeo and Juliet died tragically,' Phoebe pointed out. 'And Romeo and Juliet would probably not even be speaking to each other if they'd lived until their forties.'

Christina shook her head and carried on. 'At your age, I would have done anything for love . . . In fact, I *did* . . . which is how Alex came about.'

Phoebe pictured a young Christina catapulted into a passionate affair. She certainly threw herself at life. She admired that, in a way. If only *she* could grab experiences as Christina did. But envy was pointless, tiring, and about as much fun as eating slugs.

'Anyway,' Christina said, 'if you risk nothing, you risk *doing nothing*. Which is a terrible, terrible thought. I've reached an age where I'm not scared any more. I need to go for it, or I'll feel I've missed my chance. I do love Rupert, very much. And life is too bloody short.'

The conversation affected Phoebe quite badly, not least

because her own life seemed to be made up of risking nothing and doing nothing. There was, she reflected as she stretched out on the couch, a crazy kind of wisdom in Christina's decision. Yet, unwittingly, Christina had made her feel that her own existence was worthless. Phoebe would never experience relationships like Christina did. Mind you, she already had an inkling that no other man's love could compete with the all-encompassing, unconditional, lion-hearted love of her father.

She arrived home feeling pulpy and emotional. She sank into a chair at the kitchen table. The view from here was so pretty. Michaelmas daisies blossomed just outside the window and the rowan shone with a splendour of red berries, but she was finding it hard to appreciate any of it. Instead, she stared at a small, leggy spider as it crawled up the window frame. Al was pottering about, extracting a tin from the cupboard and muttering something about cutlery.

The effects of the massage had already worn off. Phoebe didn't know what to do with this level of pain. It was as if nails were being driven into her spinal cord. It might help if she screamed, but then she'd only feel bad about it. She could imagine the shock on her father's face. Against her will, tears pushed out through her eyes. She clamped her teeth together and tried to focus her thoughts on happy things: cherry blossom, Sherlock and his violin, Narnia, Coco, Paddy, coffee.

The spider disappeared down a crack. Phoebe moved her eyeballs the other way and looked longingly at the kettle. How lovely it would be – how unspeakably soothing – to hold a mug of coffee (or even tea) in her hands and slowly sip at it.

On the other hand, how much pain would it involve to pick the kettle up, hold it under the tap and feel it grow heavier as it filled with water? It would be too much to bear. It wasn't worth it.

Al would do it, willingly, if she asked him. But she really, really, didn't want to have to ask. And he wasn't telepathic enough to offer. It was a shame, but there it was. She'd have to go coffee-less.

'Christina's engaged to Rupert,' she blurted out.

Al gave a squawk of surprise. 'She's engaged to Rupert? But she's only been going out with him for five minutes.'

'I know,' Phoebe answered ruefully. 'She can be a bit impetuous.'

'Understatement,' he said.

'I suppose she's known him for a lot longer than we have, though.'

'True.' He attacked the tin with a tin-opener. 'Well, I hope she'll be very happy.'

'So do I.'

Phoebe looked at her father's face, a mask of loneliness.

A drop splashed on to the table.

'Phoebe? Oh, Phoebe, what's wrong?'

'Nothing,' she answered, scrunching up her face, angry at those traitorous tears. 'Nothing and everything.'

Al abandoned the tin-opener and sat down beside her. 'That's not very clear, you know.'

She sniffed. She would make no reference to the vicious prongs that were stabbing into her neck, but she'd mention the other things. 'Okay then, I'll be honest. Nothing is right. I feel weird about Christina marrying Rupert. And also . . . I've been thinking about Paddy and Coco, how they'll be separated once Coco is released. She should have his company. They should *both* be heading for a free life out in the wilds, along the banks of the Darle. But now it's not possible.'

Al patted her hand. 'You really can't take on their problems, Phoebe,' he said. 'You mustn't.'

She rubbed her wet eyes and went on. 'They're back together for now, but soon they're going to lose each other all over again, and this time it will be for ever.'

'They'll manage somehow.' He sighed deeply and leaned into her. 'They'll just have to learn to live with it.'

30

Winter

ONE OF THE parcels was very battered. The contents (the edges of a couple of picture frames, by the looks of it) were poking out of the corner. Al thought he would tape up the hole before it got any worse. He had some parcel tape somewhere. In the 'random bits' kitchen drawer, possibly?

When he opened it the first thing he saw was a jotter pad. He hadn't remembered leaving it there, and flipped through it before realizing it must belong to Phoebe. He was surprised to see so much handwriting in it; he knew that writing anything down caused her pain. The pages must be important. At the front were her theories about where Miaow might be, followed by some notes about Coco and her feeding times. One page was stuffed with information about what people were ordering in the village. He tutted under his breath. Phoebe's nosiness was terrible. He wondered if he should reprimand her about it. Reprimanding wasn't his forte, though.

He turned another page and glanced down at the words. It was a series of quite long bullet-pointed paragraphs, and he guessed she must have written it in several separate sessions.

Chronic Pain was the title.

He couldn't stop himself reading the first paragraph.

– *Pain is a robber. It robs you of days out, sports, holidays, fun. It robs you of a job and the satisfaction that doing worthwhile work brings. It robs you of friends and relationships. It robs you of your dreams. And it robs you of countless untold opportunities.*

He'd never thought of it that way before. He shook his head sadly and read on.

– *Pain strips away the shine of life. Life used to be full of shiny moments but now it just isn't any more. When good things happen, they're empty of the elation that ought to accompany them. You're hurting way too much to enjoy them.*

– *Pain induces envy. You see people going about, able to party, able to stay out late and walk miles and move without wincing and carry shopping and get things out of the fridge without any hint of hurt. Taking it all for granted. They are so bloody lucky, you sometimes resent them. You*

*look at them and you look at yourself and you
yearn to be in their shoes even just for a day,
even for an hour, and experience what it's like to
be capable of things again.*

– *Pain is JUST SO BORING. You're deprived of
so much human experience that there's nothing
to inspire or challenge you. You have nothing to
say to anyone any more. Your friends find you
dull and fall away. You can't blame them. Your
world has become a small, dark cave of pain
where nothing ever happens.*

– *Pain steals your identity. It ousts all the other
aspects of you, wrings the personality out of you
and squashes you entirely. Year after year, the
real you becomes hidden beneath this crying,
whingeing nonentity of a creature.*

– *Pain makes you selfish. You hate yourself for it,
but you're just too exhausted to care much about
other people's problems any more. You want to
be a kind, wonderful person, but it's as if your
body has reached its limit and you can't even
contemplate anyone else's sufferings. Along with
so much else, your empathy has been siphoned
away.*

– *Pain is totally, brutally, relentlessly exhausting.*

Al realized Phoebe must have been too tired to carry on
here because the next part was written in a different-coloured
pen, as if she'd scribbled it down on a different day.

- *Pain makes you tetchy and blunt. Sometimes it hurts too much to smile, even if somebody is being kind to you. Social niceties are just too much effort so the filters you would normally put up become a massive struggle. You come across as rude and grumpy when you don't mean to be.*

'Oh, Phoebe,' he sighed. 'You're not grumpy at all.'

- *Pain induces feelings of inadequacy. You're conscious that so many people do fabulous things with their lives – study to improve their wisdom and knowledge, make advances in medicine and science, create music and art, earn a living. You feel so awful that you're not doing any of it, even the basics, like cooking and cleaning. And that you're putting other people to extra work, extra worry and extra expense. That's what kills you most.*

- *Pain makes me feel guilty. All the time. Because of Dad.*

Al sank into a chair. He stared down at the words. Stared at them again. He had always known that Phoebe hated talking about her illness, and so he had never pushed it. But that meant he had never quite grasped everything it involved. All those repercussions. The pain itself was bad enough, but how come he'd never realized she was also burdened with those feelings of inadequacy and loss and guilt? All these years, she'd been holding them in, dealing with them on her own. He pressed his palms into his eyes, but the words were still there, searing into him like a brand of shame.

Never in his life had he felt such a failure.

When Phoebe came down to the kitchen, her father was slumped in a chair with his head in his hands. His shoulders were shaking. Something awful must have happened. Her mind went to Christina. Had he fallen in love with Christina after all? Then it veered back again. Coco? Had something happened to Coco?

'Dad?'

He jumped, and tried to dash the tears from his face. He pulled a handkerchief from his pocket and snorted into it.

'Dad, what is it?'

She stepped forward and put her arms around him, kissed the grey hairs on the top of his head, breathed in the earthy scent from his jumper. A noise like a sob came from his throat. He pushed at the notebook that was lying on the table, open at the page where she had once desperately scrawled.

She looked at him, horrified.

'Ah, you saw that, did you? I'm sorry.'

'Oh, Phoebe, Phoebe, I'm the one who's sorry.'

She tried to explain. 'I had to get it out of my system so I wrote it down – weird thing, how writing can help. It somehow made me feel a bit better to pin it down and put it into words. I know it was disgustingly whiney. No way was I ever going to inflict it on you.'

Al threw out his arms in a gesture of frustration. The

chair scraped along the floor as he stood up. He drew her in and clasped her tightly. 'I'm here to have such things inflicted on me. It's my job. I'm your dad, for heaven's sake. Why don't you tell me how you feel? You never tell me how you feel.'

'Dad, sometimes I want to, but I know it would hurt you too much. And what's the point in us both hurting?'

'I'm more hurt that you don't confide in me,' he moaned.

How could she make him understand? The pressure. The expectations of society, of friends, of family. Of herself.

'I have to be brave.'

He shook his head violently. 'No. No, you don't have to be brave.'

'I have to be strong.'

'No, you don't have to be strong, either.'

'I have to be positive.'

'No, Phoebe. You really don't.' He spat out the words as if they were poison. 'You don't have to be anything.'

'But I so desperately want to avoid being a negative person. Or a victim.'

'Phoebes, you're the bravest, strongest person I know. And I will always know the truth of that, even if you don't think it of yourself.'

She nestled into him. 'Thanks, Dad. You're pretty great too,' she whispered. Then she added, 'I do know I'm not completely hopeless. I make an effort with the otters, don't I?'

'You do. You really do. Thank God for the otters,' he said.

'I can still make choices within my narrow sphere, can't I?'

'Absolutely,' he said. 'Sometimes you remind me so

much of your mother, you know. Ruth used to say, "You make your choices, and in turn they make you."' He gave her another squeeze. 'I want you to make another choice now, my lovely, brave daughter. Don't ever, ever, feel guilty about me. I need you every bit as much as you need me. Where would I be without you? Don't answer that,' he added with a grimace as she opened her mouth to respond. 'Phoebe, please promise me one thing. Promise me you will not *ever* hesitate to "inflict" your thoughts, needs, feelings and worries on me in the future. I want to hear them. I want to hear them all. I want to be here for you.'

She was the one sobbing now. Great big sobs, grateful sobs. Sobs that had been waiting too long to be unleashed. 'I promise . . . but please give me time. Not sharing has hardened into a habit. It's hard to be honest about pain. I will do my best, though.'

After her breathing had calmed she realized she had something more to say. 'Dad, I want you to promise me something too. You spend so much time looking after me, and I totally appreciate it – all of it, every little thing. But I'd love you to look after yourself too, to think about what *you* want, what *you* need.'

Confusion spread over his face, as if this wasn't a concept that had ever occurred to him.

'Have a think about what would make you happy. And go for it, Dad. Promise me you'll do that?'

He gave her another tight squeeze.

'I'll try.'

Cold mists gathered and hung murkily over the river. Bracken yellowed, frond by frond, and then transformed into crunchy brown bundles that would disintegrate as the deer trampled them underfoot. The moorland exchanged its tawny cloak for a bare expanse of stubble. The prolific vegetation of the roadsides thinned and became straggly before dying back altogether. Leaves dropped and gusted away.

Winter settled in and seemed to stretch on for ever with not much in the way of frost or sparkle, just interminable greyness.

Phoebe wished she could skip over the boring bits of life, like fictional characters did. The hours of sleeping, sitting on the loo, trying to think up something intelligent to say, regretting what you *did* say, being too tired to function, waiting to feel better, waiting for the next meal, waiting for painkillers to work their magic. Sherlock and Hercule never wasted time on such stuff.

Al continued making deliveries around Darleycombe and the surrounding countryside. Christmas exhausted him, with the increased quantity of parcels, and it was just as well the seasonal visit from Jules and Jack was brief. Everyone pitched in and made something for Christmas dinner, but Phoebe didn't partake much. She only wanted to hibernate. Most of her time was spent in bed, with the curtains drawn, watching TV dramas or listening to audiobooks.

Late January brought a sweeping of snow. The air shimmered, the river swirled with crystals, the trees became a brushwork of silvers and whites. The sanctuary otters frolicked and pranced in the falling flakes, making a joyous mess of scattered pawprints. Paddy and Coco licked and patted the snow, then took turns to slither down their ice-polished bank, squeaking with glee.

Phoebe declared everything to be 'utterly Narnian' but only stayed out briefly, saying the cold hurt too much.

Al remembered how, as a child, she had dragged the family sledge up a steep slope no less than thirty times (long after Jules and Jack had finished and come back in) for the sheer pleasure of sliding down it again. He remembered her whoops and wild laughter. What a laugh she had, like a clatter of bells, so bright and uproarious that it momentarily banished all the blackness from the world. He hadn't heard that laugh for so long.

Phoebe was beginning to think her suspicions about the otter sanctuary were unfounded. Maybe she'd been wrong to blame Seth for the poisoning. It was quite possible that the button she'd found by Coco's enclosure hadn't belonged to him at all. She only had Dan Hollis's word for it, after all, and Dan was . . .Well, he might not be a hundred per cent reliable. Nothing had happened for months now. Probably the sanctuary had suffered from a few unlucky incidents and the poison had just somehow got into the water, as Carol and Rupert seemed to believe.

As time inched forwards, even the act of lifting one foot then another became a humongous effort. Phoebe felt brittle, like the miniature glass unicorn she'd once had whose legs had snapped when she'd put it down a little too firmly on the windowsill.

Pain doled itself out in ever more generous measures, blistering and burning. And there was a new rawness, as if the inside of her bones had been scraped with a rusty razor. She wondered whether to try going to a doctor again, but she just couldn't face it. There were days when she couldn't see the point in getting up at all, and only did it because her father chivvied her along. Really, what difference did it make to the rest of the planet whether she stayed in bed or got up? Her life could hardly be more insignificant.

She wore her smile like a clown's smile, a gaudy covering painted over a dark reality. She needed to re-caffeinate at regular intervals just to keep upright. It was hard to hold her eyelids open when all they wanted to do was clamp shut. More and more, she experienced that feeling of life leaving her discarded on the side of the road while others sped on busily past.

She confided some of these feelings to her father, since she had promised. He listened, his face grey. To cheer him, she told him she was practising glass-half-full techniques.

'Look, Dad. I can still move my head, even if I can only do it slowly. Just imagine if all my life I'd never been able to move it at all, but now – bingo! It's fantastic, when you think about it, being able to move your head!'

'It is,' he agreed glumly. 'Fantastic.'

She still made herself go out to see the otters as much as possible. Occasionally, she met Christina there for drawing sessions, although it was too cold to sit outside for long and she grew dizzy with the pain of holding the pencil. Carol worked hard juggling the demands of the otters with the demands of the public. Rupert helped, although he was more distracted than before, thanks to Christina. He continued to chop up the fish for Phoebe, so all she had to do was leave it in Coco and Paddy's enclosure.

She watched the cubs on video as they made new discoveries and gradually grew towards adulthood. And she knew that her role as Wild Cub Carer would soon be over.

31

Soft Release

THEN, ALL AT once, clusters of snowdrops appeared on the banks of the Darle, followed by tiny emerald specks in the twisted brown of the hedgerows. They grew into bright stitches, thicker and fuller every day, until the landscape became a tapestry of pastel and green. Cushions of primroses sprouted in the fields, their creamy yellow faces turned towards the light. Insects crawled out from their winter hidey-holes, stretched their wings and started flitting over the grass, seeking nectar. Birds made their presence known through joyful twitterings from the treetops. After months of near silence, they had plenty to say again.

Rev Lucy's voice was unusually loud and sharp as she read out the wedding banns. Phoebe (who was sitting beside her father in the congregation, thanks to

Christina's powers of persuasion) could see why the vicar might be disillusioned with the concept of marriage.

Christina had asked Phoebe to be a bridesmaid. It was a struggle for Phoebe even to butter her bread at the moment, but she didn't have the heart to say no. She observed that the aisle at Darleycombe church was short, and, provided she could sit down once she'd reached the end of it, she would somehow manage. If she was expected to carry a bouquet of flowers, though, it would have to be an incredibly light one.

As they walked out after the service, Christina, electrified with excitement, gabbled to Phoebe. 'One of the best things about getting married is the sense of new beginnings. It's like daffodils or the return of the swallows.'

'How lovely.'

'And I'm so looking forward to seeing my son, daughter-in-law and grandson again. I haven't seen them in over two years. I'm wildly emotional just thinking about it.'

Phoebe cast a look back and noticed that Al was chatting to Rev Lucy. Assuming she had been wrong in her suspicions about the vicar, could this be a Plan B for her father's love life? But she didn't now have the energy to push fate one way or the other. What would be would be.

She had zoned out of Christina's effusing, but now her friend grabbed her arm.

'I actually wanted something alternative for the ceremony, such as the old tradition of jumping over a broomstick. But Rupert insisted on a church service. I'm fine about it,' she added, noting Phoebe's frown. 'I've found a crazy, unconventional wedding dress to make up

304

for it, something that my darling Rupert has no control over at all. It's very purple and a bit like a tent, and I love it so much!'

'Great.'

Phoebe wished she could show more enthusiasm but couldn't quite remember how it was done. Luckily, Christina had enough for both of them.

She carried on listing all the details of the wedding. There would be a full contingent of bell-ringers (including Al) and the church would be decked with purple tulips and yellow irises. Her friend, Ellie, had agreed to play the Celtic harp too, although she was nervous; she hadn't been learning for long and wasn't used to performing at all. She had found a gorgeous piece of music that Christina loved and was practising hard. The harp (one that Dan had made) both looked and sounded exquisite. It would add a magical ambience to the occasion.

As for the reception, it would be an informal affair in Rupert's garden, with Rupert's brother (and best man) organizing the catering. Christina had wanted the buffet to be totally organic and vegetarian but had compromised on this, too, in the end. Certain fish dishes would be included, bearing in mind his side of the family didn't really get the vegetarian thing, but there would be no red meat.

'I had the idea of posing for wedding photographs afterwards at the sanctuary, together with the otters. Rupert wasn't keen, though. He said the guests wouldn't like going somewhere like that in all their finery. He's so practical.'

If Al had been the one marrying Christina, he would have embraced all her wackiness. He would have ensured she had everything she wanted on their special day. How Phoebe wished her plan to get them together had worked.

The river sighed restlessly. The tiles of Higher Mead Cottage shone with a slick of rain. Damp pervaded the air of Darleycombe and crept into its households. It made Jeremy Crocker hunt through his wardrobe for something fur-lined, made Rev Lucy sigh and stare out of the window as she struggled to write her sermons. It made George Bovis scowl at the bedraggled shrubs in his front garden and Spike Dobson scramble into his mackintosh before hauling his dog out of the door for the shortest possible walk, returning soon after soaked and mud-splashed. It made Christina Penrose anxiously switch on the radio to listen to the weather forecast, hoping it would improve before her wedding day. It made Al Featherstone fret for the new potato crop. It seeped into Phoebe Featherstone's sore bones, where it sat and ached and, much as she tried to stop it, sometimes leaked out through her eyes.

The time was approaching for Coco to be released back into the wild. Carol and Rupert had set up a large temporary enclosure by the riverbank in the glade where Coco was first found. They called this the 'soft release site'. When they released an otter into the wild, they always did so gradually. The otter, stressed by the car journey, would probably be reluctant to venture out immediately to explore and find food. So they would watch it and feed it for a few days first in the new situation while it settled in. It was also a measure to ensure the otter didn't keep returning to human company. An otter would endanger itself if it headed for roads and houses, or it might cause damage to property, as had happened with George Bovis's koi carp pond.

Carol was taking the first shift to leave food and observe Coco, and Rupert was scheduled to drop in the following evening. Then Carol again. After that, all being well, the door of the pen would be left open and Coco could leave for good whenever it suited her.

Phoebe wanted to play a big part in Coco's final release but, although the glade was easy walking distance from Higher Mead Cottage, it still felt a long way for her. Luckily, Al had discovered he could drive by road to a lay-by from where it was a short downhill walk through a field to get to the site.

They headed there together one morning so that she could say her silent goodbyes to Coco. Despite the extra paracetamol, pain sank into Phoebe's muscles like blades and burrowed deep inside her skull. She concentrated on putting one foot in front of the other. She had to see Coco this one last time.

It had rained again and the grass was wet.

'Do you remember the morning we found Coco?' Al asked.

'Of course,' said Phoebe. 'Although it seems aeons ago now.'

'We've certainly learned a thing or two about otters.'

'People, too.'

They stepped under the fringe of beech trees and within

a few moments found themselves in the glade. The earth sent up a rich, damp smell, almost like chocolate. Water droplets hung from the ferns and starry flowers of wild garlic, twinkling as they caught the light. Phoebe remembered how she had longed for Narnia when her father first mentioned the glade. Looking at it now, she could imagine dryads and naiads dancing across the soft moss. Or Mr Tumnus the faun, trotting home to tea. Or perhaps Aslan himself, striding under the arching hazel bows.

Instead, they found a stretch of chickenwire. But Coco was there. She stood at the edge of her pen, facing the river. Her tail was coiled in an S-shape, her posture alert, excited. As they drew closer they saw that her nostrils were flared, as if she was inhaling the scent of her imminent freedom.

'She looks ready for adventure, doesn't she?' Al whispered.

Phoebe nodded.

Coco glanced round and saw them both standing there. Two gangly humans, gazing at her, loving her, wishing her well.

Phoebe wiped her eyes. It was rare for her, this huge sense of achievement. In spite of everything, she had become an otter mother. And even if she never saw Coco again, she would know that her cub was not far away, somewhere along the course of the Darle, living her best life. And even if her own life, eclipsed by pain, never came to anything much, it helped – how it helped! – to know that she had made this happen for a fellow creature.

'Don't forget me, Coco, will you?'

But even as she said it, she realized she shouldn't be wanting it. Coco was destined to be a wild creature, free of regret – such a peculiar and unnecessary human trait. Her life would be so much purer and better if she never looked back.

32

Party Politics

THE CARD WAS decorated with gold rosebuds. It was a formal invitation to Jules's twenty-first birthday party, which she had chosen to hold not at Higher Mead Cottage (Al had offered) but at the flat in Plymouth she was renting with friends.

Phoebe wasn't going. If she went, she'd have to overload her system with painkillers and make a Herculean effort to be energetic and jolly. Jules would roll her eyes and accuse her of attention-seeking if she dared to look pale or didn't say anything for five minutes. If, on the other hand, she succeeded in being chatty, Jules would tell her friends that Phoebe always fussed about her illness yet they'd seen for themselves there was very little wrong with her.

She rang and made her excuses. Jules found them difficult to swallow. She regarded the other members of the family as her satellites whose lives should rotate around hers. In addition, she had hatched a plan to fix Phoebe up with one of her friends at her party.

'How can you fall in love with James if you don't even bother to come?' she demanded.

'James?'

'Yes, he's a biochemist and has a nice car and the kind of geeky sweetness you like.'

'Jules, wherever did you get the idea that I like geeky sweetness? It's highly unlikely I'd fall in love with this James, and even more unlikely that he'd fall in love with me.'

'Well, you'll never know if you don't come. The food will be scrummy too. Pretty much a banquet.'

Phoebe could only apologize and say again how exhausted and unwell she had been feeling recently. The conversation went round in circles a few times before she was able to change the subject.

Three days later, another formal invitation arrived that was identical to the first, except that the invitees were not 'Dad and Phoebe' but 'Dad plus one'.

Al scratched his head.

'Plus one? She knows there is no "plus one" in my life. Who on earth does she expect me to bring?'

Phoebe just sighed.

When the day of the party dawned, Al set off on his own, uncomfortable in his electric-blue velvet jacket (which Phoebe said was great, but he wasn't so sure) and bow tie. Jules had requested formal attire, and he'd taken all his dull, stuffy teaching outfits to charity shops, so it was the only option.

'I won't be back late,' he told Phoebe, who was in bed with her hot wheat pack around her shoulders, swathed in a fluffy dressing gown. He'd left a tray with a jug of orange juice and a plate of Marmite sandwiches, exactly as she had requested, and there were plenty of painkillers within reach, so she should be fine. It still felt all wrong leaving her alone for the whole evening.

'Honestly, I don't mind,' she assured him. 'Just say happy birthday and apologize again to Jules from me. And a big hug for Jack, too.'

'You'll be missed. Are you sure you won't come?' He knew she wouldn't, but he had to ask.

She patted his hand and shook her head. 'Anyway, I have thinking to do.'

She would be thinking about Coco; he knew it. It was such a shame she had to part with the otter who had provided so much welcome distraction. He felt ridiculously grateful to the dear creature.

It was a longer drive than he'd anticipated, mainly because of the rain. Most people travelling had opted to drive and there was heavy traffic around Exeter and on the outskirts of Plymouth.

He had been to Jules's flat a couple of times before. From what he remembered, the building was part of a huge, characterless complex and the rooms were filled with teddy bears, cushions and cactuses.

He managed to find a parking space a few roads down but heard the music pulsing into the air while he was still a couple of blocks away. He hoped it wouldn't be an issue with the neighbours.

Jules was stationed near the door in a shining pink

wrap-around dress, her hair curled and swept up in the style of a Jane Austen character, which suited her, he thought. She cried, 'DAD!' and flung herself into his arms.

'Happy birthday, my darling girl!' He pressed the presents into her hands.

'You shouldn't have!'

'Oh yes I should.'

'Well, yes, you should, but it's lovely of you anyway,' she giggled, adding the gifts to a mountain of others on the table. 'You didn't bring anyone, then?'

'No. Plus ones are few and far between in Darleycombe.'

'Never mind, lots of fab people here to keep you entertained.'

She introduced him to a gaggle of friends whose names immediately slipped through his head and out the other side. They were all much younger than him by a very large margin.

It didn't take him long to realize that the main aim of most of the guests was to pour as much alcohol down their throats as they possibly could. He was also slightly shocked at the skimpiness of everyone's clothes. One of the girls sported a low-cut jacket under which she was visibly wearing nothing except a lacy black bra. Another had a skirt so minute she couldn't sit down. Today's methods of attracting a partner seemed very bereft of any subtlety or romance.

Jack was charitable enough to spend a lot of time with his father, in spite of his popularity with the girls, who outnumbered the boys. Every time he went to top up his drink, he edged his way through them, saying, 'Squeeze me.' Most thought this was very funny and some obligingly gave him a cuddle as he passed. Jack could get away with anything.

Jules clapped her hands for attention and proceeded to open the mountain of presents in front of an admiring audience. It was professionally done, with great show and many exclamations of delight. Next came the sit-down meal, which was full of thoughtful details such as napkins folded into the shape of swans and a balloon tied to the back of each chair. Wine flowed, along with flippant conversations about student life. Al had little to contribute to these, and sat nodding his head and going, 'Oh, I see,' a lot. Then, in an epiphany, he suddenly realized that the people who surrounded him might like to hear about the otter sanctuary.

'My daughter and I rescued a baby otter last summer,' he said to the underdressed girl on his left.

'No, really? You and Jules?'

'Me and my other daughter, Phoebe.'

'Awesome,' she said. 'I'd love an otter.'

And, as if an electric current had been switched on, Al found that he'd become a spouting font of otter knowledge. He informed the startled girl that otter poo was officially known as 'spraint', and that an otter's nest or habitation was a 'holt'. He told her that otters produced a secretion from their anal glands which had a strong, musky scent and they used it for marking territory. He also, in case this should have put her off, told her that sea otters sometimes held hands when asleep floating on their backs in the water so that they wouldn't lose each other.

The girl drank in his words.

More and more people along the table tuned in to

314

listen to his spiel. He expounded at length about Coco, Paddy and the sanctuary. He told them, with pride and emotion, that Coco was in her last stages of captivity and about to be released. He could have gone on for even longer, but now a very beautiful cake iced with pink words ('Happy 21st Birthday, Jules') appeared.

After a ceremonial blowing out of candles, Jules gave a speech in which she touchingly thanked her amazing friends and family. A passing reference was made to Phoebe, with genuine regret that she wasn't around and, Al was pleased to note, only a tiny hint of resentment. It was hard to believe that his baby Jules was twenty-one. He beamed with pride. He wished with all his heart that Ruth, his much-adored Ruth, had lived to see this day. Al often felt like a child and had asked himself many times over the years if he was cut out to be a dad. But he couldn't have done that badly, could he, since all three of his children had turned out so well . . . 'Well' in one sense of the word, anyway.

His mind kept wandering back to Phoebe. He had asked Christina to look in on her, but she'd said she was out at her friend Ellie's that evening and muttered something about meeting Rupert later.

Phoebe had promised she'd text him. Unfortunately, when he checked his phone at nine, he found the battery was dead. He put it back in his pocket, swearing quietly. He could call Phoebe on the landline but decided against it as she was probably asleep by now.

People had started dancing. They writhed and wiggled, bounced and jolted their hips around. He didn't recognize any of the songs. Most of them were high energy with a throbbing bass and lyrics that incessantly urged him to 'pump-it-up pump-it-up'. He would have preferred some Wham! or Billy Ocean, but attempted a bit of dancing to prove he wasn't square and boring. He found himself automatically strumming at an air guitar.

'Yay, dad-dancing!' somebody cheered.

Sweating, he retreated and sank on to the sofa to recover with a glass of tonic water. Three students immediately plomped themselves next to him. They were very wriggly, and he found himself being squeezed further and further into the edge.

He struggled up and made his way through the thrashing bodies to the drinks table again. Alcohol was out of the question since he'd have to drive home, yet alcohol was clearly the only way to get through any more of this. He glanced at his watch. Maybe it would be all right to leave now. The three students on the sofa were now lying on top of each other, and he had to step over another couple on the floor as he sought out Jules to say goodbye.

He found her scrubbing at a spillage on the carpet while sharing an anecdote with a knot of friends. She blearily put her arms around him and said, 'Dad, you're the total absolute bestlest. Don't leave, pleave.'

He hesitated. She'd ignored him for most of the evening and he believed she would hardly register his absence. He'd ring her the next day to check she was all right, though. Not too early. Along with most of the others here, she would be nursing a bad headache in the morning. Jack was nowhere to be seen, but that didn't worry him. Jack could look after himself.

What a relief it was to get out into the cool night air.

He automatically checked his phone again, before remembering it was dead.

A couple of near-nakeds were snogging and smoking, propped up against the outside wall of the building. One of them shouted to him, 'Bye, grandad!' as he left the premises. It was worse than being called Big Al.

He drove back in delicious silence, his mind numb. The journey seemed to go on for ever, though.

He felt weak and wobbly when he arrived back at the cottage. He crept in, assuming Phoebe would be asleep. Everything was quiet.

Exhaustion hit him now. He ambled into the kitchen, filled a pint glass with water and gulped half of it down straight away. Scenes from the party were still jiggling around in his head. He thought again of Ruth. He knew that he'd done a fair job in bringing up the children on his own, but it would have been so much easier with her help. He brushed a tear from his eye then crept upstairs. He would take a look in on Phoebe briefly before going to bed. She'd be asleep, of course, but he needed to see her, to reassure himself, as much as anything. Even with her illness, she had always been a kind of anchor to him at emotional times.

As he reached the landing, instinctively he felt that something was wrong. He told himself not to be ridiculous.

The door of Phoebe's bedroom was open, the light off inside. He tiptoed towards it and saw by the landing light that the duvet was in a twisted heap on the floor. That was odd. Phoebe was normally too cold, not too hot. He gently pulled back the curtain and peered in. The bed was empty.

'Phoebe?'

He checked his own room, the bathroom and the spare room, then crashed downstairs again, calling her name.

She was nowhere to be seen. He looked at the pegs in the hall where they kept their coats. Her jacket had gone. Her trainers had gone too.

It was three o'clock in the morning. Where could she be? Panic rising in his throat, he opened the front door and called out into the darkness, hoping beyond hope to hear her voice calling back. There was only the hoot of an owl, the patter of rain and the wind in the trees.

He must try to keep calm, think logically. But what could have possessed her to go out without letting him know where she was going? And at this hour? It wasn't like her at all. A trickle of sweat ran down his spine.

He dashed to the phone. Sucked in a breath. Grabbed the receiver with trembling hands.

He was about to call 999 when he noticed the answerphone light was flashing.

33

Darkness

A few hours earlier

A FORMER PHOEBE would have been upset. Now she only felt relief that she wasn't going to Jules's party. Her brain felt like a vat of boiling oil and the sinews in her neck were finding it hard to support her head. They were so sore she could scarcely breathe. Even if she bombarded her system with painkillers, the party would be hard to bear. The noise alone would be torture, not to mention the impossible task of being sociable.

She told herself that Jules was probably happier without her there anyway. She had rung again earlier to atone for her absence, although even talking had become troublesome. The roof of her mouth was like sandpaper and she had to keep slurping water to lubricate the words. Not that it mattered much, because Jules did nearly all the talking. She was distracted and buzzing with all the preparations.

'Oh, Phoebe, hi. Can't talk for long. I'm hyper at the mo, running around like a headless chicken. I've got a million things to do. I need to get in some more booze – you can't trust people to bring a bottle, even though I wrote it loud and clear on the invites. My dress is badly in need of ironing. My flatmates promised to do the hoovering, but they haven't, so I'm just going to have to do it myself, and my job was actually down as folding the napkins. Swans, you know. Takes ages . . .' She reeled off a list, assuming Phoebe would be as fascinated by the intricacies of her day as she was. She didn't ask the *how are you?* question, which was just as well.

After Al had left, Phoebe watched two episodes of a Sherlock Holmes spin-off back to back. It was strange being at Higher Mead Cottage alone in the evening. If only there was a dog or a cat for company – or an otter. But, no, she couldn't wish for that. Wild animals belonged in the wild. Coco was probably now curled up asleep in her holt at the soft-release site, not far away, and soon she would be blissfully free.

A fretful wind wailed around the edges of the house. Rain thudded on the roof, dampening her spirits. Something smacked against the window, making her heart jump. It might have been a bit of branch or a disoriented bird; she didn't know. It left her feeling jittery.

She closed her eyes, trying to sleep, trying to ignore the stabbing in her spine. She couldn't get comfortable, no matter which way she arranged her limbs. Her brain ached too. A snippet of a thought was hovering at the edges of her subconscious, but she couldn't quite pin it down and look at it straight. It carried on niggling away at her.

A scene from the second TV episode was replaying itself over and over in her head. The scene was set in a garden, and a young Sherlock, strolling along with one of the suspects, stopped to admire a tree. The suspect indicated knee height with his hand and remarked, 'It was this high when I planted it.' The tree was now broad and tall, yet the man had mentioned earlier that he was new in town. This was how Sherlock knew he was lying, and the lie turned out to be the key clue in the investigation.

Phoebe reached about in her head for associations. It reminded her of something Christina had said about train sets.

In the second episode, somebody had injected poison into a fish finger, not knowing that their intended victim was a vegetarian. This, too, felt relevant. Again, the link was with Christina and fresh fish canapés that looked as if they were vegetarian but weren't. Phoebe gave a little moan of exasperation. Model trains and canapés . . . model trains and canapés . . . they jiggled around in her mind, vanished and then kept popping up again.

All at once, her imagination filled in the gaps and the pieces fitted together.

And within another beat she knew that Coco was in danger.

She hurled her duvet off and the heat pack went scudding to the floor. She scrambled into her jeans and hauled a jumper over her pyjama top, wincing with the effort. Another gasp of pain and she had pulled on her trainers.

She gulped down a couple more painkillers, almost choking in her haste.

She would have to go on foot. This wasn't going to be easy. She hurtled downstairs. As soon as she opened the front door a prickling of rain flew into her face. The sky was covered in great grey bruises. Shivering, she threw on her jacket and grabbed a torch. Down to the bottom of the garden and along the river would be the quickest route.

The grass was soaking. She should have put on wellies rather than trainers, but she couldn't delay any longer. The trees looked like battling ghosts as they whipped the air. Raindrops swarmed and scurried around her. As she approached the riverbank the sounds of the Darle became louder and angrier. During the evening, the water had risen and the bottom of the garden was awash with murky water. She splashed through and cursed as it seeped through her socks. Mud squelched under her feet. She had reached the mossy gate now, passed the fallen branch where she sometimes sat.

A shifty-looking moon stared down at her. It had a ragged edge, as if it had been torn in the branches of the beech tree, from which it still hadn't quite managed to escape. Phoebe pulled up her hood and huddled deeper into her jacket. Wet bracken and brambles caught her legs as she propelled herself forward along the path, as fast as she could. She gasped with the strain and pain of each step, but all she could think about was Coco.

The distance seemed a lot further than when she'd come here with Al last May. And it was much harder to walk when the ground was sodden and she could see so little. She tripped over a root and fell to her knees, sticking her hands out just in time to save herself from a worse fall. Shaken, she pulled herself up again with the help of a low-hanging oak, its rough bark scratching her palms. Plastered in mud, she struggled on.

The river was a flow of darkness, higher than she'd ever seen it. It seemed to be bellowing at her: 'Hurry! Hurry!'

Her bones felt as if they were warping. The rain cut her cheeks. The air stung her eyes and they kept welling up. She didn't know if they were tears of pain or fear.

At last she could make out the shape of the temporary enclosure. A human figure was standing there, an unusually tall one, who was putting on a pair of gloves, probably those thick, leather gloves he used when handling otters. Phoebe's heart beat faster. She had come out here in desperation, without any real plan. Was she intending to challenge this big, strong man – she, a thin, enfeebled girl?

She crept a little closer, then held back and watched, hiding in the shadow of a tree trunk. Rupert had no idea she was there. He said the words, 'Try this one, then,' in an unfamiliar, hard-edged voice and flung something into the corner of the pen. Phoebe crouched low on the ground, steadying herself. Now she could see Coco, lifting her head, sniffing the air. Nervously, the otter edged towards the object and Phoebe realized it must be a piece of fish. Suddenly deciding she couldn't resist, Coco pounced on it, dragged it backwards with her and started munching.

Phoebe cringed. She watched, dread coiling around her heart, wishing her reactions had been quicker. If the fish was poisoned, it was now too late. Coco had gulped down the whole thing.

Rupert was busying himself with something. She strained her eyes. What was he up to now? He lifted a section of caging and swiftly barricaded Coco into the corner. She whipped round, but not quite in time. She was enclosed in a tiny space now, with no means of escape. Rupert retreated. He walked around, stooped and picked something up. Initially, Phoebe couldn't see what he was holding. Then, as he turned, she saw by its silhouette that it was a large, heavy-looking mallet.

Posh-but-nice Rupert had become a monster.

He advanced towards Coco and swung the mallet high with both hands. His intention was clear. He was about to crash it down on her head.

'Stop!' shrieked Phoebe. 'No! Stop!'

She flung herself forwards, stumbling blindly. She crashed to the ground, pain shooting through her veins. The next thing she knew she was sprawled against the wire, a desperate, raving creature.

'What the . . . Phoebe?'

She tried to answer, but all that came out were sobs and swear words. She was aware of him throwing the mallet to one side and rushing to remove the temporary caging. Coco slipped around the edge and galloped to safety at the far end of the run.

Phoebe attempted to get up, but her legs buckled under her.

The screaming pain was too much. Her neck, her back and her head were all on fire. She was a volcano spewing out her anguish. She could hear Rupert's voice getting louder as he approached, hear him saying things like, 'For Chrissake, what's going on? Get up, girl, stop making a scene. Phoebe, what the hell are you doing here? It's me, Rupert. I was only . . . What did you think . . . ? Get a grip, Phoebe. Hey, what's wrong with you? Do you need a doctor?'

Yes. Yes, she needed a doctor very badly indeed. She was groaning and screaming in turns. She couldn't help it. It was impossible to bite back the agony any longer.

He pulled her up, gripped her arm and started marching her forwards, into the field, towards the road. Her feet dragged along the ground as the pain ripped through her. She wailed and roared. She thumped at him with her fists.

'For pity's sake, Phoebe, I'm trying to help you!'

Unable to support her own limbs, she had sunk to the ground again. She felt his strong hands scooping her up.

She was dangling like a puppet in Rupert's arms.

Now his voice took on a softer tone: 'It's going to be all right. Don't worry. My car is just up here, not far at all. I'm going to get you to hospital, okay, Phoebe?'

Her eyes were closed, her face scrunched up with pain. She could smell his skin, a sharp, musty tang. She felt his breath on her cheek as he struggled with her weight over the rough ground, felt the up-and-down bumping of every pace he made. Her own breath came in jolts and she couldn't suck in enough air. She loathed this man, hated being close to him, detested herself for her own helplessness. If only her father were here.

At last, she was hauled a little higher and deposited in the front seat of a car, Rupert's Range Rover. The door slammed her in. She heard Rupert get into the driver's seat, heard him start the ignition.

She didn't trust him. Not one bit.

That was when the panic set in. He wasn't going to take her to hospital, no matter what he said. He was going to lock her up in some terrible place where nobody would ever find her.

34

Brave

It was another hour's drive. The headlights spangled the wet road. Al felt alert now. The skin at the back of his neck prickled and alarm propped his eyes wide open. He sat bolt upright as he drove through the darkness. What mattered now was speed. He hardly slowed down for the deer that leaped in front of the car, and narrowly avoided hitting it.

How he cursed himself for having abandoned Phoebe. He should have known she was in no fit state to be left by herself. With hindsight, all the signs had been there: the way she flinched whenever she moved her head; the way she spoke in sharp, short phrases and often bit her lip; the way her eyes closed and her brow puckered up during any little gaps in conversation. How she tried to conceal it all by smiling an extra amount. There was no doubt about it: that had been her brave face.

Jules would never have forgiven him if he'd failed to attend, but how trite and trivial the party seemed now.

Why, oh why, had Phoebe gone out on her own? It wasn't like her to act so irrationally. She knew her own physical limitations better than anyone. He could only cling on to the hope that she would be all right. He'd never known fear like this.

He must be brave, for Phoebe's sake.

Christina's answerphone message had been sparse in any details. She had just said that Phoebe was 'in a real state'. At least she had told him the name of the hospital ward where his daughter been taken, apparently after a long and distressing wait in A&E.

Christina had assured him that she and Rupert would wait until he arrived.

Thank goodness they were with her. But it didn't stop him blaming himself for not being there in her hour of need.

By the time he arrived on the outskirts of Taunton, morning was crayoning soft pink streaks through the sky. He swore out loud at the traffic lights for delaying him further. The parking meter received a further barrage of insults. He sprinted from the car park to the hospital building.

Christina assailed him from the waiting area. He felt the brush of fresh cotton as she wrapped her arms around him.

'Thank God you're here, Al!'

She stepped back. 'Nice outfit!' she couldn't help exclaiming. Al was still in his velvet jacket and felt ridiculous. Still, there were more important things to worry about now.

328

'How is she?' he asked, his voice thin and shrill.

'She's sleeping now. The doctors have given her a sedative and a massive jab to ease the pain. And they've done some blood tests. The results won't be in until later today. She seems okay at the moment, but she's in a weird state of mind and she's been rambling. She wouldn't let Rupert go anywhere near her, even though it was him who saved her.'

Rupert, who had been hovering in the background, stepped up and grasped Al's hand.

'I'm only glad I was there,' he said.

Al squeezed his hand tightly. 'Thank God you were. Please tell me what happened.'

Rupert's face was puzzled. 'It was all very strange. I was at Coco's enclosure, dropping off some fish, as Carol and I had arranged. I heard this caterwauling and looked round, and there she was – Phoebe – hurtling towards me, covered in mud. She must've come on foot from your house, but for the life of me, I couldn't say why. The poor girl was screaming and shouting her head off, then she keeled over right in front of me. It was clear straight away that something was very wrong. Unfortunately, when I tried to help her, she turned on me like a wild animal.'

Al frowned. That didn't sound like his Phoebe at all.

'Anyway, I did manage to get her up the slope to my car, but it was quite a task,' Rupert continued. 'She resisted all the way. I thought it best to get medical help as quickly as possible. I called Christina first, though, because she'd help relax Phoebe. She was at Dan and Ellie's but keen to come as soon as she heard, so she drove out to meet me. Then we brought her straight here.'

Al felt so brimming with gratitude he was close to tears.

'You did the right thing. Thank you – both of you – so, so much. Thank you.'

He was not allowed to see his daughter until he had spoken to the doctor who had examined her, which involved a torturous wait. Christina and Rupert waited with him, but their efforts at conversation fell flat and petered out when he didn't respond. He was far too anxious to talk.

The consultant was a pallid, serious young man; far too young to be entrusted with so important a case, Al thought. Still, at least he listened. Al related Phoebe's background and the whole sad saga of her illness and the fact that the medical profession had so far failed to give her a diagnosis. It was hard not to sound accusatory. He expressed his hope that tonight's adventure might, at last, lead to some sort of treatment. His overwhelming fear (too terrifying to express) was that it might now be too late.

The Teenage Doctor nodded and told him to try not to worry.

After an excruciating length of time had passed and he had given every detail his brain could muster, he was allowed to look in on Phoebe. She was fast asleep, lying on her side, twisted in an odd position. Her face was paper white. He drew the curtains around the bed, wanting to cocoon her from the other patients on the ward, hoping to make the clinical tent-like enclosure reminiscent of her bed at home. Her lips were moving, and when he bent close he could hear rapid murmured words, but couldn't make out what she was saying.

He was debating whether to wake her when she flung an arm out and cried, 'Coco!' before falling back, exhausted.

He smoothed her brow. She seemed to settle down again and was silent. Her breathing slowly deepened and steadied.

Al remembered standing by another hospital bed nine years ago, drowning in grief and disbelief. Phoebe's features looked so similar to her mother's that, as he looked down on her, it seemed as if his whole ribcage would burst, the ache was so strong. The feeling was fast followed by a shudder of raw dread. He had to grab the back of the chair to steady himself.

Christina and Rupert had driven back to Darleycombe together.

'I wish I could stay,' Christina had said, 'but I can't. Miaow will need feeding.'

Al had promised to phone and keep her updated as soon as he had any news.

He breakfasted alone at one of the hospital cafés. The lardy cake stuck in his throat and had to be washed down by a gallon of coffee. He'd bought a newspaper but, as his eyes flicked along the lines of print, his brain failed to take in any meaning from the words. He took a walk round the dull, concrete environs of the hospital, registering little of his surroundings. He wondered whether to ring Jules and Jack. He decided against it, at least until he had something definite to report.

Throughout the day, he kept popping back to the ward to see if the results of the blood tests were back yet. They came through eventually and, in a meeting with the teen-age doctor, he was told that Phoebe was suffering from a very rare condition the name of which Al couldn't pronounce and immediately forgot. It was something to do with a troublesome gland which had been misbehaving and causing an imbalance in her system.

The doctor told him that the symptoms of her illness included intense prolonged joint and muscle pain, fatigue, depression, extreme thirst, a loss of libido, nausea and a loss of appetite, weakness, coldness and mental fog. Al winced as he listened to the cruel list of words. He'd only really known about the pain. Now, as he looked back, he saw that these were all symptoms he should have seen and should have listed to the doctor in the first place. Phoebe had coped with so much for so long.

It was the last symptom that he picked up on, though, one that he could scarcely have detected.

'Mental fog?'

Even on bad days, Phoebe had always seemed bright, her thought waves often outstripping his own slow brain. Now he recalled that she used to be brighter still. She had always succeeded in working out answers while others were still struggling to understand the question.

'We need to keep an eye out for kidney stones, which are common with this condition, as well as high blood pressure,' the doctor said. He swivelled towards his computer, typed in a few lines and turned back to Al, who tried not to look as unimaginably miserable as he felt. 'Your daughter is going to need immediate surgery. The chemical balance in her blood is wrong, and her levels of calcium are dangerous. The malfunctioning gland will have to be removed straight away. We'll give her a general anaesthetic for the procedure. I'm afraid it will take her a while to recover afterwards.'

As soon as the consultation had finished, Al returned to the ward, where Phoebe was still sleeping. He sat beside her, waiting.

When she opened her eyes, they were unfocused and milky. She pulled her head off the pillow in a sharp, panicky jolt. But she flopped back and relaxed when she registered his presence. He spoke to her softly, telling her they had found out what was wrong with her, that they would operate on her soon, that they would make her well.

'Dad,' she whispered, putting out her hand to grip his. 'Are they going to give me my life back? A life where I can do things again?'

'Yes, Phoebes! Yes, they are!' he said with a tremulous smile.

'Wow,' she muttered. 'Wow.'

Hope began to unfurl quiet petals inside his chest. He could see it blossoming in her, too, and it was important she should believe in her recovery. But he wouldn't let himself acknowledge it as a possibility. Not yet. He had been disappointed before and had very little faith in medical procedures.

Phoebe started rambling again. He assumed this was all part of the 'mental fog'. It must have worsened since her bad episode because she obsessively talked about Coco and Rupert in a way that didn't make sense.

'He's trying to kill Coco' was a phrase she repeated again and again. She seemed very distressed about it,

which wasn't surprising if she thought it was true. Al
tried to change the subject, without success.

'Tell Carol. Please, Dad. *Please*.'

Her voice was choked with tears.

In the end he nodded and promised. It was vital that
Phoebe had a proper night's rest before her surgery
tomorrow.

35

Fog and Starlight

LIGHT SHONE, BLURRY and white. She tried to focus. Two faces floated above her. Much-loved faces, belonging to her father and her sister. She gazed up at them for a while, unable to register anything else. As their outlines gradually became sharper she attempted to read their expressions.

Al's was apologetic.

Jules's was angry. Incandescent.

Her voice came in a low hiss. 'Phoebe, what the hell did you think you were doing? Going out on your own like that! If you were well enough to go out on your own, you were well enough to come to my party. If you'd been at my party, you never would've collapsed. You were irresponsible and just way out of order.'

She had every right to be injured. Phoebe recollected something about a party that had been a mountainous issue, and maybe she actually *had been* well enough to go . . . just. But it would have been a huge challenge; she knew that. And anyway, if she'd gone, she wouldn't have put two and two together . . . she was sure there was something about two and two being put together and adding up to . . . what? A significant realization. The precise details eluded her. Something about otters, perhaps? It was very hard to work anything out.

'I can't believe you did that. What were you thinking?' Jules's bitterness stabbed her eardrums. Her arms were crossed closely over her chest as if she was trying to keep something in.

A clicking sound came next, and Phoebe knew it was Al cracking his knuckles. His head shifted position slightly, turning to Jules.

'Shush, please, don't be harsh. She's not well, and you're not helping.'

'I'm just saying it like it is,' snapped Jules.

Phoebe tried to speak but found that she couldn't. That thing about the otters was plaguing her.

She peered at her sister's face again, which had gone a little wobbly. There was something wrong with her eyes. The skin around them crinkled and uncrinkled, the dark pupils widened. Shining pools gathered at the corners. Suddenly there were cascades pouring down her cheeks. Drops landing on the pillow. Curtains being drawn. Sobbing.

Phoebe was aware of Al reaching into his pocket and passing something over. She heard a stifled murmur of voices then the sound of a nose being blown.

Phoebe wished she could shake everything into place. There seemed to be questions everywhere: caught between the sheets, under her pillow, swarming around the

336

bedside table, circling the lamp like moths. Questions, but no answers. She wished she could communicate better with her father and her sister.

Jules gulped and leaned towards her. The ends of her hair hung down, almost touching Phoebe's face. Her shampoo smelled of chemicalized roses. Her cheeks were flushed and wet.

'Oh, Phoebe, Phoebe. I'm so sorry to be cross.'

The words were husky. They seemed to float across a wide abyss before trickling into Phoebe's brain. When they arrived, they landed in a place of surprise.

Jules had started scrubbing at her eyes and declaiming passionately, 'I love you, I just love you so much. Please, *please*, don't die.' Her voice cracked, then hardened again. 'Don't you dare die, Phoebe.'

Phoebe attempted to tell her that no way was that going to happen, but again the words refused to come out. She wasn't even sure if her mouth would smile, even though she was trying to make it. All she could do was look at her sister and try to say with her eyes, *I'm sorry too. And I do love you too. I really do, even if I might not always show it.*

Time had passed, she knew that, but she wasn't sure how much. The light had changed; the background chatter had ebbed and flowed. Bleeps and buzzes had been going incessantly and a lot of nurses had come in and stuck needles into her arm. She still felt terribly vague about everything that had happened. It must be down to the drugs.

There was a recollection of a doctor asking her the dates of the Second World War, which she had been unbelievably hazy about, and then another one (the one her father called 'the Teenage Doctor', although he was in his mid-twenties) had stuck a tube up her nose. Apparently, it carried a camera so he could see her throat via her nasal passages. She would rather have forgotten that one. There had been screamy call buttons on the ward, so shrill they hurt. And, because she was in the Ear, Nose and Throat department, there had been constant snot-gurgling noises from her fellow patients throughout the night.

Her mind kept misbehaving, too, and every so often switched into surreal mode. At the moment, she was convinced that otters knew the answer to life, the universe and everything. If only she could work out how to speak in otter language, she would be able to save the world. Immediate action was needed because the planet was due to spontaneously combust in the very near future. She'd seen it written in a diary but, to her extreme frustration, the other humans had no idea. It was up to her to check out all the details with Coco and Paddy, as soon as she could get to them. It was a huge responsibility. It was so unfortunate she was unable to walk. Her legs crumpled under her like pipe cleaners if she even attempted it.

One of the nurses came and put a steaming polystyrene cup by her bed.

'There's the cocoa you kept asking for,' she said. 'Well, it's hot chocolate, actually, but it's the nearest we've got.'

It was all very confusing.

Often Phoebe opened her eyes to find her father there, on a chair beside her bed. Jules's and Jack's faces appeared sometimes too. Jules had placed a plastic spray of carnations near her head. Jack had appeared at her bedside with a gentle red-haired girl, the new love of his life, she presumed. They had brought a bunch of bananas and a packet of chocolate-covered raisins. Phoebe had pecked at the raisins, but the bananas were speckled with brown and giving off a strong smell.

'Somebody had better eat them,' said Al.

She watched him pull a banana away from its companions, watched it stripped of its skin then, chunk by chunk, vanishing into his mouth. While he was munching, Al chatted to her about this and that. His words didn't make much sense . . . but how good it was to have him here . . .

Christina came in, too. She was talking about the rain, and what a lot of it there was at the moment. And then she was going on and on about Rupert. Phoebe had this feeling she ought to be telling her something, but she was unable to think what that something might be. The concept of 'Rupert' made her feel knotty inside. There was a darkness associated with his name. She wished she could unscramble her thoughts, but it was as impossible as unscrambling an egg.

'We have to ask the otters,' she urged Christina. Her friend just smiled and carried on talking about herself and Rupert and an upcoming wedding.

She sank her head back on the pillows.

The next time she woke up, Jules was sitting by the bed.

'Where did Dad go?'

'He's not far away, just down the corridor. He was in need of a coffee.'

'Jack?'

'Took the train back to York today. He had to set off

early but said to say goodbye and he'll be in touch soon. And I have to go back to Plymouth later, Phoebe. I'd have liked to stay longer, but there's so much coursework to catch up on. Quick sisters' selfie before I go?'

'Um . . . so long as you don't . . .'

'Post it on social media? Oh, all right, I promise. To be honest, you're not looking too great. We can do another when you've perked up a bit.'

Jules snuggled beside her and took the shot of their two heads together.

'You're through the worst, Phoebes, do you know? You're going home tomorrow, they've told us.'

The thought of Higher Mead Cottage filled her with joy; the little routines of her life there with her father. Her beautiful bedroom. The view of the hills from the window. The rowan tree. The vegetable garden. The sound of the river.

'Am I going to be well?' she asked her sister.

Jules nodded. 'Apparently, yes.'

The whole concept was just too amazing, too hard to grasp.

Jules seemed to be grappling with a thought. 'There's something I have to say, Phoebe. I know I've not exactly been sympathetic. I'm sorry.'

'It's fine.'

'It's not. I really am sorry. I honestly had no idea you were that bad. You always seemed so smiley. Too smiley to be ill.'

Too smiley to be ill? Phoebe recalled all the trouble she'd taken over years to hunt down those smiles and pin them to her face. Perhaps she'd made the wrong call all along. Perhaps she should have made an almighty fuss.

'It's okay,' she said.

She heard a little noise which she couldn't identify for a moment, and then she realized it was a sob from Jules. Her sister very seldom cried. She seemed to be doing it a lot recently, though.

'Do you remember, Phoebe, after Mum died, you used to tell us that she had gone up in a carriage to the stars?'

Phoebe did remember. The present part of her brain was invaded by fog but that chapter in the past was as clear as a polished mirror. Her childish imagination had painted the image in detail: Ruth, pulled by six flying horses in a golden chariot, her hair flying in the breeze, her eyes reflecting the points of light as they climbed higher and higher in the night sky. In her dreams, she herself was standing on her little stumpy legs gazing upwards, alongside Al, Jules and Jack. Ruth, by now a tiny silhouette, had turned to wave goodbye before she disappeared into the starlight.

Later, Phoebe had described the scene to her family. It was the one time they had all hugged and wept together with open abandon.

Now Jules's mouth quivered and she sniffed loudly. 'I kept thinking about that, and I couldn't stop worrying that you'd gone and got your own carriage, Phoebe, and were trying to follow her. It was such a beautiful image, it truly was . . . but the thought of that separation . . . The thought of losing you . . . I just couldn't bear it.'

Her eyes had gone watery again. The sisters viewed each other, no other words necessary.

Phoebe pulled her hand out from under the bedclothes and reached it towards Jules. Jules took it and brought it up to her heart. She clutched it and held it there tightly, fiercely, as if she would never let it go.

36

Doubt

BACK AT HOME in her four-poster bed, the mud inside Phoebe's head was beginning to settle.

Only now, looking at the stamped gold elephants on the headboard, she remembered that she must urgently talk to Christina.

'Dad, can you ask Christina to come round?' she begged.

'She's already been in to see you a lot, Phoebes,' Al replied. 'I don't think we should trouble her, now that you're safe back here. She's getting married in two weeks' time and I expect she's still got tons of organizing to do.' He stared at the wall.

'No, Dad. I must speak to her. It's incredibly important. She mustn't marry Rupert.'

He took her hand and stroked her hair back. 'There's nothing you can do to stop her. She has a mind of her own. A strong one at that.'

'But don't you see?' Phoebe fretted. 'It's Rupert who's been trying to sabotage the sanctuary. It was Rupert who poisoned Coco and Paddy.'

Al didn't answer, but looked despondent. Phoebe could see that he didn't believe her. He thought the drugs were interfering again.

'Dad, I'm serious,' she pleaded.

His face, his eyes and his whole posture were giving off doubt. She could see how loath he was to trouble Christina with crazed ideas about the wickedness of her fiancé.

Phoebe put on her most reasonable voice. 'Well, could you bring me the phone, so that at least I can call her? I'd like a chat.'

He raised his hands in surrender. 'The joys of not having a mobile-phone signal,' he commented. He got up and shuffled out of the room. He returned a moment later with the nearest house phone, plugged it in and placed it on the bedside table.

'Could you bring my address book, please?'

She hated bossing him around like this but couldn't recall the number. She still felt so bleary.

Christina answered immediately with a 'Rupert, darling?'

'No, it's me: Phoebe.'

'Oh, hi there.' Christina's voice, which had been drawn out and husky, pinged back to a normal, practical tone. 'Are you at home now? Are you feeling any better?'

'Yes. And yes.'

'Hurrah!'

'I need to talk to you.'

'Oh, good, because I need to talk to you too. Do you

think there's any chance you could come to the wedding after all? I know I'm being selfish, but I don't have any spare bridesmaids, you know, so it would be fabulous if you could, and just so much lovelier in every way if you were there. Not that I want you to push yourself. You mustn't come if you're still even remotely wobbly. But I'm hoping that, by then—'

'Christina . . .'

'You'll never guess what I'm doing. I wasn't convinced that my purple wedding dress was quite sparkly enough. So I'm sewing on some extra gold braid. I *know*. It's a last-minute impulse. A bit crazy, but that's me. It's looking rather stunning, though I say so myself.'

'Uh . . . ah. Right. Christina, please listen.' It seemed so mean to say it, but somebody had to tell her. 'I think you're making a terrible – a horrible – mistake.'

'No, honestly, Phoebe. It looks lovely.'

'No, not about the braiding. About Rupert.'

A pause.

'Oh God, not that again.'

'Christina, you seriously mustn't marry Rupert. Divorce is expensive and messy and not fun at all.'

There was a long pause.

'That's not a problem, is it, dear?' she said finally. 'Because I'm not going to divorce him. We are going to be blissfully happy together.'

'You're not.'

'Thanks for the vote of confidence.'

Phoebe tugged her thoughts together and made a huge effort to express herself clearly. 'Don't marry Rupert. I mean it. He's not the man you think he is. He doesn't care for the otters at all. He's been hurting them and trying to wreck the sanctuary.'

'Don't be so ridiculous!'

'I'm not! Listen . . . I saw him holding a thingy over Coco.' Why couldn't she remember the word? 'He had a thingy and he was going to kill Coco with it.'

'A thingy? A mallet, you mean.'

Phoebe gasped. 'You know?'

'I know he had a mallet, yes. But you've got it completely wrong, darling Phoebe,' Christina argued. 'Rupert told me all about it. One of the posts of the pen had gone wobbly and he was just using the mallet to bang it in more securely.'

Phoebe gave a yelp of frustration.

'He wasn't!' she cried. 'I saw him. He had Coco trapped in a corner. I saw exactly what he was doing.'

'Phoebe, it was dark, and you can't have seen properly. And you were *ill*. Seriously ill. Nobody blames you, but it's obvious you were imagining things.'

'But that's not all.' She had to try to make Christina listen. She outlined all the facts, being as clear as she could. But her tongue felt thick and swollen, her brain was full of fuzz and the words kept coming out upside-down. Some of them slipped out of her grasp altogether and she had to substitute other words which didn't quite mean the same thing. She knew exactly what she meant, but it had become impossible to express herself like a sane person.

'I'm afraid you're not making sense, dear,' Christina said in a kind but firm voice. 'I know you mean well, Phoebe, but trust me, I know what I'm doing.'

'But you don't! You've no idea!'

'Just get some sleep, and don't worry about me. I'm going to marry Rupert, and that's that.'

Phoebe's heart sank like a block of concrete as she put down the phone. She tried to go back over everything that had happened, point by point. She tried to view Rupert from every angle, in every light. She wavered between doubts that she was wrong and panic that she was right. Either way, she was unable to think of Rupert without a cold sickness in her gut. The thought of Christina marrying him was unbearable.

Her former suspicions now appeared ridiculous. The faces of George Bovis, Rev Lucy and Seth Hardwick jostled around in her subconscious, accompanied by a sense of guilt. As she dropped off to sleep, Seth's face lingered. It started to blur at the edges and then slowly morphed into the face of Inspector Morse.

She was woken up by the phone ringing.

'Yes?'

'It's me, Carol. I won't keep you. I just wanted to call to wish you a speedy recovery, and to send my love.'

Her *love*? Carol Blake? Well, that was pretty special.

'How are the otters?' Phoebe asked, rubbing her eyes and attempting to clear her head.

'All good.'

'Carol?'

'Yes, Phoebe?'

'Do you by any chance have Seth Hardwick's phone number?'

'Yes, do you want it?'

'Please.'

She scribbled it down, wincing slightly with the effort.

The minute she'd said goodbye to Carol she rang Seth before she could let herself change her mind. He answered promptly. He sounded amazed when she said who it was. Even more amazed when she told him what it was about. Again, her words came out in a jumble, but he seemed to get the gist of what she was trying to say.

'My brain is a giant soufflé and nobody will believe me, but my instinct is still pointing to Rupert. As a *Morse man*, I thought you might get it, and I just wondered what you made of it all. Do you think there's any chance at all I might be right? Do you believe me?'

The pause went on for so long that she thought he must have gone somewhere.

'I believe you.'

For some reason, that meant a lot. She thanked him, feeling rather silly.

'I'm not sure what we can do about it, though,' he said.

'No. Nor me.'

'Perhaps I could have a word with Mr Crocker . . . but without proof . . .'

She didn't have the energy to talk any more. She would have to formulate a plan once she was feeling better.

'I'll be in touch,' she said.

Al had assured her that Coco had been released, so at least *she* was safe now. Thank heaven for that. Coco was far too clever for anyone to find her in the wild.

Phoebe thought about her beloved otter a lot. She was already missing her. She could only hope that Coco was relishing her new freedom. She envisaged her cavorting in the fresh air along the riverbank, eyes shining, whiskers bent in the wind, tail streaming behind her. Perhaps right now she'd be padding over the moss or galloping through the greenery or glorying in the mud-banks. Then she'd plunge into the cool dazzle of water. Charge after a leaf as it swept by. Tumble joyfully in the rapids and become one with the dancing silvers and sparks and swirls.

And sometimes it seemed to Phoebe as if she was gazing into her own future.

37

Precautionary Measures

WHATEVER AL WAS doing, he kept his ears strained for any noises from Phoebe's room, any sign that she might need something. She should still be in hospital, but she'd been sent home early because of a shortage of beds. He crept upstairs and looked in on her often. She only really wanted to sleep and drink water.

He hated leaving her on her own even briefly. However, Jack and Jules had left an empty fridge, so it was necessary to get some provisions in. Luckily, the village shop was well stocked and only a quick drive away.

The visibility was bad and he had to keep the windscreen wipers on at high speed. He could only just make out the shape of stooping trees behind the sheets of rain. The Darle, normally so clear, looked thick and soupy. Thousands upon thousands of drops drilled holes as they met the water's surface. Thousands upon thousands of circles spread outwards.

Al noticed that Spike Dobson had sandbags outside his house, stacked neatly around the front door. So did several other houses that fronted the river.

He managed the shopping as quickly as possible, then splashed through puddles and dived back into the car with the bags. Before returning home, he pulled in at Christina's and knocked gingerly at her door. Phoebe had persuaded him to call in, although she'd given no reason apart from urging him to tell Christina not to marry Rupert – something he had no intention of doing. He would give Christina an update about Phoebe's health, though.

Christina and Miaow appeared simultaneously at the door. Christina grinned and beckoned him in. He stood, dripping self-consciously, in the hallway.

'Wow, you're soaking,' she said.

'Yes, sorry about that. It happened in a matter of seconds.'

Miaow wound around his legs, then said her name and stood on her hind legs, pushing her head towards his hand.

'Okay, here's your stroke,' he said as he stooped down and caressed her. With a loud rasp of a purr, she gazed up at him with adoration.

'I don't know why she likes you so much,' said Christina. 'She's normally funny with men. She absolutely detests Rupert. Hisses every time he goes near her.'

Al gave Miaow another stroke, feeling an unexpected surge of affection towards her.

Christina raised her eyebrows. 'I'm beginning to think

I should worry, what with Miaow not liking Rupert and now Phoebe not liking him either.' She laughed. 'Only kidding! What's really worrying me is this weather.'

'Yes, it's not good news, is it?' he said. 'Do you have sandbags? Do you need any help with them?'

He didn't have any himself, but then, he and Phoebe lived in a safer position. Higher Mead Cottage was on raised ground and would be fine, even if the bottom half of the garden became waterlogged.

'Oh, it's not going to flood,' Christina declared buoyantly. 'I'm just concerned for the wedding. Yesterday I ordered six pretty purple umbrellas so we can still pose outside the church for the wedding photos, even if it's tipping it down. So if there's a big package for me, that's what it will be.'

'I've taken a couple of weeks off work,' Al told her.

She mimed slapping her own face. 'Of course. Of course you have. How's Phoebe doing?'

When he had asked Phoebe the same question earlier, she had answered: 'Hexadecimal, thank you.'

Al informed Christina that at present his daughter was still very weak and confused, but full of hope. She vacillated between excitement at the idea of a complete recovery and dread that she'd never be able to walk again. But she'd said the pain levels were a lot more tolerable. That in itself was beyond wonderful.

'And you?'

'Cautiously optimistic,' said Al.

'I don't suppose she'll be recovered enough to contemplate being my bridesmaid?'

Al shook his head. In Phoebe's current state of mind,

even if she made it to the church, she might make a scene at the 'If anyone knows any lawful impediment' part of the ceremony. He wouldn't put it beyond her to shout 'Otter murderer!' at Rupert at the very point when he stood with Christina at the altar, about to make their vows.

'But you'll come, Al, won't you?'

He hesitated. It had suddenly become difficult to look her in the eye. He ought to support her, and he'd promised to help ring the bells, yet he had not the slightest wish to be at the ceremony.

'It would mean a lot to me to have you there. Even just the church bit, if you need to get back to Phoebe quickly?' she suggested.

'Well, I'll see how she's doing. I'll come if I can.'

He pulled at each of his fingers and made the knuckles crack, a habit that Phoebe always said he must try to avoid in public.

'Won't you come in properly and have some tea?'

Al declined, saying he had stayed out far longer than he had intended and really should be getting back now.

'Probably just as well,' Christina answered. 'It's utter chaos in here. I've got gold braid and cotton all over the kitchen table. Jazzing up the bridal dress; it had to be done. Let me know as soon as Phoebe is well enough for visitors. And give her my love, won't you?'

He drove back with care. The road shone with puddles. On the slope, the tarmac was covered in muddy ripples, cascading downwards.

It was such a shame that Phoebe's best friend in the village would be moving away so soon to be with Rupert.

Even though it wasn't far, Christina would inevitably be paying his daughter less attention once she was married. He hoped Phoebe would still go and draw the otters, even if she had to do it on her own. Otter therapy was so good for her.

How odd it was that Phoebe had developed all these delusions about Rupert. She was wrong, of course. Rupert was a great guy, everyone thought so. Al had never much warmed to the man himself, but that was no doubt due to paranoid feelings of male inadequacy to do with height. If Rupert hadn't been there at Coco's soft-release site that night, would Phoebe even still be alive? She couldn't have walked any further, so she would have been stuck there for goodness knows how long. In spite of Phoebe's resistance, Rupert had done the responsible thing. He'd taken her to hospital straight away and kindly brought her close friend along too.

Al would have to take Rupert out for a drink, or send him a bottle of whisky at the very least, to say thank you.

Nevertheless, he felt a lurking undercurrent of distrust for Rupert. Phoebe's anti-Rupert rants over the last few days must be getting to him. Perhaps the bottle of whisky would be the better option.

As soon as he got in, he called up: 'Back home now, Phoebe! Lots of goodies to eat!'

A faint voice called back from upstairs. He unloaded the shopping into the fridge and went up to see if she was ready for a meal. He was hungry himself.

Phoebe had finished all the water in the glass by her bed and asked for more. She wasn't keen on the idea of food but agreed to try a small slice of omelette if he was making one anyway. He assured her that he was and headed back to the kitchen.

When he'd cooked it and taken it up, she didn't even manage all of the small scrap he'd put on her plate. He polished it off himself in one mouthful. As he was stacking up the plates, she pulled the duvet higher around her shoulders.

'Dad, can I ask you a favour? Would you mind staying in my room tonight? You could maybe sleep in the armchair? I'm probably being silly, but I feel . . .' She trailed off then took a breath. 'To be honest, I feel scared. I think something awful might be about to happen.'

He stared at her. 'Gosh, don't talk like that, Phoebe. That's not like you at all.'

'No, I suppose it isn't,' she said, gnawing at her lip. 'It's just that last night I dreamed that Rupert came into my bedroom with a mallet. He lifted it over my head and . . . It was horribly real.'

Al frowned. 'They gave you a pretty strong cocktail in that general anaesthetic, didn't they?'

Still, he was glad that she had told him about her fear, glad that she had reached out to him for help. If she wanted him to spend the night in the armchair, then that's what he would do.

38

Captivity

'Dad?'

His voice replied out of the darkness. 'Yes? Are you okay, Phoebes?'

'Yes . . . Well, no . . . I don't know. I feel very odd.'

She had been dreaming that she was locked in a cage, with people trooping past, looking at her; people who had no idea how badly she longed to be free. The cage wasn't like the enclosures at the sanctuary, with space to run around. It was so cramped she couldn't move at all. Not her arms, not her legs: nothing. The dream was vile and the horror of it lingered. And that wasn't all . . .

At night-time, reality always became blurry. Night was when monsters of the mind arose to torment you about problems that melted away with the daylight. Yet Phoebe was sure her mind wasn't playing tricks on her this time.

She didn't want to be alarmist, but she couldn't just lie there and ignore what was happening.

'You know the doctor said we must contact the surgery straight away if I got tingles in my fingers and toes? Well, I've got tingles in my fingers and toes.'

Al stirred in the armchair, where he'd settled with a blanket over him.

'How bad is it?' He sounded groggy.

'Well . . . Just a tingling so far. It doesn't hurt,' she added, which was definitely a reason to be cheerful. Still, the tingling worried her. She had no idea how serious it was. She was hoping Al would make a decision.

She heard him struggling to his feet, and a moment later the light flicked on. It was so bright her eyes automatically closed again. When she opened them, his face was looking down on her, his eyebrows drawn together. The fabric of the chair cover had left a pattern imprinted on his left cheek. His eyelids were drooping.

He consulted his watch. It was three o'clock in the morning.

'We can't ring the local surgery now. It will be closed.'

'Shall we wait a while and see if the tingles go away?' she suggested.

He perched on the side of the bed, his eyes fixed on her face. She hated herself for waking him, especially as she'd made him spend the night somewhere so uncomfortable and he'd probably only just got off to sleep. Was she acting like a spoilt brat? If so, she couldn't help it. Everything had been so upsetting and abnormal recently. She had no control over her mind or her body, no idea whether she could still trust her own instincts.

The tingling continued. She tried to wriggle her toes to relieve it. They wouldn't cooperate. Experimentally, she tried to stretch her index finger. It wouldn't cooperate either. In fact, none of her fingers or toes would move at all.

Al was hanging his head and looking as if he was about to drop off again.

'Sorry, Dad, but I think I need help.'

'I could take you to A&E, if you're sure?' he said, rousing himself.

'Maybe best.'

She tried to sit up and managed it, just.

It would be seriously embarrassing to go to A&E in her unicorn pyjamas. She started reaching for the heap of clothes on the upright chair, but her arms couldn't manage the task. They felt as useless as discarded chicken bones.

'Dad, can you help me dress, please?' The words sounded so pathetic.

'Of course,' he murmured.

He helped her lift the pyjama top over her head, easing her arms out of the sleeves. This was all too surreal. Never in her life had she felt so peculiar and helpless. He pulled her clothes around her, tugging and pushing her limbs as if she were a puppet.

It was so ridiculous that she burst into hysterical laughter.

'Let me just get a coffee,' he mumbled. 'I don't think I'm safe to drive without having one first.'

He must have concluded she wasn't too bad because of the laughter. He disappeared downstairs for a few moments. By the time he was back, every part of her was paralysed. She wasn't laughing now. It was as if she'd been filled with molten metal that had suddenly hardened. The skin on her face had become tight, stretched over her skull. Her tongue was stuck, too, and her whole palate was numb.

Al was glugging coffee from his mug. He had no idea she was unable to speak.

'Let's get you to the car, then,' he said.

She didn't reply, didn't move.

She had become a statue. He was cottoning on now. 'Um, can you manage to get downstairs, Phoebe?'

She tried to shake her head. She couldn't.

He plonked down the coffee and hoisted her in his arms. It was just as well she'd lost so much weight and he was strong. Her body sagged, a useless bundle. She leaned against his chest, worried, as he carried her downstairs, that he might drop her. She could sense his fear and exhaustion, hear his gasping breath. But how much better it was being carried by her dear father than by that rat Rupert.

Al leaned her against the wall as he opened the front door. She flopped forwards as he picked her up again. The night air gusted through her, filled with cold spears of rain.

He posted her into the passenger seat of the car, strapped her in. Now her eyes had gone fuzzy. She couldn't see a thing. Blindness, immobility . . . what on earth was happening to her? It was baffling. Terrifying. She kept trying to form words, but they wouldn't come out. Her lips and tongue simply refused to function. She wrestled with them, desperate to let her father know there wasn't much time left. At last she managed to push out the word 'Ambulance!'

Al's voice came to her ears, faint but sure. 'No, Phoebe, it'll be much quicker if I take you myself.' He pressed her palm with his own. She heard the car engine splutter and start.

Thank goodness her hearing was still okay. She felt as if there was an iron rod inside her. Her face had frozen completely.

This was it; this must be it: the beginning of the end. A sad realization. She would loved to have done more with her life.

She wasn't scared of dying, though. Who knew – it might be rather nice? She didn't hold any religious beliefs as such, but for all she knew she might be heading for some sort of afterlife, and it would be an adventure. Jules had reminded her of her childhood belief that her mother had gone up to the stars in a carriage. She imagined the same horse-drawn carriage touching down to collect her and sweeping her up. How wonderful it would be if she did, somehow, get to see her mother again. Or maybe her spirit would just drift on the wind, unconscious, at one with the world, freed from this wretched block of a body at last.

She felt upset for her father, though. Al would miss her terribly. He would be heartbroken for a long, long time and might never recover. If only she had managed to get him together with Christina! She would have done much to ease his loneliness. Thank goodness he still had Jack and Jules.

Al's fingers gripped hers as he drove one-handed, letting go only occasionally to change gear.

'You're doing great, Phoebe,' he said. It was far from the truth, but she loved him for saying it. What a dear, dear man he was, the very best and most devoted of fathers. She was determined to appreciate being with him these last few hours. Or moments. She silently thanked him for the comfort he provided, for everything he had done throughout her short existence.

Then she was struck by a thought, a terrible possibility. Her body might refuse to let go. It might hang on to life yet remain in this state of complete paralysis. She could live on for decades, trapped inside a useless, non-functioning lump of flesh. The idea of it made her scream inwardly. She imagined her whole life stretching into the future like this: unable to move a muscle, unable to communicate in any way, kept alive on a machine. No, God no, she couldn't bear it.

Alongside the panic, she was assailed by a memory. She had once seen a TV programme about a man who had lived in whole-body paralysis for years, fed by drips, lying stationary in a hospital bed. His wife (surely an angel) had possessed the perfect combination of patience and stubbornness. She had stuck with him, visiting him daily and talking to him, even though she had no idea if he was aware of her presence at all. Yet he seemed to look at her, and she believed he could still use his brain. The only way he could convey anything at all was to blink. And somehow, they had worked out a blinking language together. Phoebe remembered that a slow single blink meant yes and a double blink meant no.

Al had watched the programme too, but she doubted he would recall the details. Still, if anyone asked her whether they should turn off her life-support machine, she knew already that she would give a slow, deliberate single blink. That was assuming she was able to open her eyes at all . . .

The terror of this thought was the last thing she experienced as they drove through the night, on and on, into the relentless, beating rain.

39

The Dress and the Peugeot

AL DROVE IN a state of shock. He had assumed everything would be all right now, and that the only thing he'd have to do was feed Phoebe and wait for her recovery. What the hell was going on? Nobody had suggested she might go downhill so quickly. 'A tingling' was all the doctor had mentioned. That sounded pretty mild. How he wished he'd asked more questions.

When he'd dressed Phoebe he had been horrified to see that both her arms were blackened with bruises from all the blood tests. Even more horrifying was the fact that now she could neither speak nor move. He squeezed her small, fragile hand. It didn't squeeze back.

The clatter of rain on the car roof drilled into his ears. As he drove, he caught glimpses of the dark river, running alongside the road, engorged but greedy. It grabbed twigs and stones and anything within its reach, tearing up young saplings from their roots, sweeping all manner of debris along in its clutches. In several places it had burst its banks and he had to drive through floods stretching across the road. He couldn't see the tarmac at all in the headlamps, just a shining wing of water splayed across it.

'God, why now? Why now?'

He bit his lip and wished he hadn't said it aloud. Phoebe had enough to worry about. She didn't respond. When he glanced across at her, he saw in the watery moonlight that her eyes were clamped shut. Her face looked strangely pinched.

He must talk to her. He must find something reassuring to say.

'We're just coming to the middle of Darleycombe now, and it's lovely weather for the duck couple.'

No ducks were in sight, however. As he drove further into the village, he saw that a fallen branch had blocked the flow under the bridge, sending another massive swell of water over the surrounding land. The water had already claimed half of the village green.

'This is a bit of an adventure, isn't it, Phoebes?'

He detested the thin flippancy in his voice, so added: 'Everything's going to be all right.'

Let it be true, he prayed.

He wasn't sure whether it was best to go fast through the deep flood to keep the momentum of the car going or to proceed more slowly. At the moment, with Phoebe in this state, speed seemed like the best option. He accelerated a little and told himself to keep it steady. The tyres shifted unhappily, losing contact with solid ground. He was about halfway through when the engine spluttered and conked out.

'Oh God! Oh God, no!' he groaned.

Automatically, he reached for his phone and switched it on, but of course it told him there was no mobile signal. *Damn, damn, damn.*

He turned the ignition on and off a few times. It coughed weakly and wouldn't engage.

'Looks like we're in a pickle, Phoebe.'

At least they were in a populated area rather than the middle of nowhere. He did a quick recce of his surroundings and realized that, in fact, they were very close to Christina's cottage.

He pushed open the car door and jumped out. His feet plunged into icy water.

In a moment he was round at the other side of the car. Phoebe was terrifyingly still and quiet.

'Can you move at all?' he asked her. There was no answer.

'Come on, Phoebes. I need you to try.'

Silence. To get Phoebe to dry land he would have to carry her again.

'Okay. Sorry about this.'

It was more difficult getting her out than it had been getting her in. He twisted his back as he heaved her weight towards him, then couldn't avoid trailing her feet in the water. Eventually, he had her in his arms again, in a firm hold. She was light for her age, but with the water pulling him about and her complete inability to cooperate, he wobbled a bit. A memory rippled through his head of giving her a piggyback when she was a toddler. He had bounded with happiness then, so delighted he was almost flying. Not like now.

He sloshed along, the thudding of his heart almost as loud as the swish and roar. Cold pellets of rain struck his head and arms. He wanted to shield Phoebe from them but didn't have enough hands.

As he approached Christina's cottage, a flotilla of random objects was bobbing in the water around him. He couldn't see them clearly enough to identify them, but he hoped these were items from people's gardens rather than their houses. In normal circumstances, he'd go and help the flooded residents cart sandbags around and move their valuables upstairs, do whatever was needed. Now he could only think of getting Phoebe to hospital.

Christina would help, he was sure of it. Her purple Peugeot was in the drive. Although it was the middle of the night, lights shone through her curtains. Water was lapping against the front door. He was nearly there when a soft, sodden shape brushed against him. It wrapped itself around his legs, making it difficult to proceed. He hauled Phoebe up over his shoulder and yanked at the thing to try to remove it.

A glint of gold braid shone in the moonlight.

'It's only Christina's goddamn wedding dress,' he muttered.

He managed to scoop it up, clutching Phoebe hard, and dangled it over his other shoulder before pounding on Christina's door.

No answer. He wondered if she must be at Rupert's house after all. But after a few moments, curtains were drawn back and her silhouette appeared at the window. It opened.

'Oh, it's you, Al. Thank heaven you came!' Her voice was taut. 'I made the mistake of opening the front door ten minutes ago and was hit by a tsunami. My floor is inches deep in water and half my stuff has escaped. And I can't find Miaow. What the hell are you carrying . . . Oh . . . Oh my Lord, Phoebe!'

'Please can you open up, Christina. She's in a very bad way. My car is stuck in the flood and we have to get her to hospital quickly.'

She disappeared and, within three seconds, the front door opened, letting another great gush past her and into the house. Al splashed in. The whole ground floor was awash with grey water.

'I found this,' he said, draping her heavy, wet wedding dress on the banister.

'Oh cripes, thanks!' she cried, at the same time putting her arms around the dishevelled hump that was Phoebe.

They briefly discussed calling an ambulance before deciding to try Christina's car.

'An ambulance would have to come all the way from Taunton, so this way we'll be quicker,' she said. 'If we can get through this flood, we'll be on the high ground. And when we get to the top of the hill there'll be a mobile signal so we can call an ambulance from the road if the worst comes to the worst. I'll drive.'

'Thanks. Thanks so much. Great,' said Al. Nothing was great, in fact, except for Christina's cooperation. Without a second's hesitation, she was prepared to abandon her flooded house and her drowning possessions and even the missing Miaow in order to get Phoebe to hospital.

They bundled into her car. She drove like a maniac and, with the engine roaring, powered through the flood and up the hill beyond.

'I'm so glad you were in,' Al confessed. 'I thought you might be at Rupert's.'

'No, I haven't managed to get hold of him,' Christina answered. 'He'll be at the otter sanctuary. The barriers there are right on the water's edge, so Carol will need his help making everything secure.'

Al was grateful for her company as they sped through the storm, even though they didn't talk much. Christina spoke more to Phoebe than to him.

'I wonder how Coco is getting on now,' she said, making her voice sound remarkably cheerful. 'I expect she'll be just fine. She is so much better equipped than us humans to deal with the elements.'

If anything could rouse Phoebe, it would be talk of Coco. But there was never any answer.

40

Lifelines

THE MEDICAL STAFF lifted Phoebe in on a stretcher, just as the sun was rising. Al's heart quailed to see his daughter laid out, motionless like a church effigy. Of course, none of the medics in A&E knew the history and it was up to him once more to try to explain her long illness, sudden collapse and subsequent surgery. He was so shattered and upset he could hardly string words together. He prised the information out of his limp brain, spoke slowly and hoped he hadn't missed out anything important.

The earnest young nurse, predictably, decided a blood test was the correct thing to do. When she pushed up Phoebe's sleeve, needle poised, she couldn't find any patch of skin free of bruises. She searched both arms and selected a tiny area where the skin was not quite as grey as everywhere else. The needle slid in but, even after prodding and angling, she failed to extract any blood at all.

'Never mind,' she said chirpily. 'We'll try again, some-where else.'

She kept trying. Needle after needle punctured Phoebe's flesh up and down both arms until Al couldn't bear to watch any more.

Christina had been told to stay in the waiting area. He popped out to update her.

'Nothing. They won't give her any treatment until they get a blood sample, and they can't manage to get a blood sample.'

'They'll keep on until they do. You look shaken, Al. Let me get you some tea.'

She filled a cup from a machine and made him drink before he went back in. The tea was dung-coloured and -flavoured, but the shot of warmth was very welcome.

Fifteen minutes later he came out again. Christina sat staring into space with her hands folded in her lap. How glad he was of her company. Her presence helped steady him. She looked up at him expectantly.

He shook his head. 'The nurse has given up and sent in another nurse. He's not managing to get any blood either. They must have tried a dozen times between them. She's still . . .'

He covered his face, distraught.

He had lost his wife. He could not lose his daughter. He could not.

Christina sprang up and engulfed him in a tight hug. 'Poor Phoebe!' she cried. 'And poor you. But she'll know you're there with her, I'm sure of it. You're doing great.'

He tried to reply, but putting anything into words was like trying to build a house out of water vapour. He let himself be held, his eyes half closed. A sob swelled in his throat. He swallowed it back down, with effort, but it kept on rising again, threatening to overtake his whole body.

How could he even begin to comprehend a world without Phoebe? His heart cried out that it was impossible, yet his head insisted it might happen. It might happen very soon. Despair surged through him in a great, black tide that was so fierce it knocked the air from his lungs. He must get back to her. He must be at her side . . . but he was empty of the strength required to keep seeing her suffering, to keep standing by, powerless to help.

With a slight glugging sound, he made himself let go of Christina.

She pressed something into his hand. It was a new pair of men's Argyle socks, olive green and very thick. 'Got these from the hospital gift shop,' she said. 'Your feet are soaking . . . and a father with foot rot isn't going to be much help to Phoebe, is he?'

Al looked down. It was true. His trouser legs were caked in mud, his shoes were claggy and chafing, his socks still sodden. In his anxiety, he hadn't even noticed. He glanced around, unsure if he could get away with changing his footwear here, unwilling to spend time seeking out the hospital conveniences.

'I've always liked Snickers,' one middle-aged woman was telling another, while a young couple fiddled with their phones and a silver-haired man turned the page of his newspaper with a huff of disapproval about the rise in fuel prices. Snapshots from other lives, lives oblivious of the dramas that were going on in his own.

'Just do it here,' said Christina.

370

He quickly peeled off his shoes and socks. The touch of the new socks was so warm and soft it brought tears to his eyes.

He crept back in. How he wished there was something – anything – he could do for his daughter. She was still lying there like a discarded doll, her hair a tangle, her face white as ash. He touched her fingers. They were cold.

The nurses were discussing the case, the lack of a blood sample. Their voices were grave. Their faces registered frustration. They were clearly not used to this situation.

'How about getting it from her legs . . . or a foot?' Al suggested, trying not to sound like an old fool in tears.

They frowned. 'Not a good idea,' one of them replied. 'That would be extremely painful for her.'

Several more unsuccessful attempts to extract blood from her arm and they were willing to try, though. The needle was inserted into a vein in her foot. Al watched, breathless, through scrunched-up eyes. Phoebe didn't flinch.

A tiny thread of red appeared in the phial.

The results of the test were through.

'They've decided to give her a shot of calcium.'

Christina nodded encouragingly. 'I expect that's the thing, then.'

Al's hope was faint as the dose was administered. Calcium was the sort of mild ingredient you got in a vitamin pill, surely not a cure for sudden-onset whole-body paralysis?

He sank into the chair beside his daughter, his eyes glued to her face.

What followed didn't seem real. It had the quality of a miracle. It reminded him of a passage from *The Lion, the Witch and the Wardrobe* that he'd read to her when she was a child: the scene in which Aslan breathed on stone statues and, bit by bit, colour spread through them as they transformed and became living, breathing creatures again.

Phoebe's fingertips stretched. Her toes wriggled. Her mouth twitched. A faint flush of pink appeared on her cheeks.

The first nurse was watching too, fascinated. 'Oh, look at that!' she exclaimed after a moment, unable to contain her surprise. 'Her face is changing.'

It was! It looked less rigid. More fleshed out. More like Phoebe.

'She's smiling!' cried the nurse.

As life gradually seeped back through his daughter's bloodstream, relief spread through Al like a warm current.

'Phoebe?' he said. 'Phoebe.'

Her eyes fluttered open.

'Dad!' she murmured. 'Hi. I think I'm back.'

His heart brimmed over and over with love. He leaned down and planted a kiss on his daughter's forehead, but was too choked up to say anything more.

41

Luminescent

AL FETCHED CHRISTINA, who jumped up and hugged him again, thrilled at the news.

'She's in observation now,' he said. 'We can both go and see her.'

They went to the ward together and sat with Phoebe for a while. She didn't communicate much, but beamed at them hazily until her eyelids drifted closed.

'She's asleep,' whispered Al.

Christina gave him a thumbs-up. 'She will be all right, you know.'

'Yes. I believe she will.'

They went in search of the hospital canteen, both badly in need of coffee and breakfast. He treated Christina to a vegetarian full English and got one for himself too. He was surprised at how delicious it was. And for the first time, the sense of it struck him: why eat dead pig when vegetable protein tasted this good? He would certainly be trying a few more veggie meals in the future.

'And how are *you* doing?' he asked Christina.

'Oh, I'm tip-top.'

He didn't believe it but had to admire her spirit. She was looking shattered, and now he remembered that she had dire concerns of her own. Her house, by now, would be even more flooded. Her possessions were swimming around. And who knew what had happened to her beloved Miaow?

She could have gone back to Darleycombe long before now.

'What I do want to know,' she said, 'is what has happened to Rupert. He might have called, even if he *is* busy helping out at the sanctuary.' She twisted and twiddled her paper napkin between her fingers. 'I've tried phoning him and left loads of messages, but I haven't heard a squeak from him.'

Al pulled at his collar, overcome by a barrage of guilt. 'Please don't feel you have to stay here now. You'll need to get back and find him. And find Miaow, and check on your house. I wish I could help, but I feel my place is here with Phoebe.'

'Absolutely!' she cried. 'Understood. But you can't stay here for ever. How will you get home?'

'I'll take a bus or a taxi later. I'll find a way. Christina, I can't thank you enough for your help today.'

He involuntarily took her hand across the table. She let him hang on to it. If she noticed that he was still a bit tearful, she didn't mention it.

He walked her back to the Peugeot.

'Please send me updates,' she said. 'I'll check my phone whenever I'm anywhere with a signal, and check my landline too, when I'm back home. I love Phoebe too,' she admitted. 'I need to know how she's doing.'

His voice came out scratchy. 'Drive safe, and good luck.'

He was sorry to see her go. The barriers between them had come down during the night. *What a mosaic of different parts is Christina*, he thought as he headed back to the ward. She was made up of emotion and high spirits and kindness and passion and courage. And she really cared about what was important . . . such as Phoebe. He wished she could have stayed here by his side.

He bought a gardening magazine and went back to wait by Phoebe's bed. He turned the pages silently, glancing at his daughter every so often, heartened that her sleeping face looked so peaceful. Eventually, he saw that her eyes were open and she was gazing back at him. She looked reflective.

'Dad,' she said. 'I'm still here. How nice. I thought I was a goner.'

He didn't like to say, 'Me too,' so he said: 'Of course not. You, Phoebe? Never! I was never going to let that happen. Neither was Christina,' he added as an afterthought.

Thank you, she mouthed.

'How are you feeling?' he asked.

She shifted position slightly and gave a wry smile. 'I'm amazingly crepuscular, thank you. And you?'

'Quite . . . quite luminescent, thank you, Phoebes.'

She closed her eyes for a second then opened them again. 'Life's interesting, isn't it?'

'It certainly is, Phoebes.'

'And good, on the whole.'

He considered the horrors of war, famine, crime and the thousands of people suffering all over the world at any one minute. He glanced inward at the deep scars left by the loss of his wife. He looked back on all Phoebe's years of pain. Life was unjust and fickle and spiteful and vicious. And yet, when you had moments like this, moments of intense relief that were so good they hurt . . . when you experienced miracles that shone like stars in the darkness of human existence . . .

'It is good, Phoebe, yes. It absolutely is.'

He returned, wet-eyed, to the hospital newsagent's and sought out a detective novel for his daughter. He sat with her for most of the day and read the first few chapters aloud, even though he wasn't sure she was taking in much. He updated Christina regularly, going outside to roam the car park, sending texts and voicemails.

Phoebe is doing fine. Much better. Talking about the otters. How's the house? Any news of Miaow? Rupert?

The first he heard back was a text. *Phew! I'm so glad she's okay. Give her all my love.*

No news from her, so he asked again.

A message pinged back. *House is not good. Miaow and Rupert both missing. Must stay hopeful. Phoebe is okay – that's the main thing.* Her words were followed by a row of smiley emojis.

Of course, there were no buses that would take him all the way to Darleycombe, but he let her know he would be taking a taxi back at seven, when the hospital wouldn't let him stay any longer. He would be at her service as soon as he arrived back, to help in the hunt for Miaow, at the very least.

She replied by voicemail. 'Al, don't take a taxi. I'll come and pick you up. Nothing to do here. Let me know you've got this message.'

He answered immediately with a 'Thank you so much' and an 'Are you sure?'

Yes, sure.

When she arrived to fetch him she was full of questions about Phoebe. He answered as many as he could.

They drove out of town and into the Exmoor hills. He gazed out of the window at the tired, torn landscape.

Christina said, 'Things are bad in the village. It's not just my house and the immediate neighbours. I visited the sanctuary this afternoon. One of the outside barriers has been washed away. Most of the otters have gone.'

'Gone?'

'Swum away. Upriver, downriver, who knows?'

'Oh no!'

'I'm afraid so. Seth Hardwick was helping Carol make safe the enclosures that were left, but she's devastated. She doesn't think the otters can survive in the wild. Some of them aren't even native to this country, and none of them are used to hunting for themselves. Quercus has gone, and he can't run fast because of his injury. Rowan, Holly, Hawthorn and all the Asian otters are gone too. It's just so awful.'

'I'm so sorry.'

It was all he could say. What a horrible twenty-four hours it had been. He was still so relieved about Phoebe that there was little energy left for mourning the otters, but that new, cold truth would sink in later. Phoebe would be gutted when she found out. The otter sanctuary meant so much to Christina, too. She hadn't mentioned Rupert again. Al presumed he must have been with her there this afternoon. He couldn't bring himself to ask.

The rain had eased off at last. Trees hunched at the roadside, crippled by the wind, and everything was browner than before. They passed fields drenched with water. A heron, looking rather pleased with itself, had settled on one of them.

Christina fixed her eyes ahead. 'I'm going to go via the back road into the village to avoid that big flood. Your car is still there, by the way.'

'I'll call out the AA tomorrow. I'm just too knackered to deal with it tonight.'

'Of course you are. I'd invite you in for a meal, but my house is rather . . .'

'Christ, sorry, of course it is. You're welcome to stay over with me tonight . . .' He stumbled over his words. 'There's at least one spare bed . . . But I expect Rupert has already got you sorted . . .'

She shook her head. As if they'd been waiting for the cue, tears sprang from her eyes and gushed down her cheeks.

'No. Bloody Rupert still hasn't contacted me, even though I've left a million messages. And he wasn't at the sanctuary either. I checked with Carol, and she hasn't seen anything of him since the flood began. So I drove to his house after I visited the sanctuary. Nobody was in. His car wasn't there either. I'm so worried something awful has happened.'

Al longed to comfort her, but the right vocabulary eluded him. He could find nothing to say other than 'Blimey!'

'Sorry, Al. You don't want to be worrying about this now.'

'No, no, you go ahead and cry. Don't mind me. It's quite understandable.'

Now she was openly sobbing.

'Not that anything bad will have happened,' he added quickly. 'I expect . . . I expect something came up and he'll be on the phone to you as soon as he has a minute.'

She gulped. 'I hope you're right.'

'Do come over to Higher Mead Cottage in the meantime. Only if you want to, of course.'

'Yes, please,' she whimpered. 'I'd be so grateful. I really don't want to stay in a flooded house tonight. I could call on Dan and Ellie – they're on high ground – but they don't have a spare room and their place is overflowing with harps – you can hardly move for them. Not to mention Ed's toys and the pet pheasant, who is always coming in and out. It would be hard for them to squeeze me in. I'd love to come back to yours, if you really, truly, don't mind. But would it be all right if I pop back home first, just to see if Miaow has turned up?'

'Of course,' he said. 'Of course, Christina, we must do that.'

They were passing the fish farm. Christina turned her head and pointed through the windscreen.

A huge tree had been uprooted and blown down across the area. The end of one of the buildings was crushed. Its walls had crumpled inwards and the roof sat skewed with a great gash across it. A length of fencing was squashed and laid flat, its posts sticking out at all angles. Brown water lapped across the yard, cluttered with debris.

'Looks like they're in trouble too,' Christina said. Then she let out a gasp. 'That's Rupert's car! What on earth is he doing here?'

She swerved into the drive and pulled up next to the Range Rover.

They got out. Al could hardly keep up with her, she was striding so fast towards the buildings, heedless of the mud that was splattering up her trousers with every pace. Before long they caught sight of a couple of figures. Rupert was standing, viewing the devastation and gesticulating towards it, deep in conversation with another man.

As soon as he saw her, he took a step forward. 'Christina!'

'Oh, thank God you're all right!'

She was about to plunge into his arms but halted abruptly just short of him. There was something odd about his expression that Al couldn't quite make out but which had stopped her in her tracks.

'Rupert, what's going on? Why are you here? Why haven't you answered my messages? I've been sick with worry about you.'

'I . . . There have been a few problems,' he blustered. He made as if to embrace her, then didn't, seeing Al with her. Al knew he wasn't looking his friendliest.

The other man had walked up too. 'Hello, Christina.'

At once Al spotted the resemblance between the two men. The brother was a little stockier but had the same

380

height, facial features and imposing presence. Christina ignored him, firing questions at Rupert.

'Didn't you read my texts or hear my calls? My house is flooded, and Miaow is missing, and Phoebe's in hospital again.'

Now his face displayed concern. 'So very sorry to hear that. I haven't managed to check my messages. No signal here, as you know, and I've just been unbelievably busy helping my brother out.'

'And the otter sanctuary . . . you must have heard?'

'No.'

'Terrible damage, and most of the otters have gone.' Her eyes veered towards the other man. 'Hang on, what did you just say? Helping your brother out? You're something to do with the fish farm, then?'

Rupert and his brother exchanged glances. Neither of them spoke.

'Just tell me, please,' Christina begged. 'I'm so tired and confused.'

The brother viewed her with what might have been compassion. 'You should really know the truth, since you're going to marry Rupert,' he said softly.

'The truth?' she echoed, gazing at them both. Rupert was stock still now.

Al watched, aware of an odd, clammy chill in the region of his heart.

'Yes, we jointly own this fish farm,' the brother answered. 'Although I don't know where we go from here. The flood and the fallen tree have combined forces and pretty much ruined the business. Ironic, really, after all Rupert's efforts.'

Rupert eyed his brother with a minimal shake of his head.

Christina stared at him, everything about her demanding answers. 'I . . . I can't take this in! You own the fish farm?'

'Family business,' he said. 'My brother does the practical side and I do the accounting, mostly. I was waiting for the right moment to tell you.'

'But . . . this is so weird. We've been together all these months, we're about to get married, and you didn't even tell me this key thing about your life?'

He shrugged. 'Sorry, my lovely,' he said to her. 'I had to try and win you over somehow. I had to show you only the best of me. And you always were more enthralled with otters than with fish.'

She threw her arms up. 'You're not making sense.'

'I know, I've been a first-class idiot. But it was for the best of reasons.'

'What reasons? I'm a vegetarian, yes, but I'm open-minded. I wouldn't hold this against you.'

'No, no, of course,' he said, scratching his neck. 'I was being paranoid. Stupid, really.'

Christina's confusion was converting into anger now. 'I've been stressed out of my mind about Phoebe and Miaow and my house and . . . and *you*, Rupert. Imagining you'd gone and got yourself drowned in the floods. Didn't it occur to you I might be worried? Did you even try to contact me? And now I find you here, of all places.'

'Sorry,' he mumbled.

'To keep something like this from me is crazy . . . deceitful. I honestly don't think I know you at all, Rupert

Venn. It seems like you don't know me either. I'm beginning to wonder if you even love me.'

'Yes, yes, I do. Christina, of course I do!' He put on a silly, patronizing expression that was designed to be coaxing and humorous and put out a hand to her. 'Come on, old bean! You know I do.'

She glowered at him.

Rupert's smile flickered and went out. Now fear was plainly visible in his eyes: fear of losing her. He changed tactic, suddenly resolved. In a dramatic gesture, and to everyone's shock, he dropped down on his knees in the mud. 'I truly am sorry I didn't tell you, and I know I don't deserve you . . . And of course I would have come over to yours if I'd known you were flooded. I'd do anything for you, Christina, anything at all. I'd walk to Rome on my knees. I'd . . . Just tell me what to do to make up for it.'

Al put his hands in his pockets and then took them out again, feeling he owed it to Christina to show respect for this startling outburst. Not that it made any difference, because her eyes were riveted on Rupert anyway.

She seemed deeply affected by the grand gesture made by her fiancé, this muddy creature at her feet who was pleading and gesticulating. She wavered.

'To be honest, I don't know what to think. I'm just gobsmacked. I can't pretend to understand it, Rupert.' Now she added with a degree of scorn, 'But for heaven's sake, get up. No point in ruining a decent pair of trousers. You're embarrassing everyone here as well as making a complete fool of yourself.'

Rupert pulled himself out of the mud. He looked at her fawningly. Then he spoke in a more practical tone.

'Well, there's nothing else I can do here now. Come back to mine and we can have a brandy and a cuddle and chat about it all. Please, Christina.'

Christina did look as if she could do with a stiff drink and a cuddle. Her eyes became unfocused and she swayed on her feet for a moment so that Al feared she was about to faint. But her words came out sharp as razors.

'No, Rupert. I'm not coming home with you. There will be no cuddling or chatting. I'm going back to Al's tonight.'

42

A Few Overnight Things

AL HAD GIVEN up on sleep, despite his exhaustion. He clambered out of bed and systematically googled the words that had been thrown at him by the medics: hyperparathyroidism, hypercalcemia and hypocalcemia. He pored over stories from people who had suffered from these conditions. It would be useful to understand the intricacies of Phoebe's condition, but none of it made for happy reading. These were descriptions of pain, disability and despair.

Once again, he had to be grateful to Rupert, who had undoubtedly saved Phoebe. He must remember to send that bottle of whisky.

All the same, he hated the way Rupert had kept parts of his life hidden from Christina. It was almost funny that he'd been working for the opposite factions of the otter sanctuary and the fish business. But his dishonesty didn't bode well for their marriage.

Al had also used up some night-time ponderings on Christina and what he might do to help. Her cottage was in need of a major clear-up and she wouldn't be able to live there for some time.

On the way back from the awkward scene at the fish farm, Christina had been uncharacteristically quiet. They had driven straight to her house to check out the flood damage and to search for Miaow. They were met by a scene of devastation. Most of the water had drained away, but, as they stepped in, Christina's hall carpet squelched and belched and oozed putrid, brown slime. The wedding dress was still drooped over the bottom of the banister, stained and tatty-looking. The air stank.

After a thorough search and much calling, they had discovered Miaow snoozing inside an upturned straw hat on top of the wardrobe in Christina's bedroom. She had let out a disgruntled squawk as Christina lifted her down, as if outraged to be cossetted and cared for again.

'Oh, Miaow! Why didn't you just call out your name, then I would have known you were there,' Christina had said, holding her tightly, plunging her face into the soft fur. A velvety, ginger paw crept over her shoulder. 'When she finds a new place that she loves, she just keeps going back there,' Christina explained to Al.

'She likes to keep you on your toes, doesn't she?'

'You never said a truer word, Al. Well, thank goodness she's here! I don't think I would've coped with losing her again at the moment.'

Al had invited Miaow to come and stay as well. It

seemed unreasonable to leave her in the flooded house, even if she did appear to be quite content in her new hat bed.

Christina had thrown a few overnight things into a rucksack while Al waited for her. She also, he noticed, thrust the soggy wedding dress into a polythene bag and brought it with her, muttering something about lovely silky material which might be preserved if hand-washed with care.

Miaow had whined at them in the car, on Christina's lap, all the way to Higher Mead Cottage. Christina reprimanded her. 'Al is rescuing us, Miaow. Where is your gratitude? I haven't brought you up to use language like that.'

Miaow just gave her a dirty look and continued swearing.

It was only on their arrival that Al remembered the dearth of clean sheets because Jules and Jack had stayed while Phoebe was having surgery and laundry had hardly been a priority since then. Phoebe's four-poster was still made up, though, and he thought she wouldn't mind her friend sleeping there, given the circumstances. Miaow and Christina had settled in for the night quite comfortably. Al hoped they'd slept better than he had.

First thing in the morning, he picked up the phone with clammy hands and called the hospital. His enquiry wouldn't leave his lips to start with, then came out as no more than a hoarse whisper. But the answer made him punch the air with joy. Phoebe was doing fine. She could come home. In case she had any more 'episodes', Al was to collect some tablets, to be administered only if the tingling sensations returned. Her system had been un-balanced for many years. Now it was in shock and needed time to adjust.

At eight thirty, which he reckoned was not so early as to be annoying, he brought Christina a cup of tea with a soft knock on the bedroom door.

'Come in!'

She sat bolt upright in bed, billowed in a huge dressing gown gathered around her. The design on the dressing gown was extraordinary; it looked as if a troop of aubergines and gooseberries were throwing a party. It suited her, though. Her hair was draped gloriously and untidily around her shoulders, but her expression was shell-shocked. Miaow lay snuggled into the crook of her arm. If a cat could smirk, Miaow was definitely smirking.

'How are you?' Al asked, out of habit.

Christina replied: 'I'm pretty well, considering. Slept like a baby in this king of all beds.'

He told her the news about Phoebe. She clapped her hands.

'Phew! Thank heavens!'

Once again, Al was ambushed by a barrage of emotion as he stood there in the doorway. He would have liked to climb into the bed next to Christina, put his head on her warm, cushiony bosom and cry like a baby. That wouldn't really be on, though, would it? So he just stood rooted to the floor.

'Al,' she said. 'Give me that tea, would you?'

He obliged and noticed her hands were trembling as she took it. After a quick sip, she wrapped her fingers around the mug and stared down at it. 'I think my brain has been processing things while I was asleep. And do you know what else I think?'

'No.'

'I think I've been an idiot.'

Al started to protest, but the words faltered. In his opinion, she actually *had* been an idiot, at least when it came to a certain very tall man. And it might be a good thing if she acknowledged it.

'Al, please don't stand there looking like a muppet,' Christina said petulantly. 'Look, I'm quite decent and there is an armchair over there . . . and I'd like to talk to you.'

He went over and sat on it, the same armchair where he'd tried to sleep . . . wow, had it only been a couple of nights ago? He waited to see what she had to say.

She looked down again and studied her tea. Miaow, annoyed that the mug was being given all the attention, stretched and jumped off the bed. She headed across the room to Al, dived into his lap and circled twice before settling. He stroked her behind the ears, eliciting a loud, rumbly purr. Her close proximity seemed to strengthen his connection with Christina.

Christina continued in a low voice: 'I am relieved, so relieved, that Miaow is safe. And more thrilled than I can say that Phoebe is all right. My cottage will be all right, too, eventually. I have insurance. I adore my arty things, a lot of which are irreplaceable, but there's nothing like disaster for putting things in perspective. Loved ones are so, *so* much more important . . . Phoebe, and Miaow . . .' She paused. 'As for Rupert, I need to think some more.'

'About your impending marriage?'

'I note the way you use the word "impending" there, Al, a word that normally goes with the word "doom".'

Al's automatic response would be to apologize, but again he stopped himself. The truth wasn't in need of any veiling at the moment.

'My vocabulary reflects my feelings,' he answered. 'You should have been Rupert's first concern in the floods, not that wretched fish farm.'

'I think so too. He has behaved very oddly,' she admitted, now looking Al in the eye.

'Rupert saved Phoebe,' he made himself say, as a reminder to them both.

Even so, he just couldn't get himself to like the wretched man.

43

Denouement

PHOEBE CAST A look back over the years. So many years, so many precious, precious years of her youth. All lost.

She could recall very little about them. They had congealed into a sort of amorphous mass which contained too much sleep and too many pills and far too much pretending. It was only with the advent of Coco that the perspective had started to change and clarify. Coco, by some miracle, had stirred her into action. This tiny, squeaking package of fur and tail and whiskers had made Phoebe realize how worthwhile it was to push herself, no matter how hard that might be. And Coco had shown her how much utter joy could be found in the littlest things.

She had also taught Phoebe the value of freedom.

The future stretched ahead, an unknown path. But even as she lay in the enclosed cell of a hospital ward, Phoebe was aware of possibilities beginning to blossom.

One day soon she, too, might run wild. She, too, might dive into a whole new landscape of adventures.

It occurred to her that she hadn't really lost those years, those precious years. She had just been using them in a different way. She had been learning how to be patient and how to hang on to hope. She had developed an inner strength through her outer weakness. And now, having been held back for so long, she sensed she would spring forward, much further than she would have done if her life had been normal.

Today, once the doctor had seen her, she would be going home. At her bedside, Al talked to her about many things. He updated her on the progress of the broad beans and his aim to resume the nightly slug runs. He reminisced about the times when she, Jules and Jack were children. He expressed his hope that the substitute delivery driver was managing all right. He chatted about the villagers. He informed Phoebe that Rev Lucy was in hospital too, just a few corridors away. She was on her rounds, visiting patients, praying with those who wanted it and administering Holy Communion to a few religious souls. She had sent her greetings and said she would pop in and see Phoebe.

'Apparently, she is getting a divorce.'

Phoebe wasn't surprised. 'I'd like to see her again.'

'I could do with a leg stretch,' he said, rising stiffly from the chair. 'Since you're awake and up for it, I'll see if she can come now.'

He came back ten minutes later, accompanied by the vicar. He left them alone to chat and pottered off again on a quest for tea.

Rev Lucy looked smaller than she had done, and greyer somehow. She didn't try to smile at all, and that was fine by Phoebe.

'I actually had no idea you were ill, Phoebe, but I hope you'll be very well again soon.'

'Thank you.'

And all at once, words were tumbling out of Phoebe's mouth and she confided in Rev Lucy how she'd been covering up her pain for the last four years and how hard, how unbelievably hard and cruel and exhausting that had been. Rev Lucy listened.

Then Rev Lucy told Phoebe about her own troubles and Phoebe listened. She explained how weary she'd become of her husband's infidelity. She had ignored it for long enough. When she had confronted him, he'd been apologetic, smugly so. He'd said the affair was just a game and he would never leave her. She had replied that she didn't like that kind of a game and *she* was going to leave *him*. She would be taking the children with her. And the dog.

'Well done,' said Phoebe.

'It wasn't easy,' said Rev Lucy.

'No, I don't suppose it was.'

'I'll be leaving the parish, too.'

'Oh. I'm sorry to hear it. You'll be missed.'

Phoebe worried for a moment that Rev Lucy was going to offer to pray with her and was relieved when she didn't. Rev Lucy was holding a book, which she had been fingering throughout the conversation. As she stood to leave, she placed it on Phoebe's bed. Phoebe smiled sadly when she saw the title: *God and Coping with Disaster*.

How could Phoebe ever have suspected such a dear, kind woman of terrible, heinous actions? As soon as she was well enough, she would get something nice for Rev Lucy, as a leaving present. A little token that would just say: *I care*. She knew what would do it perfectly. One of Dan Hollis's beautiful candlesticks. She hoped the future would shine more brightly for Rev Lucy.

As Phoebe pictured Dan, a smudge of a memory appeared in her head. She homed in on it, with all the concentration she had available. As she scrutinized it, the memory seemed odder and odder. And now she cursed herself for never having thought it through, never having appreciated the significance of it. She supposed, at the time, she must have been distracted by Christina's announcement of her engagement. But now this tiny detail might clinch everything.

She must speak to Dan Hollis.

The river had retreated again. It was gurgling along contentedly, as if it had changed its mind after a wild escapade and decided that its normal routine was quite acceptable after all. The silver skirts of water had withdrawn from the fields. Only a few shreds remained, caught in the ruts and dips of land. They shimmered rebelliously and reflected the sky.

On the way home, Phoebe absorbed several interesting facts related by her father: that Christina had stayed at Higher Mead Cottage last night because her own house was flooded, that Miaow was there too, that they had slept in Phoebe's room but had now collected Christina's bedclothes and would be based in the spare room for the next few days. Also, that they had discovered the fish farm was part-owned by Rupert and run by his brother. Drained as she was, Phoebe had a feeling answers to long-asked questions might finally be within reach.

Al hadn't mentioned the otter sanctuary at all. She had to ask. He shrugged his shoulders and tried to change the subject. At last she wheedled it out of him.

'So Rowan's gone, and Quercus, and Paddy, and the Asian family . . .'

'I'm afraid so.'

She swore under her breath and said no more. When Al next glanced across at her, she had her eyes closed. He didn't know if she was sleeping or deep in thought.

Pale, watery sunshine was breaking through the clouds as they pulled up in the driveway of Higher Mead Cottage.

Christina flung her arms around her as soon as she came in, leaning on her father's arm. 'How are you, Phoebe?'

'I'm quite . . . quite Holme-ogeneous, thank you.'

Christina looked nonplussed at this, until Al explained: 'As in Holmes. Sherlock. Phoebe must be feeling better if she's deducing things again.'

He insisted that Phoebe go straight to bed, and she didn't argue. She still couldn't walk without support and felt as if every last dreg of energy had been sucked from her body. What she needed was a glass of water and a good, long sleep. But after that . . .

When she woke, Al and Christina were murmuring quietly downstairs and certain facts had lined up neatly in her head. But behind every brainwave was a strong cup of coffee. Once she was sufficiently caffeinated, she needed to make a phone call or two. And after that she would consult the oracle of all wisdom: Google.

She called out: 'Any chance of a coffee?'

'Yes, of course!' Al and Christina choroused.

They were prompt in bringing it to her. She had to beg to use the phone, though, and they took ages to leave her in peace again to make the calls.

The first call was to Seth Hardwick. He was marginally less surprised to hear from her than he had been last time. She went through everything with him, just for the sake of a second opinion from a self-proclaimed Morse man.

'Does it sound sane to you?' she asked him.

'It does,' he said, which was all she needed.

For the next call it was Ellie who picked up. She understood at once that Phoebe was tired and only needed a quick word with Dan.

'Hello, Phoebe-Featherstone-the-Wild-Cub-Carer,' came his voice, gentle and clear down the line.

'Dan. I'll get straight to the point. You probably won't remember this . . . it was a long time ago . . . but you once met my dad in the lanes and stopped for a conversation out of your car windows. And you gave him a button for me to give to Christina.'

'I do remember. It was a Tuesday morning in September and Al-Featherstone-Your-Father had a small scratch on his forearm that showed up white against the tan of his skin. There was a dried splash of bird poo on the bonnet of his car. He had seven parcels left to deliver, which had toppled and were splayed out behind him in the back. Standing in the meadow on the other side of the hedge, there was a cow the colour of a ripe chestnut who was busy munching grass in a very sideways-mouthed fashion.'

'Wow, you *do* remember, don't you! But what I want to know is, why did you give Dad the button?'

'To give to you to give to Christina to give to Rupert.'

'To give to Rupert?'

'Why, yes. Christina was engaged to him, so she would be seeing him soon, I presumed.'

'But why did you want Rupert to have the button?'

'Because he collects buttons.'

She paused. Rupert, a collector of buttons? 'How do you know?'

'Because I saw him picking one up in the garden at Christina's barbecue and wrapping it in a handkerchief as if it was very special. I collect fir cones and pennies. Rupert collects buttons.'

'Okay. Thank you so much, Dan. That is very interesting.'

Dan was brilliant at observing details, but less good at interpreting them. What a detective team they could be, working together! *Hollis and Featherstone Investigate.* She could see it as a TV drama.

Now for a bit of googling . . .

Phoebe called a meeting in her bedroom, just as Poirot always did when it was denouement time. Al took his place on the armchair. Miaow immediately took up residence on his lap. Christina perched on the upright chair, sitting on her hands.

'Let us face the facts,' Phoebe said. She steepled her

fingers and pressed her fingertips together (how lovely that they weren't tingling). She focused on Christina, who was looking as if she'd swallowed a lot of uncomfortable truths in the last twenty-four hours.

'Christina, you have to listen to what I say now that you've seen evidence with your own eyes. Also, because I'm a recovering invalid and deserve some attention. Are you ready to hear this?'

'I know what you're going to say. Rupert wanted to kill Coco. You already tried to tell me, many times.' Her face underwent a series of contortions. Her voice came out raw and jagged. 'And do you know what? I'm beginning to wonder if you could be right, Phoebe. He's clearly not the man I thought he was. But I feel as if I'm going mad. It's hard to believe that of Rupert.'

'Well, you must try. Because he is guilty as hell. And now, at last, I know why he acted as he did. He had it in for the sanctuary from the beginning, from the day he walked in and introduced himself to Carol. I realized he was a liar when I remembered something you mentioned about his train sets being in the garage for the last eight years – yet when we met him he'd said he was new to the area.'

'He'd told me that, too. I just didn't really think about it . . .'

'I suppose the lie made it easy for him to be vague about his past and just talk about doing accounts for "various businesses". Nobody would be bothered much exactly which businesses if they weren't local; nobody would ask questions. But they – or rather it – was right on our doorstep. And it was his family business.'

'And a very fishy business it was too,' Al put in.

Christina gave a half-smile, followed by a long sigh.

'I also remembered the fish canapés you ate by mistake, Christina,' Phoebe said, 'and Rupert's expertise in everything fish-related, and it struck me that he might have something to do with the fish farm.'

Christina shuffled and released one of her hands to nibble on a thumbnail. 'But trying to kill Coco? So brutal, so extreme! Surely he couldn't really have attempted such a thing? To such a sweet, innocent, lovely creature?' Her voice became a thin wail. 'He was working with otters for months and seemed to love them as much as I did.'

'He was a very good bluffer. He pretended hard.' Phoebe gave her own sigh.

Christina stared at her, turning the unpleasant thought over and over. 'But anybody can see that the sanctuary was a good thing, not just for the otters, but for the local community, too. Not even that bad for the fish farm, I would've thought. I just don't get it at all.'

'We need to delve into Rupert's past to understand him,' said Phoebe. 'I've been looking up fish farms associated with the name "Venn" and it seems that his family have always worked in the industry. His parents, his grandparents, even back another generation or two. Here's the thing. Twenty years ago, when Rupert was a young man, a team of otters raided one of their fish farms night after night. They stole vast numbers of fish and caused complete havoc. Rupert's father tried to barricade them out, but the otters just kept finding ways in. Because of the laws protecting otters there was nothing else he could do. It was a disaster for the family and the last straw for a failing business that went bust soon afterwards.'

Christina frowned. 'He did mention that at one stage his family had fallen on terrible times and had to leave their beloved home, and soon afterwards his parents split up. His mother moved to Australia and she died there not long after. It left him devastated. He always clammed up if I asked about it. Now I understand why.'

'I'm guessing Rupert blamed the otters for it all. After their parents' death, he and his brother decided to rebuild something in the only trade they knew about. They moved to this area and set up the fish farm on the Darle. It was a sad irony that, unknown to them, Carol was simultaneously setting up the otter sanctuary with her friend a few miles up the river. Because of Carol's successful reintroduction of otters into the wild, the local otter population then steadily increased. Rupert, once he realized, knew well the potential risk facing his business.'

Phoebe paused, worn out by her long narration, and took a sip of water. Christina and Al remained riveted, waiting for her to go on. Miaow purred.

'Rupert kept a careful eye on the sanctuary and looked for his opportunity. As soon as he heard about the departure of Carol's friend, he saw a way of undermining the sanctuary and its work: to get a job there himself. His main purpose was to stop Carol releasing otters near the fish farm, but he was also trying to get the sanctuary closed down if he could.'

Christina gulped several times as if something was stuck in her throat. She shook her head, incredulous.

'And there he met me. It must have been tricky keeping up the pretence, bearing in mind how I love otters.'

'I'm thinking his duplicity was complicated,' said Phoebe in an attempt to soften her horror. 'I'm thinking he's neither as posh or as nice as we thought, but he does have some sort of heart. He does love you, Christina, and he *was* kind to me, chopping the fish for me. He may even have liked the otters. He just didn't want them released. It must have been inconvenient for him falling in love with you. I wonder if he would ever have come clean to you. Probably not.'

She considered. 'He could never have admitted to trying to sabotage the otter sanctuary. Although it must have to have come out soon that he part-owned the fish farm.'

She waved Phoebe on.

'Do you remember Carol telling us about health-and-safety inspectors coming in? Well, it was Rupert who arranged it, and he deliberately moved the warning signs in order to "clean them" that day so that their report would be bad. Luckily for Carol, it wasn't quite enough. After that, he staged a robbery. It was easy for him because Carol trusted him entirely. He'd been given control over the takings, and he was a good actor, too. I met him occasionally, coming back from the wild otters' pen. I'm sure he was spending time with them so that they'd become imprinted. I just thought he was fond of them! He decided to be affable, and that's exactly how he came across. We all fell for it, didn't we?'

'The scoundrel!' cried Al, in a voice reminiscent of old

films. Phoebe sensed that, underneath the shock, he was rather enjoying the drama.

She explained that it had been Rupert who had written the letter to the local press that had prompted the animal-rights activists to stage their protest. His absence that day had been deliberate, nothing to do with sheep on the road. Then, as the time for Paddy and Coco's release came close, he had turned to more desperate measures.

'I realized something dodgy was going on, but I had no idea who was responsible. By the time of your barbecue, I'd already voiced my suspicions to a few people, Rupert among them. He found Seth's button by chance and seized on the opportunity. He planted it later by Coco's enclosure and made sure I found it there when I was sweeping up. But, of course, it wasn't Seth who was responsible for the poisoning. It was Rupert. He soaked fish in rat poison before Coco and Paddy's feeding time. I think he got the idea from you, Christina, when you told him about the feud between George Bovis and Spike Dobson that all began with rat poison.'

Christina let out a moan. 'I can't believe I went and handed him the idea. And to try and pin it on Seth, too . . . What a devious, shitty thing to do. I hate his guts more and more.'

'His plan worked,' Phoebe continued. 'Just a small quantity of poison, not enough to kill an otter but enough to make him need close care and become dependent on humans so he could never be released.'

'Poor Paddy!'

Phoebe thought of the happy hours she had spent getting to know each of the otters, how she adored Paddy, but what a tragedy that he had now become too human to survive in the wild. Now, ironically, having escaped in the floods, he *was* in the wild. She gritted her teeth.

'Perhaps it was this success that prompted Rupert to try something yet crueller and more drastic. He'd attempted, when left alone with Coco, to turn her into a domestic creature too. When this failed and she was about to be released, he decided to kill her at the site, hide her body and pretend she had escaped. He couldn't risk poison again because if her body was ever found it would be detectable, but a bang on the head could have been caused by all sorts of things.'

'Thank God you stopped him,' Christina cried, leaping forward and seizing Phoebe by the hand. She crouched beside the bed, burying her head in the covers.

Al had gone very quiet. He was obsessively stroking Miaow, but his eyes were fixed on his daughter.

'I did stop Rupert, to my own detriment,' Phoebe said, reeling at the terrible memory. 'But hey, it led to a diagnosis and surgery. And that, in turn, seems to have – fingers crossed – led to my recovery. So thank you, Coco. A million times, thank you!'

She said it quietly, but in her heart a little trumpet of joy was sounding. She had a second chance at life. She was going to be well. If only the otters were all right . . . and if only Christina could be happy . . .

Christina raised her face again. It was crumpled with emotion. She rose to her feet. 'Phoebe Featherstone, I admire you more than I can express. You – only you – saw the truth.'

'I only wish I'd done it faster!'

Christina balled her fists until the knuckles turned white. Her words came out in jabs. 'And Rupert – God, what a sorry excuse for a human being. What an evil toe-rag and vile, loathsome worm. I never want to set eyes on him again.'

44

Consequences

A MAGNIFICENT BOUQUET of roses and carnations had arrived at Higher Mead Cottage, addressed to Christina. She had promptly binned it.

'After his radio silence yesterday, now he won't stop emailing me,' she told Phoebe. It was Rupert's only other means of contacting her, as she wasn't at home to answer the landline, there was no mobile signal and he didn't have Al and Phoebe's number. 'I read the first few, but it was all excuses, excuses, saying he didn't exactly lie, he just didn't tell the whole truth. Asking me to come over to his place. Wanting to make up. He doesn't know that I know about the otters.'

Phoebe looked at Christina's distraught face and had to give her a hug.

'Rupert is despicable, but the single good thing about him is that he loves you. I really believe he does.'

Christina sobbed out like a baby, 'Well, I hate him!'

Together with Al, after much discussion, they had agreed to call Jeremy Crocker. Rupert's actions were criminal and he must not be allowed to get away with them. It was a matter for the police but probably easiest if they went through Mr Crocker, who had, after all, volunteered his services many times. When Al phoned him, he listened gravely and promised the police would be knocking on Rupert's door very soon.

Al had retrieved his car from the dip in the road in central Darleycombe. He wouldn't be using it for deliveries for some time yet. Not while Phoebe still needed him so badly.

One trip was compulsory, however. It was not going to be pleasant, but Phoebe had insisted. She would have gone herself if she'd been well enough to venture out. He left Christina and Miaow to look after her.

The village, as he drove through, looked as if it had been newly scrubbed clean. The trees shone emerald green and the ducks scooted through the sparkles on the pond, passing enthusiastic quacks backwards and forwards to each other.

Yet as he drew closer to the sanctuary, a cloud lunged across the sun. The whole landscape seemed to take on a more sombre air.

A new sign was nailed to the gate. It read: *We regret that this sanctuary is now closed.*

He went in anyway. Carol was expecting him.

He found her outside the pens, a bucket in her hands. Of the otters, only Twiggy and Willow were still there. They seemed less active than usual, as if they were aware of all the dramas and fully partook in the humans' anxiety.

'You must be gutted,' Al said, aiming for empathy but not excelling in diplomacy.

Carol remained thin-lipped. He noticed she had hosed down the mud from all the enclosures.

They had already spoken on the phone. Apparently, Rupert had skipped work and hadn't contacted Carol at all in the last few days. Neither had he answered her calls. She had begun to wonder about him.

She did not register much surprise when she learned the truth. 'Rupert has always been an obsessive person,' she said. 'It looks as if destroying the sanctuary became his major obsession, only seconded by his obsession with model trains . . . and his obsession with Christina. I am only shocked that I was fool enough to be taken in.'

Al shook his head sadly. 'So is she,' he said.

The wedding had, of course, been cancelled.

Christina spent a lot of time weeping as she adjusted to this new turnaround in her life. Phoebe watched her closely. What happened to love when it received so great a shock? Did it promptly vanish? Did it gradually fade, sputter out and cease to be? Or might it be refocused in another direction? She couldn't be sure.

Watching endless detective dramas with Phoebe did little to cheer Christina up. In a bid to help, Al invited her friends, Dan and Ellie, to dinner at Higher Mead Cottage. Phoebe, who could still barely manage to walk, was too tired to join them for the meal itself. Al helped her downstairs to sit with them for a short time afterwards, since she was keen to see Dan.

When she entered the sitting-room, Christina was in full flow, telling her friends how horribly guilty she felt for having fallen in love with Rupert, even though she had played no part in his vile actions.

'Well,' said Ellie, 'you wanted very much to believe in human kindness, so that's what you saw in Rupert. Nobody makes good choices all the time. Sometimes it's impossible to see people for who they truly are.'

Phoebe somehow felt that this might be the voice of experience.

Christina was still railing. 'I cannot believe that at forty-something I am still so bloody blind,' she cried. 'What is Cupid playing at?'

Ellie tried to soothe her. 'None of this is your fault. Cupid is very . . . Cupid can be quite . . .'

'Stupid,' said Dan. 'Cupid can be stupid.' Evidently pleased with the rhyme, he repeated it several times. 'Cupid is stupid. Stupid Cupid. Stupid, stupid Cupid.' Then, struck with another truth, he added: 'Not all the time, though. Cupid is stupid and careless and miscalculates badly, but then later he realizes his mistake and he starts sending all his love arrows in the proper direction and then everything's good again.' He looked adoringly at Ellie, who returned the look.

Oblivious, Christina rocked to and fro in her chair, furiously biting her lip. 'How could I ever have been such a terrible judge of character? I don't think I'll ever, ever, trust a man again.'

'You will,' said Phoebe. Christina was a natural truster, she knew that much.

'Anyone want a big, bling, gold-and-purple wedding dress?' asked her friend.

They shook their heads.

'There's no way I'm ever going to wear it now. I wish you'd never bloody saved it from the bloody flood, Al.'

Al raised his eyebrows. Phoebe gave him a look which she hoped would convey: *Please don't take her words personally. She knows that you were acting in her best interests and, really, she's grateful. She's just mixed up and upset at the moment. Bear with her. She'll get over it, and who knows? One day, her lonely but lovely heart might be ready to reach out again.*

She doubted that Al could detect everything she'd said in that look, but she hoped he got the gist of it. Romance for her father was still a possibility, wasn't it? Love, like cheese, just needed time to mature.

To lighten the mood, Phoebe asked Dan about his woodwork. It was soon decided that he would make a fine, sturdy candlestick for her to give to Rev Lucy.

'Maybe not one with an otter or a cat. It's too upsetting to think about the otters now, and Rev Lucy isn't a cat person. Could you do a candlestick with a Labrador, like her faithful friend?'

Dan nodded solemnly. 'I could indeed. And I will.'

After he and Ellie had left, Christina sighed a deep, shuddering sigh. 'They are so happy together,' she sobbed.

Phoebe decided it was time to put forward a suggestion which she hoped might bring some closure.

'I'll take the dress off your hands, if you like.'

'Thank you, Phoebe. You're welcome to it. Although I

wouldn't have thought it would be your style. For your sister, perhaps?'

'No, not for Jules. It's not really her style either. Christina, can you keep a secret?'

Christina perked up visibly. 'Oh yes. Absolutely yes. Do tell!'

The next day, Christina spent an hour with her needle, letting out the newly washed dress and adjusting the sleeves. Then, in Phoebe's bedroom and under her direction, she folded it carefully, wrapped it up in coloured tissue paper and ribbons and laid it in a long, shallow cardboard box. She encased the box with brown paper and tied it up with string and handed it to Phoebe, who wrote the name and address in capital letters on the front.

As they were finishing the task, Al knocked on the door.

'What are you two up to in there?'

'Come in and see for yourself,' Phoebe called. '*Brown paper packages tied up with strings*,' she added, pointing to the box as he joined them. 'That's your cue, Dad.'

Al duly performed his Julie Andrews impression, much to Christina's mirth. Phoebe looked on with satisfaction.

Then she asked her father if, on his next round, he would deliver the parcel to Jeremy Crocker's house.

To give them a break, Christina was hopping around Darleycombe, staying with different people. She was popular with the residents and had more invitations than she knew what to do with. At the moment, she was chez the Dobsons.

410

An extraordinary thing had occurred during the floods. The Bovises had been without sandbags, while the Dobsons had far more than they needed. Spike Dobson had no intention of helping out his neighbour after all the recent hostilities. However, his wife, Felicity, had other ideas. She staged a kitchen sit-in, refusing to cook anything or talk to her husband or even look at him until he agreed. He wouldn't go round with the sandbags himself, but eventually, weary of the silence and lack of dinner, had said that if George Bovis wanted to come and fetch a few sandbags, he would raise no objection. Felicity joyfully delivered this message to Marge Bovis by phone. Soon after, George Bovis arrived at the door, crimson-faced, grudging the favour but nevertheless extremely grateful.

After he had uttered the magic words 'thank you', Spike, rather overcome with his own virtue, had been moved to apologize for various occurrences involving hydrangeas and dog wee. George had, in turn, apologized for occurrences involving summerhouses, mowers and hosepipes. The two men had even gone so far as to help each other manoeuvre the sandbags.

The ladies had a celebratory cup of tea together.

'Let's hope it's the end of this silliness,' Marge Bovis had said.

'Yes indeed,' Felicity Dobson had replied. 'I believe it will be. It's quite incredible what the words "thank you" and "sorry" can achieve.'

All of this, Christina had relayed to Phoebe as she was recovering.

It was now a week after her operation, and she could almost feel the cells in her body regenerating.

'I told my fifteen thousand followers that you nearly died,' Jules informed her via Zoom.

'It's true,' said Phoebe, who had googled her condition. 'But I somehow managed not to. I think it was all due to the otters, you know. They kept handing me little parcels of joy just when I needed it. And joy is seriously good for your health.'

She still wasn't ready for any visitors, apart from Christina, of course. She was popping round all the time. That was partly because Miaow was still residing at Higher Mead Cottage. (Miaow was not willing to meet the Dobsons' Jack Russell, being no great fan of canines, particularly those tiresome individuals who never stopped barking.)

Miaow was doing much to soothe Phoebe's spirits, since there was now a dearth of otters in her life. Although it was Al who was the favourite of the opinionated feline.

There were no more roses for Christina. Jeremy Crocker informed them that Rupert had been arrested. As yet, he was admitting nothing but, with Carol's help, the evidence was stacking up.

And then, on the village grapevine, the news came to them that a certain fish farm had been raided by otters. Perhaps this was not surprising in view of the fact that so many otters had recently escaped into the countryside, otters who were not in the least bit afraid of human habitation, and who were used to a good daily supply of fish. What glee they must have felt on discovering such a banquet!

The fish farm in question had already been near-ruined by flooding and damage from a fallen tree and was now forced to fold altogether. This was a turning point for the older Venn brother, who had been struggling with his conscience for the last year. He had never condoned Rupert's actions but had known about them, and now he begged him to confess everything to the police. Rupert finally obliged.

Jeremy Crocker informed the Featherstones that Rupert's immediate future would be spent in prison. According to village gossip, his brother was done with fish and now intended to start up a lavender farm in France. The plan was for Rupert to join him there in a few years' time.

Christina, who firmly believed in the healing powers of lavender, said she was glad. She was also glad that France was a very long way away from Darleycombe.

45

The Attraction of Fish

THE DOORBELL RANG with urgency, again and again.

Al scrubbed the earth off his hands (he'd been repotting strawberry plants) and rushed to answer. Christina stood on the step. Her hair was twisted into a knot on the top of her head, but little tendrils of it fell around her face. Her eyes were wide and shining.

'You have to come, both of you. Now.'

'Where to?'

'I'm not saying. Just come.'

Phoebe was in the sitting-room with a book. He called her and she struggled up. They followed Christina outside to the drive, where her Peugeot was waiting.

'Hop in.'

They roared down the road. The fields whooshed by in a bright blur and the Darle looped and glittered alongside them. They blasted through the village and past the green, the shop, the bridge. They turned sharp left down a lane and now Phoebe recognized the route.

'Oh no, please no. It's too sad,' she said. She wasn't ready. Surely it was time to look ahead now, not back.

'Humour me,' Christina answered. Her lips twitched briefly, as if they were desperate for more exercise, but she was determined to give nothing away. She parked the Peugeot askew in the empty car park.

Phoebe got out with a sinking sensation. She leaned heavily on her father's arm as they made their way towards the entrance. He had told her that the otter sisters, Twiggy and Willow, were still there. It would at least be good to see them again. She guessed that Christina thought they'd cheer her up, that the Otter Effect from two of them would be enough. This would be a good opportunity to commiserate with Carol, too, she supposed, although it would be hard to find the right words.

Phoebe viewed the sign that read: *We regret that this sanctuary is now closed*, and a snag of sorrow caught in her throat. She stopped, not sure she could bear to go in.

Christina jostled them forward. 'Go on. Carol needs to talk to you, and I said I'd bring you over. She'll be disappointed if you don't turn up.'

They headed through the building. Carol was nowhere to be seen.

'She's probably outside,' said Christina.

As they walked out to the public area, Carol's back view appeared. She was in her anorak and wellies, leaning over the wall of one of the enclosures, looking in. Her grey hair was loose, for once, and tumbling around her shoulders. As they approached they could hear her

415

talking in a low voice. But who was she talking to? Hearing their footsteps, she turned.

'Oh, it's you.'

Her face was dimpling with an expression Phoebe had never seen on it before.

Sheer delight.

Christina dragged her friends forward. Phoebe blinked and wondered for a moment if the effects of the anaesthetic still hadn't worn off and she was imagining things. Because there in front of her were several brown, furry, romping shapes. Twiggy and Willow . . . and . . . Surely it couldn't be?

She let out a gasp.

Was that or was it not Quercus? Yes, it *was* him. He scampered up with his lopsided gait to examine them. His head moved up and down and he seemed to be giggling. And there was Rowan, right behind him. And there, racing round in circles, was the whole family of short-clawed Asian otters. And that was Holly, frisking about with Hawthorn. And there, patting the ground with widespread toes as he came up to say hello, was Paddy.

Phoebe threw out her hands. The ground tilted under her feet and she had to grab hold of her father. It was the Otter Effect, surging through her with such strength it almost winded her. Her heart thrilled.

'They've come back!' Christina cried, gesticulating wildly. 'They've come back home.'

'I hoped they would,' Carol said. She wiped her eyes. 'I thought they just might. Having gorged on their ill-gotten spoils at the fish farm, they were obviously finding the rest of the river less satisfactory. And they asked themselves where else could they find food? I have left fish out in the pens every day, and fresh hay in the holts, and made sure there was access from the river for them, just in case. They love it here, and they feel safe.'

'And they *are* safe,' Christina declared.

The Asian otters swarmed into a tunnel and out again the other side. Hawthorn dived into a pond and corkscrewed through the water. Holly rolled on to her back and kicked her legs in the air. Paddy took a pebble between his front paws, chucked it upwards and caught it again, as if to show how clever he was.

Phoebe laughed loudly, a laugh of relief, of pure joy. An earthquake of a belly laugh that exploded out of her.

'That laugh,' murmured Al, and he listened, transfixed, as if he had spent the last century longing to hear it. Then he started laughing as well, great big grunts of happiness. The ripple effect spread and set off Christina too, and then even Carol. The laugh gathered momentum, becoming more and more uncontrollable, until they were all snorting and crying and holding their sides and clutching on to each other. And as soon as they'd finished they started all over again.

Finally, when it was impossible to laugh any more, Al pulled out a hanky and mopped his brow. He squeezed his daughter's arm. 'All's well that ends well, eh, Gromit?' he said in his best Wallace Yorkshire accent with toothy grin to match. Then, in his own voice: 'Worth coming, heh, Phoebes?'

'Oh, otters!' Phoebe cried, not caring who heard, not caring if she came across as sentimental. It had to be said. 'I love you. I bloody love the whole lot of you! Welcome home!'

46

Wild Thing

AL FEATHERSTONE DROVE through the lanes. It was good to be back on his rounds again. The hedgerows were packed with flowers: buttercups, dandelions, vetch and campions, vivid dots of yellow and pink against the green. Wagtails skimmed the air and launched into wild acrobatics. A tractor trundled in front of him for a couple of miles before turning into a side road.

The morning sped past, with numerous drop-offs on the well-worn route. Al accelerated up the hill and then followed the winding road back down into Darleycombe.

A removal van was parked outside the vicarage. No deliveries there today.

Spike Dobson and George Bovis were chatting over their garden hedge. They were so engrossed they were oblivious to the loud barks within the Dobsons' house.

Al dropped off a package for Felicity, which Phoebe had told him was books. Then he dropped off a package for Marge, which Phoebe had told him was a new yoga mat. He moved on to Jeremy Crocker's, where he stepped past the chickens and stopped for a while to talk about the bell tower in Florence and a holiday Mr Crocker had once taken in that city, then Mr Crocker received his parcel, which, according to Phoebe, was a new handbag.

As he drove beside the river, Al wondered if Coco was anywhere nearby, if she had met her otter friends when they escaped, if she had helped them in the raid of the fish farm. He could only hope that she was alive and revelling in her freedom, somewhere along the course of the Darle.

Christina stayed alternately with friends in Darleycombe and in B&Bs, but she called in at Higher Mead Cottage every day to see Miaow.

Miaow lapped up all the extra attention she was getting. She consumed six meals a day and regularly demanded strokes from Al and Phoebe, who were happy to oblige. Al had given Christina a key to Higher Mead Cottage. He understood that Miaow was her family and you should be able to see your family whenever you wanted, shouldn't you? He and Phoebe almost felt they were Christina's family too now.

Except that your heart didn't normally do a backwards flip in your chest when you saw your mother or sister or daughter, did it? And that was exactly what his heart kept doing. It was trying to tell him something, and he couldn't ignore it any more.

He had gone and fallen in love with Christina.

He couldn't understand now why it had taken him so long both to do it and to realize it. It could have been because of the car-pranging the first time he met her. Or it could have been that he was so focused on Phoebe that he didn't register much else. Or that Rupert Venn got in the way. Or just his own pig-headedness. Whatever the reason, love now burst in on him and seemed to take over his every thought and deed.

The sensation was something he'd almost forgotten about, and it brought with it a range of emotions. Often a kind of honeyed softness enveloped him, and he spent far too much time dreaming up delicious scenarios featuring Christina and himself. There was also a good deal of worry that sometimes bordered on panic. This spilled over into nervousness, and in her presence he kept turning into a shy teenager, getting tongue-tied and dropping things. Other moments shone with sheer, giddy elation.

He had no expectation that Christina might feel anything similar for him. She had recovered well from the whole disgraceful Rupert episode, and he rejoiced in the fact that he could see her so often and that she considered him a good friend. He lived in anticipation of the sound of the key turning in the front-door lock and her voice calling: 'Hallooo, it's me!'

Then, one cloudless morning in August, it was time for her to move back into her own house, taking Miaow with her.

'We'll miss this little madam,' Al said, holding Miaow and caressing her under the chin as they gathered in the hall.

'That I can understand,' said Christina. 'Please come round whenever you like to see her. It's not as if I live far away. You and Phoebe are always welcome.'

'We'll come ever such a lot, won't we, Dad?' said Phoebe, hugging her friend tightly. 'You won't be able to get rid of us. A kind of revenge on you for plaguing us for so long.'

Christina, having mimed slapping her, squeezed her back. 'Good. That's the kind of revenge I like.'

Al thought she was about to hug him, too, but she didn't. She turned her face back towards Phoebe. So he leaned forward to give her a peck on the cheek. At the same time, Christina turned her head again, and the kiss accidentally landed on her lips.

'Oops,' he said, giving an awkward huff of laughter. Miaow miaowed.

Christina laid a hand on his arm. 'Oh, Al.'

It would be nice to read meaning into those two little syllables. He kept listening to them long after they'd finished, asking himself if they contained a hint of anything non-platonic, but he couldn't trust his own judgement on that one.

In the meantime, Christina pulled the protesting Miaow from him and wrestled her into the cat basket. She walked quickly out to the Peugeot and placed her companion on the passenger seat. Then, with two hoots of the car horn, she was away.

Al stood with Phoebe on the drive and they waved until the engine sound had trailed into nothing and Christina was a purple dot vanishing round a bend.

The world grew a shade blanker.

A crow who was sitting on the roof gave a dissatisfied squawk and flew off.

A wrinkled berry dropped from the rowan tree and landed at their feet.

Al cracked his knuckles.

Phoebe looked at him piercingly. 'Dad, two things. One, don't do that.'

'Sorry,' he said. 'I'll try not to. And two?'

She whispered something in his ear.

His eyes widened. Now his heart was dancing a jig.

'Do you really think so?'

She nodded. 'Definitely.'

'Surely not.'

'I've been right before, haven't I? Trust me,' she said.

The next day, Al caught himself singing in the shower: '*Birds do it, bees do it, even scruffy retirees do it. Let's do it . . .*'

Phoebe's voice rang out from down the landing. 'Are you going to ask her, then?'

'Mind your own beeswax.'

'Never!' she exclaimed.

Al had no idea that, shortly before she had whispered in his ear how much Christina adored him, she had whispered in Christina's ear how much *he* adored *her*.

Now the honeyed sweetness filled him completely, accompanied by a quivering excitement. He thought he might do as Phoebe suggested, now that he had a faint inkling that success wasn't completely out of the question. But how? He'd like to do something truly romantic, but flowers seemed naff, and anyway, Christina might still associate them with Rupert, which was the last thing he wanted. He did have an idea at the back of his mind. But he wasn't sure if it was genius or just plain stupid.

'The words "faint heart" and "fair lady" come to mind,' Phoebe called through the door.

'Leave me alone,' he called back.

However, his head wouldn't let it go until he had convinced himself that the plan must be implemented. The worst that could happen was that he'd make a fool of himself, and he was quite used to that.

So while Phoebe was taking a nap, he sneaked out of Higher Mead Cottage. He felt too nervous to drive, so he jogged the route along the river. His steps thudded on the path. Trees swished above his head. The water swirled and rumpled over the rocks, twinkling at him.

When he reached Christina's front drive, he didn't stride up to the door. He crept round to the back garden. He loitered behind one of the tall willow structures, catching his breath and summoning as much courage as he could. He needed to act with conviction or there was no point in doing it at all.

A slight movement beside the hedge caught his eye. It was Miaow, busy washing. She was perfectly poised with one leg up in the air and her head bobbing up and down as her tongue worked its way through her fur. He watched, mesmerized. Aware of his presence, she took her time. Once she had completed her task, she strolled towards him in a straight line, tail pointing skyward.

Reassured by her company, he gave her the required

stroke, then put a finger to his lips. 'Don't let on I'm here, Miaow.'

He marched forward until he was outside the living-room window. He hoped he wouldn't alarm Christina.

He started with several strums on his air guitar, using a *brmm brmm* sound to represent the chords.

He had thought long and hard about the song. It couldn't be anything too slushy because slushiness would make him feel even more embarrassed than he already was, and it needed to have words he could remember and a tune that would work even if it was *out of* tune. Quietly, while Phoebe was engaged in Sherlock Holmes, he had tried out a few options in his bedroom with the door closed. He'd decided that his rendition of 'Wild Thing' was marginally less bad than the others.

Madly pounding at his air guitar, he now launched full into it at the top of his voice. Startled birds rose from the trees. Miaow bolted across the lawn and plunged into a hole in the hedge. A door banged from somewhere inside the house.

Al carried on, slightly wishing that the earth would swallow him up but determined not to show it. As his voice sawed the air like a rusty blade, it struck him how right the words were. Christina was – in her wonderful, unique way – a wild thing. She *did* make his heart sing, and she *did* make everything groovy. He was getting into it now.

He had just reached *GROOOOOOVY* when the window opened and Christina put out her head. Her hair was loose and luscious. She was wearing her buttercup-yellow sarong. How he'd missed it! Her cheeks were flushed. Tears were streaming down her face.

She was crying with laughter.

He continued strumming with one hand and reached the other hand out to her, crooning and waggling his head. He knew he was ridiculous. He could only hope it was a brand of ridiculous she liked. He crescendoed as he reached the key line. It was important she didn't miss the point.

I think I love you.

Her wonderful hair blew across her face for a moment so he couldn't see her reaction. Her hand went up to the window. Was she going to shut him out?

No. The hair gusted back and he could see her face. It looked happy.

Now she was singing with him, her voice punctuated every so often by wild giggles.

I wanna know for sure.

And now she had hoicked up her sarong and stuck her dainty foot out of the window, followed by her leg.

And now she was climbing out of the window to join him.

And now she was stumbling towards him across the grass, with her arms flung wide open.

'For heaven's sake, Al, stop that god-awful noise!'

And he had to stop, in fact, because it is completely impossible to sing and to kiss at the same time.

47

The Otter Effect

'HOW WAS IT?' asked Seth.

'Incredible!' Phoebe cried from behind him.

She climbed off the motorbike and removed her helmet. Her hair, now thick and shoulder length, had been squashed down, and her knees felt a little shaky, but what a sense of invigoration! She had kept throwing her arms out in the air, so that Seth had to tell her to stop it and hold on. Soaring through the Devon countryside, she had felt as if she was made of wind and fire.

Seth parked his bike, opened the garden gate and shouted: 'No, Boz! Down!' at the Alsatian who had careered full pelt into Phoebe.

'Hi, Boz,' said Phoebe. She ruffled the dog's coat affectionately, unfazed by the huge, scrabbling paws and flying slobber.

Al and Christina were just leaving the sanctuary, ambling along the road ahead of them, holding hands.

'It doesn't take much of a detective to see what's going on there,' muttered Seth.

Phoebe hailed them.

'Hey, Phoebes, good to see you still in one piece. How was it?' asked Al.

'Fantastic. Loved it, loved every minute.' She turned to Seth. 'Will you teach me to ride?'

'A motorbike?'

'No, an elephant! Of course, a motorbike.'

'Seriously?'

'Seriously. You will teach me, won't you? Please say you will.'

He glanced uncertainly at Al. But Al was wearing the look of a father who, despite his concern, could not deny his daughter anything.

Seth's eyebrows spread wide and his face broke into a grin. 'Of course I will. Liking your attitude, Phoebe Featherstone.'

'Look at you,' Christina said approvingly. 'The new Phoebe. Or, rather, the real Phoebe. Fast, fluid and joyous. Didn't I always say the otter was your spirit animal?'

'You did indeed.' It was an enormous compliment.

Christina gave Seth a nudge. 'Don't forget our appointment tomorrow at five o'clock, Seth.'

Al turned a questioning face towards her. She tapped her nose mysteriously, but Phoebe knew what all this was about. Christina had been doing an online course on hypnotherapy and had offered to try out her new-found powers to help Seth with his blushing problem.

Phoebe and Seth told each other nearly everything these days. She had discovered that he wasn't anywhere near as grumpy as he looked. In fact, in her updated opinion, he didn't even look grumpy. His face just possessed a certain, not unpleasing *gravitas*. And who else was prepared to engage in endless conversations about the comparative merits of Morse and Sherlock?

'Are you going out together?' Jules had asked. Phoebe had given an elusive answer because the last thing she wanted was Jules trying to fix her up with any of her Plymouth friends. To her brother, Jack, she had told the truth. She had every confidence that she'd find somebody to love when the time was right, but Seth wasn't that person. He had become a firm friend, a friend she trusted, and a friend of her own age: something she hadn't had in a long while.

After she'd thanked him and said goodbye, she turned to her father.

'So how are you, Dad?'

'Quite allegorical, thank you. And you, Phoebe?'

'I'm . . . I'm *very well*, thank you.'

It was not quite true yet, but it was close to the truth. Things were, at last, heading towards normality. Maybe soon she could stop pretending altogether.

Phoebe gloried in her new life. It was as if all her senses, blocked off for years, had opened up again. Salt tasted saltier. Bark felt rougher. Flower petals were silkier. Hills looked greener. The sun on her face felt warmer. The river sounded . . . It sounded like the most beautiful music she had ever heard.

Everything had sprung into focus and now she was able to see with clearer eyes the lives of all the people around her, none so dear as her own father. Al had been transformed by her recovery too. There was a new buoyancy about him. His verve for gardening had increased and was irrepressible. He reeled out Kermit the Frog impressions nearly every day, which was a true sign that he was happy.

Much of this happiness was due to Christina. Their relationship had blossomed into something fiery and passionate and wonderful, full of days out, dancing, very bad singing, the cooking of herby, healthy vegetarian meals, and frequent outbursts of wild laughter. Christina had even coaxed Al to start yoga. It was doing him good. His spine was straighter and his shoulders were less hunched, as if he had finally laid down a mighty yoke. He occasionally even gave the impression of being tall.

Miaow basked in the ever greater quantities of affection that were lavished upon her. She had started bossing Al about almost as much as she bossed Christina about. They both adored her.

They visited the sanctuary nearly every day. Carol had lost Rupert's help – which, as they now knew, was in fact hindrance disguised as help – but she had gained many more willing volunteers who only wanted the otters to prosper. There had been several fundraising events for the sanctuary. One was an art exhibition featuring sketches and oils by Christina Penrose and woodwork by Dan Hollis. Another was a concert that included a solo from Ellie on the harp. A good sum was raised, since so many villagers attended, including the Bovises and the Dobsons. Jeremy Crocker also supported each event. (He had finally confided in Al that, every night after nine, he became Jemima Crocker. He hadn't told another soul about it ... but somebody must know because he'd anonymously received a gorgeous, silky, gold-braided dress in the post. It was one of the loveliest things that had ever happened to him.)

When he went out on his deliveries, Al was now circulating a flyer that asked people to have a look in their garages for anything that might be recycled for the otter sanctuary. He gathered all sorts – skateboards, drainpipes, fire guards, rabbit hutches, a pile of bricks. Christina, with her artistic eye, had painted leaves, acorns and fish on any flat surface available, mostly sticking to natural colours although, occasionally, a little purple or gold crept in. Together with Al, she had created a fabulous otter playground that was greatly enjoyed by the otters and greatly admired by their audience. If Carol thought they had gone a bit over the top, she kept the thought to herself.

Was ever a group of otters so indulged? Phoebe doubted it. The tourists loved it, and the sanctuary had become incredibly popular and quite well known. Not that Carol cared that much. She just wanted the otters to be happy. Geoff Pickles, the vet, came round whenever he was needed, and confirmed that they were remarkably healthy, too. Just occasionally a wild otter was brought in, and everything possible was done to ensure its safe release back into the wild.

'I think I'm ready now,' Phoebe told Al and Christina.

Al regarded her, eyebrows aloft. 'You don't mean . . .'

'Yes.'

She had not yet been back to the glade where they had first found Coco, which was also the site of her release. The place had been marred by unpleasant memories. Yet now she was filled with a desire to return there, to live through the memories both good and bad. To try to put the bad ones behind her and focus only on the good.

Besides, Al had said he'd seen paw prints on the bank last time he was there.

'Let's go now, then, before you change your mind.'

The three of them strolled together along the winding path, under the greenery of oak, beech and hazel. Afternoon sunshine dappled the ground and floodlit the etched intricacy of every leaf. Bright ripples ran beside them. Threads of light interwove a wobbling lattice in the clear water.

The distance was much shorter than it used to be. The glade had also undergone a transformation since the last time Phoebe was here. Instead of a prison barred with sinister shadows, it had become a gilded island glowing with light and colour.

'Just like Narnia,' Phoebe murmured.

'Told you so,' said Al.

They stood and faced the Darle. A cloud of tiny gnats, floodlit like specks of gold, jiggled wildly just above the water's surface. They flitted around with speed and precision, and Phoebe thought how incredible it was that they never bumped into each other.

'What's the river saying now, do you think, Phoebe?' asked Al.

Phoebe put her head to one side, which she could do without her neck hurting now. She nodded slowly. 'It's saying that sometimes bad things happen so that later good things can happen.'

She let Al and Christina go ahead on the way back while she loitered on the edge of the glade, not wanting to leave quite yet. If she was very still, very patient and very, very lucky . . .

Quietness bloomed, full and warm and rich.

Phoebe listened.

After a few moments – or maybe hours – she heard a soft splash to her left. Saw a trail of bubbles. A dark arrow gliding under the water.

A face popped up. A furry brown face with a tiny smudge of white fur like a milk moustache just above the mouth. The whole head dipped under immediately, but a minute later reappeared even closer, whiskers dripping. Phoebe was sure there was a spark of recognition in those alert eyes. And she felt it more strongly than ever before: the Otter Effect, hurtling through her veins, flooding her with joy.

For a moment Coco held her gaze, and then she was gone in a scattering of silver ripples. Her life was wild and free, just as it should be. Whatever lay ahead for her, Phoebe wished her well, with all her heart.

And what lay ahead for Phoebe herself? She didn't know. University, probably. She'd had offers from four so far and hadn't yet decided which it was to be. She could study maths . . . or linguistics . . . or psychology . . . or almost anything. And beyond that she sometimes thought she might become a private detective . . . or a keeper in a wildlife park . . . or perhaps even an artist . . . The possibilities were endless.

Acknowledgements

This, unbelievably, is my fourth book. Yet I'm only just beginning to grasp how many people it takes to get ideas sprouting, feed them with research, pull them into a structure, dissect, hone, polish, present and send them out in the shape of a novel. Although my name is on this cover, I am part of a much, much larger team. So here are some giant thank-yous for these amazing people:

My editors, Francesca Best and Alice Rodgers. You have prodded my thoughts in all the right directions, shone a light on this story and brought out vital elements that would never have manifested themselves otherwise. You are inspirational and it is a joy to work with you.

All the others at Transworld who have been involved in producing and publicizing this book. I know there are many of you and I'm indebted to each and every one of you. What a team!

My agent, Darley Anderson. I am so glad you took that risk on an unknown and ignorant hopeful all those years ago. Thank you. Your guidance and knowledge on everything book-related is unparalleled. And huge thanks to Mary, Kristina, Georgia and Kira for securing so many foreign deals for me, to Rebeka for your loveliness and efficiency and to Rosanna for kindly ensuring some money comes my way!

My fellow authors who have advised, encouraged, endorsed and supported me, far too many now to mention by name, but you know who you are. Thank you with all my heart.

Book bloggers, for your hard work reading, thinking and writing your reviews. I hope you know what an incredible difference you make.

Booksellers and librarians. All of you. Where would we be without you?

Readers. I'm so happy you picked up this book. You will all see completely different things in it and get completely different things out of it, but I do hope those things are good!

Everyone who works at Dartmoor Otters and Buckfast Butterflies. Thanks go to David Field for giving me so much time, for showing me around and generously sharing a wealth of otter know-how, as well as to Sue and the otter team (Keira, Aimee, Taz and Rachel) for your help. Every visit has brought new insights and so much joy. A big, fun-filled, fish-flavoured thank-you, of course, goes to the otters themselves (especially Sammy).

Mark and Louise Bolland, however can I thank you for all the information and anecdotes about delivery driving? And (not to be sniffed at) for sparking the idea in the first place?

Gina and Elisabeth, thank you so much for the fun times in Devon, the 'level 5' discussions and the memories.

My other friends and family, thank you, as ever, for your wonderful, invaluable support. Special thanks and love to dear Jonathan and Purrsy for being with me through all the ups and downs. There have been plenty of both. You are everything to me.

A final note to anyone suffering from chronic pain. You are braver than anyone knows, but remember that sometimes the bravest thing you can do is to ask for help. Please keep holding on to the good things, however small they seem. Maybe, if you can, go and visit some otters. I hope you will experience the Otter Effect. And I hope that, like Phoebe and Coco (and like me), you will one day be free. Miracles do happen.

HAZEL PRIOR lives on Exmoor with her husband and a huge ginger cat. As well as writing, she works as a freelance harpist. Hazel is the author of *Ellie and the Harp-Maker*, the number-one ebook and audiobook bestseller *Away with the Penguins* and its follow-up, *Call of the Penguins*. *Life and Otter Miracles* is her fourth novel.

Meet Ellie. She's perfectly happy living her quiet life with her husband, Clive. Happy to wander the Exmoor countryside and write the occasional poem that nobody will read; happy to dream of all the things she hasn't yet managed to do.
Or is she?

Meet Dan. He thinks all he needs is the time and space to make harps in his isolated barn on Exmoor. He enjoys being on his own, far away from other people and – crucially – far away from any risk of surprises.

What Ellie and Dan don't know yet, is that a chance encounter is about to change all of this.

This book also contains a pheasant named Phineas . . .

'Uplifting and full of heart. Perfect for fans of *Eleanor Oliphant is Completely Fine*'
JO THOMAS

'A beautiful love song of a story, wonderfully told with a warm heart and much hope'
PHAEDRA PATRICK, author of
The Library of Lost and Found

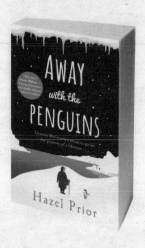

Veronica McCreedy lives in a mansion by the sea. She loves a nice cup of Darjeeling tea whilst watching a good wildlife documentary. And she's never seen without her ruby-red lipstick.

Although these days Veronica is rarely seen by anyone because, at eighty-five, her days are spent mostly at home, alone.

She can be found either collecting litter, trying to locate her glasses or shouting instructions to her assistant, Eileen.

Veronica doesn't have family or friends nearby. Not that she knows about, anyway . . . And she has no idea where she's going to leave her considerable wealth when she dies.

But today . . . today Veronica is going to make a decision that will change everything.

'Unflinching, stubborn, funny and moving, Veronica is an unlikely heroine who will sneak in and capture your heart.'
TRISHA ASHLEY

'A glorious, life-affirming story. I read it in a day.'
CLARE MACKINTOSH

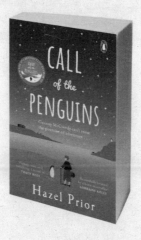

Fiercely resilient and impeccably dressed, Veronica McCreedy
has lived an incredible eighty-seven years. Most of them
alone in her huge house by the sea.

But **Veronica** has recently discovered a late-life love for family
and friendship, adventure and wildlife.

More specifically, a love for penguins!

And so, when she's invited to co-present a wildlife
documentary, far away in the southern hemisphere, she jumps
at the chance. Even though it will put her in the spotlight, just
when she thought she would soon fade into the wings.

Perhaps it's never too late to shine . . .

'Funny, wise and touching. I loved it.'
TRACY REES

'Beautifully written by a born storyteller.'
LORRAINE KELLY

'The perfect fireside read. Hazel Prior's novels
always make me smile.'
TRISHA ASHLEY